Danvis Tales

Other Works by Rowland E. Robinson

Forest and Stream Fables (1886)

Uncle Lisha's Shop (1887)

Sam Lovel's Camps (1889)

Vermont, A Study of Independence (1892)

Danvis Folks (1894)

In New England Fields and Woods (1896)

Uncle Lisha's Outing (1897)

A Hero of Ticonderoga (1898)

In the Greenwood (1899)

A Danvis Pioneer (1900)

Sam Lovel's Boy (1901)

Out of Bondage and Other Stories (1905)

Hunting Without a Gun and Other Papers (1905)

Silver Fields and Other Sketches of a Farmer-Sportsman (1921)

Hardscrabble Books—Fiction of New England

DANVIS TALES

Selected Stories

☛ by Rowland E. Robinson

edited by David Budbill

with an Introduction by Hayden Carruth

University Press of New England

Hanover and London

University Press of New England publishes books under its own imprint and is the publisher for Brandeis University Press, Dartmouth College, Middlebury College Press, University of New Hampshire, University of Rhode Island, Tufts University, University of Vermont, Wesleyan University Press, and Salzburg Seminar.

Published by University Press of New England, Hanover, NH 03755

Library of Congress Cataloging-in-Publication Data

Robinson, Rowland Evans, 1833–1900.
    Danvis tales : selected stories / by Rowland E. Robinson ; edited
by David Budbill ; with an introduction by Hayden Carruth.
      p. cm.
    "The definitive source for this abridged edition of Rowland E.
Robinson's stories is the seven volumes of the Centennial Edition of
his complete work published by Charles E. Tuttle Company of Rutland,
Vermont, between 1934 and 1937"—P. ix.
    ISBN 0–87451–718–4 (alk. paper)
    1. Vermont—Social life and customs—Fiction.   I. Budbill, David.
II. Title.
PS2719.R68A6   1995
813'.4—dc20   95–13841
♾

Contents

Acknowledgments

Hayden Carruth's monograph, *Vermont's Genius of the Folk, Rowland E. Robinson*, was originally funded by the National Endowment for the Humanities, and an abridged version of it was first published in *Vermont History: The Proceedings of the Vermont Historical Society*, Volume 41, Number 4, Autumn 1973.

The editor wishes to gratefully acknowledge generous support from The Vermont Community Foundation for his work on this volume.

The definitive source for this abridged edition of Rowland E. Robinson's stories is the seven volumes of the Centennial Edition of his complete work published by Charles E. Tuttle Company of Rutland, Vermont, between 1934 and 1937.

The seven pen and ink drawings included in this book are by Rowland Robinson's daughter, Rachel Robinson Elmer (1878–1919), and were done for the original edition of *Hunting Without a Gun*.

The photograph of Rowland Robinson is credited to The Huntington Studio.

Editor's Preface

I first read Rowland Robinson in the early 1970s when my friend Hayden Carruth urged Robinson upon me. I fell in love with him immediately, with his elegant and graceful prose, his precise eye for describing the minute details of the natural world, and with his delightful, complex, and real people.

At the time I began reading Robinson I was working as a day laborer in the woods of northern Vermont and living a kind of modern version of the lives folks in Danvis lived a hundred and fifty years earlier. At this time also, I was just beginning to write the poems that would become my own late twentieth-century version of the *Danvis Tales* and would be collected twenty years later under the title *Judevine*, the name of my own, Danvis-like, quasi-imaginary town. While I was working in the woods I came to know a number of French Canadians, and I fell in love with their accent and their creative use of English, and when I came to invent my own French Canadian character for *Judevine* I named him Antoine in honor of Robinson's own outrageous and delightful Antoine.

Robinson's prose is different from what we are used to today. His writing is elegant and graceful. The syntax of his sentences makes music out of words. We have abandoned this sense of musicality, this elegance and grace, in our modern writing in favor of sentences that are too often nasty, brutish and short. It is a delight to read Rowland Robinson's careful, stylish, and lyrical prose.

Robinson's visual sense, his ability to make the written word paint vivid and accurate pictures of this world, is uncanny. When Sam Lovel's hound dog returns to camp having been shamefacedly chased there by a vixen fox, Sam says, "'Oh, Drive! hain't you a spunky dawg, a skulkin' hum with yer tail atween yer laigs afore a nasty little bitch fox not quarter's big as you be!' as the hound came up to him and endeavored to explain the peculiarities of the situation with whimpers and more deeply corrugated brow, and quick, low-swung tail beats that shook all his lean anatomy." Or this on red squirrels: "Sam's neighbor, the red squirrel, was in high spirits with such sunshine after storm, and flung at him a shower of derisive jeers and snickers from the trunk of a great hemlock where he clung with spasmodic jerks of feet and tail." Anyone who has seen a red squirrel piqued to a fit, as they always seem to be, knows the accuracy of Robinson's description. On a day of rain, "a May day with April weather," the posture of the barnyard chickens seems to articulate the universal disappointment with this step backward in the seasons: "a group of fowls stood, bedraggled and forlorn, with shortened necks and slanted tails." Or this: "a kingfisher hung steadfast for a moment on vibrant wings above the shallows, then dropping like a plummet, arose almost with the upbursting splash of his plunge, and presently proclaimed his good luck with a metallic clatter of his castanets."

Almost all of the *Danvis Tales* were written after Robinson was totally blind. No doubt Robinson's ability to describe the natural world comes from his desperate urgency to "see" the world through words. His blindness was an overwhelming burden to him and he felt cut off, as if he were already dead. At one point, Uncle Lisha tells the story of Kit Jarvis, a blind man, who says, "I been the same as dead this ten year, . . . the world a-rattlin' raound me 'thaout no more 'caount on me 'an if I wa'n't in 't, my own flesh an' blood grown up 'thaout my knowin' haow they look, er seein' my ol' womern's face er my nighest friend, er seein' the grass an' the trees leaf aout er shed the' leaves, er ever p'intin' a gun er hookin' a traout an' jest a-setting' an' harkin' in the everlastin' dark! It's lunsome, I tell ye. A blind man's uselesser 'n a dead man, an' you can't bury him aout'n the way an' be perlite." These stories I am sure were Robinson's way of getting back to his days of roaming forest and field, lake and stream, hunting and fishing and trapping and "seeing" the magnificence of all creation; these stories were his way of being, as Sam Lovel puts it, "a mournin' for the feller that was himself oncte."

Among the few who still know Robinson, he has, I fear, a reputation as a folksy, funny, down-home kind of writer. Although all of those adjectives apply, I want to suggest, as Hayden does in his Introduction, that there is far more to Rowland Robinson than that.

Robinson is candid, for example, about the relations between men and women. There is more than a little tension, and some open animosity, between the sexes in these stories. One of the reasons Sam Lovel is forever going into the woods is to escape his hateful stepmother and in general to just get away from the "womern." And in *Uncle Lisha's Outing* when the wives come down to the lake to join their husbands at their

duck hunting camp, the air of chagrin hanging between the lines is pal-
pable. The women like it also when the men are gone. As Aunt Jerusha
says, "When folks gits settled daown to the tussle o' livin', there be times
when it's restin tu hev men folks aouten the way. Women wants a chance
tu talk about their consarns, an' argy their own way. Somehaow men can't
argy, but keep a-givin' their reasons an' their whys and wherefores." Well,
in this modern age of inflated vocabulary we would no doubt call what
goes on between men and women something like anguish or struggle or
grief and not a "tussle," but if one attends to what Hayden says about
understatement—"Reticence is the key"—it should be clear that even
though there are a hundred and fifty years separating us, we are all talking about the same thing.

Hayden points out that Rowland Robinson "tells us what we as Americans and New Englanders are: our character, our heritage, our predicament." And much of what Robinson tells us about ourselves makes us
uncomfortable. He tells us, sometimes inadvertently, that we "white
folks" are obsessed with notions of race and ethnic differences, that we
think anyone who isn't "white" is inferior.

Where Robinson stood on the racism and ethnic prejudice rampant
in these stories is sometimes difficult to say. Certainly regarding Black
Americans he stood with the Quakers in the story who run the Underground Railroad and with Margaret Bartlett who says to Sam Lovel, "I
wish thee wouldn't call colored people niggers." Yet Robinson gives us,
as any real writer would, the full spectrum of attitudes toward American
Blacks, including the Virginia slave hunter up in Vermont to capture the
runaway, Bob. But according to Sam Lovel, and no doubt Robinson also,
the lowest of the low regarding race hatred is the Vermonter who helps
the Virginian try to find Bob. As Sam says, "Oh! you cussed slinks! I don't
lay it up so much ag'in that other feller, for that's the way he was brought
up; but you—V'monters—huntin' niggers! Damn ye! I'd lufter sink ye
in the mud!"

The real "nigger" in these stories, however, is the French Canadian—
the "White Nigger of the North." There is evidence in *Danvis Tales* that
Robinson did not think too highly of the Canadian imports in his midst.
Uncle Lisha for all his love of Antoine, for example, exclaims, "Take a
match er a splinter an' light yer pipe like white folks . . . ," and later, one
evening in the shop about dusk, he says, "Wal, we're gittin' all of a color,
white folks an' Canucks, 'n' I guess we'd better hev a light. . . ."

Robinson also deals with varying attitudes toward Indians. Sam Lovel has an open hatred for Indians, while Pelatiah Gove clearly admires them and sees painfully the injustice being done to them. At one point the conversation turns toward "the Indian" and Sam says, "I wish 't they was all sick 'n' dead, consarn 'em! See haow they're cuttin' up aout West 'n' in Floridy!"

> "I don't keer what you say 'baout red men, ef I was a Ninjun as I be a white man," cried Pelatiah, rising and smacking his mittens together, "while 't there was a pale face on the face of the U'nited States of Ameriky, I wouldn't never lay daown my bowarrers, my tommyhock, an' my wampum: never, no, never!"

Robinson himself was interested in what Indians remained in the Champlain Valley, in their history, artifacts, language, customs and so on. It is easy to hear Robinson's own voice in Pelatiah's heartfelt and passionate defense of the Indian's militancy.

Yet in these stories, Indian-hating Sam Lovel is the one most interested in Indians and the one most eager to get to know them and their culture. Sam is also the one who persists in referring to American Blacks as "niggers," yet he is the one who helps the runaway Bob escape to Canada. In short, the character of Sam Lovel has what Julia Alvarez calls the "dignity of complexity." Toward the end of *Uncle Lisha's Outing* Uncle Lisha says to Huldah, Sam's wife, after they have met and visited with a Black man while they are all boating on Lake Champlain, "Why, yes, that's one o' your husband's friends, Huldy. You'd admire tu see what comp'ny he keeps when he's daown here,—Injins an' niggers an' I don't know what all."

It is painful to read overtly racist passages even when they are spoken in the name of good will. Painful yet necessary; we need to look squarely at the assumptions of white supremacy in the literature of our past, because, although we no longer use such blatantly racist language, the attitudes beneath the language persist.

It should be remembered that this kind of language was not unique to Robinson. During the time in which Robinson wrote, what we now consider racist language was commonplace in literature even among the liberal, social reformers of the day. Jacob Riis, the great photographer, journalist, and reformer, was a contemporary of Robinson's. His influential *How the Other Half Lives*, which exposed the squalid living conditions on New York's Lower East Side and was published in 1901, a year after

Robinson's death, is riddled with what we would now call racist and ethnic slurs. Intolerance and fear of nonwhite people has been a part of the white American psyche for centuries. I hope that looking straight at our own racism, painful as it is, will help us come to grips with our own prejudice and our own past. It is my hope that Rowland Robinson's stories can help us in this way to know ourselves.

Perhaps Rowland Robinson's most significant and notable contribution to the important issues of our age is as a ecologist and conservationist. *Danvis Tales* are filled with appalling brutality toward the natural world and its nonhuman inhabitants. You needn't worry that to read these stories is to repair to the bucolic gentleness of some sylvan dream: here you will find butchery abounding. We too-often-self-righteous New Englanders don't need to look to our western countrymen and their slaughter of the buffalo for examples of barbarism—it was right here in Vermont, fully and furiously abroad in the land of our progenitors, such as, for example, the macabre habit of "crusting" deer—an annual outing of sorts into the deer yards in March when the snow is deep and crusted over so that men on snowshoes can go on top of the snow, and the deer cannot, in order to club dozens of deer in a single morning into senselessness and then slit their throats for no other purpose than the "enjoyment" of the activity. Against this and snaring partridge and catching bass off their spawning beds, Sam Lovel protests vigorously, yet when Sam shoots the last otter in Otter Creek he says simply, "Well, there ye be!" Robinson and his protagonist, Sam Lovel, are both, as we all are, a bundle of contradictions.

Because Rowland Robinson lived close to the natural world as a farmer and as one who loved the outdoor life, and no doubt also because he was a Quaker, he believed that in each of us there is an "uneliminated atom" that "still holds us to kinship with nature, and though it may not be the best part of us, without it we should be worse than we are. He who loses all love for our common mother is, indeed, a wretched being, poorer than the beasts." Such a wholistic and ecological world view certainly has great relevance for us today.

If Robinson is such a wonderful writer and of such enduring importance to us and to the basic issues of contemporary life, why then is he completely neglected, totally forgotten? Some would say that his dialect writing makes him inaccessible. To that I would say: anyone willing to give Robinson twenty minutes will easily see how his apostrophized dialect writing and his spelling methods work, and once that is understood a world will open to the reader full of the delights of interesting stories and entertaining people, and all of this surrounded by writing so acutely sensitive to the natural world that Rowland Robinson surely must be one of the best nature writers who ever lived.

Inaccessibility is not the issue; snobbery is. Robinson was not a member of a big city intelligentsia; he was a farmer and he wrote about ordinary people doing ordinary—some would say disgustingly ordinary—things. In fact, he was one of those ordinary persons himself. Had Robinson lived in Paris or New York and written about Vermont, or lived in Vermont and written about Paris or New York, he might have gotten on better with the literary snoots. Also, the popularity Robinson's books enjoyed with ordinary folks both during his lifetime and shortly after no doubt convinced many of the elite that he could not have been, by virtue of his popularity with the commoners, a really serious writer. On this subject, let John Farrar, late of Farrar, Straus and Giroux, writing in 1934, have the last word: "I find [Rowland Robinson] more exciting than Thoreau, and in reproduction of dialect more adroit than Thomas Hardy. . . . If a great many of us hadn't been literary snobs for the past 50 years, we would have canonized this simple man many moons ago."

Danvis Tales is an abridgment of four of Rowland Robinson's books written over a span of ten years from 1887 to 1897. They comprise in my opinion, and in Hayden's, the essential and best of Robinson's extraordinary story telling. Of the six books that make up the stories about the people of Danvis, I eliminated the first, *A Danvis Pioneer*, and the last, *Sam Lovel's Boy*, as the first comes well before the bulk of the stories and the last well after, and also because it is generally agreed that these two are noticeably weaker than the others. For those reasons I worked with the middle four—*Uncle Lisha's Shop, Sam Lovel's Camps, Danvis Folks*, and *Uncle Lisha's Outing*—since these four books are more or less continuous. I've reduced 950 pages to a little more than 250. To do such a thing one must make painful choices at every turn. I have had to eliminate whole stories and entire characters and truncate mercilessly many of the stories and the people who remain. Some may object because I have excluded this or included that. I have been guided by my own taste, for which I make no apology. I have also and more importantly tried to fairly represent *all* aspects of Robinson's writing in this selection while trying, at the same time, to create as seamless and continuous a piece of "fiction" as possible. If what you find here is interesting, I urge you to pursue Robinson's complete works by going to the seven Centennial volumes published by Charles E. Tuttle Company of Rutland, Vermont, between 1934 and 1937, where you can read to your heart's content.

Finally, there is a unique joy in championing the rediscovery of a forgotten writer. I hope you will join me in this joy and step out of the momentary now, out of current cultural assumptions and back into a world of a hundred and fifty years ago. It is with great pleasure and enthusiasm that I welcome you to Danvis and to the lives of the people in this particular place on the western slopes of the Green Mountains and down into the broad valley that stretches to the shores of Lake Champlain, this particular place fully real yet also fully within the imagination of Rowland E. Robinson.

D.B.

Introduction
Vermont's Genius of the Folk, Rowland E. Robinson

Hayden Carruth

> No, on the contrary, it is for words to serve
> and follow; and let Gascon get there if French cannot.
> —Montaigne

I

Rowland E. Robinson was born at the Robinson homestead, called "Rokeby,"[1] in Ferrisburgh,[2] Vermont, on May 14, 1833, and died in the same house—some say the same room—on October 15, 1900. On his father's side he was descended from early settlers in Rhode Island, Quakers who had sought the sanctuary offered by Roger Williams and who had later, when Rhode Island became merely a state among states, joined the wave of emigration to northern New England during the first quarter of the nineteenth century. On his mother's side, his family had belonged to the minor aristocracy of Virginia. They too were Quakers.

Not much is known of Robinson's boyhood. He attended district school, a one-room affair that met, according to New England custom, for short terms both winter and summer. Later he went to Ferrisburgh Academy, a public high school, but he was an indifferent scholar and did not graduate. He is said to have got his education at home where he read "the novels of Scott and other tales of adventure" in his father's library; which of course is what is said of every nineteenth-century American who rose to prominence from humble beginnings. An examination of the books in the Robinson homestead today that were published before 1840, when Robinson was seven years old, shows far fewer novels than

Quaker tracts and books of theology and moral philosophy. In such a context one novel might go a long way, however. We cannot make a balanced judgment concerning what the boy might have read or what literary influences might have touched his imagination. What we do know is that he was brought up in a region where literary pretensions were generally unheard of, but in a house where both books and periodicals were read, where speech was probably fluent, and where a certain skill in verbal improvisation, as at a Quaker meeting, was undoubtedly esteemed.

Beyond this we know that the boy's principal interest was not literary but pictorial. He liked to draw. Though he had no instruction his work was good enough to win Quakerish toleration if not out-and-out support at home. When still in his teens Robinson left Vermont for New York City. We know little about the circumstances surrounding this adventure, either before or after his departure. Doubtless it was attended by the whole allegory, still alive in the new republic, of the young man setting forth to seek his fortune. Once in the city Robinson went to work for a draftsman, in whose shop he learned the rudiments of "perspective," "shading," etc., and also the trade of engraving on the head of a hardwood block with a steel burin and needle, which was the principal means at that time for making commercial reproductions of graphic illustrations. In effect Robinson thereafter earned his living as an engraver while trying to graduate to the rank of illustrator. It didn't work. He sold only a few comic drawings, and before many years had passed he became discouraged and returned to the farm in Ferrisburg.

In 1866, however, when he was thirty-six years old, he returned to New York, again to work as a draftsman and engraver, but this time he had better success with his drawings, which began to appear regularly in *Frank Leslie's Magazine, The American Agriculturalist, Rural New Yorker, Hearth and Home*, and others. His work was in the popular convention of the time: line drawings based on rural life, comic in intent, though not what we would call cartoons today, since they lacked the punch of modern humor with its reversals and double meanings. Their comedy was what has been called "situational," and their real aim was moral and homiletic. To a modern observer they seem completely undistinguished in either content or execution. The drawing is too literal, lacking flair or style. It gives no intimation of the quality of Robinson's oil paintings, a few of which can still be seen at Rokeby. They are charming in the best sense of the term, fluent and warm with a suggestion of emotional depth, especially in the miniature landscapes, usually ovals, which he did in conformity with the prevailing taste of the mid-nineteenth century. They are not overlooked masterpieces by any means, but neither are they primitives; they are modest and good.

In New York Robinson signed a business contract which he thought would permit him to work at home as an engraver and illustrator, and in 1873, at the age of forty, he returned to Rokeby. The arrangement fell through. But apparently Robinson had had enough of the city. He remained the rest of his life on the farm, which was now his to manage, and although he continued to make drawings for the magazines, most of his income must have derived from the products of the land, especially butter and wool. To what extent Robinson engaged in actual farm work we do not know. He is said to have taken more interest in his orchards and buttery than in other aspects of the farm, but we know that the farm supported three flocks of sheep, descended from the Merinos his grandfather had imported from Spain in 1806, as well oxen, horses, poultry, gardens, and so forth. One gathers, however, that much of the work and perhaps the management was performed by others, though Robinson advertised his butter by drawing cartoons on the lids of the wooden tubs in which it was shipped to market in Boston and New York. At one time a number of these lids were hung on the walls of a wholesaler's office at Faneuil Market, a little gallery of "folk art" that attracted considerable attention.

At about this time, the mid-1870s, Robinson began writing, but except that his wife—a Quaker woman from East Montpelier, younger than he—had urged him to do it, we do not know the reason. It was not need for money; the farm was still prosperous. Perhaps Robinson merely wanted more prestige than his work as an illustrator could bring him. For my part I think it likely that he wanted, probably not consciously at first, to work in more detail and with greater imaginative freedom than his pencil, brush, or engraver's burin could afford, and with his own proper subject, namely, the natural environment of northwestern Vermont and the people and animals inhabiting it. He set to work on his first literary sketch, "Fox Hunting in New England," a topic recommended by his wife, and when it was written he sent it, with appropriate illustrations, to *Scribner's Magazine*. It was promptly accepted.[3]

If the event seems incredibly lucky to young writers today, it should be remembered that Robinson was in his forties at the time, and his subject had been maturing in his mind for more than two decades. Mrs. Robinson had needed no special shrewdness to suggest it, as her husband had been a fox hunter for years: not, as he took pains to point out, the aristocratic equestrian in fancy dress from Virginia, but a proper New England fox hunter—one man with one dog and one gun, a muzzle-loader, prowling the woods and rocky ledges, searching for signs, studying the runways, and above all savoring the passionate solitude of life in the wilderness. This was Robinson's delight. It was also his serious concern: the place of the human species in the natural scheme. But he had to pursue this not only on his own and largely without precedents but also in the face of long-standing American disdain for hunters, who from Rip Van Winkle to the advent of the Hemingway hero were regarded by the genteel as lazy, slovenly, lying creatures.

Robinson followed up his first success with a steady production of sketches and essays, chiefly about hunting. Some of these he sold to the literary magazines of the day, *The Century, Lippincott's, The Atlantic*, but he wrote more than this market could absorb. Before long he was a reliable and settled contributor to magazines of outdoor and rural life, especially *Forest and Stream*, whose publishers were the first to collect and issue Robinson's work in book form. *Forest and Stream Fables* was published in 1886. Thereafter his books appeared regularly, published chiefly by Houghton, Mifflin and Company, which also acquired rights to the earlier books. However, Robinson continued writing for *Forest and Stream*, the magazine, regularly until his death. His writing for the first four or five years was limited to accounts of fishing and hunting in New England, miscellaneous sketches of rural folk and their ways, a few bucolic fables or attempts at fantasy, but most of this production, though valuable historically and full of interesting observation, is no more than apprentice work to the heart of Robinson's achievement. The first of his "Danvis tales" appeared in *Forest and Stream* in 1884. These, continued in several sequences and later published in several volumes,[4] give Robinson his claim to our attention and his stature as genuine artist.

Meanwhile Robinson's eyesight began to fail. His daughter, Mary Robinson Perkins, in a biographical memoir that she read before a women's club in 1921, said that her father had suffered an accident to one eye in childhood, with a resulting lifelong weakness of vision in that eye. She ascribed his failing eyesight to this cause; others who knew him have mentioned his years of intensely close work as an engraver and miniaturist. A modern layman is likely to think of glaucoma. At all events Robinson began to lose his vision in 1887 and was completely blind by 1893.

What is astonishing is that these years and those remaining until his death in 1900 were his most productive; nearly all the "Danvis tales" were written after 1887. According to his daughter's memoir, Robinson worked by means of a special composition board that had been pressed to give it a grooved surface. By laying his paper on the board and using the grooves to guide his pencil, he could turn out legible manuscript, which his wife then read aloud to him, making corrections as she read. From this corrected manuscript she made a fair copy for the publisher. It seems a clumsy method, yet it worked. Robinson's style showed steady improvement in his last years, greater concision and more vigor. This would have been extraordinary if he had worked only with descriptive or narrative prose, what used to be called "expository writing." When one considers that most of the "Danvis tales" were written in orthographically reproduced dialect—and not in stereotyped or slapdash dialect either but in dialect used creatively and with meticulous attention to distinctions of pronunciation and phrasing—one sees what a feat the work of these final years really was. Leaving aside questions of stylistic and substantial value, Robinson's effort in his last years was the concentrated imaginative endeavor that we call literary heroism when we find it in a self-conscious artist, preferably living in Paris. Is it any less heroic when it occurs in a Vermont farmer?

II

When I try to pin down formative cultural influences on Robinson's work, I find myself groping in the dark. Even the simplest inferences are suspect. The truth is that *no* reliable biographical research has been done on Robinson, just as *no* serious critical attention has been paid to his writing. What we know of his life comes from the appreciations of his friends and relatives, mostly brief, after his death, homely contributions to the historical journals and local papers of Vermont. The "critical" examinations of his work are mostly superficial exercises in local pride, done by newspaper editors, college professors, and other publicists.[5] In addition one unpublished master's thesis exists at the University of Vermont,[6] and I have been told a doctoral thesis is in preparation at a midwestern university. The only work I have found that makes any pretense to critical objectivity is a paper by Terrence Martin.[7] But Professor Martin's opinions are pedantic, smug, and without much value.

In short, nothing in print helps us in our estimate of the man and his work. Robinson's correspondence, manuscripts, and other private papers remain unpublished, for instance; not only that, they remain uncatalogued, unmicrofilmed, unread—stored in little packets at Rokeby, in desks and cupboards, subject to damage of many kinds. His library has never been catalogued. The books are jammed on shelves in the living room at Rokeby, usually two rows to a shelf, in only the roughest semblance of order. One cannot tell what books by his contemporaries Robinson may have read. In glancing through the collection I could find no Melville or Whitman, for instance, no Emerson, no Muir, only a few books by Burroughs, looking as if they were unread. There is a complete Thoreau, but it too looks mostly unread. On the other hand, the works of Francis Parkman were clearly of great interest to Robinson, and the poems of Tennyson and Longfellow were well read. I looked in vain for early writings in the "local color" convention, by Bret Harte, Edward Eggleston, Joel Chandler Harris, or others, but this does not mean they were not there. And the only author of dialect writing I spotted was Artemus Ward. What conclusions may one safely draw from this? Virtually none. Possibly that Robinson, though a New Englander, was decidedly a back-country Yankee, a pragmatist, not attracted to the cultivated down-country Transcendentalism of Concord and Cambridge. Of the two authors who had lived in the wilderness, Robinson seems to have preferred Parkman, activist and historian, to Thoreau, the contemplative. But it would be impossible to make even this broad statement with any assurance if it were not well supported in Robinson's own writings.

Robinson's published texts must be our chief resource, not only in literary matters but in our search for the author's personality. He did not write a real autobiography, but he did leave a number of sketches and essays based explicitly on boyhood experiences. By putting these together with the few publicly ascertainable facts and with what we can infer from the rest of his writings about his ideas, prejudices, beliefs, and general attitudes, we may, I think, make two inferences that will be safe and helpful.

First, although Robinson was a Yankee born and bred, he resembled many people who come to New England from elsewhere: he admired and even envied the "strength and serenity" of Yankee character without being able to enjoy it in his own right. His was at once a gentler and more complex personality, more sensitive, more hesitant, more aware of ambiguities in traditional Yankee values. He was far less single-minded than the stereotyped Yankee, as is shown in his vacillations between New York and Ferrisburg, and even more in his ambivalent attitudes toward nature. For although Robinson loved hunting, he feared what hunting would do. He deeply regretted what it had already done. And although he admired the simple vigor of his neighbors in northern Vermont, he feared the effects of their pragmatic, narrow methods in their use of land. He praised Vermont and its inhabitants, and celebrated Yankee virtues more consistently than any other first-rate writer in Vermont's history, at least until the emergence of Robert Frost; yet in reading his works we recognize at once that he was no chauvinist, no vainglorious booster. He was aware of Yankee defects too, and troubled by them, and he wrote of them more and more poignantly as he grew older. In short, Robinson was more than a farmer and an artisan, he was an artist. And one of the signs by which we recognize him, as in the case of almost every other artist of the post-Renaissance world, is his alienation from the society in which he found himself. No matter if it was slight or great: for our purposes it is less relevant to ask the degree of alienation—obviously not enough to drive him away—than to notice that in him, as in others, this friction between social environment and individual sensibility was at least partly responsible for engendering the artistic impulse. Art is a product of irritation. Those patriotic Vermonters who try to make Robinson into a simple native product, as forthright as Vermont cheese, as pure and sweet as maple syrup, are misguided in their intentions and wrong in their effects.

The second inference is this: that the greatest single influence on Robinson was his parents' religion. This is difficult to prove. Doubtless other more amorphous cultural and social influences produced broader effects. But Quakerism seems to me the one unified cultural force that can be identified in his later attitudes. It was absorbed early, for we have no evidence that Robinson participated actively in any religious observances during his adulthood. In his "Recollections of a Quaker Boy,"[8] Robinson wrote of the Quaker community in the latter part of the nineteenth century:

> Except by a few of the oldest members, the peculiar distinctive dress is no longer worn nor the "plain language" spoken. In the meetings one sees fashionably dressed congregations and hears singing and organs, but no testimony against "steeple houses"

and a "hireling priesthood," and but little is said of the great
guide, the "light within." To one who remembers Quakerism as it
was sixty years ago, its forms are not recognizable nor befitting its
name, and its peculiar spirit seems to have departed.

Clearly Robinson did not care to take part in a church he found so degen-
erated; equally clearly, I think, though not as explicitly, he indicates his
own loss of faith, or at least loss of interest, in those aspects of Quakerism
that he places within quotation marks. The piety of his father's household
was gone; the eighteenth-century zealotry of his grandfather's household
was even farther in the past. Rokeby in the author's time had become a
nineteenth-century household where religious feeling lingered in a certain gentleness of conduct and in certain moral and social attitudes, but
less and less in formal observances.

This is corroborated in Robinson's stories, in which the Quaker characters are never agents of religion as such, but rather the representatives
of moral, social, and political attitudes. In short, they are Abolitionists.
They are advocates of gentle and nonviolent but resolute civil disobedi-
ence, in contrast to non-Quaker Vermonters who liked to earn a dollar
by endorsing law and order and turning in runaway slaves. We know that
Rokeby was a station on the Underground Railway during Robinson's
boyhood.[9] We know that William Lloyd Garrison was a visitor there,
perhaps more than once, and was in correspondence with Robinson's
parents. Here is a passage from a letter of Garrison's, dated 30 November
1835: "Accompanying this, is an excellently written epistle . . . from Rachel Robinson, wife of Rowland E. of Ferrisburgh, Vt. Not a particle of
production of slave labor, whether it be rice, sugar, coffee, cotton, molasses, tobacco, or flour, is used in her family." If Garrison's list is correct,
Robinson's mother was a marvel at finding substitutes, for we know the
family lived well; but the point of the quotation is the way it illustrates
Quaker seriousness and quiet militancy—they would have found no
contradiction in the term—with respect to antislavery. And this was exactly the aspect of Quakerism, rather than the sectarian theology, that
was impressed on the young Robinson. It derived very directly in
America from the writings of John Woolman, whose works I could not
find in the library at Rokeby, though all my instinct tells me they must
be there. Woolman's selfless humility and gentle mysticism were exactly
the qualities that Robinson's Quaker characters, in the stories about the
Underground Railway, display *par excellence*; Woolman's exquisite toler-

ance toward all human beings together with his submissive acceptance of the natural world were mirrored in the best inhabitants of Danvis. Woolman had written of the ways by which he had tried to "learn to Exercise true Justice and Goodness, not only toward all men, but also toward the Brute Creatures"—an extraordinary statement for an American of the eighteenth century—and the words are a succinct expression of Robinson's own ideal.

Obviously I cannot prove the extent of Quaker influence on Robinson. On one hand the doctrinal aspects of Quakerism had worn away by the time Robinson came to the expression of his mature beliefs, while on the other a different or more general origin could be found for the same attitudes toward nature and society. The generalized and somewhat diluted romanticism that had reached America from Europe in the first third of the nineteenth century could account for much of Robinson's later development as a writer. The later poems of Philip Freneau and the writing of Cooper, Bryant, Irving, and others of their generation might have given Robinson his esthetic and philosophical directions. Yet these same romantic threads were woven into far different fabrics in other sectors of American artistic life during Robinson's years of development: into the gothicism of Poe, the symbolism of Hawthorne, the theatricality of the Hudson River painters, and the entire transcendental joy and agony of nineteenth-century America. Robinson seems to have escaped these darker elements of American experience. We cannot say he was insensitive to them, or unaware of them; he lived in New York for at least ten years during his formative period, and he read and contributed to the magazines that were *au courant* with American intellectual development. I think the answer is his Quaker background. The intrinsic evidence of his work together with external evidence of his known biography make a convincing case. Quakerism gave his sensibility the direction of its development toward realism, acceptance, tolerance, and concern, and preserved it from transcendental or neo-metaphysical *Sturm und Drang*.[10]

In an essay titled "Cleaning the Old Gun,"[11] Robinson gives us an anecdote of his boyhood, amusing yet like all his work imbued with modesty and truthfulness. It shows us the quality of life in a proper Quaker household. Robinson was loading his first gun, he tells us, an old flintlock which had been "clumsily changed to the incoming percussion fashion." He was in the kitchen at Rokeby, where grandfather Robinson, with his back turned, stood gazing out the window and "dreaming an old man's dream of the past." After the boy had rammed home the charge, shot, and wad in the barrel, he pulled the trigger with his finger and lowered the hammer gently with his thumb, since "hammer down was the rule of safety in those days." But his thumb slipped, the hammer struck hard, the percussion cap ignited, and "the house was shaken with the discharge, the shot driven like a bullet through the panel of the kitchen door and [into] the ceiling of the hall." His grandfather, "serene amid the uproar," turned from the window and said, "What is thee trying to do, boy?"—and that was the whole extent of the child's reprimanding.

Perhaps another way to approach Robinson's personality would be to say that he was raised permissively in the midst of a rural society that held the extreme opposite idea of conduct in children and in every department of life.

But inevitably our clearest image of Robinson, as of most authors, is not as a boy but as an old man. Then, when his reputation was at its height, visitors came flocking to see him and to write their accounts of him afterward; photographers came asking to take his picture. We have a number of portraits of Robinson when his hair and beard were white, and his eyes blind, including one in which Mrs. Robinson also appears, looking much younger than her husband, almost another generation. They sit together, she reading aloud, he gazing unseeingly at the skies; a portrait so profound in its unposed mystery and dramatic sorrow that it could serve as archetype for the blind poet and his muse. We are told that writing was the chief pleasure of his blindness, but that smoking his pipe remained a pleasure too, and walking in familiar lanes and fields with his left hand on the right shoulder of one of his children. His eyes, though blind, remained "a clear blue and full of expression." [12] Robinson bore his affliction courageously; the few times when he wrote about it seem more poignant for their rarity. In 1893, soon after the last of his vision faded, he wrote to a friend: "'I'm dead, I'm dead' as my schoolfellow, Charley R., shouted when he got a licking; and I know something how it seems to a man to hear the world going on around him, and he lying under the grass." [13]

The final year and a half of his life were bedridden. Robinson was taken by a slow, painful cancer of the stomach that made him cry out involuntarily in his room, as he continued working with his grooved writing-board. In this way he completed two more books and a number of essays and sketches before he died, hurrying to say all he had to say about the splendors of the world.

III

The materials I have called by the working title of "Danvis tales," though Robinson did not use this title himself, consist of more or less connected sketches falling into six sequences, plus a few miscellaneous pieces collected elsewhere. They comprise somewhat less than half of Robinson's total production. Yet they are by far the more important part, since they alone raise Robinson to the stature of an artist. Virtually all the rest of his work is magazine jobbery and historical studies done for the glorification of Vermont. Only in the "Danvis tales" did Robinson discover not only a form but an entire expressive matrix that was exactly suited to his creative personality and to what he as an artist could reasonably expect to do within the limits of time and energy he could devote to it, that is, the last twenty years of his life. It was not, we may be sure, a purposeful discovery; the ways of art are not that rational. It was a spontaneous and natural and, in the circumstances, remarkably swift evolution of personal insight, for which we may be thankful.

We are told[14] that when he was ten years old Robinson accompanied his father on a one-day excursion, a business trip from Ferrisburg, which is situated on the littoral plain near the shore of Lake Champlain, up into the Green Mountains to the town of West Lincoln. It was a distance of no more than twelve miles or so as the crow flies, but considerably farther in a one-horse wagon on twisting mountain roads, and farther yet in terms of economic and social gradations. The farmers of Ferrisburg held large tracts of bottomland, rich and level, and they sold their produce in the cities for cash. But the farms of the mountains were small, stony, and hilly, the "towns" were no more than settlements, and the people lived in poor self-sufficiency in an economy dominated by barter. Culturally, they were isolated: not totally, of course, but close to it. Indeed, West Lincoln would have presented a dismal enough appearance in most respects. Yet in others its appeal was great. The countryside was still largely unspoiled, and the people were still a hardy pioneering stock, whose vigor of body and spirit was expressed in their architecture, speech, and general comportment. Young Robinson was impressed. He was impressed so deeply, if the story is true, that forty years later when he came to write the "Danvis tales" he described West Lincoln, under the name of Danvis, with an accuracy recognizable in the features of the town today. This strikes me as somewhat exaggerated, I confess. From the deeper verisi-militude of event and character in the "Danvis tales," beyond any matter of pictorial authenticity, I surmise Robinson visited West Lincoln and adjacent regions many times again before he lost his sight, on fishing and hunting expeditions or in search of local history and folklore. Other towns too must have contributed to the composite Danvis. But there can be no doubt of the locus of the "Danvis tales" high on the western slope of the Green Mountains, somewhere "back" of Ferrisburg between the Lincoln Gap on the south and the Appalachian Gap on the north.

The point is not that certain ingredients of Robinson's Danvis are ac-tual while others are fictional, but that the amalgam he made of them, forged in affection, is neither fact, in the statistical sense, nor fiction, in the novelistic sense; it is simpler but purer. Doubtless at a modest level, it is truth enlarged, the kind of superreal generalization at which all imag-inative writing aims. Robinson achieved his minor triumph precisely through the simplicity of his expressive matrix, which incorporated and absorbed his defects. Thus he instinctively avoided a complex narrative, such as his formal history of Vermont had forced on him, and chose instead the loosest episodic structure for his sequences, held together by a thin thread of continuity. The thread is there; his "Danvis tales," though seeming no more than random strokes of memory and insight collected without other restraint than that imposed by good sense and relevance, nevertheless do have narrative consistency, as David Budbill's selection from them makes clear. It's a loose narrative, spontaneously developed, yet it confirms Robinson's artistic intelligence, which is a point worth making.

One cannot say with precision what the "Danvis tales" are about—they are about almost anything. One can at best note their coordinates. In time they make a chronology of events in the lives of several families from about 1830 to the outbreak of the Civil War, with one lesser se-quence, A Danvis Pioneer, extending backward to the first days of settle-ment before, during, and after the Revolution. In place they convey a sense of both mountain and littoral, since several sequences deal with fishing and hunting excursions to the marshland where Otter Creek, Dead Creek, and Lewis Creek empty into Lake Champlain. Their persons are Sam Lovel, a young farmer; his wife, Huldah; their boarders, Uncle Lisha, who is a cobbler, and Aunt Jerushy; Gran'ther Hill, Revolutionary veteran and oldest in the community; Mrs. Pur'n't'n (Purington), Hul-dah's mother; Solon Briggs, a long-winded Yankee Mrs. Malaprop; Pelatiah Gove, a young man thwarted in love; Joel Bartlett, a Quaker; Antoine, a French-Canadian; and a score of lesser inhabitants. Their ambience is the natural environment, Vermont's forests and fields, animals and birds, rivers and mountains, seasons and weathers, the entire external reality, which is in fact more than an ambience in these tales; it is the substance of them, as it was the substance of experience in Danvis, the very fullness of being, within which human words and feelings were as insubstantial as chimes on the wind. Finally the focus of these tales . . . but let Robinson speak for himself, in an explanatory note, dated 1894, prefaced to *Danvis Folks*:

> . . . It was written with less purpose of telling any story than of recording the manners, customs, and speech in vogue fifty or sixty years ago in certain parts of New England. Manners have changed, many customs have become obsolete, and though the dialect is yet spoken by some in almost its original quaintness, abounding in odd similes and figures of speech, it is passing away; so that one may look forward to the time when a Yankee may not be known by his speech, unless perhaps he shall speak a little better English than some of his neighbors. In truth he uses no worse now, nor did he ever, though he is accused of it. Such as it was, some may be glad to remember, and chiefly for them these papers have been written.

When I first read this note, it seemed a case of *déjà vu*, so strong was my impression that I had read it before—which was impossible. I had never read anything of Robinson's before. I had never heard of Robinson. My sense of something already seen must come from another source entirely. And before long I thought of a similar note to a more famous book: Mark Twain's "Explanatory Notice" at the front of *Huckleberry Finn*. There Twain had given special emphasis to his seriousness of purpose in reproducing the various dialects of Missouri, just as Robinson had affirmed his own concern for preserving the speech of rural Vermont. And both authors had disclaimed a more exalted purpose, Robinson by saying simply that he did not aim at storytelling, Twain by a comic offer of punishment to anyone who could find either motive, moral, or plot in his book. *Huckleberry Finn* was published in 1884, the year when the first "Danvis tales" were serialized in *Forest and Stream*. Robinson's original conception of his work could hardly have been influenced by Twain. But

Robinson did not write his note until 1894, the year when *Danvis Folks* appeared in book form; and he could have read *Huckleberry Finn* well before then. In fact it would be astonishing if he had not read it. This is not to suggest that his note at the beginning of *Danvis Folks* was a conscious imitation of Twain's at the beginning of *Huckleberry Finn*; yet certainly Robinson's reading of Twain's masterpiece could have given him a firmer notion of his own artistic aims in the "Danvis tales," from which the similarity of notes would follow naturally.

Indeed, many similarities exist between *Huckleberry Finn* and the "Danvis tales." There are many differences, too, of course, differences of tone, subject, intensity, and so forth. Twain was a man of wit, of tensions and despairs, Robinson a man of gentle melancholy. Twain was a fiercely devoted artist, who said that "the difference between the *right* word and the *almost* right word is the difference between lightning and the lightning bug"; we have little evidence that Robinson's literary conscience was anywhere near so acute. Twain gave us in the figures of his book—the dark river, the raft with its irreversible motion, the symbiosis of slave and white boy, the themes of escape and regeneration—our primal American experience in a stroke of mythopoetic genius, as many critics have pointed out; Robinson's tales contain no such penetrating and concentrated vision. Yet both *Huckleberry Finn* and the "Danvis tales" are loosely episodic narratives or sequences; both are conscious endeavors to reconstruct the folk manners and customs of a particular region at a particular time; both emphasize the creative value of local patterns of speech; and both were written from intimate and affectionate personal knowledge. Though in substance the two are largely not related, as in effect they are not comparable, certainly in many ways they are parallel. And I think in one respect, his creative use of dialect, Robinson's work is far from the paler construction, while in another respect, his awareness of the environment and of the American's peculiar relationship to the wilderness, it is more modern and more profound, imbued with a doleful spirit of prophecy.

IV

Yet even with respect to their linguistic experiments the comparison of our two authors, Twain and Robinson, is unfair to them and only valuable to us if we recognize its narrow limits of applicability; although both men professed the same objective, that is, a serious and accurate representation of the dialect speech of their respective regions, their methods differed greatly. Whereas Robinson endeavored to *reproduce* the dialects of northwestern Vermont, by means of orthographic manipulation of the standard English alphabet, Twain tried to *suggest* the dialects of eastern Missouri, through the use of local idiom, syntax, and speech rhythm, while retaining standard English spelling in all but a few unavoidable cases.

Twain's was the more professional method, as we would expect. He was remarkably successful and exerted a profound influence on later writers. In the generation of Hemingway, Faulkner, and Frank O'Hara, for instance, although many writers were dealing with regional materials and dialects, few resorted to misspellings. The entire Bre'r Rabbit school—if I may so name it—had passed out of favor. It was now considered unprofessional to force the reader to put up with unconventional orthography. Behind this change lay the belief that no method of linguistic notation, neither standard alphabet nor the most complex phonetic alphabet that academic linguists could contrive, can reproduce human speech. Only the preservation of actual sounds, by mechanical recording, can do it. The best one can hope for in print is a suggestion.

To this Robinson would have replied that nobody was striving for perfection, least of all himself. True, he might have said, no typographical notation can more than suggest the sounds of real human speech, but is this a reason for making the suggestion less suggestive? If spelling can help suggest actual sounds, then why not use it?

At any rate, Robinson spelled his dialects. But an important distinction must be made at the outset of any consideration of his success. He was *not* imitating the humorists. From Royall Tyler and Thomas Chandler Haliburton down to Artemus Ward and Bill Nye, the humorists had used misspelling for comic effect in the portrayal of rustic Yankee characters. But those misspellings were conventional, stereotyped, with little attention paid to actual sound values. Many were intended simply to show ignorance of book learning, as "rite" for "write," "ruff" for "rough," and so on. Robinson's procedures were entirely different. Although his sketches are often comic in intent, they almost never derive their humor from verbal practice alone. There are no puns, no verbal misunderstandings, and the closest thing to pure verbal humor is the speech of Solon Briggs, whose nonsensical malapropisms sometimes convey an alternative sense unknown to the speaker; but this would be just as effec-

tive in standard speech as in dialect. In short, Robinson never condescends to his dialects, as he never condescends to his characters. His
attitude is serious and affectionate. The dialects he records are real lan-
guages, still close in many respects to the Tudor speech of the first New
England settlers. Robinson sensed this, though he was not a linguist—
he could not have been in his lifetime. He was a writer, an artist working
with language; he had an ear for sound and cadence. He knew the speech
of his region. He recognized the integrity and humane value of that
speech, and this at a time when the dominant gentility of America insisted that such speech could be nothing but vulgar.

The question is, did Robinson succeed in his effort to record the
speech of northwestern Vermont?—which is difficult to answer. We don't
know what that speech was. More than a century has passed since the
time of the "Danvis tales," and though old speech habits persist in isolated
parts of Vermont, nowhere today is the local dialect what it was. About
all we can say is that the experts are agreed on what the speech of northwestern Vermont is *not*. It is not part of "New England dialect." Draw a
line from the Canadian border down the spine of the Green Mountains
and the Berkshires to lower Litchfield County in Connecticut, thence
eastward to the Connecticut River and southward to Long Island Sound:
New England dialect, they say, is confined to the east of this line. If by
"New England dialect" we mean the broad, flat vowels and jerky, elided
consonants of the typical Boston and Down East accents, then the experts
are easily borne out by amateur observation. Down East can be heard
today as close to northwestern Vermont as the eastern slopes of the Green
Mountains, in such towns as Peacham and Chelsea; but in the Champlain Valley and along the inlets of the Winooski and Lamoille Rivers
and on the still sparsely settled western slopes of the mountains, we hear
something else. The vowel sounds are more complex, not flat but diph-
thongized, with a range of pitch from nasal to guttural, and although the
r's are slurred or elided ("pa'tridge," "butt'nut"), there is in general a fuller,
spikier use of consonants. Diphthongization, as in the "oi" sounds, sometimes makes northwestern Vermont seem closer to Brooklyn or New Or-
leans than to Boston.

No one can prove that Robinson's ear was as sensitive to colloquial
speech as we have every right to believe it was on the basis of circumstantial and textual evidence alone. The circumstantial evidence consists
largely of the testimony of his readers, particularly those who read his

works as they were first published. We have a considerable mass of such testimony.[15] Its tendency is unanimous, and it confirms our judgment that Robinson has been most appreciated by those who have lived in or near his region of Vermont. Again and again we read the statements of living persons who recall how the "Danvis tales" were read aloud in their homes when they were children, read by some older member of the family who was both verbally talented and familiar with the speech of the Green Mountains. I suppose these performances were in the nature of "recitations," that great source of entertainment during the decades of American "gentility," but do we have any reason to look down on them for that? The performances may have contained elements of absurdity—extravagant gestures and forced intonations—but they were at bottom designed to exploit the peoples' genuine awareness of language and their delight in its creative use. All the testimony of his readers reveals their firm conviction that he was not indulging in stereotyped "dialect-writing," but was sympathetically and accurately recording the speech which they themselves knew and frequently heard, though presumably they, being book-readers, represented a "higher" culture than that of Danvis and hence were not themselves the primary users of the speech in question. They knew it, however, and they could tell what Robinson was doing with it.

Robinson was an instinctive linguist; he understood the value of listening carefully and recording faithfully. And we may say as a matter of course that he applied the same care and fidelity to the larger aspects of his material, to idiom, syntax, and speech rhythm.

When Sam Lovel and his friends are camping on the shore of Lake Champlain, they find some aspects of lowland living less attractive than what they are used to in the mountains. One morning Pelatiah Gove, who has just joined the party, kneels on the shore to wash his face in lakewater and then turns to Sam:

"Wha' d'ye du for suthin to drink? this 'ere water hain't fit! I hain't hed a decent drink o' water sen I come off 'm the hills. This 'ere stuff 'raound here don't hit nowheres!"

"Julluk me," Sam answered, "when I fust com' daown here. The well water an' sech didn't squench my thirst no more 'n it 'ould to open my maouth an' let the moon shine into 't. It's hard, all on 't; you can't suds a pint on 't with a barrel 'o soap! But I'm

a-gittin' use to 't an' the's a brook back here 'at dreens the snow
aoutin the woods that you'll find toll'able satisfyin' 'f you drink
tew three pailfuls on 't . . ."[16]

This is calculated writing by a man who knows his people. He does not
write "fit to drink," but merely "fit." Notice the use of "'ere" and "here"
in the same sentence, and such terms as "suthin," "sen," "squench," and
"dreens": these are far from the stereotyped usages of literary or comic
dialect-writing, though some of them might be found in other works of
other writers. Taken altogether they give the distinct impression of language actually heard. Notice that Robinson writes "off 'm," not "offen" or
"off'n"; this is accurate for the region, as I myself have verified among
older inhabitants. But the most telling elements of Robinson's skill are the
least demonstrable, his sensitivity to the syntax and rhythm of colloquial
speech. Notice the interplay of long and short breath-units in these sentences, and the mixing of grammatical structures, clause and phrase, different verb moods, and so forth. Only a very complicated chart could
reduce all these elements to a form of linguistic analysis, but they are
what account for both the verisimilitude and the esthetic liveliness of this
speech. The truth is that Robinson's dialogue, which is the largest and
most important part of the "Danvis tales," is invariably better writing than
his descriptive and narrative passages in the standard overblown English
of his day.

When Uncle Lisha wishes to tell his friends how plentiful the muskrat
are at the mouth of Little Otter Creek, he says:

> I've seen their haousen on the ma'shes in fall an' winter thick as
> ever ye seen hay cocks in a medder, 'most, an' hundreds of acres
> o' ma'sh with 'em sot jes' so thick.[17]

That "'most," set where it is in the sentence, is pure Vermontese. The
characteristic Vermont syntax, reflecting the characteristic Vermont humor and turn of mind, is what might be called the "modifier as after-
thought," tacked on almost too late to catch the main impetus of the
sentence. When Uncle Lisha asks Joseph Hill if his grandfather, who had
been at the taking of Fort Ticonderoga in his youth and was known for
his garrulous accounts of it, still "has spells o' takin' Ti":

> "Well, yis," Joseph answered with a tone of resignation. "Reg'-
> lar onct a week, an' I do' know but oftener; seem 's 'ough. Some-

times I most wish him an' Ethan Allen hadn't never took the pleg-gid ol' fort, seem 's 'ough I did a'most." [18]

Which gives us two examples of the commonest locution of all in Green Mountain dialect, "it seems as though." It is never given full pronunciation. The actual sound is: *seem'zo*, with the slightest of hesitations between "m" and "z." Usually Robinson gives it in standard elided spelling, as here in the quotation from Joseph Hill, but sometimes he tries variations, and he seems never to have been satisfied with any of his approximations. This is a more obvious case than most of the unspellability of Green Mountain dialect in the standard alphabetical signs.

However, the dialect is distinctly not a matter of particular words, phrases, or idioms, nor of any collection of particular devices put together by way of artifice; it is a matter of the wholeness and flow of the language, heard spontaneously in Robinson's inner ear.

"I was kinder runnin' things over in my mind arter you was here t'other night," said Uncle Lisha, rolling a length of shoe thread on his aproned knee and then carefully splicing it to a split bristle, "an' I got tu thinkin' 'baout ol' Bart Johnson's scrape wi' the wolves up on Tater Hill. He was a kinder half-cracked ol' critter 'at useter come a-wanderin' raoun' here abaout onct a year when I was a young feller, an' useter stop tu aour haouse, off an' on, fer a week or two at a time, an' poke 'raoun' on the maountain days, a-lookin' for his treasure, as he called it. He'd ben a soger in the ol' French war, endurin' which he went on a expedition ag'in the Canady Injins under a Major Rodgis, I b'lieve his name was. Wal, they s'prised the Injins an' destr'yed the village an' fetched away lots o' stuff 'at they'd got from aour folks, trinkets an' silver an' gold an' money an' a silver idolatry imidge 'at weighed more 'n twenty paounds—jest clean silver. Wal, off they started back, a-luggin' the' booty, wi' a fresh lot o' Injins arter 'em, so 't they headed off towards the Connect'cut River. Pooty soon they begun tu git short o' provision an' they divided up inter small parties, each one shiftin' fer himself, an' they come tu terrible straits, grub-bin' fer rhuts an' gnawing bark, an' most on 'em hove away the' plunder an' hedn't no thought o' nothin', on'y savin' the' mis'able lives, which was more n' some on 'em done. But ol' Bart hung tu what he'd got, a lot o' money an' I do' know but the silver imidge, an' he wandered off by himself till he come tu the top of a high maountain, an' seen the lake an' knowed where Crown P'int was. An' he came daown this side a piece, an' bairied his stuff, an' arter a spell he got tu Crown P'int, nigher dead 'an he was alive. When the war was ended he begin tu look fer his plunder an' he consaited Tater Hill was the maountain he'd left it on, an' so year arter year, as long as he lived, he'd come an' s'arch an' s'arch for the stuff 'at was goin' tu make a rich man on him. . . ."[19]

Well, there's no need to reprint all of "ol' Bart's" search for his buried loot or his run-in with the wolves, though the story is worth reading. What needs pointing out to modern readers is that this tale is told by Uncle Lisha, no pariah, not by any means, but a literate artisan, a man of substance; his speech is the *standard respectable mountain speech* of Vermont in the early nineteenth century. If the tale had been told by a degenerate member of the town, Robinson would have made the speech considerably more slurred ("hiss'f" instead of "himself," etc.). It is also worth noting that the expedition of Major Rodgers against the St. Francis Indians in Canada and the extreme hardship of the return journey are historical events. But whether or not there was such a soldier as Bart Johnson, I don't know. In miniature, the tale is a good example of the way Robinson put together the whole of the Danvis sequence from historical and observed fact, with a mixture of imagination in the telling.

The degenerate element of Danvis, if there was one, appears only very sparingly in Robinson's stories, and in fact he speaks of Danvis as belonging to "the old times when none were rich and none were poor, and all were . . . dependent on each other." If this seems idyllic, a part of our eternal romance with the "olden days," we have reason to believe nevertheless that Robinson was not romanticizing; he was accurately describing social and economic conditions in the early settlements of Vermont. There was one apparent exception, however, the family of Antoine Bassette, the town's French-Canadian immigrant: a large, ever-burgeoning family. Poor, happy-go-lucky, full of wood lore, Antoine is a boaster and story-teller, whose speech, if not degenerate, is such a tangle of Vermont idiom and French syntax, salted with wildly incorrect verb forms, that it can scarcely be understood by those who have not heard it. Yet it is authentic. Since no research whatever has been done on French-Canadian speech, the proof would be even more difficult to bring forth than a proof of the authenticity of Robinson's Danvis dialect, if we couldn't still hear the French-Canadian dialect in all its "purity" every day. New immigrants arrive with every generation. There isn't a town north of the Winooski River that doesn't have its family of Antoines.

Granted, at first one thinks that Robinson uses the French-Canadian's irregularities of grammar for comic effect, and consequently that he may be open to the charge of exaggerating them. My own feeling, after looking at many examples of Antoine's speech and matching them against what I hear from my French-Canadian neighbors, is that this is not the case. The speech is set down pretty much as Robinson heard it. The comic effect comes simply from the setting down—there *is* an element of comedy in mangled speech, though in these days of touchy national sensibilities one can scarcely point to it without appearing to condescend—and also, of course, from the substance of Antoine's tall tales and bragging expostulations.

Here is Antoine defending himself:

> "Haow many tam Ah'll gat for tol' you Ah ant never lie? M'sieu Mumpson, he'll read me 'baout George Washin's son chawp a happle-tree wid hees new saw, an' tol' hees fader he'll do it 'cause he'll can' lie. Ah'll chawp more as forty happle, prob'ly feefty tree 'fore Ah'll lie, me. Yes, sah."[20]

Even "George Washin's son" is no exaggeration, but a linguistic probability. As for the rest, it is absolutely characteristic. When the prospect of going fishing is mentioned, Antoine cries: "Bah gosh! Ah wish Ah ketch some bullpout or heel, bose of it, Ah don' care which, me!"[21]

Perhaps the best of Antoine's stories about the life he left behind in Canada is the one told while he, Sam, and Pelatiah are sitting in their shelter at their camp on the creek called the Slang:

> "Dat mek me tink," said Antoine, coming in from a brief in-spection of the chowder, and nursing a coal that he had scooped out of the ashes in his pipe bowl, "mek me tink one tam me ma brudder-law keel one dat panter in Canada. We was go huntin' for deer. Ah guess so, an' da was leetly mite snow on de graoun'. Wal seh, we'll see it track, we ant know what he was be, an' we'll folla dat, oh, long, long tam. Bamby he'll go in hole in rock, leetly laidge, you know, 'baout tree, fo', prob'ly seex tam big dis shantee was. Wal, seh, boy, Ah'll left it ma brudder-law for watch

dat holes, an' Ah'll go 'raoun' back side laidge see all what Ah'll see. Ah'll look veree caffly, an' what you tink Ah'll fin' it? Leetly crack in rock 'baout so wide ma tree finger of it, an' dat panter hees tail steek off of it 'baout so long ma arm, prob'ly, where he'll push hind fust in dat holes. An' he'll weegly hees tail so," waving his forefinger slowly. "Wal, Ah'll tink for spell what Ah do. Den Ah'll go cut off strong steek so big half ma wris' an' two foots long. Den Ah'll tek hol' dat tails an' tied knot in him, veree caffly, den Ah'll run steek t'rough an' pull knot hard! Ah, bah gosh! you'll oughty hear dat panters yaller an' holla! Wus as fo' honded tousan' cat! Yes, seh! Oh, he'll hugly, Ah told you! But he can't help it, he can' gat it loose 'less he pull up hees tails off. Wal, seh, Ah'll lafft at it, Ah can' help it, mos' Ah'll split off ma side. Den Ah'll go 'raoun ma brudder-law, an' he'll be scare mos' dead, an' goin' runned way, Ah'll tol' heem, Ah goin' in dat holes shoot dat panters. 'Oh, gosh!' he'll ax me, 'he tore you dead more as forty piece!' Ah'll say, 'Ah so good man Ah'll don't 'fraid me.' Den Ah'll crawl in dat holes an' Ah'll shoot it, boom! right 'tween hees head! An' bamby pooty soon he ant yaller some more, he be all still as mices. Den Ah'll come off de holes an' Ah'll tol' ma brudder-law he'll crawl in an' pull off dat panters. He'll pooty 'fraid for go, but bamby he go. He touch hol' of it, he can' pull it cause hees tail tie, but he ant know. 'Bah gosh!' he say, 'dat pant-ers more heavy as two ton! Ah can' pull it!' Den Ah'll go 'raoun' an' taked off dat steek, an' holla 'pull!' an' ma brudder-law pull more harder he can—boom! he go tumbly on hees back, dat panters on top of it! Oh! 'f he ant scare, ma brudder-law. Yas seh! Wal, seh, boy," after a pause during which no one spoke, "'f you ant mek b'lieve dat stories you go Canada 'long to me Ah show you de steek. Ma brudder-law he'll saved it. Ah ant never tol' you stories so true lak dat, seh!"[22]

And as any Vermonter knows, this story was told at a pace about equal to a machine gun. Incidentally, "caffly" for *carefully* is standard Vermontese, either native or French-Canadian, and not exaggerated in the least. Again incidentally, when Antoine uses two forms of the negative in one sen-tence—"can't help" and "can' gat"—this is not Robinson's carelessness, as some readers might think, but dead-on accuracy. The "t" would appear before the partly aspirated "h" but not before the hard "g."

Robinson was not always consistent, however. He was not working from a glossary or following principles of systematic transliteration, not even in his own mind. He was listening to what his ear told him was right. In some books Antoine says "sah" and in others "seh," though the former is closer to proper French-Canadian English as spoken today. I believe Robinson refined his techniques for recording dialect as he progressed from book to book in the Danvis sequence. He worked ever closer to what he heard, which is extraordinary when you consider that in his blindness he could not even read what he himself had written. I've noticed, for what it's worth, that in the early tales Robinson wrote "keptin" for *captain* and "gardin" for *garden*, but in later tales he moved closer to actual Vermont usage, as still heard today, by changing the words respectively to "kepting" and "garding."

No doubt Robinson's dialectical spelling is an impediment to some readers, perhaps to many. Today we're not used to this degree of distortion. But let me say as plainly as possible that any reasonably literate person can become accustomed to Robinson's language in five pages. I mean it. Just pronounce what you read, as if you were reading music. And if you take this small, easy step to meet Robinson, he will return your effort many times over. The "Danvis tales" are not a novelty, not a piece of subclass folk material. They are first-rate comic literature.

V

If we make allowances for Robinson's place as a Vermont farmer within the general cultural situation of America—a provincial within provincialism, so to speak—what allowances must we make for the particular milieu of the years in which he wrote? We know that during the second half of the nineteenth century in America a great wave of Victorian gentility swept across the country. By 1890 it had begun to recede in New York, and perhaps also in Boston, where William Dean Howells, with his advocacy of mild realism in literature, had succeeded the older arbiters of taste, the Cambridge circle of Lowell, Longfellow, and Holmes; but in most of the rest of the country the wave had hardly reached its crest. We know that in reading any literature of the nineteenth century, English or American, Dickens and Thackeray or the lowliest frontier scribbler, we must almost automatically make certain corrections and substitutions. When Robinson has one of his characters say "goldumb" we read "goddamn." We know that "Jeems Price" means "Jesus Christ." We know, or can guess, a good many other quaint euphemisms. And we feel quite certain in our minds that the conversation of the men gathered around the campfire or in Uncle Lisha's workshop—since eighty percent or more of the episodes in the "Danvis tales" is confined to a masculine cast of characters—contained a great many more references to sex than Robinson had reported, a much larger proportion of "smut" and "vulgarity" (to use outmoded terms). Shall we criticize Robinson on this account? Shall we say that although, as we have established, he was faithful to the language of his region, in other respects he lacked realism? Two main points need to be made, one negative, the other affirmative.

First, it is much too easy for us to misconstrue the actual temper of mind prevailing in America during the latter half of the last century. Most Americans whose tastes and attitudes have been formed in the movement of liberalized manners that began in 1914 and is still unfinished cannot imagine the inner patterns of mental and emotional response that governed the behavior of average Americans a hundred years ago, and I mean both men and women. I remember one summer I fell into conversation with a man my own age who lives near one of northern Vermont's many beautiful lakes. He was a workman who made his living from logging and farm labor. I asked him, somewhat idly, how the swimming was, but got only an evasive answer. Without realizing that I had committed a *gaucherie*, I pursued the matter, until my friend finally said he didn't *know* how the swimming was, he had never *been* swimming. I was astonished. The water was virtually at his doorstep. I asked why not. More evasions; then at last, with a look of heroic despair, he blurted: "I bin private all me life and I means to keep private." Frankly, I could have talked to this man for half a day, and if he hadn't told me, such a reason for not swimming would never have entered my mind. Yet there it was. And I am convinced now that the extreme modesty represented by his attitude is not only common but *prevalent*, at least among people over sixty who live in rural northern Vermont. Call it extreme inhibition if you wish, for although this raises Freudian specters we cannot pursue here, you won't be far wrong, and your conclusion will tie in plainly with other evidences of social malaise in the backwoods of Vermont (the north's "Appalachia"). The backwoods Vermonter today *is* inhibited, he is ultra-inhibited, and his inhibitions function with respect not only to sexual behavior but to ninety percent of the rest of bodily existence, and to the whole area of social custom and cultural reference arising therefrom. Finally, it hardly needs to be said that the backwoods Vermont of today is the remnant of all rural Vermont a century and more ago (with a strong reinforcement from the Catholic Puritanism of French Canada), including the society of Danvis.

All of which in turn may mean that Robinson in his reticence was more realistic than we think. Just possibly in 1840 men like Sam Lovel and Uncle Lisha did *not* sit around the campfire and discuss their wives' anatomies, though such topics are heard commonly in the society of modern hunters. Just possibly men raised under the energetic, unquestioned authority of fundamentalist religion, even though they themselves later made no show of religious enthusiasm, *were* content with such profanities as "goldumb," or with Sam's customary "By the gre't horn spoon!" or Uncle Lisha's "Good airth an' seas!" At any rate the commonest epithet in the "Danvis tales," "dumb" or "dum" (Robinson spells it both ways), is still standard for *damn* among many farmers of Lamoille and Franklin Counties, as I can attest from my own hearing.

Reticence is the key. The one critic who has made a serious if rudimentary attempt to read Robinson's works, Professor Martin,[23] goes astray on just this point. After concluding that Robinson could not depict real relationships between people, and that life in the "Danvis tales" is too "serene," Martin continues: "It would have taken a great burst of creative energy (which he does not show that he possesses) for Robinson to express dramatically the fundamental principles which bring persons together and cleave them apart. To bare the heart of Danvis, or even the heart of one person, he would have had to expose the various stresses at play upon human life. This he does not do." But Martin is wrong on two counts. First, it is patently not necessary to "expose the various stresses at play upon human life" in order to convey themes of human conflict and attraction; most good writers avoid such exposure like the plague and strive to attain their ends by indirect means. There is plenty of strong feeling in Danvis, obviously—Sam Lovel's feeling for his Huldy, Pelatiah Gove's feeling toward the girl who jilts him, the enmity between Gran'ther Hill and Mrs. Pur'n't'n, the homesickness of Uncle Lisha after he has moved to Wisconsin, the feelings of Joel Bartlett and other Quakers on the issue of slavery, Sam's radical despondency when he is in danger of losing his farm, and so on. These feelings are there, no reader can doubt them, they are the armature on which the sequence of "Danvis tales" is wound; but they are not dramatized, not shouted out loud, because Robinson chooses other means to develop them—in general, understatement and indirect suggestion. Second, Martin is wrong in his misunderstanding of Vermont character. Robinson could not realistically "bare the heart" of Danvis because Danvis would never "bare" its own heart. Social order was maintained in Danvis without resort to violence or the use of law enforcement agencies, precisely because strong feeling was held in check by reticence, by the custom and manner of reticence.[24] This is Yankee character *par excellence*. When Mrs. Pur'n't'n has said something that is in fact extremely offensive to Uncle Lisha, he replies: "Wal, wal, ef folks didn't talk, they wouldn't say notin', an' I don't take no pride in what you said."[25] This is standard behavior for a Vermonter. Indeed, it has become the stock demeanor for the back-country Yankee in popular literature and the movies, from Mrs. Partington to David Harum (though he was nominally a Yorker). The stereotype has been used so often that it has lost its credibility: a paradox of the popular imagination. Real Yankees still exist, but the fictional type has disappeared.

In my reaction to Professor Martin's shallow misjudgments I do not wish to go too far in the other direction. Robinson was *not* a novelist. Whether or not he possessed the technical means to sustain suspense in his stories, he never tried it. When I say there was plenty of strong feeling in Danvis, I do not mean that these feelings are consistently exploited by Robinson, even with the means of understatement and suggestion that he demonstrably did have at his disposal. In the ordinary novelistic sense there is no "problem" in Robinson's sketches, not even something as simple and fortuitous as the freedom of Jim in *Huckleberry Finn*. The sketches are held in sequence, not by internal development, but by the consistent and recognizable characters of the persons who appear in them. Professor Martin has, first, imputed to Robinson a kind of writing he did not attempt; second, criticized Robinson for failing to meet the standards of that kind of writing; and, third, failed to understand why the kind of writing Robinson actually did choose to practice was right and suitable for the materials he dealt with.

Other considerations too lead us to credit Robinson's realism. In comparison with much of the writing of his time, Robinson's work has a straightforward, businesslike quality that cannot be overlooked. He used too many unnecessary adjectives, granted. But he did not use as many as most popular writers of the day, and even in the matter of euphemisms his "dumbs" and "goldumbs" are sprinkled through his sketches more liberally than perfect gentility would have permitted. We must remember that even though the affluence and security of the American middle class in the second half of the nineteenth century had induced a certain interest in the folklore and local color of social classes that had formerly been shunned as primitive or too close to the frontier, Robinson was still denied a truly genteel audience by the nature of his material—the vulgar pursuits of hunting and fishing—and by the periodicals in which his sketches mostly appeared—the sporting press. In other words, since he had never acquired genteel readers to begin with, he need not fear offending them. We see the results in the realism of his descriptions of nature, which are genuinely appreciative but never hyperbolical. He could deal with the death or maiming of a wild animal in a detailed, matter-of-fact way that seems harder to take, sometimes, than the purposely shocking descriptions of violence in our own fiction today. Similarly, there can be no question of his glossing over the appearance of his characters or of the place where they lived, shoddy enough in both cases. Given these aspects of realism, I see no reason to reject the idea that Robinson was equally faithful in his portrayal of the more nebulous elements of the civilization he was representing, what we generally call manners and morals.

Robinson recorded the manners and morals of the folk civilization he was concerned to present to us with the same fidelity that he used toward its speech. I don't by any means suggest that the eroticism, prurience, and sexual conflict we do *not* find in the "Danvis tales" were not present in the civilization either. Those people were human; presumably they behaved like the rest of us. We must make allowances in reading Robinson, to correct his portrait. But I insist that the correction is slight and easily made; it is no more than the ordinary application of common sense. We can supply what is lacking. We have no need to apologize for Robinson, as we would for the host of writers of his time who trimmed their work to meet the popular genteel demand. We see, when we ourselves take a realistic view of the historical Vermont character, that Robinson was close to its truth in his reticent or indirect approach to violent feeling and his suppression of overt sexuality. The small discrepancy that remains becomes easily bridged when we look at it in the light of historiographic or sociological criteria.[26] And I think when we look at it in terms of art, it becomes no discrepancy at all, but merely a factor of temperament, both the author's and the civilization's, that merges with the other necessary formal limits of his work.

VI

Any reader of all Robinson's work cannot fail to be struck by a sense of ongoingness and self-generation. We are reminded more of such modern works as Robert Duncan's "Passages" or Robert Lowell's "Notebooks," open-ended random sequences in which the onrush of experience is taken as the risky substance of meaning, than we are of the rounded-off, self-contained novels of Victorian literature. (Henry James was almost Robinson's exact contemporary.) Robinson was no innovator, nor was he ahead of his time. He was behind it. In important ways his technique was closer to Washington Irving's than to the evolving novelistic modes of his own era. Yet because Robinson escapes the categories of Victorian literature, and because his life concerns were inevitably those of his own time, not Irving's, he does seem closer to us than, say, such mannerist and local-colorist writers as Eggleston or Harris. We can see that Robinson was working his way through the problems of his world and doing so there on the page, from day to day, and from this we get a sense of effort, evolving intelligence, and integrity, a well as a kind of bedrock avoidance of artifice and a humane responsibility, which make his work, though far from modern, nevertheless amenable to modern sensibility. I realize I am expressing in awkward, imprecise language a generalized feeling I experienced while reading Robinson's books: namely, that here was a man closer in mind and heart to me than anyone else from his period whom I had encountered in a long time. And I have the impression from reading the awkward, imprecise statements of other admirers of Robinson that this is the experience of most of them.

What was the "problem" of Robinson's world? Not so different from ours, though we hope we have a clearer view of it. The place of human beings in nature. And if we see the problem more clearly than Robinson did, or at least more broadly, we must give him credit for being one of the first to see it at all, that is, in terms that prefigure our own concern. We recall that Robinson began his literary career with an encomiastic essay on the pleasures of fox hunting, and this remained a prominent theme in his writing until the end—not simply the hunting of foxes, of course, but hunting and fishing in general. Sam Lovel, who in spite of the foolish assertions of several critics[27] is not Robinson's alter ego, but who is nevertheless clearly the protagonist of the "Danvis tales," is presented to us under several aspects, as husband, father, and farmer, but chiefly and from first to last as hunter and fisherman. The pleasures of the hunt again and again drive Sam from his chores into the woods and fields with his dog, significantly named "Drive." And let there be no mistake, part of the "pleasure" is the kill: the well-aimed shot from skillfully chosen cover that takes the fox by surprise and tumbles him in bloody death, and then the skinning out of the carcass, the bearing home of pelt and brush as trophies for general admiration. There simply cannot be any equivocation about this; the quality of Robinson's prose, its pace and color, invariably sharpens when he describes, as he does scores and scores of times, the death throes of animals, birds, and fishes killed for sport. And it is definitely a sport. The hunter may sometimes eat the game he kills, but there is never a suggestion that this is from necessity, nor that Sam eats the foxes he shoots, nor that the many instances in the "Danvis tales" and elsewhere of the useless killing of crows, owls, squirrels, and other harmless wildlife is for any purpose but the killer's fun. All this is incontestable. It is there on the pages of Robinson's books.

Yet equally incontestable is the fact that Robinson was appalled by what he saw as the indiscriminate waste of wildlife by bloodthirsty hunters and the destruction of the natural habitat by careless farmers and woodsmen. He put into Sam Lovel's mouth several notable condemnations of hunters who take game out of season or hunt a particular species to extinction. Robinson was a conservationist in the emerging tradition of American naturalists like John Burroughs and John Muir (who were both close contemporaries). He loved the Vermont environment and he knew a lot about it.[28] A frequently quoted passage is the one in which Sam denies that his primary object in the hunt is the game he brings home. "Wal, then, Samwill," asks Uncle Lisha, "what on airth du ye go fer? Ye hunt more 'n 'most anybody I know, an' ye git more game." To which Sam replies:

> I can't hardly tell, Uncle Lisher. It comes nat'ral for me tu run in the woods. 'F I du git more game tu show for it 'n some does, I git suthin' besides 't I can't show. The air o' the woods tastes good tu me, fer't hain't ben breathed by nothin' but wild creeturs, 's 'n ole feller said 'at useter git up airly daown in Rho'dislan', where my folks come from. I luffter breathe it 'fore common folks has. The smell o' the woods smells good tu me, dead leaves 'n' spruce boughs, 'n' rotten wood, 'n' it don't hurt it none if it's spiced up a leetle bit with skunk an' mink an' weasel an' fox p'fum'ry. An' I

luffter see trees 'at 's older 'n any men, an graound 't wa'n't never
plaowed 'er hoed, a-growin' nat'ral crops. 'N' I luffter hear the
stillness of the woods, fer 't is still there. Wind a-sythin', leaves
a-rustlin', brooks a-runnin', birds a-singin', even a bluejay a-
squallin', hain't noises. It takes folks an' waggins an' horses an'
cattle an' pigs an' sech to make a noise. I git lots o' things a huntin' 't I can't show ye nor tell ye abaout, an' a feller that don't, don't
git the best o' huntin', cordin' to my idee.[29]

Later—around 1890, more than a century ago—Robinson wrote:

Of all living things, only man disturbs the nicely adjusted balance of nature. The more civilized he becomes, the more mischievous he is. The better he calls himself, the worse he is. For un-
counted centuries the bison and the Indian shared a continent,
but in two hundred years or so the white man has destroyed the
one and spoiled the other.[30]

This was Robinson's dilemma: on one hand his love of hunting and
his commitment to all that hunting signified in the human instinctual
drive to power and dominion in the natural world; on the other his
awareness of the value of the environment in terms remarkably close to
those of modern ecology. In his writing he worked nearer and nearer to
the metaphysical heart of his dilemma, but he never reached it. Some of
his strategies seem pitiful today, all the more because of their basic hon-
esty. His belief that he might solve the dilemma through remedial conservation, for instance: the enforcement of game laws, he hoped, would pre-
serve not only the "balance of nature" but the very means for keeping
alive his beloved blood sport—the supply of killable animals. This has
seemed, as we know, a reasonable reformist program to sportsmen and
even some naturalists for years and years. Yet there is at least some evidence that Robinson was dissatisfied with such a compromise, that he
recognized or half-recognized the absurdity at its heart. Was not a "man-
aged wilderness" a contradiction in terms? Was not the very concept of
man's dominion at odds with the functional "balance of nature"? Was
there in the heart of the race a self-division that turned the impulse of
life into a destructive, even suicidal force? Robinson had been raised a
Quaker. He does not say so, he probably could not have seen this deeply
into his own dilemma, but I suspect that at its heart lay the injunctions

against violence that he had heard so often in boyhood. Robinson was caught in a bitterly powerful love/hate relationship with his own violence, symbolized by his gun.

Occasionally—more and more toward the end—he went all the way over to nonviolence. The best example is the essay "Hunting Without a Gun," in which he recommends the pleasure not of killing but of looking, just as many naturalists since then have recommended using a camera instead of a gun. Other essays extol the virtues of walking at different seasons in woods and fields, or describe different species of songbirds and plants that have only the appeal of beauty or rarity. Most of these essays are included in the volume of the Centennial Edition entitled *In New England Fields and Woods* [with] *Sketches and Stories*, which contains the whole range of Robinson's outdoor and sporting essays, from the original "Fox Hunting in New England" through many similar hunting and fishing essays, proposals for game conservation, pleas for the establishment of reserves and other conservational measures, to "Hunting Without a Gun" and similar essays. It is a strange, confused, self-contradictory volume, put together by other hands and issued after his death.

Robinson had plenty of opportunity to see the results of man's depredations. Vermont in his day was a better place to study environmental mismanagement than Vermont today, in spite of the destruction wrought in recent years by developers of ski resorts and housing tracts. Men still living in Ferrisburg in Robinson's boyhood could tell him what the Champlain Valley had looked like when settlers first came, he could see the vast spoliation that had already occurred, and during his lifetime he saw it become drastically worse. He was personally acquainted with the man who had shot the last otter on Otter Creek, which is actually the longest and one of the loveliest rivers in the state. The salmon, which once had made the creeks and brooks churn in spawning time, were gone. The white-tailed deer was declared officially extinct in Vermont in 1877. (The present herd was restarted with animals imported from the Adirondacks.) The great forests were gone, the brooks were lower and more sluggish. Moose, caribou, wolves, black bears, panthers, lynx, and other magnificent animals that had ranged freely in the Green Mountains were gone or almost gone; ospreys and eagles and owls, pike and pickerel, the buttonwood and the great white pine, beaver, mink, fisher, and many, many other species were greatly reduced. Even the foxes, Robinson's favorites, had vanished from many hills and ledges where they had formerly run at large.[31] Today the populations of a few of these species—dear, bear, moose, beaver—have somewhat revived, while others have disappeared completely, probably forever.

Remember, these ravages had been wrought in a span of time hardly longer than a normal human lifetime. Robinson knew who was responsible for them. He was well acquainted with Vermonters who saw only the plenitude of the wilderness and indulged their lust for sport with no thought of the future. But it is doubtful that he, or anyone else in his time, pursued the matter to its nucleus, which lay even deeper than his personal dilemma as a Quaker hunter. And this is the point at which the "Danvis tales" connect with the rest of Robinson's writing, the essays dealing expressly with hunting, fishing, and conservation; this is where we begin to understand what it is that we have half-heard occasionally in the tales, an ominous, troubled undertone that gives them a resonance we had not been led by their surface qualities to suspect. It is there all right, unless I am much mistaken; a sadness that is more than Victorian sentimentalism, a sorrowing for the lost primitive world, a reverberation of moral despair and metaphysical mystery. We are aware that something, we scarcely know what, is at work to counteract Robinson's admiration and affection for his Danvis folk. He could not see it, perhaps happily for him, but now we can tell that it was his own unrecognized awareness of what these people really were, these mountain folk, hardy, pragmatic, independent Vermonters, exemplars of every Yankee virtue, including tenderness and compassionate understanding—these were exactly the people who had slaughtered the animals and destroyed the forests. In the heart of their innocence an evil lurked. For they had done it in the very necessity of their selfhood; their virtues were their vice. These farmers had destroyed the trees, overworked the land, sold their holdings to the first buyer who offered a dollar above market value, speculated in their own land, bored mines in the fields, built woolen and paper mills to pollute the streams, and they were only beginning. When horses and oxen gave way to tractors, when tractors gave way to monstrous earth movers and log skidders, when mountainsides gave way overnight to files of pastel-colored ranchhouses and chalets, it would be this same mentality at work, the Yankee, the pioneer. Deep in Vermont, deep in America, the paradox inheres. The virtues we celebrate, the virtues of our pioneering hearts, are exactly the products of our will to power and dominion, our unwillingness to compete with other species equally. The hand that brought honest thrift and industry to the continent was the hand that felled the tree, broke the sod, opened the earth to erosion and pollution, and from this hand it is a mere logical extension to the gun that massacred the Indians and the whip that drove the slaves. In short, Sam Lovel was as pure a specimen as Lorenzo de Medici before him; in Florence and in Danvis, in the fifteenth century and the nineteenth, Renaissance man had gloried in humanistic self-aggrandizement, and had looked at the universe as an anthropocentric structure, in effect a huge material resource accessible without limit to his greedy exploitation.

Robinson, like all Vermonters, had a perfect example to study in the founding of his own state. But he could not see the truth of it; only a stroke of unequaled foresight could have put him that far ahead of his time. Instead, in his historical writing about Vermont he consistently played the patriot, not to say the chauvinist. As much as anyone he is responsible for the popular image of Ethan Allen as a dashing, intrepid, democratic, impudent, free-thinking, independent pioneer and soldier, the first Green Mountain Boy and prototype of all the rest forever. Not until the 1930s and 1940s did historians begin to uncover the truth about Allen and his brother Ira and their followers, namely, that they were land speculators on an immense scale, whose activities during the latter third of the eighteenth century were motivated less by ideological considerations than by a burning desire to save their claims to hundreds of thousands of acres in the Champlain Valley and throughout northern Vermont. These were the men whose interests in the land were empirical and economic, who bought it for little and sold it for much, who encouraged the wasteful spoilage of the magnificent climax forest of white pine for the sake of a little timber and potash—and who, incidentally, were dickering with the British considerably before the Battle of Lexington in an attempt to improve the value of their land by means of a separate peace. This is known now, and has been for some time; it has been written about by both popular and scholarly historians.[32] But no one has drawn from this knowledge its logical conclusion, that Yankee character to this day remains as it was fixed by its originators, a melding of reciprocal good and evil, and that the strength of mind which built a free and orderly society—that historical miracle—was a product of the will to power and human dominion in the natural world. We see the outcome. Only a brave man could promote such a hypothesis in the face of the outraged patriotic howls that would ensue. But something must be done. And is outrage required? Ethan Allen's virtues remain, no one disputes them or denies them. Perhaps it is best to abandon terms like good and evil, virtue and vice, and to speak instead of the multiple strands of our heritage, some of which have proven unserviceable as our social and ecological predicament unfolds. We must unravel ourselves. Then we must reweave the threads in a design more suitable to our needs.

I have strayed a long way from Robinson and Danvis. Yet this, I am convinced, is the context in which the "Danvis tales" must be read. For the people who bought their pitches from the Allen brothers' land company, who fought with the brothers as Green Mountain Boys, who drove out the "New York, cutthroatly, jacobitish, High Church, Toretical Minions of George III, the pope of Canada and tyrant of Great Britain,"[33] who won the wilderness and made it yield its bounty, these were our friends of Danvis: the Hills, Lovels, Pur'n't'ns, Goves, Peggses, hunters and fishermen all, farmers and woodcutters, tough-minded, pragmatical, independent, quiet-spoken Green Mountain men and women to a T. And what they were, *all* that they were, Robinson intuited as well as we.

VII

In our own convulsive epoch, literature has become such a deadly serious business that it is difficult for us to imagine the artistic motives of a man like Robinson. Our stories are studies in violence and obsessive behavior, and our novels are many-layered structures of metaphysical anguish and social retribution. The forms themselves have changed or worn away. The "sketch," which was once the mainstay of thousands of literary and journalistic careers, has passed out of existence. Today a serious writer who sat down at his desk with no purpose but relating a simple story or recording the manners of a particular segment of society would be accused of frivolity and bad faith—and rightly so if we assume, as most critics do, that one function of literature is to give us back a true image of ourselves. The issues of our time have turned us into bedrock people, struggling on every front with the barest requirements of survival. Even our humor, such as we have, springs from the grimmest possible view of reality.

We are almost relieved when we find statements from another epoch echoing our anxieties. We feel less lonely. In the late 1840s Herman Melville wrote: "There are certain queer times and occasions in this strange mixed affair we call life when a man takes this whole universe for a vast practical joke, though the wit thereof he but dimly discerns, and more than suspects that the joke is at nobody's expense but his own."[34] A very Kierkegaardian statement! And how exactly we still understand it!

Rowland Robinson would have understood it too, though we cannot tell if he ever read it. We have been accustomed to the superficial view of Robinson propounded by his so-called critics in the years following his death and glibly promulgated in the public schools of Vermont to this day. It is certainly an injustice. Robinson was a man and writer in a fuller sense than his appreciators have allowed. His Quaker background, his blindness, and above all his awareness of what was happening in the natural world made him sensitive to the profundities of human experience. These were the aspects of his life that turned him away from naturalism in the philosophical sense, to which it might have seemed that he was particularly fitted to turn, being knowledgeable of the glories of nature. But he was no Darwinist, no Spencerian; he looked upon the natural world without the optimism and faith of the great nineteenth-century scientists and philosophers. He was, in fact, far ahead of these eminent men in his awareness of the *tragedy* of nature. He was almost a man of our time, rather than his own. He knew there was no place of solace for mortal man in the great mechanisms of nature. From his blindness he wrote, concerning the slowness of the years of youth: "Heaven knows they were long enough to count as years go now, when I wait and wait for what will never come."[35] His blindness was an analogue of universal blindness, the mechanistic blindness of the stars. Concerning what had happened to the hunting grounds of Vermont during his lifetime, he wrote: "There are too many shooters, too little cover, and yearly the horde of the one increases, the acres of the other become fewer, and the game laws, game preserves and game protectors cannot long avert the day of annihilation . . ."[36] Could anything be more lucid? In a dramatic way the hunter was closer to natural—and human—tragedy than the great natural scientists of the day.

At the same time it is necessary to make clear Robinson's place in the New England tradition. He was not in the mainstream. He read, we know, at least some of the works of Thoreau, and probably, though we cannot be sure, he was acquainted with the main elements of Emerson's lectures. But Concord Transcendentalism did not touch him deeply. Critics often speak of "the New England tradition" as if it were a unitary force in American literature and all New Englanders were the same. That is not true now; it was less true in Robinson's time. The gulf between the back-country and the metropolitan center was nearly unbridgeable, culturally, socially, and philosophically as well as geographically. The pragmatic, independent spirit of Yankees in western New England's hills and mountains was far from the spiritual self-reliance conceived by Emerson and his followers in Cambridge, Boston, and Concord. Thoreau's experiment at Walden Pond must have seemed curiously futile, trivial, if not downright effete, to people living in far more primitive conditions on the Green Mountain frontier. The Emersonian sense of a spiritual universe, as derived from German romanticism and the Vedantic tradition, could not touch Yankees who were still living in an eighteenth-century world, and whose spiritual lives were shaped by a strange, pragmatic combination of Methodistical or Quakerish enthusiasm and Deistical free-thinking, as bequeathed to them by Ethan Allen along with his other benefactions. It was a poor amalgam perhaps, leading to the Sunday piety of characteristic Yankee horse traders and land speculators, spread by them throughout the nation, until it formed the Rotarian mentality from Boston to San Francisco. No wonder Robinson shunned it. But he did not turn away from his region either to adopt the Transcendentalism of the southern New England core, as some other outlanders did; one thinks of Emily Dickinson in Amherst and Herman Melville in Pittsfield. We may look at this in one way as a pity, because the powerful insight of Emerson might have given Robinson, as it gave the others, a more articulate means for expressing the metaphysical undertow beneath his work. But in another sense we may be grateful that Robinson evaded the characteristic systematicism of the prominent New England symbolist writers, since this leaves him more accessible to our own essentially secularist and unenclosed imaginations.

At any rate Robinson belonged to a different strain of New England writers, the outlanders, humorists, journalists, from Artemus Ward in Maine to Charles Dudley Warner in Hartford, and he is the only native Vermonter with a good claim to admittance into even this circle. Yet if my contention is right that Robinson saw more deeply into the meaning of life than most of his readers have believed or wished to believe, his place is not exactly with the humorists either. In my search for comparisons I find myself turning, not to American literature, but to English, specifically to Thomas Hardy, who was ten years Robinson's junior. The difference between them is enormous, of course. Hardy was an educated Englishman, Robinson an almost untrained American. Hardy worked in literature all his life, producing novels and poems of great power and distinction; Robinson came to writing only as an old man, working in blindness and illness, and produced only short works in haphazard sequences. Yet the Hardy of *The Return of the Native* and the novels of Tess and Jude bears somewhat the same relationship to the people, speech, and manners of Wessex as Robinson bears to the people, speech, and manners of Danvis. The two imaginary locales, based so firmly on reality, are domains in which their authors have discerned the basic values of earthiness, creativity, and ultimate tragedy. Hardy brought these qualities more vigorously and dramatically to the page, yet if we read Robinson with these considerations in mind the comparison, especially in view of his limited ambition, need not be invidious to him. On the contrary we will understand him better. If, as I believe, his genius was genuine though inhibited by the circumstances of his life, it cannot be hurt by our analytical or comparative studies.

But is there after all any point in studying a backwoods American contemporary of Strindberg, Brahms, Van Gogh, Nietzsche, Cézanne? The years in question gave us one of the great surges of the questing spirit. What can Robinson contribute? Hadn't we better concentrate on the masters? The answer is that we are in no danger of neglecting them; they are forever before our eyes. Robinson is the one we have neglected, seriously and shamefully. And if his contribution is small compared to that of the great foreigners, it is nevertheless crucial to us, because it tells us what we as Americans and New Englanders are: our character, our heritage, our predicament. We find three principal components in the lesson of Robinson. First, the man himself, the quality of his imagination, the cultural and social antecedents that shaped his sensibility. Second, his work, his actual accomplishment, both as an indispensable record of speech and manners among our forebears and as an early intuition of the conflict at the heart of humanistic civilization that now becomes more apparent to us every day, seen by him from the vantage point of America's ruined frontier. Third, the inhibiting forces in Robinson's social and cultural ambience that prevented his artistic genius from flowering as it should. In each of these areas we have much to learn.

I end with a plea for greater consideration of Robinson. Both general readers and scholars are needed, and the more the better, especially in his native state. I hope that soon the work of more and better criticism can begin. We need textual studies of all kinds, comparative, stylistic, linguistic, to give us the actual information required for sharper critical discriminations. I hope the next general estimate of his work will not be written in the enforced ignorance that qualifies so much of this one.

Finally, I hope some enterprising publisher will soon see the value of bringing out a one-volume selection of the best of Robinson's writing. The big Centennial Edition is a splendid monument and has great value to scholars and critics; I could not have written this paper without it. But we need a handy one-volume edition of the "Danvis tales." Let it be done soon.

[Postscript, 1994]: And here we are—twenty-three years later. The wheels grind slowly but they do grind. So we must rejoice, and must rejoice especially in the difficult, painstaking editorial job David Budbill has done so well. To reduce the "Danvis tales" to a one-volume selection while retaining consistency and some degree of narrative reference has been an arduous, though I think enjoyable, labor. For my part I must apologize for this "introduction," which was originally written as a monograph in 1971 and published, in part, in the papers of the Vermont Historical Society. I have cut it to scarcely more than half its original length, I have added a few small passages, I have made rearrangements and new transitions, but although I have looked at the extremely sparse bibliography of works about Robinson published since 1971 I have been unable to consult them. I hope the result will nevertheless be useful. It should be noted also that the conditions at Rokeby Museum are much improved from what they were in 1971. Robinson's papers have been microfilmed and his books properly stored.

Notes

1. Rokeby is maintained as a public Museum by the Rowland E. Robinson Memorial Association.

2. Robinson continued all his life to spell the name of his town with an "h." But the spelling without "h," which had begun to take hold in his time, is now universally preferred.

3. Published in *Scribner's* for January 1878. I don't know how long the piece was held between acceptance and publication.

4. *Uncle Lisha's Shop* (1887), *Sam Lovel's Camps* (1889), *Danvis Folks* (1894), *Uncle Lisha's Outing* (1897), *A Danvis Pioneer* (1900), *Sam Lovel's Boy* (1901).

5. Robinson has been noticed in passing by a few writers of more than local reputation, especially Sinclair Lewis, Fred Lewis Pattee, and Dorothy Canfield Fisher. Mrs. Fisher was genuinely interested, but her talents lay in other directions than literary or historical analysis; the remarks of the others are perfunctory. It is worth noting also that Van Wyck Brooks discussed Robinson's work for two pages in his chronicle of New England culture; see *New England: Indian Summer* (New York, 1940), pp. 457–58. Brooks wrote: "Danvis is a fictional name for Ferrisburgh," from which we may judge pretty closely how much of Robinson's work that eminent critical fraud actually read.

6. "Rowland Evans Robinson, Portrayer of Vermont Background and Character," by Genevra N. Cook, master's thesis, 1931. A pedestrian but adequate investigation of some verifiable cultural antecedents to the "Danvis tales" but it tells us almost nothing useful.

7. *Vermont History* (Vermont Historical Society), January 1955.

8. Published in *Out of Bondage and Other Stories* (Boston, 1905). I do not know when this essay was first written, but presumably after 1890. I have taken my quotation from the Centennial Edition of Robinson's works, edited by Llewellyn R. Perkins (Charles E. Tuttle Co., Rutland, Vt., 1933–1937), p. 254 of the volume named; and unless otherwise noted all further quotations from Robinson will come from the same edition.

9. Much that has been written about the "slave's room" at Rokeby seems nonsense. Unless the old part of the house was considerably altered at some later date—and this is not evident—the room can never have been "secret," nor can the back stairway leading to it. For that matter, Ferrisburg is no more than fifty miles from Canada, and during much of the year the journey could be made by water after dark, with no danger of detection. A slave who had safely reached Ferrisburg could be reasonably sure that no southern agents would have come so far north in his pursuit, and although precautions still were taken against the treachery of local southern sympathizers, the extreme subterfuge practiced at stations farther south was no longer needed. Granted, Robinson does introduce southern agents into one or two of his stories about runaway slaves in Ferrisburg; but of all the characters in his *dramatis personae* these strike me as least credible, closest to the stereotypes of Victorian melodrama.

10. When he set out as a young man to seek his fortune, Robinson went to New York, not to Boston, which was then, as it remains today, the natural metropolitan focus for all New England. His unusual choice may have arisen from the fact that the Yearly Meetings for Quakers of the northeast were held in New York. Robinson's parents attended them, though he apparently was left at home. Perhaps Quaker friends or acquaintances in New York offered to look after young Robinson during his first weeks in the city. In any case this cultural orientation

made a sharp division between Quakers and other Vermonters, and it must have been very evident in the Robinson family, as it is in Robinson's later writings; this is a further minor but significant corroboration of the part Quakerism played in the author's life.

11. *New England Fields and Woods* [with] *Sketches & Stories*, p. 172. (The Centennial Edition combines more than one title in most of its eight volumes.)

12. Mary Robinson Perkins.

13. See also *Danvis Folks*, p. 168, for a fictional account of blindness, doubtless influenced by Robinson's own experience.

14. By Genevra Cook, in her master's thesis, op. cit.

15. Especially reminiscences and appreciations published by his friends at the time of his death and after, and also statements from many others published from time to time in *The Rokeby Messenger*, which is the quarterly newsletter of the Rowland E. Robinson Memorial Association; e.g., statements by Mrs. Stephen K. Perry, Vice Admiral George L. Russell, and Frances E. Holmes in issue no. 44, Autumn 1970.

16. *Sam Lovel's Camps*, pp. 39–40.

17. *Uncle Lisha's Shop*, p. 226.

18. *Danvis Folks*, p. 53.

19. Ibid., pp. 120–21.

20. *Danvis Folks*, p. 171.

21. *Uncle Lisha's Shop*, p. 228.

22. *Sam Lovel's Camps*, pp. 59–60.

23. Op. cit.

24. Well, not always, but almost. The exceptions—axe-murders in remote mountain cabins, the whole dark remnant of New England's Puritanical satanism—are rare enough and quite terrible enough to prove the rule.

25. *Danvis Folks*, pp. 68–69.

26. To my mind the most serious lack of realism in the "Danvis tales" has little to do directly with manners or morals. It is simply the lack of any adequate treatment of the most prominent environmental fact in Danvis, the season of winter. The importance of winter hardship in the practical affairs of Danvis, and in the cultural and temperamental properties of its inhabitants, is strangely absent.

27. Especially Professor Duane L. Robinson (no relation) of Middlebury in his "Rowland Evans Robinson, An Appreciation," *The Vermont Review*, vol. II, no. 5 (May–June 1928), pp. 114–18. He writes: "In Sam Lovel, the hunting farmer, we have perhaps the character that is most the embodiment of Rowland Robinson himself." But to say that Sam is "most the embodiment" of Robinson is to say nothing at all, for clearly the author was a far more complex, troubled, modern man than the rudimentary mountaineer whose character he created.

28. Natural conservation was in the air at that time, of course, especially in New England, and I do not mean to credit Robinson with attitudes not found

also in the works of such other nature writers as Bradford Torrey, Frank Bolles, Wilson Flagg, or President Charles Eliot Norton of Harvard. Urban blight in Boston and New York was already alarmingly apparent in the 1870s, giving rise to pressure for the creation of municipal parks, such as Olmstead's Central Park in New York, and to the establishment of nature sanctuaries on abandoned farms throughout the northeast. At this time, too, many great collections of native flora and fauna were begun, such as the collection now housed in the Fairbanks Museum at St. Johnsbury, Vt.

29. *Uncle Lisha's Shop*, p. 215.

30. *In New England Fields and Woods*, p. 41. This seems to show the influence of Parkman, especially *The Oregon Trail* (1849), as well as of the naturalists. The essential idea became, of course, a staple of conservationist theory as developed in the years immediately following Robinson's death by Gifford Pinchot (see his *The Fight for Conservation*, 1909) and others. For that matter, it has a very contemporary ring in 1972. On the other hand, Robinson shows elsewhere that he understood the dangers and absurdities built into conservationism and was less than optimistic about man's ability to undo the folly of his own existence.

31. What Robinson would have said if he could have foreseen the mass extermination of foxes in Vermont by poison and bombs is not hard to guess. With his knowledge of ecological balances he would have realized what the Vermont Department of Agriculture has failed to suspect, that the danger from rabies in the fox population is far less than many other dangers implicit in the eradication of the region's last effective wild predator.

32. See, for example, *Independent Vermont*, by Charles Miner Thompson (Boston, 1942), and *Vermont in Quandary: 1763–1825*, by Chilton Williamson (Montpelier, 1949).

33. Solomon Harvey of Dummerston in 1772, referring to the "judges" and other officers sent from Albany into the territory now called Vermont, to enforce the Yorkist land patents.

34. The opening sentence of Chapter XLIX, *Moby Dick*, published in 1851.

35. From "Cleaning the Old Gun," *In New England Fields and Woods*, p. 173.

36. Ibid., p. 180.

Danvis Tales

Author's Foreword

The boundaries of the township of Danvis are not more clearly defined than the limits of the county of Charlotte, in which it is situated. Suffice it to say that it is in the state of Vermont, backed at the east by the mountains that gave the state its name, and shut out from the valley of the Champlain by outlying spurs of the same range. Thus fortified against the march of improvement, its inhabitants longer retained the primitive manners, speech, and customs of the earliest settlers of Vermont than did the population of the lake towns, whose intercourse with the great centres of trade and culture was more direct and frequent.

It is all changed now: Danvis has daily mails, the telegraph almost touches its border, and its mountains echo the shrieks of locomotives and the roar of railroad trains. The people, generally, wear as fine and modern clothes as any country folk, and it is doubtful whether there is one adult who has not seen something of the bustle and life of at least one of Vermont's two cities, if not those of even greater marts. An aristocracy has sprung up, and people are losing the neighborly kindness of the old times when none were rich and none were poor, and all were in greater measure dependent on each other. In fact, the Danvis folk are no better now than their lowland neighbors, who therefore no longer despise them.

Rowland E. Robinson

from Uncle Lisha's Shop

In Uncle Lisha's Shop

U ncle Lisha Peggs was the owner of a small farm lying so near the
Green Mountains that his woodlot was on a westering slope of one
of their spurs, and the "black growth" of balsam and spruce crept
down to the upper edge of the sugar bush. His acres were too few to keep
him steadily employed in their tillage, and so, in slack times, as well as
in evenings and rainy days, he mended the boots and shoes of his neighbors, and was sometimes persuaded, as a special favor, to exercise the
craft to the extent of building a pair of leathern conveniences.

Uncle Lisha's shop had long been, a sort of sportsman's exchange,
where, as one of the fraternity expressed it, the hunters and fishermen
of the widely scattered neighborhood met of evenings and dull outdoor
days "to swap lies." Almost everyone had a story to tell, but a few only
listened and laughed, grunted, or commented as the tale told was good,
bad, or of doubtful authenticity. And so one October evening, as the rising hunter's moon was streaking the western slopes with shadows of evergreen spires and long paths of white moonlight, Uncle Lisha's callers
began to drop in by ones and twos. The first comer got the best seat, the
broken-backed chair, the next the second best, so accounted, the chair
with three legs, though the occupant had to give so much thought to the
keeping of his balance, that he sometimes tumbled to the floor when the

laugh came in. The later comers had the choice of seats on a roll of sole leather, the cold box-stove, or a board laid across the tub in which Lisha soaked his leather, and the latest the floor, with the privilege of lying at length upon it or setting their backs against the plastered wall. So were disposed a half score of the old cordwainer's neighbors, thus far doing little but smoke, chew, and silently watch Lisha as he hammered out,

shaped, and pegged on the tap of a travel-worn boot as intently as if they were taking lessons in the craft, when Antoine Bassette entered with a polite "Good evelin, Onc' Lasha; good evelin all de zhontemans." Then as he looked about he drew forth from one pocket his short black pipe, from another his knife, with which he scraped out the pipe and emptied it on the stove hearth, then he got out from another a twist of greenish-black tobacco, and whittling off a charge and grinding it between his palms, filled and lighted his pipe at Lisha's candle with such sturdy pulls that the little dip seemed likelier to be quenched than to longer "shine like a good deed in a naughty world."

"Git aout! ye dummed peasouper," Lisha shouted, after pounding his fingers instead of a peg in the uncertain light, "you'll hev us all in total moonlight fust ye know! Take a match er a splinter an' light yer pipe like white folks, stiddy suckin' my candle aout. Don't ye know what the feller said 'at was goin' t' be hung in ten minutes, when they gin him a candle t' light his pipe with? He says, says he, 'Gimme a match, if ye please, 'taint healthy t' light a pipe with a candle,' says he. Take keer 'f yer health, Ann Twine, f' that 'ere Canady Gov'ner 'll want yt' be wuth hangin', when he gits a holt on ye."

"Hah, naow, Onc' Lasha," said Antoine, "dat wus too bad faw you talk so to me. Who help you w'en dat bear keel you, hein?"

"Wal, yes," Lisha rejoined, "ye did help, sartin; the bear an' I done the fightin' an' you done the runnin'. You larnt how to du that in the Pap'neau war, an' ye larnt it well, Ann Twine; ye don't need no more lessons."

"Wal, Ah do, seh. Ah wan' some bodee show me haow Ah run wid dem boot you mek me.

"Haow d' ye 'spose any body could fit yer dummed Canuck feet arter ye'd wore souyaas* ever sen' ye was weaned, ker-splash, ker-spotter, till yer feet's wider'n they be long? You git ye some babeesh† an' I'll give ye tew sides o' sole luther, an' then ye can make ye some souyaas, 'n' then put on yer ole trouses 'at ye could carry a week's p'vision in the seat on, an' be a Canuck; ye can't be a Merican, no ways."

"Ah, Onc' Lasha! You pooty bad hole man. Haow you feel dat time you tink you dead? Wha' you tink you go? A'nt you sorry you don't was been mo' gooder? Wha' you tink you go, hein?"

"I do' know," Uncle Lisha slowly responded; "but I hoped I'd go where the' wa'n't no Canucks!"

"Dah! dah! Onc' Lasha; you so weeked no use talk to you," cried Antoine, when the laugh in which he joined had subsided; "'f you tole dat leet'ly story you beegin dat night, Ah won't said no mo'; you leave off rat in meedly w'en de bear shoot heself, an' you see Ah got so Yankee Ah mos' come dead 'cause Ah do' know de en' of it. Dat story, you know, 'bout man dat cut bread so fas' wid shoe-knife. You rembler?"

"Le' me see," said Lisha, scratching his head with his awl; "Oh, yes, I remember! Wal, I s'pect that's a true story, Ann Twine, an' 'f I tell it ye got t' b'lieve it."

"Oh, sartin, Onc' Lasha; Ah don' b'leeve you tole lie no more as Ah do; no, sah."

"Humph!" Lisha grunted. "I never knowed but one Canuck but what 'ould lie."

"An' dat was me, Onc' Lasha?"

"No, sir! He was a dead one! Wal, the' was a shoemaker 't lived in Connecticut, an' my father knowed him, 'at hed a knife julluk this"— holding up his longest knife—"the cutest thing t' cut bread with't ever was, but he would n't let nob'dy but his own self use it, so they use ter send fer him to all gret duins t' cut the' bread fer 'em. Wal, arter he'd ben a-cuttin' raoun' for three, fo' year, they sent fer him one July to go t' Colonel Leavenworth's gret shearin'. He kep' a thousan' sheep, an' hed twenty

*Moccasins.
†Rawhide used for sewing moccasins.

shearers, an' made a big splonto, 'wine in quart mugs an' strawb'ries rolled in cream, 'he use ter brag about, but they wan't on'y pint mugs 'n not filled very often at that, an' the wine was cider, an' the' wan't more 'n tew strawb'ries apiece, 'n' they was dried apples. Wal, the shoemaker come with his knife keener 'n ever, an' the han's an' comp'ny hed all got washed up for dinner with the' clean clo's on, an' stood raound watchin' on him cut the bread, ker slice, ker slice, faster 'n a gal could pick up the slices, off'm a loaf 't he hel' agin his breast. He done it so neat 't they cheered him, which he got kinder 'xcited, an' tried t' cut faster 'n ever, an' the next lick he gin the loaf he cut hisself clean in tew, an' the man 'at stood behind him clean in tew, an' badly waounded the next one. They sot tew an' stuck 'em together so 't they lived, but it spilte the shoemaker's bread-cuttin' business, an' he hed to go back to shoe-makin' an' starvin', julluk me."

"Wal, sah, Onc' Lasha," cried Antoine, emphasizing every word with a gesture, "Ah b'lieve dat story, 'cause Ah promise, baht Ah tink 'twas 'cause you goin' tole it dat bear scrape you so bad. You see, sah, bear is send for punish bad folkses. An't you hear haow bear keel fawty leetly boy 'cause dey call hol man he don' got no hair on top hees head of it— what you call heem—bal'? Ah spec' dey be nudder bear long 'fore soon for ketch hol man what tole such story, an' den tell Frenchman he don' lie honly w'en he dead!"

"Good airth an' seas!" Lisha roared, "I du blieve one on 'em would hev the last word 'f he was deader 'n a door nail."

A long young man, whose arms and shanks seemed to have lengthened beyond his means to keep them clothed, ventured to say as he looked admiringly upon his new buckskin mittens, too precious to be taken off his hands, but kept opening and closing and turning on them just before his eyes, "The's a painter a-hantin' on Hawg's Back, I du raly b'lieve; I hearn the gol darndest yollupin' up there t'other night, julluk a womern a hollerin', 'n' I hollered, 'n' it arnswered, an' kep' comin' nigher, 'n' then I started my boots fer hum, I tell ye!"

"Sho! Sho! Peltier, you git aout!" Lisha roared, for he was apt to think it his exclusive right to see and hear all strange things first. "'Twan't nothin' but a big aowl, I bet ye!"

"'Twan't no aowl," cried Pelatiah, clapping his mittened palms together with a resounding smack; "'twas a annymill! Guess I know an aowl when I hear 'im!"

"Wal, mebby 'twas a lynk. A lynk 'll git up a c'nsid'able 'f a skeery yowlin'. 'N' mebby 'twas tew ole tomcats a-fightin' up 't ye' west barn. D'ye ever hear, boys," Lisha continued, without waiting for any reply from Pelatiah, "baout Joel Bartlett's Irishmun 't he sent up int' the aidge o' the parster a-choppin' one day? Didn't ye, none on ye? Wal, up he went, and bimeby he come a-runnin' back scairt half ter death, an' hollerin' 'Murther! oh, murther! it's a painter I seen, sure's me name's Pat Murphy!' 'Show!' says Joel, 'haow 'd he look, Partrick?'

"'Wal,' says Pat, 'he was yolly, sur, an' he had a long tail on 'im.'

"'Wal, naow, Partrick, wa'n't it aour ole yaller tomcat?'

"'Be gob, sur, it moight,' sez Pat, an' he lit his pipe an' went back to his choppin' 's contented 's if the' hedn't never been a painter in V'mont."

Pelatiah's panther, being thus contemptuously disposed of, the conversation turned for a time to owls.

"Those 'ere saw-whet aowls," Solon Briggs remarked, clearing his throat, "is a curosity thing—a frik o' natur' comin' daown to her onsignificantest teches—a nart'ral fewnonnymon, so to speak. A puffick aowl, minus the gretness of the die-mentionist kinds."

"Wal, they be small, but reg'lar aowls," said Sam Lovel. "Cut the head off 'm one 'n' he 'll lack a ounce o' weighin'. I shot one on 'em outen a tree jes' to see what he was, 'n' he come a-floatin' daown julluk a bunch o' feathers."

"An' their vocal voice," put in Solon, "is the fact smile of sharpnin' a saw."

"Guess 't is," said Sam, "egg-zack! Makes me think o' one time t' ol' Mist' Van Brunt f'm New York 's up here a-lookin' arter his lumbrin' intrus. 'Twas long airly 'n the spring 'n' he was ridin' 'long hoss back 'n the evenin', 'n' when he got daown int' Stunny Brook holler, he hearn, someb'dy a filin' a sawmill saw, *screet er screet, er screet er*. 'Some o' them dum maounting Aribs,' says he, 'hes got a sawmill right here in the hairt o' my woods! Hello you!' he hollered, but the file kep' a-goin', *screet er screet, er screet!* 'You owdacious villing!' says he—he allus used high duck langwuage—'you owdacious villing! I'll prosecute ye to the extents o' the law,' says he, and he rid his hoss int' the woods where he hearn the noise, 'n' his sto'pipe hat ketched on a limb an' tumbled off, 'n' his hoss stumbled agin a ruht 'n' throwed 'im off, 'n' then the noise o' filin' stopped, 'n' then in two, three minutes it begin agin furder off. 'The pirutical scoundril,' says the ol' gentleman, 'hez got his dum sawmill on wheels!' 'n' he got back int' the path an' rid ont' the tarvern 'thaout no hat. When he got there he tol' Hamlin (he kep' it then) what he'd hearn, 'n' Hamlin he laughed, 'n' says he, 'Mist' Van Brunt, 't wa'n't nothin' but a saw-whet 't you hearn.' 'A saw whet!' says th' ol' gentleman, 'I know it, but a two-legged saw-whet, sir.' 'Yes,' says Hamlin, 'two-legged, but he wears feathers stiddy clo's,' 'n' 'xplained. Then the ol' gentleman laughed at hisself, an' treated the hull craowd, a dozen on 'em, to ole Jamaiky sperrits 't he brought with him f'm York—twenty ye'r ole, they said 't was."

"Gosh!" ejaculated Joseph Hill, with a watering mouth, "Wish 't I'd a ben there!"

"Ben where?" asked he of the inquiring mind.

"The study of nart'ral hist'ry things," Solon remarked, "is a most stumenduous subject, cal'lated to fill the human mind of man with—er—er—ah—"

"Puddin' an' milk," shouted Lisha, as he drove the last peg in the wide sole of the boot, "'n' I 'tend to ha' some an' go to bed."

So saying he took off his battle-scarred apron, and his guests departed, and faded with silent footsteps into the dusky whiteness of the snowy night.

A Rainy Day in the Shop

One gloomy day in November several of Uncle Lisha's friends, realizing the fact that it rained too hard to "work aou' door," that it was too wet even for comfortable hunting, and that it was too late in the season for fishing, betook themselves singly and in couples to the shop to pass away the time which hung with unendurable heaviness upon their hands at home. There was a genial warmth radiating from the full fed rusty little stove, and a mild sunshine from the kindly face of the old shoemaker that made the rude interior seem exceedingly comfortable in contrast with the dismal chill and dampness of the outdoor world, and the clatter of the hammer on the lapstone was a much more cheerful sound than the leaden patter of the rain on roof and pane and fallen leaves. But though the newcomers gave some impassive signs of appreciation of the change from outdoor discomfort to indoor comfort, they seemed to have brought in with them too much of the exterior atmosphere; it exhaled from their wet garments and dulled spirits till their host felt it and resented it.

"Good airth an' seas, boys, what's the motter ails ye, all on ye? Ye ain't no sociabler 'n a passel o' snails holdin' a meetin' 'n under a cabbage leaf! 'Tain't a fun'el. By mighty, it's wus, for the' hain't no preachin' ner singin', ner even sighthin' ner cryin'. Why don't some on ye up an' die an' kinder liven up things a leetle mite, hey?"

While Solon Briggs was swelling up with explanatory words too big for speedy utterance, Joseph Hill remarked, as he searched all his pockets for the pipe and tobacco that he never knew where to find, "I 'spect, as Joel Bartlett says when he takes a notion to start off on a preachin' taower, 'at we've all on us got a weighty consarn on aour mind, Uncle Lisher."

"Wal, Jozeff hes spoke, an' that's incouragin'. Naow, let another, as Brother Foot says in prayer-meetin'."

"Jozeff's speakin'," continued Uncle Lisha, after waiting a moment for a response, "puts me in mind o' his dawg 'at he uster hev, 'at nob'dy never knowed to du nothin' on'y eat an' sleep, an' bark a' folks goin' 'long baout the' business, an' at the moon nights, when folks was extry tired an' wantin' t' sleep more 'n common but couldn't, 'caount o' his 'tarnal bow-wowin' an' yollopin'. Jozeff, howsever, was allus a-tellin' what a good dawg he was, an' even went the len'th o' sayin' 't he was harnsome! A yaller dawg, an' harnsome! Hain't that so, Jozeff? Don't ye deny it!" he roared, glaring at his visitor between his eyebrows and the rims of his spectacles, at his visitor between his eyebrows and the rims of his spectacles, as he began to fashion a slow, dubious "wal" with his lips. "Yes," he continued, "good an' harnsome, he said he was. You never seen a man 'at hed him a dawg 'at wa'n't a-braggin' 'baout him on some pint. That's one reason 'at I don't hev me a dawg. I hain't no gift o' braggin'. 'Nuther is, I hain't no use for a dawg in my business. Wal," picking out the soggy "heel" of his pipe with a crooked awl, "one day when Samwill here an' 'mongst 'em was exhaltin' of the' horns an' a-blowin' on 'em 'baout the' haoun' dawgs, Jozeff he up an' begin blowin' his'n abaout his'n. Someb'dy nuther ast him, 'What'll he du? Did he ever tree a coon?' 'No.' says Jozeff. 'Er hole a woo'chuck?' 'No.' 'Er drive a k'yow er a hawg?' 'Wal, not ezackly drive 'em.' 'Er ta' keer o' the' haouse?' 'Wal, he's allus there, but I do' know 's he raly takes keer on't.' 'Wal, then, what on airth is he good for?' 'Wal,' says Jozeff, says he, arter c'nsid'able c'nsid'rin', 'he's comp'ny!' An'," said Uncle Lisha when he had blown through his pipe after clearing the stem with a waxed end, "I'll be dum'd 'f I wouldn't druther hev Jozeff Hill's ol' yaller dawg for comp'ny 'n t' hev sech a consarned mumpin' set as you be."

The only responses were a general though feeble and perfunctory laugh and an apologetic remark from Solon Briggs that "when the caloric of the warmth had penetrated the water aouten their garments they would be more conversationabler," which Antoine endeavored to make more easily comprehended by explaining, "Yas, Onc' Lasha, when we'll gat aour froze t'aw aout we'll got aour speak t'aw aout."

A little later the constant searcher for information broke the silence by asking Joseph Hill, "Whatever be become o' that 'ere dawg 'at Uncle Lisher ben speakin' on?"

"M'ri sol' him tu a peddler," said Joseph, with a sigh of regret for his lost companion. "M'ri didn't never set no gret store by dawgs, though the' be women 'at likes to hev a dawg 'raound, for all the' makin' b'lieve hate 'em—likes to hev 'em 'raound to lay things onter, bad smells an' sech, an' broken airthenware, an' t' 'buse—wal, I do' know as 'buse ezackly, but tu vent the' feelin's on. But M'ri never 'bused Liern, though I don't think he raly 'nj'yed her comp'ny, 'specially moppin' days an' when she was sweepin' aout."

"Wal, I do' know's I blame anybody much for mumpin' sech weather," said Uncle Lisha, relenting, as while he ground the pegs from the inside of a newly tapped boot he gazed abstractedly out of the rain-pelted little window upon the blurred landscape; the sodden dun fields bounded by the gray wall of mountain with its drifting coping of mist—all dun and gray but for one poplar that shone like a pale flame among the ashy trunks and branches of its burned-out companions, and when a gust fanned it, showered down its yellow leaves like sparks from a flaring torch. "I do' know 's I blame any on ye much; sech weather 's turrible hefty on the sperits. 'F I hed me a pint, er mebby a quart o' cider brandy, er ol' Jamacky sperits, I raly b'lieve I'd git so condemned boozy 't I couldn't see aouten the winder—'f 't wa'n't for makin' an' mendin' these 'ere dum'd ol' boots an' shoes, I would, by golly blue!"

"I snum! I sh'ld like ter help ye, Uncle Lisher," said Joseph Hill, smacking his lips.

"'N' it's mos' Thanksgivin' time," Lisha went on; "I b'lieve the day's ben sot by the Gov'ner, hain't it? Seem's 'ough I seen it in the last *V'monter*. Jerushy!" He called so loudly and suddenly that it startled all his guests, and again "Jerushy!" with a roar that made the battered stove-pipe jingle. "Be you deaf or be you dead?"

"What—on—airth?" asked the mildly astonished old matron as she opened the door just wide enough to let her nose and voice into the shop.

"Gim me that 'ere last paper; I wanter see 'f Thanksgivin' Day's 'pinted. It's eyther in the stan' draw, erless in the cub'd, 'f ye hain't got some o' yer everlastin' yarbs spread onter it in the chahmber."

"Yarbs!" Aunt Jerusha replied from the "house part," where she could be heard wrestling with the refractory stand drawer, and then rummaging among papers, "why, good land o' Goshen, Lisher, my yarbs was all dried an' in the' bags 'fore ever that 'ere paper thought o' bein' printed! Naow, seem 's 'ough you took it to wrap up Miss Bartlett's bootees in t'other day. Oh, no, here 't is"—reappearing in the doorway—"I b'lieve, le' me see," "tromboning" the paper to get the proper focus of her glasses, "October the thirty—yes; here, Lisher," groping her way to her lord through the tobacco smoke and rubbish and legs of visitors, and then as through the reek she began to recognize one and another—"Oh, hope I see ye well, Mr. Briggs an' Mr. Hill. Miss Briggs an' Miss Hill, be they well? Turrible spell o' weather we're a hevin' on. Why, haow do you du, Samwill? Be you well, Antwine? an' haow's your womern? My! haow you men du smoke! I can't scasely see who's who. Wal, I s'pose terbarker is comfortin' sech weather for them 'at c'n stan' it, but I never could," and she retreated, tapping her snuffbox as she went.

"As if snuff wa'n't terbarker!" Uncle Lisha snorted after her. "Le's see," spreading the paper on his knees and staring at it naked-eyed while he wiped his glasses on his shirt sleeve; then, adjusting them astride his nose with unusual care. "Le' me see—'Scott an' Raymon' offer—m—m—'Partrick Foster, groceries an' p'visions' (an' hoss rum) m—m—m—'B. Seym'r, hats an' caps an' highest price fer fur'—oh, here 't is—'Proclermatiern by the Gov'ner—Cordin' to suthin' nuther usage 'n' so f'th, 'n' so f'th, hm—m—m—I du hereby 'pint Thursd'y the twenty-sev'mph day o' November as a day o' thanksgivin'.' Wonder what they allus hev it come a Thursd'y for, and Fast Day Frid'y? Dum'd 'f I know. An' 'lection day an' taown meetin' an' the leegislatur' begin settin' a Tuesd'y. Mebby that's so 's 't the men c'n hev clean shirts on; though the' hain't time for i'nin on 'em—more likely it's cause the men folks is fresh f'm the disciplyne o' washin' day, an' more cal'lated to du the' duty. Hm! so Thanksgivin' comes tew weeks f'm nex' Thursd'y, hey? What be I goin' t' du f'r a turkey, I sh' like t' know? We hain't raised none, an' I can't 'ford to buy one, an' I've got tu ol' an' dim-sighted t' shoot one tu a-shootin' match—do' know 's the' 's goin' t' be one, anyway."

"Yas," some one said, "Hamner 's layin' 'aout t' hev a turkey shoot, Thanksgivin'."

"Ya-us," Joseph Hill contemptuously assented, "he's a cal'latin' tu hev what might posserbly be called a turkey shoot. He's got him fifteen er twenty leetle teenty tawnty faowls 't he calls turkeys—hatched in August, do' know 's they was fore September, nary one on 'em bigger 'n a cardy bird*—do' know but they be bigger 'n cardy birds, but pleggid little to speak on, an' he'll set 'em up forty rod, I do' know but fifty, at a York shillin' a shot! The' haint nob'dy, erless it's Sam here, c'ld hit one shootin' a week that fur off. 'N' one on 'em would n't more 'n go 'raound 'mong tew hearty folks—do' know 's the' 'ld be 'nough for tew. He hedn't ort to set 'em up not to say more 'n fifteen er twenty rod, ner ast over 'n' above fo'p'nce ha'p'ny a shot, at sech leetle teenty tawnty insi'nificant creeturs, an' then he'd make money aout on 'em."

"I tell ye what you du, Samwill," Uncle Lisha said. "You gwup to Hamner's turkey shoot an' git me a turkey—git tew 'f ye'r a minter, an' come t' aour Thanksgivin'. The' 'll be a turkey for me an' Jerushy, an' one for you—one for us tew an' one for you tew, 's the Irishmun said when he was dividin' the four dollars 'twixt himself an' his tew frinds. Er she c'n hev the necks o' both—she's allus a-tellin' haow the necks is the bes' part of a faowl, an' you 'n' I'll take the stuffin' an' what's left. I'll pay for tew shots an' you pay for tew, an' 'f you can't git tew turkeys aout o' four shots you hain't the man 't I take ye t' be. What d' yo' say, Samwill?"

"I'd a good deal druther git ye some patridges, Uncle Lisher. Dum this blazin' away at a poor mis'able turkey sot top of a barrel with his laigs tied, scairt half to death with the balls zippin' raound him. 'Taint no fun for me. I'd druther go out in the woods an' git ye tew three patridges."

"Well, patridges then," said the shoemaker; "I don't keer, on'y patridges ain't ezackly sech reg'lar Thanksgivin' meat as turkeys is."

"But the' 's more meat in one good Tom patridge 'an the' is in the hull flock o' Hamner's turkeys," said Joseph Hill. Then, after a little consideration of this statement, "Wal, I do' know's the hull on 'em, but half on 'em, say."

"Wal, then, call it patridges," said Uncle Lisha, with a sigh of resignation. "We'll go it on punkin pie an patridges. Will ye git 'em, Samwill?"

"You sh'll hev 'em, Uncle Lisher," Sam said, sitting upright from lean-

*Nuthatch.

ing against the wall, his promise emphasized by the creak of the roll of sole leather he sat upon, "'f the's any in the woods."

"Oh, the woods is popular with 'em," said Solon.

"I scairt one aouten my woodshed yist'd'y mornin', er mebby 'twas day 'fore yist'd'y mornin'—any ways, I scairt one aout on't when I went aout arter kin'lin', an' I tol' M'ri on't."

"Proberly the's so much wood in your shed, Jozeff, 'at he thought he was in the woods," said Uncle Lisha, whittling a plug of tobacco on his cutting-board.

"Bah gosh!" cried Antoine, who had long suffered with silence, "'f dey don't tick in de hwood! an' he don't 'fraid more as hen was. Bah gosh! 'todder day, seh, when Ah'll was be choppin' in de hwood dey was one of it flewed raght in ma face, an' Ah'll bite hees head wid ma mouf! Ah'll peek ma toof more as two nour fore Ah'll got de fedder off of it. Bah gosh! Ah 'll got all de patridge Ah 'll wan' for heat more as dis year, dat tam, me."

"Git Antwine to set his maouth an' ketch ye some," Joseph suggested.

"He'd pizon 'em with his dum peasoup lies," growled Uncle Lisha, as he brushed the tobacco into his hand and began grinding it between his palms. "Say, Samwill, haow was you a-cal'-latin' to spend yer Thanksgivin' this year? Naow, 'f yer goin' huntin' for me, I want ye t' 'tend right tu yer huntin' an nothin' else."

There was a roguish twinkle in the corner of the eye nearest the reclining hunter as the old man asked, "Boys, I do' know's I ever tol' ye 'baout this 'ere gret hunter's agoin' foxhuntin' one Thanksgivin' Day back o' Pur'n't'n's, did I?"

"Uncle Lisher," Sam drawled in a slow, impressive monotone, "if you raly want me tu git you some patridges for Thanksgivin', you don't wanter tell no stories 'baout my Thanksgivin's."

"You mean it, Samwill?" Lisha asked, pausing in the lighting of his pipe till the match began to fry the wax on his thumb.

"Sartinly I du," Sam answered.

"Wal, then," said Lisha, "I want them patridges, an' I got t' hev 'em," and though Antoine cried, "Tol' it, Onc' Lasha, tol' it! What you cared? Bah gosh! Ah'll know where dat turkey Hamny's roos', an' 'f Ah don't gat you more turkey as you'll heat an' A'n' Jerrushy in four day, Ah'll give you masef for roas'! Ah'll bet you head, boy, dat Sam shoot fox an' he'll ant hit heem!" and though all beset him importunately, the old man utterly refused to tell the story, and presently his visitors departed in as bad humor as they had come. As they separated at the door yard gate to go their several ways, the inquirer turned back to ask, "Say, Jozeff, haow much did M'rier git for that 'ere dawg?"

The Turkey Shoot at Hamner's

The morning of the day before Thanksgiving was bright and still, promising such a day as a rifleman would wish for target-shooting, and before the middle of the forenoon almost every man in Danvis who owned a rifle, and some who did not, but were enough in favor to borrow one of owners too old to use one, or too impecunious to share in a sport that called for a "York shillin'" a shot, was at Hamner's hostelry, or hurrying toward it across lots or along the rough, frozen roads. And as many or more than these were those who went with hands in pockets, otherwise empty, to look on enviously, and rugged-faced old mountaineers whose dim eyes could no longer sight a rifle, and whose palsied hands had shaken off all their cunning, to criticise the younger shooters and tell marvelous tales of what they could do and had done in bygone years; and also penniless and stingy topers who scented occasional free drinks among the possibilities of the meeting.

The outbuildings of the tavern straggled along the bank of the intervale, on the broadest part of which was room enough—too much, some thought—for the range. Beyond the stable was the stand, which was simply a plank with one end resting on a horse, the other on the ground, and out toward the furthest curve of the little river stood a dry-goods box on which the turkeys were to be placed. "Thunder in the winter!" John Dart ejaculated, as he looked over the range with a half-shut, calculating eye, "you call that forty rod, Hamner? M'asured it with an injin-rubber string, didn't ye, 'n' pulled like a yoke o' stags? I sh' like t' buy the interv'l 'cordin' to that m'asure. But set one up!"

The long, lank, sharp-faced publican directed an assistant to bring out a turkey, and after a fluttering commotion in the stable he reappeared with a half-grown one under his arm, and took his way across the flat toward the dry-goods box. "Oh, what a turkey!" Dart shouted. "Haint ye got no aigs ter set up? Wal, Hamner, you be tough—tougher 'n a biled aowl! But nev' mind, I'm a goin' ter shoot—that's what I come here for. But a feller might jes' 's well shoot at the moon—'t ain't much furder off, an' it's bigger."

"Wal, yes, some bigger, John," said Joseph Hill, taking off his hat and scratching his head meditatively, "leastways when it's full, which it don't seem as 'ough that turkey was."

"Oh, you shet up, Joe Hill!" Hamner snarled. "Turkeys is what's called for, an' that 'ere 's a turkey, haint it?" and he glowered a sidelong glance at the giant Dart, who, good-natured as he was, looked too big to quarrel with.

"Sartinly, Mr. Hamner," said the amicable Joseph, "that's the name on 't, I haint no daoubt. A turkey's a turkey soon 's he's hatched."

"Say, Bill!" Dart shouted after the bearer of the turkey, "got any lunchern in yer pocket! You'll git hungry 'fore you git there. An' say, Bill, holler when ye git yer gobbler sot up, so 's 't we'll know. He's most aout o' sight naow!"

At last the poor bird was placed in position, Bill retreated to a safe distance and the cover of the river-bank, and Dart, lying down on the plank, rested his rifle across the end of it. After much sighting and squinting he cocked his piece and, taking careful aim, fired.

"Sol', for a nimep'nce!" he proclaimed, as the turkey was seen to flutter and fall prone upon the box.

"Don't b'lieve ye teched him! He's only scairt!" Hamner snarled, unwilling to believe that his turkey had gone for so little money. But all doubt on that score was removed when Bill took it down and began his journey toward them, a dozen of the party running out to meet him.

"'T won't take more 'n half on ye tu bring in that turkey," Dart called after them. "Naow, Hamner, you be ketchin' another tu set up. I want a mess while I'm 'baout it an' got my hand in."

"Not by a gol darned sight you don't hev another shot! You s'pose I'm a goin' tu hev the bread took aouter my maouth that way? One turkey 's 'nough for anybody but a darned hawg!"

"You're jest right, Hamner. One turkey 's as much as anybody 'd ort tu eat tu oncte, an' all I want is one apiece for the fam'ly. The' 's five on us, none on us very hearty t' eat only gran'maw 'n' the baby, an' five turkeys is all 't I want. But the' haint nothin' small 'baout me only my feet," holding out a No. 12 "stogy" for inspection, "which you may not think they be, but a feller's boot haint his foot. Mine 's small, but a big boot fits 'em best. I don't push for the nex' shot. Here's Mr. Putnam, which he's got him a rifle 'at cost him thir-ty-five dollars in money, an' Varney made it, which that means all you've got t' du is tu show it a turkey an' it fetches him! An' Mr. Putnam wants a few. 'N' here's Peltier Gove, he's got the Widder Wiggin's rifle, which it was Pete's, an' he give Hatch the price of a ye'rlin' colt for it, an' the' 's some 'at says haow Hatch c'n make jes' as good a gun as Varney any day, an' Peltier wants tu find aout. An' here is Jozeff Hill; he's a luggin' 'raound one o' Seaver's ol' fewzees which they say he *hes* hit a barn with it, bein' 'at he was on the inside on 't an' all the doors shet. An' the' 's lots more on 'em 'at hes tu heng on t' the' guns tu keep 'em f'm goin' off arter turkeys. I'm willin' for half on 'em tu hev a chance while I rest my gun a spell, for it's turrible strainin' on a gun t' shoot so fur. Wal, here's Bill mos' tuckered aout a luggin' of that turkey aout there 'n' back 'thaout restin' much 'n' nothin' t' eat all the time. Le' me see where I hit him. Right in the butt o' the wing! That's where I allus hit 'em— when I don't miss on 't. Haint he an ol' sollaker! Sary Ann 'll hefter put the stuffin' on the aoutside—the' haint room 'nough on the inside."

Meanwhile Sam Lovel was out in the woods, where he had been long before the shooting began, in pursuit of Uncle Lisha's promised partridges. The frozen leaves, showing a crinkle of brown and here and there a streak or patch of yet unfaded October red and yellow through the light powdering of snow, were noisy under the lightest tread. The squirrels scampering over them, in quest of their Thanksgiving fare, could be heard thirty rods away, and a dozen partridges went whirring and crashing away unseen through the haze of gray branches and dark clouds of evergreen boughs before Sam drew a bead on the head of an old cock who strutted an instant too long on his last spring's drumming log, and then verified the truth that pride goeth before a fall as he tossed up a flurry of leaves and snow in his death-struggle. So our hunter went on through this range of wooded hill, exhausting its present possibilities of game when he had killed another partridge, but all the while enjoying his solitary tramp. He heard the intermittent popping of the rifles at Hamner's, and in soliloquy mildly anathematized the shooters as "a pack o' dum'd fools." In a different spirit Joel Bartlett, hearing the frequent reports as he foddered his cattle in the barnyard, sighed loudly and sorrowfully, and said in the sing song tone that would now certainly be heard next day in the Fifth Day meeting, "A snare of the evil one, an' a-nother pitfall digged for the feet of the onwary! These men a-shootin' at innocent faowls of the air, is a-follerin' of a custom, an' a practyse, an' a observance o' them 'at hung Mary Dyer, an' grievously pussecuted many formerly."

When Sam had come to the top of the hill, the shortest way to the next likely hunting ground lay past Hamner's and a natural curiosity drew him to the shooting ground.

Fortune had frowned on all the contestants but the amiable giant, Dart, who by his weight and good-nature and the possibly better gift of luck, seemed always to make his way, and having now got three turkeys Hamner was disposed to debar him from another chance.

Poor Pelatiah was in doleful dumps, having fired three shots without getting a turkey, and now debating with himself whether he should hazard the remainder of his treasure on another. "I hit a nine-inch ring three times aout o' five, forty rods as I paced it up behind the barn t' hum, yist'd'y, wi' that gun," he confided to Sam, "Widder Wiggin's rifle, the best one the' is in Danvis, so ev'b'dy says, an' tu-day, Samwell, I can't hit a ten-acre lot!"

"It's fifty rods f'm here to that box if it's a rod," said Sam to Pelatiah, and partly to himself. "The dum'd ol' cheatin' cuss! Look a here, Peltier, if you wanter try agin I'll pay for yer shot if it's a miss. Don't ye be in no hurry. You might," measuring the distance to the hill across the road with his eye, "you might forgit tu put any cap on, an' snap tew three times, an' then hol' high! Aim at the top o' 'Tater Hill 'f you'r a minter—'tain't nob'-dy's business if your shot 's paid for. But don't ye graound your ball this side o' the turkey!"

"Goin', Mr. Lovel?" Hamner asked, as Sam shouldered his ponderous gun, known far and near as the "Ol' Ore Bed"; "I was a-hopesin you 'd jine us."

"No," Sam replied; "I can't hit a turkey forty rod off. I'm goin' up on your hill tu try 'f I c'n git another patridge. They 'pear tu be turrible scase t'day."

"Tell ye what, Lovel," said Dart, "I b'lieve Hamner's chick-a-biddied 'em all intu his barn wi' a ha' bushil o' buckwheat, an' sot 'em up for turkeys! These things we ben a-shootin' at is patridges, an' the scruff eends o' litters at that!"

Sam left and made speedy way to the hill which overlooked the whole range.

Pelatiah bestowed his ungainly length upon the plank once more, and three times pulled the trigger with no responsive explosion of cap and charge. "G—o—s—h!" he exclaimed, with well-simulated surprise; "I never thought tu put no cap on." This oversight having been duly remedied, at the next pull the Widder Wiggins's rifle responded with its wonted spiteful crack, which was more loudly repeated from the hill behind, and the turkey, with a few feeble flaps of its wings, sank upon the box.

"Sam Hill! What an e-cho!" Joseph ejaculated, taking in vain the name of a possible ancestor, and then looking toward the rough steep beyond the road he saw a thin film of smoke wafted upward through the evergreens. After one breathless moment of open-eyed and wide-mouthed wonder, he doubled himself up in a paroxysm of smothered laughter.

When the turkey was examined some one remarked that the "Widder Wiggins's rifle made a onaccaountable big hole," but Pelatiah bore home his prize in triumph and with unquestioned right.

Sam Lovel's Thanksgiving

As hunting was dearer to Sam Lovel than feasting, it very naturally happened that on the morning of Thanksgiving Day he was out on the hills with Drive rather than at home enduring the fuss and bustle of the "women folkses'" preparation of the great dinner.

As he took his way across the narrow fields to the woods, the dun grass land, the black squares and oblongs of fall ploughing, the gray of the deciduous trees, and the "black growth" of the woodlands were blurred together in the first light of the early morning, nothing distinct but lines and patches of the first snow, left by the ensuing warm days, and the serrated crest of the mountain now sharply cut against the eastern sky. The hound, quartering the way toward sunrise, came into sight and vanished, now to the right, now to the left, first white spots and then a dimly defined dog, then white spots and no dog, nor any indication of his nearness but his loud snuffing and the crisp crush of the frosty herbage under his feet. Presently he gave tongue on a cold scent, puzzling out with his miraculous gift of smell the devious course of the fox over knolls and through swales of matted mouse-haunted wild grass, and by and by, when daylight had set well-defined bounds to field and forest, led his slowly following master to the ridge of the first hill. Then the sun began to burn its way up the sky with so intense a flame that it seemed to be consuming the stubby trunks and low-spread branches of the stunted evergreens bristling in blurred silhouette on the mountain crest. Sam followed the trend of the long ledge that formed the top of the hill, a sheer steep abutting toward the west, a long rough slope slanting to a dark gorge on the east. Out of this came from time to time the tuneful baying of the hound as he worked southward on the scent, so cold that only in those places that held it best it greeted his nostrils with an aroma strong enough to bring forth his bugle-like challenge. The intervals of silence became longer between the bugle notes, sounding now fainter and farther away, till at last unheard at all, though the murmur of a mountain brook changing with wafts of the light breeze, the monotonous song of the evergreens swelling and falling with its varying touch, and a hundred nameless mysterious voices of the woods fooled the hunter's ear now and then. But he had an abiding faith that at last Drive would get up the fox and bring him back along this ridge, and so he listened and waited, sitting on a moss-cushioned log while all the chickadees of the neighborhood came and visited him with inquisitive friendliness, and the jays, at more respectful distance, squalled a protest against his intrusion on their haunts. A solitary crow, belated in his migration, discovered the silent and motionless figure, and made as much pother as if it had been a featherless owl or a furless fox; but when his clamor failed to bring any response from the brethren now far beyond the sound of his voice, he flapped away in silent disgust. A red squirrel scampering over the matted leaves in quest of buried treasure sat up at the toe of Sam's boot, and after a short inspection of this queer black stump ventured onto it, and then as far as Sam's knee, whence a wink of the hunter's gray eye frightened him in a sudden panic, from which he recovered sufficiently when he had gained the vantage of a tree trunk to rattle out a volley of abuse. When these visitors had all departed and Sam had listened long in vain, he moved on to a bald peak of the hill from which a portion of the valley could be seen, with its cleared fields and wooded cobbles, and farm houses and outbuildings strung along the frozen black road like nests on a slender leafless branch. Some were as deserted today as the vireo's nest that hung in a fork of the witch hazel beside him, the inmates away for one day's thanksgiving as the birds were for months of it. But from the chimney of one red-painted homestead, which Sam's wandering

glances always came back to, a banner of smoke flaunted, denoting occupancy.

"Someb'dy stayin' t' hum t' Pur'n't'ns," he soliloquized. "Guess most on
'em 's gone some'eres tu Thanksgivin', f' the' hain't nob'dy stirrin' 'round
aou'door. Guess they hain't keepin' on 't there, for 'f they was, ol' Granther
Pur'n't'n's shay 'ould be a-loomin' up 'long side o' the barn like a tew
storey haouse afire. Wonder 'f the' hain't nob'dy t' hum, 'n' the dum'd
haouse is afire"—as the chimney belched forth a greater volume of
smoke. "Do' know but what I'd better go an' see. That 'ere fox is an ol' N'
Hampsh'r traveller, an' he'll tow Drive clean t' the C'net'cut River 'fore he
gives it up an' comes back, an' I'll be dum'd' I'm a-goin' to set 'raound
here a-waitin' for him till t'morrer night. I b'lieve that dum'd ol' haouse
is afire!" And listening one moment more for the voice of the hound,
almost afraid that he might hear it, he started down the sheer hillside,
checking now and then his headlong course with clutches on bushes,
saplings, and tree-trunks, till he reached the level of the alder-bordered
brook that wound along the base of the hill. The red winter berries
glowed there in vain to catch his eye, and he crushed unseen beneath his
feet the scarlet cones of the wild turnip drooping on their withered stalks
as he breasted the tangled sprawl of the alders. When beyond them he
came in sight of the house again, he caught a glimpse of a trim figure as
the kitchen door opened for an instant, the flash of a dishpan and the
glitter of its discharged contents, and a few notes of a clear voice singing,
"The Girl I Left Behind Me." The figure and the voice made his heart beat
quicker, but he slackened his pace as he taxed his wits for an excuse for
his call. When he crossed the chips in front of the woodshed, he had
decided that his first idea was the best to act upon, and that if he did not
quite believe it now, he really had believed that the house was on fire.
He knocked at the kitchen door and waited long enough for flames to
have made great headway, while he listened to the voice singing with all
the freedom from embarrassment of one who sings without a listener,
and for the singer's sole pleasure—

> "If ever I chance to go that way,
>   And she has not resigned me,
> I'll reconcile my mind and stay
>   With the girl I left behind me."

He did not knock again till the words ended and the singer began to
hum the tune in a lower voice. Then the singing and the accompanying

clatter of dishes and swash of "wrench water" suddenly stopped, and Sam knew that in the ensuing hush Huldah was wiping her hands on the towel behind the buttery door, that the few quick footsteps took her to the looking-glass in the door of the clock, whose ticking he could now hear, and now she was coming. When she opened the door such a bright pleased surprise shone on her pretty face that he could compare it to nothing but the brightness of that morning's sunrise.

"Why, good land sakes alive! Samwell Lovel, where on airth did you come from?"

"Wal," said Sam, his cheeks as red as hers, "I was a-huntin' up on Pig's Back, an' I seen the smoke a-tumblin' aouten your chimbly at sech a rate 't I was afeared the haouse was afire. I thought most likely 'at you'd all gone off t' Thanksgivin', an' suthin' nuther hed ketched, an' so I come ri' daown. I'm sorry 't I troubled ye, but I'm dreffle glad 't the' hain't nothin' afire. Guess I'll be a-goin' naow."

"Why, what's yer hurry, Mr. Lovel? Come in an' seddaown an' rest ye a spell. Aour folks is all gone, father 'n' mother 'n' Sis, up to Gran'ther's, an' lef' nob'dy t' hum but me 'n' the cat. I didn't keer no gret 'baout goin', an' so I staid t' hum to keep haouse. Come in an' seddaown a minute, won't ye? while I gwup stairs an' look o' that sto' pipe—it *hes* ben kinder aouter kilter. Come in an' take a cheer. The kitchin looks like all git aout" [it was as neat as a new bandbox], "but I wa'n't 'spectin' nob'dy, an' the' hain't no fire in the square room. I'd take yer gun, but I dassent—set it in the corner, er heng it up on the hooks over the mantel-tree there. Father's gun's gone t' V'gennes, a-bein' altered over tu a—a cap-lock, is 't you call 'em? He thinks they're better 'n flint-locks. Du you think they be, Sa—Mr. Lovel, I mean?"

"Wal, they be handier an' sartiner to go off, but I do' know but what a flint-lock gun is 'baout as good—to heng up, as yer father's does mostly," Sam answered, looking up contemplatively at the hooks where his own gun now hung.

"Make yerself t' hum, Samwell—why, haow I du keep a-callin' on ye by yer fust name! excuse me, *Mr.* Lovel—while I gwup an' see 'baout that 'ere sto'pipe."

The stovepipe must have been found in satisfactory condition, for Huldah presently reappeared in a smart new calico gown, and with her hair neatly brushed and fastened with a high tortoise-shell comb.

"Is it usuil, Mr. Lovel," she asked, after she had set away her dishes, and drawing a chair to the stove, sat down and folded her hands in seemly fashion over her check apron, "for folks to knock at the door when they think a haouse is afire?"

"I wa'n't a-knockin'!" Sam said, dropping his abashed eyes from her roguish glance, "I was a-beginnin'—kinder mawdret, ye know, to bust open the door. I didn't wanter skeer nob'dy, s'posin' the' was anyb'dy t'hum, which I hedn't no idee the' was."

Huldah could not help laughing at this absurd explanation, nor could Sam help joining her, and when they had had their laugh out they found themselves much more at ease and became very sociable. When Huldah again corrected herself for addressing him by his first name, he reminded her of their old school days when she had never thought of calling him anything but Sam. "We was putty good frien's them times, Huldy, but I'm afeared you hain't a-feelin' so frien'ly tow-wards me naow, a-Misterin' on me so. I do' know who folks is a-talkin' tu when they says Mister Lovel; seem's 's 'ough they was mistakin' on me for father or gran'ther."

"Wal, then, Sam, 'f 't suits ye any better!" cried Huldah; and he declared that it did suit him better, "a dum'd sight."

"I hedn't made no cal'lations on gittin' a reg'lar dinner tu-day, bein' 'at the' wa'n't nob'dy here but me," Huldah apologized, looking up at the clock as it warned for eleven. "I'm dreffle sorry 't I didn't naow, but I'm a-goin' t' git ye some nutcakes an' pie an' cheese, an' you'll hafter stay yer stomerk wi' them. You mus' be hungrier 'n a bear, eatin' of your breakfas' 'fore daylight, I s'pose, an' a traipsin' raound in the woods all the fo'noon," and she bustled away to prepare the lunch, in spite of Sam's protesting that he "wa'n't the least mite hungry, an 'ould druther set an' talk 'n t' eat."

"It does beat all natur'," she said, with an emphatic and rather petulant toss of her head, as she returned from the pantry with a pie and a plate of doughnuts, "at anybody can enj'y traipsin' raound, up-hill an' daown, all day long, arter a leetle insi'nificant fox! An' shoolin' an' stumblin' raound the lots all night arter coons! Ketch me, 'f I was a man. But you men folks du beat all creation!"

"Shouldn't wonder 'f we did, putty nigh, 'xceptin' the womern part on't. That beats us all holler. But I'd a good deal druther ketch ye jest as ye be. I hain't hed a chance tu speak tu ye 'lone 'fore in a dawg's age!"

"I do' know 'f nothin' 'at the' 's ben t' hender, 'f ye wanted tu," Huldah said, pouting her red lips, "erless you'd forgot where we lived. You hain't ben a-nigh f'r I d' know haow long, an' ye wouldn't t'day 'f you hedn't a-thought the haouse was afire 'n' nob'dy t' hum," and the pout changed to a smile.

"If I c'ld raly b'lieve 'at the time seemed long sence I'd ben here t' anyb'dy but me, I sh'ld be turrible glad on 't, an' the' wouldn't be no need o' settin' the haouse afire t' fetch me. But ye see, Huldy, yer father he don't set no gret by folks 'at goes a-huntin', no more 'n his darter does, 'n' so I hain't felt ezackly free 'baout comin'."

"Why, Samwill! I wa'n't sayin' 'at I hed anythin' agin folkses huntin'; I was on'y wonderin' what makes 'em lufter."

"Wal, it's kinder natur', I s'pose, borned inter some on us, same's 't is inter haoun' dawgs, an' we can't help a-runnin' off int' the woods. Suthin' takes us. An' when 't 'ain't none tew pleasant for a feller t' hum, like 'nough he goes off a-huntin' er a-fishin' oftener 'n he would 'f 'twas pleasant. Naow, 'f I hed a haouse o' my own an' someb'dy t' keep it—wal, say as this is kep'," looking around the neat kitchen with a look of admiration that grew as it returned and lingered on the bright face of the young housekeeper, "An' wa'n't allus a-scoldin' an findin' fault, I p'sume to say I wouldn't go a-huntin' more'n onct a week in the season on't, 'thaout 'twas when oncommon good days come oncommon often."

"The' hain't no daoubt," Huldah said, rising in some confusion, and taking the tea-kettle from the back of the stove, going out to fill it, talking back through the open door as she went to the pump, "but what you c'ld *hire* someb'dy nuther to keep haouse for ye"—then the squeaking and gurgling crescendo of the pump's voice drowned hers. "I'm a-goin' t' make ye a cup o' tea," returning with the kettle and setting it on the stove, and giving the fire an enlivening punch.

"I wa'n't a-meanin' no *hired* help," Sam said—"no, don't make me no tea—I'd druther you wouldn't take no sech trouble—no, not no hired help, but someb'dy 'at 'ould—'at thought they could stan' it tu—tu go snucks along wi' me a-ownin' of a haouse, an' keepin' on it for me an' her."

"Why, Samwell Lovel! Haow you du go on! Did anybody ever!" cried Huldah, glowing with blushes. Then she held her breath to hear what, she was sure, her lover now must ask. But Sam was frightened into dumbness by his own unwonted boldness; and at last when the silence was becoming painfully awkward, she not knowing what else to say, broke it with the unfortunate remark that "The' was some other nat'ral borned hunter up on the hill, she guessed, for she hearn a haoun' dawg a-yollupin' up there." Sam hurried out to listen, and she followed him.

"Wal, by the gret horn spoon!" he exclaimed, as the familiar long-drawn notes of his own hound struck his ear, "I'll be dum'd if that hain't Drive, as sure as shootin'! He's brung that 'ere fox back f'm the Lord knows where! Yes, sir," as the musical cry swelled louder from the nearest ridge, "he's jest a-shovin' on him, 'n' he's a-goin' t' cross by the Butt'nuts, 'n' I b'lieve I c'n head him!"

Sam was in the kitchen and out again with his gun in an instant and speeding across the fields toward the well-known runway, where three great butternut-trees crowned a knoll with a widespread of thick, ungraceful ramage. Sweetheart and doughnuts were forsaken, love almost forgotten and hunger quite, in the ardor of the chase, though it must be said in palliation of Sam's abrupt departure that he longed to give Huldah an exhibition of his skill as a hunter, to shoot the fox before her eyes and presently bring her the furry trophy of his prowess. But alas for his hopes! Before he was within the longest possible gunshot of the knoll he saw the fox crossing it, halting for a moment to look back at the bellowing hound, and then disappearing with undulating lopes on his way to the western range. He would probably play when he reached those lines of ledges, Sam thought, and after a little hesitation and more than one wistful glance back to the red house, he went forward. He was ashamed to return now, so unsuccessful.

"My!" Huldah said to herself, as with her plump hand shading her eyes she watched the receding form of her lover, "I hope to goodness he'll git him!" Then when the fox appeared and disappeared far out of Sam's reach, she exhaled her long-held breath in a great sigh, not wholly of disappointment. "Wal, I don't care, he'll come back naow." But when he went on with a swinging stride that speedily took him out of her sight, her eyes filled with tears of vexation. "The 'tarnal great fool! I hope 't he won't never come a-nigh me again 's long 's I live an' breathe, an' I hope 't that won't be long—I do! What a plegged fool I was t' up an' tell o' hearin' a haoun'! I wish 't the' wa'n't a haoun' dawg ner a fox in this wide-livin' world for men t' go shoolin' an' runnin' an' traipsin' arter when they might be a-duin' suthin' wuth while. He cares more for a mis'able sneakin' fox 'n he does for me, or anything on airth, to run off arter one an' leave me jest when—I wish 't I was a fox, an' then mebby—Oh! wouldn't I keep him a-moggin' a spell—I won't never speak to him agin so long 's I live an' breathe! Let him hev his ol' haoun' an' his foxes an' his hateful ol' gun an' his everlastin' huntin' 'f he likes 'em better 'n he does me. I don't care, so there, naow!" But she was choking with alternating tearful fits of sorrow and anger all the afternoon, and when her father and mother and little sister returned from the Thanksgiving at "gran'thers," they wondered to find her so woebegone.

"I hedn't no idee," said her father to her mother after furtively watching her as he sat warming his hands at the stove, "'at Huldy keered a row o' pins 'baout goin' t' father's."

When miles away on one of the farthest ridges of the western hills, Sam at sundown shot his fox, and gave the dying brute a spiteful if merciful finishing kick in the head, he said, "Blast yer pictur', I wish 't you hed ha' gone clean t' N' Hampsh'r', 'n I never 'd see er heard on ye, dum ye! You've cost me more 'n any fox ever cost a man afore sen the' was foxes an' men an' women folks in this world!" He bore an aching heart for many a weary day before he forgave himself or was forgiven by Huldah.

One day in the winter Huldah came to Aunt Jerusha on an errand. "I wanter borry your wool caards, Aunt Jerushy, to caard some rolls for father some socks. Aourn is lent, we do' know where." In the conversation that accompanied the borrowing and lending of the cards, Aunt Jerusha asked when Huldah had seen Samwill Lovel, to which Huldah replied with a show of spitefulness that her wistful eyes belied, that she had not seen him since about Thanksgiving Day, "an' didn't wanter, as she knowed on!" Whereat Aunt Jerusha was surprised and grieved, for it was her cherished hope that these two, her favorites among all the young folks of Danvis, would some day make a match. After some coaxing Huldah told her old friend her grievance, and so Uncle Lisha came to know in part the story of Sam's Thanksgiving.

Little Sis

"Good Lord o' massy! if I hain't jest baout clean tuckered aout!" Mrs. Purington gasped, exhaling a longdrawn sigh as she dropped her portly person into a creaking splint-bottom chair in her own kitchen, then flopped her sunbonnet into her short lap, and stroked the hair back with both hands from her heated brow. "Whew! 'f 't ain't hot, jest a-roastin', bilin' hot! Huldy, reach me a dipper o' water, won't ye? I'm e'en a'most choked. I sot that ere pitcher o' emptin's on the winder stool; you ta' keer on em, won't ye?" Huldah brought her mother a quart dipper full of cool water from the pump, that with its dolorous squeaks and hollow groans always reminded her now of last year's Thanksgiving Day.

"Lord o' massy! I b'lieve I *be* roasted," Mrs. Purington exclaimed, regarding her scarlet reflection in the bright interior of the tin dipper, after she had taken a long draught.

"You be dreffle mumpin' this summer," said Huldah's mother, after waiting a little for her daughter to speak. "It's jest yis an' no with ye, an' ye never laugh ner sing a mite 's ye uster. I b'lieve I'd orter steep up some boneset an' hev ye take some; *I* b'lieve yer stomerk 's aouten order."

"Why, mother, I'm jest as tough as a bear," Huldah declared, blushing and making a brave effort to laugh; she could not help smiling at the thought of boneset as a remedy for her ill—heartsease would be more to the purpose, it seemed to her.

"It is a turrible job tu fix them ol' pertaters fit for cookin'," said Mrs. Purington, now apparently just noticing her daughter's occupation. "Seem 's 'ough we'd ort tu hev some new ones by this time. Wonder 'f yer father 's dug int' any hills tu see? Where's Sis?" she asked, after looking thoughtfully at Huldah and the potatoes as she went to hang the dipper and sunbonnet on their respective nails. "I hain't seen nor hearn nothin' on her sen I come in." It was indeed noticeable that the six-year-old pet of the household had not even in so short a time in a wakeful forenoon in some way made her whereabouts known, and her mother wondered now with a maternal qualm of conscience that she had not sooner remarked the absence of the child's voice, talking to herself, or asking endless unanswerable questions, or singing her rag doll to imaginary sleep. She suddenly realized how still it was, that there was no sound in the kitchen but the buzzing of the flies, the ticking of the clock, and the fluttering splash and chip, chip of the potato washing and paring, and that from outdoors came no sound but the lazy "crating" of the hens, the dolorous mixture of peep and cluck wherewith the half-grown chickens expressed their contentment, the dry clap of a locust's wings, followed by his long, shrill cry when he had lighted in the chip-littered yard, and from farther off the faint ringing of the mowers' whetted scythes.

"Why," said Huldah, coming with a start out of a maze of troubled thoughts, "she was a-tewin' 'raound an' a-pesterin' me half tu death 'baout this an' that she wanted t' du, an' at last I gi'n her her little baskit 'at—'at she thinks so much on, an' tol' her she might gwup in the stump lot a-blackbaryin' a spell. I tol' her she mustn't gwaout o' sight o' the haouse."

"Wal," Mrs. Purington said, looking out toward the hills, "I guess you hedn't orter let her. I d' know 's she'd orter gwup there 'lone. She'd better ben a-watchin' the ol' hen turkey an' her young uns. If they git up tu the aidge of the woods the foxes 'll ketch every identical one on 'em. Oh dear me suz! Seems 's 'ough the pleggid foxes hed ort tu git some scaser, wi' Sam Lovel an' mongst 'em a-huntin' an' a-haounin' on 'em half the year; but they don't. Seems 's 'ough that young un ort tu be some 'eres in sight er a-comin' hum by this time. Haow long's she ben gone?"

"She's ben gone," Huldah answered, looking at the clock—"why, it's most an hour an' a half! Mother, 'f you'll put the pertaters in the kittle, I'll go an' git her. 'F I don't git back soon 'nough, the pork 's all cut an' in the fryin'-pan ready for freshnin'." So putting on her sunbonnet she went out, her mother following to the door to say, "Jes' 's like 's not she's over in the medder 'long wi' yer father 'n' the rest on 'em." With this hope Huldah went out toward the meadow till she could see her father and the two hired men swinging their scythes with even strokes, but there was no little sister there, and she went on quickly, crossing the brook where its summer-shrunken current wimpled among the stones in the shade of a thicket of young firs. She saw a print of a small shoe in the soft gravel, half filled with water, and pointing toward the berry lot. Surely, she thought, she must soon find her now, and listened a moment with the expectation of hearing the child prattling to herself or rustling among the bushes. But she heard nothing but the hum of insects, the chirp of crickets, and an occasional bird note, and calling, got no answer. But she must see her presently, for it was impossible to keep out of sight in the field that the axe had swept all tree growth from only two years ago. But when she entered it, after beating along its lower edge for a while, she was surprised to see how tall the sprouts and bushes had grown since she had last been there. It now seemed hopeless enough to look here for one grown to full stature, much more so to find a child whose head would be overtopped by the lowest of the blackberry brambles that reared themselves with rampant growth about every blackened stump and log heap.

Perhaps Polly had fallen asleep on some inviting bed of moss by the brook. Nothing was likelier, and it was strange she had not sooner thought of it. Returning, she followed all the turns of the little watercourse along the border of the stump lot, but saw no living thing she cared to; nothing but a scared trout flashing across the shadows of a pool; heard nothing but the warning cry of a mother partridge and the startling whir of wings when the old bird and her well-grown brood burst away in brief flight, and then the lisping call that gathered the scattered family. Why would not her little chick of a sister hear and answer her call? Huldah went back into the brush and swiftly threaded the maze of cowpaths, and with laborious climbing gained the tops of the tallest stumps, whose height showed how deep the snow was when the trees were felled, and scanned all the thickets she could overlook, always hoping to see somewhere among the tangle of stalks and leafage the little pink sunbonnet moving about. Once she thought she had surely caught sight of it, but on approach it proved to be only the full-flowered spike of a willow herb nodding to the breeze or bending under the shifting weight of the bees. She called loudly and often, but was answered only by the mewing of a catbird that flitted near yet unseen in the thickets, and by the sudden jangle of a cowbell as its startled wearer crashed away through the brush. Sometimes the mysterious murmurs of the forest would fool her ear for a moment; then when she listened they seemed to come from everywhere and could be located nowhere. One moment she was so vexed and impatient that if she had come upon the little wanderer her first impulse would have been to give her a scolding; the next she was choking with a swelling ache of dread that she would have given the world to have cured by a sight of the yellow-polled pet and tease, whom if she might but find alive and well she would never scold again. So she hurried on in her fruitless search till she came to the upper end of the half-cleared field where the lofty branches of the great trees linteled the doorway of the ancient forest, whose depths and darkness and mystery she feared, but would dare to enter, if there was one promised chance of her finding the lost child there. Yes, lost. The fact with all its terrible possibilities forced itself upon her, and horrible visions floated in a swiftly returning procession before her misty eyes of the little form lying dead at the foot of a precipice, or drowned in a brook pool, or torn by wild beasts, or at best stumbling blindly onward in a craze of fright perhaps to a worse death by starvation and terror. It would be only a waste of precious time for her to go into the woods. There was nothing for her to do but to hasten home and rouse the neighborhood for the search. She mounted a great boulder for one more unrewarded look, and to make another unanswered call. She could see her home basking in the August sun with such a restful air as if it was never to shelter the sorrow that was soon to enter it; and a wood thrush filled the cloisters of the woods with his sweet chime of silver bells as if there were naught but peace and happiness in their quiet depths. Huldah was no saint, and she felt an angry resentment of this mockery of her trouble. She could have wrung the thrush's neck to end the song so ill-attuned to her feelings, and it would have been a slight relief to see some token of disturbance about the house, though it would not have quieted her self-reproach. If this wrathful feeling had not been overpowered by the stronger emotion of grief before she reached home, it might have been somewhat appeased by the pervading air of anxiety that brooded over the household. Her father, watching for her as he smoked his after-dinner pipe, came out to meet her, questioning her with a troubled face. She only halted to say in a choked voice, "O father, she's lost! Hurry, an' raout aout everybody!" and answered the inquiring look of the hired men who stopped their meditative whittling and arose from the doorstep at her approach with, "Polly's lost! Go an' tell 'em all tu come an' find her!" Her mother, meeting her at the door, heard this, and retreating to the nearest chair, sat down, spreading a helpless hand on either knee. "Oh dear me suz! Huldy, I don't see haow on airth you ever, ever come tu let her go!"

"O mother, *don't*! Is the' any tea left? I'm a-chokin', an' tuckered." She poured out a cupful from the teapot, swallowed it at a draught, and went quickly out. "I'm a-goin' tu Joel's an' Solon's an' Hillses' an' that way 's fur 's I can tu tell 'em," she said to her father, who was hurriedly consulting with the men. "You an' John an' Lije go t' other ways. I searched and hollered all over the stump lot, an' never seen nothin' on her but her track where she crossed the brook, a-goin'," and she hastened down the road.

"Thee don't say so!" Jemima Bartlett said, her placid face full of pity when Huldah briefly told her errand. "The poor little precious! I'll call the men folks right off up aouten the medder. They'll come tu rights when they hear the horn. Thee'd better come in an' sed daown an' rest thee a spell, thee does look so beat aout, poor child."

But Huldah sped on while the blasts of the conch-shell were echoing from the hills, and when she looked back as she turned into Solon Briggs's yard, she saw Joel and his hired man trudging along the road toward her home.

Solon happened to be mending his "hay-riggin'," and, dropping his tools on the door-yard chips, he hastened away as soon as he heard her message, stopping only to ask if it would be "more essifactious for him tu go an' help her raise a human cry?"

Joseph Hill came to the door in his stockings trying to rub and gape away the leftover sleepiness of an after-dinner nap. When he had slowly pulled on his boots he was ready to go; he hardly knew which way till he had "told M'ri," who came with the youngest baby in her arms, and two a-foot tugging at her skirts and peeping from behind them, while she offered her condolences. The whistling growl of Gran'ther Hill came from where he sat in his arm-chair at the back door, asking many questions: "What is 't yer a-talkin' 'baout, M'rier? Somebody lost? Who is it? Purin't'ns' young un? Don't Purin't'ns' folks know no better 'n tu let a baby gwoff int' the woods? Why didn't they chuck her int' the cist'n? Then they 'd ha' knowed where she was! Wal, I s'pose we all got tu turn aout an' sarch arter her," and he came stamping through the house with his hat on and his cane in his hand. "You needn't talk to me, M'rier!" he said, glowering fiercely at his daughter-in-law when she mildly protested against his going, "I hain't ol', nuther, I tell ye. Eighty-five year hain't nothin' tu a man 'at's ben where I ben, when the's babies lost in the woods! I've tracked Injins, an' I guess I c'n track a foolish little young un!" and he marched off with his son with as much alacrity as he had responded to Ethan Allen's call in the long past May of his youth.

Presently Huldah was at Uncle Lisha's telling her sympathizing old friend, Aunt Jerusha, of the loss of the child, and she added, as she had not before, "It's all my fault—I let her go a-baryin'!" The old man was in the shop mending a piece of harness, and the door between the shop and the house being open, as it usually was when he had no visitors, his ears caught the girl's voice and something of her story.

"Good airth an' seas! Huldy, what's that you're a-sayin'? Sissy lost? Haow? Where?" he shouted as he suddenly appeared in the doorway with the tug in his hand. Then she told him all she could, repeating that it was all her fault, for she found a little comfort in making this confession now.

"Wal," pitching the tug back into the shop, and untying his apron and sloughing it off on the threshold, "I'll go an' du what I can. I c'n waddle 'raound in the woods arter a fashion, an' I c'n holler c'nsid'able, an' I tell ye hollerin' caounts sech times. Fust I'll go an' holler fer Tawmus. Say, Huldy, I'll tell ye," he said, turning toward her while one upstretched hand groped along the pegs for his hat, "the's one man in Danvis 'at I druther hev a sarchin' for Sissy 'an all the hull caboodle on us, ol' an' young, big an' little. He knows the woods julluk a book, an' c'n read every sign in 'em—an' that 'ere man is Samwill Lovel! You're spryer 'n I be, 'n' some spryer 'n Jerushy, I guess. You cut over to his haouse an' start him!"

"O Uncle Lisher, I can't!" Huldah gasped, her hot, tired face paling an instant, then burning redder with blushes, "I can't! Someb'dy else 'll tell him. You go an' tell him!"

"I tell ye, Huldy, *you* mus' go! The' hain't no time for me tu turkle over there, an' you comin' this way they'll depend on you tellin' on him! Good airth an' seas! gal, this hain't no time for stinkin' pride 'f you *be* aout with him. He'd sarch tu the eend o' the airth if you ast him—he warships the graound you tread! Go right stret, an' clipper, tew!" and having got his hat on he took her by the shoulders and gently pushed her outdoors, and as far as the gate, facing her the desired way. She went on, accelerating her pace till she was running when she came to the door of the Lovel homestead, caring for nothing now so much as the finding of her lost sister.

Mrs. Lovel, Sam's stepmother, a gaunt, hard-featured woman, came to the open door, beating the threshold with a broom to frighten away some intruding chickens. "Shoo! you pesterin' torments! I wish 't the aigs o' yer breed was destr'yed! Why, massy sakes alive! Huldy Pur'n't'n! What be you in sech a pucker 'baout?" she cried in astonishment when Huldah's swift approach diverted her attention from the objects of her displeasure. "Why, you look 's 'ough you'd ben dragged through a brush heap, an' scairt aouten your seben senses!"

"Oh, Miss' Lovel, Polly 's lost in the woods. Where's Samwell? I want him tu help find her. Where is he?"

"Polly lost!" Mrs. Lovel repeated, regarding Huldah with a reproachful severity in her countenance that the poor girl felt she deserved. "Up back o' your haouse? Wal, I shouldn't wonder a mite 'f you never faound her a-livin'. Like 's anyways she'll tumble off 'm the rocks an' break her neck, 'f the' don't suthin' nuther ketch her afore. Some on 'em was a-tellin' o' hearin' a wolf a-haowlin' an' a-haowlin' t' other night, an' some thinks the' 's a painter a-hantin' 'raound. The' 's allus bears, an' they du say 'at the' hain't nothin' 'at bears likes better' t' eat 'n child'n."

Huldah, with raised hands and averted face, asked again for Sam.

"Sam! Humph! Sure 'nough, where is he? You tell. Him an' his father finished up hayin' yist'd'y, an' of course he hed tu put off a bee-huntin' the fust thing arter breakfus' this mornin'; nob'dy knows which way. He'd a 'tarnal sight better ben a-fencin' the stacks so 't the kyows c'ld be turned int' the medder. An' Lovel, he's a-putterin' 'raound daown in the back lot 'baout suthin' 't hain't no vally, I'll warrant. O my eyes an' Betty Martin! If these men hain't 'nough tu drive any womern distracted! Haow ol' *was* Polly?" as if the bright little life was assuredly ended.

"Six, the twenty fourth o' June," Huldah answered, and turning away went wearily homeward, half the hope dying out of her heart, now that there was no hope of finding Sam.

When Joel Bartlett arrived he went in and shook hands with Mrs. Purington as solemnly as he performed the same ceremony when he "broke the meetin'" on First and Fifth Days. "I wanter tell thee, Mary Pur'nt'n, tu keep quiet in thy mind," he said. "Aour Heavenly Father, withaout whose knowledge not a sparrer falls tu the graound, will ta' keer of a precious little child; an' I feel it bore in upon me 'at thy little darter will be restored tu thee. Sech poor insterments as we be o' His'n, we will du aour best indivors. An' naow, Mary, keep quiet in thy mind, an' seek for stren'th in Him tu help thee tu bear this grievous trial o' waitin' on His will."

The rescue party had been quickly mustered, and the plan of search agreed upon. It heartened Huldah when she reached home to know that twenty-five or thirty stalwart men were already ranging the woods in quest of her lost sister, all so inspired with neighborly kindness that they would spare themselves no pain or hardship in the search.

But oh, if the keenest and bravest woodsman among all these hills were only on the same quest! Why of all the days in the year must he have chosen this most anxious one of a lifetime wherein to go bee-hunting? Huldah mentally relegated the bees to that limbo whither she had long before in like manner banished the foxes.

Sam Lovel's Bee-Hunting

Away up on the mountain-side, where some hopeful pioneer had hewn out of the wilderness a few acres with slight and remote possibilities of a future pasture, Sam Lovel was wallowing at noon among the golden rods, willow-herbs, and asters that filled this wild garden with yellow and pink and blue and white bloom, yet more varied with the heightening and deepening of their colors by sunlight and shadow, and contrast. The bees were making the most of such bountiful pasturage; the clearing droned with their incessant hum, and the drowsy murmur of their toil seemed to have lulled the forest to sleep, so still were all its depths. Sam had no trouble to imprison one of the busy horde in his bee-box, but more to line his liberated captive and the mates returning with her, for the little square of sunlit sky was flecked with hundreds of hurrying brown specks. But his sharp eyes were not easily foiled when he set them fairly to their work, and he had not lain long on his back among the ferns before he caught the airy trail of the bees that carried their burdens of sweets from his box, set on the nearest tall stump. He did not follow far into the woods before he found the great tree where they were hoarding their wealth. "Tu easy faound for fun," he said, as he lighted his pipe and began to cut his initials on the trunk of the old maple, "but bee-huntin' 's better 'n no huntin', an' more fun 'n fencin' stacks 'at c'n jes' 's well wait a spell while the rowen grows, er a-hearin' everlastin' tewin' an' scoldin'. An' it helps tol'able well ter keep a feller's mind off 'm onprofitable thinkin'. Wal, there you be, Mister L.," slowly pushing his knife shut against his thigh as he critically regarded his carving, "an' you 're the best letter I got in my name, for the' 's an l in Huldy. I sh'd like tu put tew more on ye in her'n. Ho hum! Wal, come, you dum'd ol' long-laigged fool of a S. L., le's go an' find another bee tree." And he took himself back to the clearing. He captured a bee on the first "yaller top" he came to, and soon established another line, but it took much longer to trace it to the bee's home, and when he had set his mark on this, it was time to be going to his own home. He took his unerring course through the pathless woods, stopping now and then to rest on a log or knoll that seemed to be set with its cushion of moss on purpose for him. During one of these halts, when half way through the woods, he heard a cry, so strange that he paused to listen for a repetition of it while his lighted match went out before it reached his pipe, or the pipe his mouth. Once more the distressful wail struck his ear, whether far away or only faint and near he could not tell. "Wal," letting out his held breath and striking another match, "'f I've got another painter on my hands, I wish 't I hed the ol' Ore Bed 'long. But like 'nough 'tain't nothin' but a bluejay 'at's struck a new noise—I thought they hed 'em all a'ready, though." And he went on, pausing a little at times to listen to and locate the voice, which presently ceased. "'F I hed a gun I'd go an' see what kind of a critter 's a-makin' on't," he said, and then half forgot it. He had come to where he got glimpses of the broad daylight through the palisades of the forest's western border, and where long glints of the westering sun gilded patches of ferns and wood plants and last year's sear leaves, when his quick wood-sight, glancing everywhere and noting everything, fell upon a little bright-colored Indian basket overset in a tuft of ferns, with a few blackberries in it and others spilled beside it. "Why," he said, picking it up and examining it, "that's the baskit I gin' little Polly Pur'n't'n last year! It hain't ben dropped long, for the baries is fresh, 'n' there's a leaf 't ain't wilted scacely. She dropped it, for there's some puckerbaries, an' the' wouldn't nob'dy but a young un pick them. Haow com' that little critter 'way up here?" Then he heard men's voices calling and answering in the woods far away at his left. "God A'mighty, she's lost!" he exclaimed, as he quickly formulated the sounds he heard and the signs he saw. "That was her 'at I hearn! What a dum'd fool I be!" He dropped his bee-box, marking the spot with a glance, and sped back into the heart of the forest so swiftly that the inquisitive chickadees which had gathered about him knew not what way he had gone. He spent no time in looking for traces of the child's passage here, but made his way as rapidly as possible to the place which the cry had seemed to come from, listening intently as he glided silently along, for he knew that if she had not sunk down exhausted with wandering and fright, she would be circling away after the manner of lost persons, from where he had heard her. Moving more slowly now and scanning every foot of forest floor about him, he at last saw a broken-down stalk of ginseng, its red berries crushed by a footstep, and noting which way it was swept and how recently, found on a bush beyond it a thread of calico, then a small shoe-print in the mould, and farther on a little garter hanging to a broken branch of a fallen tree. According to established usage in such cases, he should have put this in his breast, for he knew that Huldah had knit it, but he only placed it in his pocket, saying, "If she hain't never faound it'll be a sorter comfort tu 'em tu see this—but I'm a-goin' tu find her—I got tu!" He was assured of her course now, and thought she could not be far off, but he did not call, for he knew with what unreasoning terror even men are sometimes crazed when lost in the woods, when familiar sounds as well as familiar scenes are strange and terrible. While for a moment he stood listening he heard the distant halloos of the searching party—then rushing away from them, a sudden swish of leaves and crash of undergrowth, and then caught a glimpse of a wild little form scurrying and tumbling through the green and gray haze of netted shrubs and saplings. He had never stalked a November partridge so stealthily as he went forward now. Not a twig snapped under his foot, nor branch sprung backward with a swish louder than the beat of an owl's wing, and there was no sign in glance or motion that he saw as he passed it, the terror-stricken little face that stared out from a sprangly thicket of mountain yew. Assured that she was within reach, he turned slowly and said softly, "Why, Sis! is this you?

Don't ye know me, Sam Lovel? Here's yer little baskit 'at you dropped daown yunder, but I'm afeared the baries is all spilt!" and then he had her sobbing and moaning in his strong arms.

"This is the best day's huntin' ever I done," he said, his voice shaking with the great thankfulness of his heart. He called again and again to let the searchers know that the lost child was found, but if they heard they did not heed or understand his calls.

When he came to Stony Brook with his burden asleep on his shoulders, he seated her on the bank and bathed her hot face and gave her grateful draughts from a dipper that he made in five minutes with a sheet of birch bark folded and fastened in a cleft stick, and here he shouted lustily again, but got no answer.

"Come, Sis," after listening, stooping and reaching out his arms, "we must be a-moggin'!"

"I be awful heavy, Samwell, but I can't step a step," she said apologetically, as he took her up. "Oh, how good you be!"

Sam's long shadow had ceased following him, and was blurred out in the twilight when he crossed the door-yard chips that his feet had not trodden since that Thanksgiving Day. Polly was asleep again in his arms when he entered the open door of the kitchen which bore a funereal air, with a dozen neighboring women sitting against its walls speaking to each other in hushed solemn voices, one standing beside Mrs. Purington, ready with a hartshorn-bottle when she should take her apron from her face. The poor woman was reaching out blindly with one hand for the comforting salts when Sam, unseen by any till now, set Polly in her lap, and then casting a longing look along the line of gaping, speechless women, he disappeared before the feminine chorus of "Ohs!" and "Mys!" and little shrieks had swelled to its height.

Huldah was out in the back yard trying to comfort herself with listening to the faint halloos of the searchers, and with watching the occasional glimmer of their lanterns and torches, dim stars of hope to her now, when she heard the indoor stir, and hurried in expecting to find her mother in a fainting fit. But there was her little sister with her mother crying over her and scolding her in the same breath, and all the other women letting out their pent-up speech in a hail storm of words, wherewith fell a shower of tears. When she had hugged Polly and kissed her, and sprinkled her with the first tears she had shed that day, she asked, "Who fetched her?" and out of the confusion got this answer: "Sam Lovel, an' the great good-for-nothin' cleared right aout an' never said one word!"

He could not have gone far. "Samwell! Samwell Lovel!" she called softly, running out toward the road.

"Was you a-callin' me, Huldy?" a low voice answered out of the dusk.

"Won't ye come an' blow the horn tu call 'em hum, Samwell? The' can't none on 'em in there blow nothin'—O Sam!"

The tall form of her lover came out of the gloom, and the big sister was in the strong arms that had just brought home the little sister.

The search of the rescue party was prolonged a little before Sam's blasts on the conch-shell were tossed far and wide from echoing mountain to echoing hill to call them home.

"Sam," said Huldah, half an hour later, "you hain't never tol' me whether no you got that 'ere fox?"

"I hain't never hed no chance!" he answered.

In the Shop Again

At the next gathering in Lisha's shop, Antoine was present, and when the old cobbler became aware of him, he gave him a hearty welcome, for though he was always cracking rough jokes upon the Frenchman, he had a real liking for him for his good nature.

"Hello, Ann Twine! Buzzhoo musheer! Cummassy vau! How dy do? Glad t' see ye agin. Oh, you've missed it 't ye hain't ben here t' aour meetin's! Sech stories as the boys has tole, an' Solon Briggs has tole us lots o' things 't we didn't know—nor he nuther."

"Wal naow, Onc' Lasha," asked Antoine in a low voice, as he edged onto the corner of the shoe-bench, "w'at kan o' langwizh dat was, M'sieu Brigg he spik it, hein? 'F dat was Anglish Ah can't nevah larn 'em. He broke ma jaw off. Guess he Sous 'Merican, don't it?"

"Nev' mind, Ann Twine, you c'n onderstand it jes' 's well 's any on us—'n jes' 's well 's he ken, I guess. It don't hurt us none, 'n' it does him lots o' good to let off them 'ere booktionary words. Wal, Ann Twine, it's your turn naow. You got to tell a story er sing a song. Le's hev Pappy no, come. 'Pappee no sa bum pay-raow.'" Lisha sang with a roaring voice the first line of that once popular Canadian revolutionary song. "Tune 'er up!"

"Bah Gosh, Onc' Lasha," Antoine said with a sorrowful voice and face, "Ah can' sing, nor tell storee, Ah feel so bad!"

"What's the motter, man? Ye inyuns froze, er terbacker gin aout?"

"No, sah, Onc' Lasha, Ah got plenty onion, plenty tabac, plenty, plenty. But Ah have such bad dream las' nahgt! Oh, Ah feel so sorry, me!"

"Tell it, Ann Twine, tell it," Lisha shouted, and all the others joined in the request or demand.

"Ah don't lak tole it, mek you all feel so bad jes' lak me, Ah fred. Wal, don' you cry. Las' naght w'en Ah go bed Ah'll freegit pray. Den Ah'll go sleep. Bambye Ah'll dream Ah'll go to l'enfer, what you call it, hell?"

"Guess 't was 'baout mornin' when you dremp that dream, Ann Twine. Mornin' dreams comes true, they say," Lisha put in.

"W'en Ah'll gat dah," continued Antoine, only noticing the interruption by a shrug and a wave of the hand, "de Dev' he come as' me what so good man Ah'll be come dah faw? Ah'll say Ah'll honly come faw fun, see what goin's on, me. Den he say, 'Se' dawn, se' dawn, M'sieu Bissette, mek it youse'f to home.' So Ah'll sit in ver' warm place an' look all 'raoun'. Bambye one hole man come, he don't got any clo's on it, honly jes shoe mek it tool ond' hees arm. Dev' he say, 'What you want it?' Hole man say, 'Dey a'nt have it me on tudder place, so Ah'll come heear, see 'f Ah'll can git it jawb mek it you some boot.' Dev' he stick it aout bose hees foots, one of it lak man's, one of it lak caow's, den he say, 'You can mezzhy only but one of it for mek bose boot; tek it you choose.' Hole man he say, 'Guess ah'll tek it de bes foot,' so he mezzhy de man foot an' go work raght off. Pooty soon raght off, bambye, he have it de boot all do, an' Dev' he try it on, an', bah Gosh, de boot fit de caow foot bes', an' he won't go on tudder one 't all, no, sah! Den Dev' he mad, an' keek dat poo' hole man aou' door in col'; an' Ah'll feel so sorree for it Ah'll run raght back here an' git it some clo's, an' fus' one Ah'll git hole of it was Onc' Lasha clo's, an' bah Gosh! you b'lieve it me, dat clo's fit dat hole man jes' if dey been mek it for him, yes, sah!"

The laugh which the relation of this dream aroused was made louder by Lisha's roaring "haw, haw, ho," at the end of which he said, glowering at the narrator through his spectacles, "You dremp that wide awake in the daytime, Ann Twine. You been studyin' on it up ever sen' you was here?"

"No, sah, Onc' Lasha, Ah'll dream dat in a mawnin'; an' he come true, you say? Wha' you s'pose dat hole man go? Dey won't have it in de good place, dey won't have it in de bad place—wha' you s'pose he goin' go, hein?"

"Guess he'll hafter go t' the 'Hio," Lisha answered, with a laugh that ended in a sigh; "to the 'Hio, where his on'y chick an' child is. Canucks," he continued "don't never die, 's fur's heard on, 'ceptin' the one 'at I spoke on. When they git old 'nough to die they go to Colchester Pint. Forty, fifty years f'om naow you'll go there, Ann Twine."

"Wal, da't pooty good place to feesh, don't it? Ah'll rudder go dah as come dead."

"Fish! Yes; fish 'n' inyuns 'n' terbacker 's baout all a Canuck keers for. Ann Twine, you're the furderest Canuck f'om where ye c'n ketch bull-paouts an' eels 't I ever see. Give 'em them an' inyuns an' terbacker, an' an ole hoss, 'n' a wuthless dog, 'n' they're happy."

"You call it ma dog don't good for somet'ing, Onc' Lasha? You tole him dat he bit you, den he show he good. He fus' rate dog, sah. He lay in haouse all a time honly w'en he barkin' at folks go 'long on road, 'n' he jes' fat as burrer."

"Good qualities, all on 'em," said Lisha, "p'tic'ly in a Canuck dog, bein' as fat 's butter."

"Those 'ere French," Solon Briggs remarked to Pelatiah, who sat beside him, "is a joe-vial an' a fry-volous race."

"Yus," said Pelatiah, sadly regarding the palms of his mittens, much soiled with handling cord-wood since sledding had come, "I s'pose they be pooty smart to run."

Solon, disgusted with his unappreciative listener, raised his voice and addressed the Frenchman. "Antwine, didn't your ant-sisters come from France?"

"No, M'sieu Brigg, ma aunt seesters an' brudder, too, all bawn in Canada. Ma mudder one of it, seester to ma aunt, prob'ly."

"You misconstrowed my inquirement, Antwine," said Solon. "I meant to ast you, wa'n't their prosperity 'at was borned before 'em natyves of France—reg'lar polly voo Franceys, so tu speak?"

"Ah do' know—yas, Ah guess so, Ah guess yes," Antoine replied at random, having no idea of Solon's meaning.

"Shah! fur's any conjoogle satisfactualness is consarned, if a man hain't a lingoist he might 's well talk to a sawmill as one o' these furrin Canucks," said Solon, and added, "I b'lieve I'll take my department an' step outside."

"Ah do' know 'f Ah got it raght, zhontemans," said Antoine, as the wooden latch clattered behind the departing wise man, "but Ah tink wat you call Solum in Anglish was dam hole foolish, an't it?" There was not a dissenting voice, but Lisha said apologetically, "Oh, wal, Solon means well!"

"I'll be darned if I know what he does mean," Sam Lovel said.

"Wal," said Lisha, "I s'pose he 's a well-read man, an'—"

"Dum the *well* red men!" Sam broke in, "I wish 't they was all sick 'n' dead, consarn 'em! See haow they're cuttin' up aout West 'n' in Floridy!"

"Oh, wall," Lisha continued, "we're well red o' him an' them, so le's don't bother!"

"I don't keer what you say 'baout red men, ef I was a Ninjun as I be a white man," cried Pelatiah, rising and smacking his mittens together, "while 't there was a pale face on the face of the U-nited States of Ameriky, I wouldn't never lay daown my bow-arrers, my tommyhock, an' my wampum: never, no, never!"

"Guess ye'd hev tu lay daown yer wampum 'f I mended yer boots, Peltier," said Lisha. "Wal," Samuel said, after getting his pipe in full blast, "I seen suthin' on the North Hill 'at 's an oncommon sight now er-days."

"What was that?" one asked, and others guessed "a painter," "a wolf," "a woolyneeg," or the tracks of the animals named.

"Was it the footprints of some avarocious annymill, or the annymill hisself?" Solon Briggs inquired as he reentered the shop.

"Nary one," said Sam, and added after a few deliberate puffs, during which the curiosity of his auditors grew almost insupportable, "a deer track."

"Good airth an' seas! You don't say so, Samwill? I hain't seen nor hearn tell o' one a-bein' raound in five, I d' know but ten, year. Did ye foller it, Samwill? It's a tol'able good snow fur still-huntin'."

"Foller it? No!" Sam answered emphatically. "What would I foller it for? I wouldn't shoot a deer on these 'ere hills 'f I had a dozen chances at him!"

"I swan I would," said Pelatiah.

"Yas," said Sam, with contemptuous wrath, "you would, I ha' no daoubt on't, an' so would three quarters on 'em shoot the las' deer 'f he come to their stacks an' eat along with their cattle, jes' as Joel Bartlett did, consarn his gizzard! I wish 't was State's prison tu kill a deer any time o' year, an' hed ben twenty year ago. Then we might hev some deer in these 'ere woods, where the' hain't one naow tu ten thousand acres, 'n' where forty year ago the' was hundreds on 'em 'n' might jes' as well be naow, if 't wan't fer the dum'd hogs an' fools. I knowed critters 'at went on tew legs an' called 'emselves men, 'at when I was a boy useter go aout in Febbary an' March an' murder the poor creeturs in their yards with clubs, twenty on 'em in a day, when they wa'n't wuth skinnin' fur their skins, say nothin' baout the meat, which the' wa'n't 'nough on tew carcasses tu bait a saple trap. An' some o' them things is a-livin' yit, an' would du the same again if they hed the chance. If they was gone an' a wolf left in the place of each one on 'em, the airth would be better off, a darned sight. Cuss 'em, they're wus 'n Injins!"

The stillness that followed this outburst of the hunter's righteous indignation was broken by Solon's rasping preliminary "Ahem! That 'ere last remark o' yourn is an on-dutible fact. The abregoines would not perforate sech an act, because in so a-duin' they would ampitate their own noses off, deer a-bein' their gret mainstayance, both intarnally an' out tarnally—that is to say, both food an' remnants."

"Wal," said Lisha, as he soused a tap in his tub, "the' can't nob'dy say 't ever I crusted deer, but the' was 'nough on 'em 't did, twenty, thirty year ago, an' mis'able murderin' business it was, tew. The' was one man, though," he continued, after some vigorous pounding of the tap on his lapstone, "'at got cured o' crustin' for his lifetime, which it shortened it, tew."

"It ort t' been shortened afore ever he went a-crustin'," said the relentless Sam. "Wal, haow was 't, Uncle Lisha?"

"Wal," said Lisha, taking the last peg from between his lips and driving it home, "I guess it's gittin' ruther late t' begin a story t'night, hain't it?"

Noah Chase's Deer-Hunting

After the soft snowfall the grip of winter tightened with sharper weather, and it was a nipping night when Lisha's friends, the creaking of whose coming footsteps he heard twenty rods away, again entered the shop. Each as he came in made his way quickly to the ruddy, roaring stove, and hardly one failed to shrug his shoulders with a shivering "booh!" rub his hands, stamp his feet, and proclaim in some form of words that the night was cold, as if that was something which needed every man's testimony to establish as a fact.

Pelatiah asked Sam Lovel, "'S this col' 'nough for ye, Samwel?" and Sam answered, as he fanned himself with his fur cap, "Cold 'nough? No. I want it cold 'nough tu freeze the blaze of a match tu a pipe. I'm most melted, 'n' wish 't I could set top o' 'Tater Hill 'n hour er tew 'n' cool off."

"And naow," said Solon Briggs, when Lisha had established himself in the polished leathern seat of his bench, "arfter the preluminary remarks 'at you made at aour prevarious meetin', it is confidentially expected 'at you will preceed to dilate your narrowtyve."

"Yas," Antoine urged, "you goin' fill up you promise, don't it, Onc' Lasha, hein?"

"Wal, boys, 'f I must I must, I s'pose," said Lisha, pulling hard at his pipe between words, "but I hain't no gret at tellin' stories. Ye see"—after some silent back tracking of memory—"'twas baout Noer Chase; he was the fust one in taown 't hed a pleasure waggin, 'n' they uster call it Noer's Ark. He'd ben sellick man three fo' years, 'n' sot in the leegislatur' onct—cousin t' Jerushy, tew—'n' orter ben in better business 'n goin' crustin', but he went 'n' more 'n onct. So one March the' was the alfiredest crust, 'n' he hedn't nothin' tu du much, 'n' says he, 'I guess I'll hassome fun,' says he. So he got him a club, an' put on his snowshoes an' put 'er fer a basin up in the maountin where he knowed the' was some deer a-yardin'. I know the ezack spot, an' so du you, Samwill. Right up where the east branch o' Stunny Brook heads. He got Amos Jones tu go 'long with him, 'n' they got there an' faound the deer, twenty on 'em or more, a-yardin' 'raound in the little spruces, 'n' all poorer 'n wood. Wal, they schattered 'em aout an' went at 'em. Amos he seen Noer knock down ten on 'em and cut the' thruts, 'n' then he telled 'im for tu stop, 'f that was 'nough. But Noer he laughed 'n' said he was jes' beginnin' tu hassome fun; 'n' then he put arter a doe that was heavy with fa'n, 'n' as he run up 'longside on her, she stumbled in the crust, her laigs all a-bleedin', an' rolled up 'er eyes turrible pitiful tow-wards him, an' gin a beseechin' kind of a blaat. An' Amos he hollered aout tu Noer t' let 'er lone, but Noer he on'y laughed 'n' said haow t' he was goin' ter kill tew tu one shot, 'n' he gin 'er a lick on the head with his club 'fore Amos co'ld git tu him."

"Damn 'im!" growled Sam.

"Amos didn't hardly never cuss, but I s'pose he ripped aout then 'n' gin it tu Noer hot 'n' heavy, 'n' said he was a good min' tu sarve 'im 's he'd sarved the doe; 'n' jes' then he happened tu see that Noer was standin'

'long side o' the doe, right onderneath an onlucky tree, 'n' then he said
he knowed suthin' 'ould happen tu 'im, 'n' tol' 'im so. But Noer on'y
laughed at 'im, 'n' called 'im a sup'stitious chickin-hearted ol' granny, an'
took aout his knife tu cut the doe's thrut. Amos couldn't stan' it tu see no
more sech murderin', 'n' so he cleared aout and went hum. Wal, Noer
finished the doe, 'n' then took arter a-yullin' buck next. The buck started
daown the maountain, 'n' bein' putty light he skinned it 'long putty good
jog, so 's 't Noer couldn't ketch up with 'im 's easy 's he hed with t'other
ones. So Noer 'gin to git mad, 'n' doubled his jumps, 'n' went tearin'
daown hill lickerty split, 'n' hed mos' ketched up tu the deer, when the
toe of his snowshoe ketched int' the limb of a blowed-daown tree, an'
he fell, kerlummux! 'n' struck his laig on another limb on 't an' broke
his laig."

"Good!" cried Sam.

"His laig pained him onmassyfully, 'n' like 'nough he hurt his head
tew, for he went inter a swound, I s'pose," continued Lisha, after nodding
to Sam, "an' he lay quite a spell 'fore he come tu, 'n' 'twas mos' night. Fust
thing, he tried tu git up; but he couldn't make it aout till he got holt of a
saplin' an' pulled hisself up, 'n' then he couldn't take a step. An' while he
stood there a-considerin', that 'ere doe appeared right afore him, lookin'
at him jes' as she did when he run her daown! He said, 'Shoo!' but she
didn't stir a mite, and then he reached daown an' picked up his club an'
hove it at 'er, 'n' he said it went through her jes' 's if she'd ben a puff o'
smoke, an' it went a-scootin' over the crust twenty rods daown the hill,
'n' she never stirred! He tried to walk agin, but he couldn't step a step,
an' then he goddaown on all fours an' crawled 's well 's he could tow-
wards the clearin's, an' that ere doe kep' allers jes' so fur ahead on him,
allers lookin' at him jes' as she did afore he knocked her in the head. An'
when it began tu grow duskish the' was a wolf set up a-yowlin' behind
him as he snailed along a-groanin' an' a-sweatin' like a man a-mowin', an'
not goin' more 'n a rod in five minutes, 'n' then tew more wolves jined in
a yowlin' so clus tu him 't his toes tickled, 'n' when he looked over his
shoulder he could see the dum'd critters a-shoolin' 'long arter him like
black shadders, 'n' every naow 'n' then sittin' up on their rumps an' yowlin'
for more tu jine 'em. An' all the time that 'ere doe kep' jes' so fur ahead
on him, allers a-lookin' at 'im jes' so mournful. Bimebye arter dark, he
got tu the clearin', 'n' he couldn't go no furder, so he sot his back agin a
tree 'n' sot there an' hollered with his club in his hand, for he'd picked it
up in his crawlin', an' there he sot, 'n' there the wolves sot, an' right be-

twixt 'em stood the doe, which the wolves never took no more noticte on her 'n' of a shadder. Arter a while—seemed 's 'ough 't was a week t' Noer—someb'dy hearn the rumpus, wolves a-yowlin' an' man a-hollerin', an' Aar'n Gove an' Moses Hanson 'n' mongst 'em rallied aout an' went up, an' faound him an' fetched 'im hum. They got a darkter an' sot his laig, but he was sick for three months, 'n' many a time, they said, he seen that 'ere doe a-lookin' in 't the winder 'n' hearn the wolves a-yowlin' raound the haouse, but the' could none o' the rest on 'em see her nor hear the wolves. Bimebye he got better, an' so 's 't he could git aout raound. An' then his son, the on'y one 't he had, went off t' the fur West a-trappin' an' a-tradin' fer furs an' skins, an' got killed by Injins, an' then his oldest darter run away with a wuthless, drinkin' goo'-for-nothin' creetur; an' his other darter married an Irishmun, an', wust of all, so Noer said, Amos Jones come up tu see him, and said, 'I tol' yer so!' Then Noer got wus an' run int' the consumption, 'n' arter lingerin' an' lingerin', he died."

"All of which," said Sam Lovel, "sarved him right, and," lifting to his lips the broken-handled pitcher of stale water that stood on a shelf in the corner, seldom replenished but never quite empty, "here's a hopesin' that all crusters may forever meet the same fate. Amen!"

"Haow long," put in the inquirer, "haow long did Noer Chase hev the consumption?"

"Ten year," Lisha replied.

"Was that all?" said the inquirer.

"I don't b'lieve," said Pelatiah, wiping his nose with his right-hand mitten, "'at ever I'll crust hunt a deer's long 's I live and breathe."

"I don't b'lieve ye will nuther," said Sam, "not in these parts, for ye won't hev the chance. But I wanter tell ye one thing, Peltier, the nex' wust thing tu crustin' deer is snarin' patridges! One day in the fall I was huntin' up through yer father's woods, an' I come acrost a leetle low brush fence with snares sot in the gaps. I tore it all daown, an' one gret cock patridge 't I faound a-hangin' by the neck I hove off int' the woods for the foxes t' eat. You sot them snares, Peltier, 'n' you hadn't ort t' done it. Every time I find any sech contraption, I'll spile it, no matter who sot it. 'Xceptin' ugly and mischievous critters 'at won't let ye hunt 'em no ways decent, give all God's creeturs a fair chance. Foller 'em up an' shoot 'em ef ye can, in the times 't they'd ort tu be shot, but not no other times. Not no nestin' good birds nor breedin' an' sucklin' beasts that's wuth a-savin'. Then when ye die, 'f you've ben honest an' decent tu folks, ye won't hev nothin' tu torment ye. Naow, Peltier, you remember what I tell ye, an' don't ye never snare no more patridges, or less ye 'll hav an ol' hen patridge a-hantin' on ye jes' as that 'ere doe did Noer Chase."

In the Sugar Camp

The first warm days of spring had come, when for all the chill of the frosty nights, the sky and the white clouds drifting across it looked soft and hazy as in summer. The voice of the crow had become a familiar sound again; the first robin had been reported; more than one bluebird had sung its short sweet song in the valley; and Lisha had seen a phebe perched on a dry sunflower stalk in his garden, and making thence her unerring swoops upon the flies that, thawed to life again, buzzed about the sunny side of the fence. The snow was deep in the woods yet, but it had grown coarse-grained, and all the winter litter of branches and twigs and latest fallen leaves seemed to be upon its surface, and it was gray in patches with myriads of ever-moving snow fleas. In the open, whole southward-sloping fields were bare and brown except their borders of drifts, and here and there bits of the road were dry and firm, most pleasant to feet long accustomed to the uncertain and slippery footing of wintry ways. Here and there at a homestead a man or boy in shirt-sleeves was working up the great pile of sled-length wood into fuel, but most of the "men folks" were away in the sap works gathering their great harvest of the year.

Among the tall maples that grew on some hillside of every farm the smoke of the sugar camp drifted upward, and the daily and nightly labors there of all Lisha's friends had for some time prevented their customary visits to the shop. Lisha having, as he said, "got tew ol' an' short-winded tu waller raound in the snow, an' never could git the heng o' snowshoein'," had hired Pelatiah to do his sugar-making, while he attended to his shoemaking and mending. But getting very lonely with his solitary labors, during a slack run of sap he sent his henchman out among his friends with a verbal "invite" to a sugaring off at his camp on a certain evening. Accordingly at "airly candleligh'in'," the guests came straggling in, and were loudly and warmly welcomed by their host. "I'm dreffle glad tu see ye, boys! I hain't sot eyes on ye fer a month o' Sundays, seems 'ough. Make yerselves tu hum, an' I'll sweeten ye up tu rights." The little open-fronted shanty faced a rude fireplace, a low wall of rough stones enclosing on three sides a square yard wherein burned a rousing fire that shed a comfortable warmth into the farthest corner of the shanty, and lighted up the trees for rods about. To one side stood the "store trough," a huge log hollowed out to hold the sap as gathered. The great potash kettle slung by a log-chain to its monstrous crane, a tree trunk balanced on a stump, was swung off the fire, and the syrup was bubbling in a smaller kettle, carefully tended by Lisha and Pelatiah.

"Wal, boys," the old man said, after testing the syrup for the twentieth time by pouring it slowly out of his dipper, "it begins tu luther-ap'n, an' I guess it's baout ready. Peltier, you put aout an' git tew three buckets o' clean snow; Samwill, ketch a holt o' that 'ere stick an' help me histe this 'ere kittle off. Naow then, fetch up some seats, the' is sap tubs 'nough layin' raound. Samwill, Jozeff, Solon, some o' ye, the' 's a baskit of biscuit in back there under my cut, an' a bowl o' pickles; won't ye jes' fetch 'em aout?"

So bustling about, he at last got his guests seated around the kettle of hot sugar and the buckets of snow, and they fell to, each in turn dipping out some syrup, and pouring it in dabs upon the snow, when it presently cooled into waxy clots ready for eating.

"Pass raound them 'ere biscuits, Peltier—ta' keer, don't tip the kittle over wi' yer dum'ed hommils! Mos' 's good 's wild honey, hain't it, Samwill?" Lisha asked, smacking his lips after disposing of a big mouthful.

"I d' know but what it's jist as good t' eat," said Sam, "but the' hain't much fun a-gittin' on it."

"Naow, du you r'aly think the' is much fun in bee-huntin', Samwill?" Lisha asked.

"Sartinly I du. 'Tain't so excitin' as fox-huntin' an' sech, but it takes a feller int' the woods in a pleasant time o' year, an' it's interestin' seein' the bees a-workin' an' seein' haow clust you c'n line 'em and cross-line 'em, an' a feller's got tu hev' some gumption, an'—wal, I'd a good deal druther hunt bees 'an tu lug sap."

"By gol! so 'ld I," said Pelatiah. "My shoulders is nigh abaout numb kerryin' the gosh darned ol' neck-yoke."

"Wal naow, boys," Lisha said, after all had plied their paddles silently but diligently for some time, "this is what I call bein' kinder sosherble agin. 'Tain't quite so cosey as the shop, but we've got all aou' doors for room."

"Not inside on us, we hain't—leastways I hain't"—said Joe Hill; "this 'ere maple sweet is turrible fillin'."

"Take a pickle if y'r cl'yed, Jozeff, an' begin agin," Lisha urged, on hospitable deeds intent, but Joe declined, and soon all but Pelatiah desisted and tossed into the fire the little wooden paddles which had served as spoons.

"This is what I call raal comfort," said Sam Lovel, after lighting his pipe with a coal and stretching himself on the evergreen twigs in the shanty. "The' hain't nothin' like an aou'door fire an' a shanty like this an' a bed o' browse fer raal genywine restin' comfort!"

"Wal, it hain't bad for onct 'n a while in pleasant weather; but fer a steady thing, I'd a leetle druther hev a good ruff over my head, an' plarstered walls raound me, an' a fireplace or a stove," said Lisha, and then to avoid unprofitable discussion—"Samwill, I s'pose ye don't git much huntin' naowdays. Tew late fer huntin' foxes an' tew much bare graound fer trackin' 'coons. Git a patridge onct 'n a while, though, I s'pose, don't ye?"

"No, sir," said Sam, with emphasis; "hain't shot a patridge in a month, I want the' should be some next year. I killed a fisher, though, t'other day."

"I wanter know! Shoot him? 'Tain't often 't a feller gits a chance tu shoot one o' them critters. Awfle hard tu git a shot at, they be, I s'pose?"

"Yes, and hard tu kill when ye du git a shot at 'em. Drive treed this one, an' he went a-skivin' through the tree-tops baout as spry 's a squirrel. I let 'im hev it on the run—hed in buckshot an' three Bs—an' disenabled him so 's 't he couldn't jump; but I hed tu shoot him twict more 'fore he come daown, an' then hommered his head a spell 'fore he'd quit a kickin'. Then I tied his hind laigs together an' slung him on my back an' started fer hum."

"Wha'd ye wanter lug his carkiss for? Why didn't ye skin 'im?"

"Oh! I—ah," said Sam, stammering and blushing, "I wanted tu show him tu—tu—some o' my folks 'at hedn't never seen the hull critter; nothin' but the skins."

"H-m. Some o' my folkses' names begins with H-u-l-d-y P-u-r—"

"'N 's I was a-tellin' on ye," Sam broke in hurriedly, "I hed him on my shoulder slung ont' my gun berril, an' hed kerried him much 's half a mild, an' goin' 'long through some little thick secont growth, suthin' ketched an' most pulled the gun off 'm my shoulder, and I'll be shot if 't wa'n't that 'ere cussed fisher come to agin an' ketchin' holt of a saplin' wi' one of his fore paws!"

"Wal, I say fer 't," said Solon, "be they so terminatious o' life as that?"

"What for you ant tole him he dead, Sam? Dat all what was de matter wid it, he ant know when he dead!"

"Wal, I hed tu go tu work an' kill him agin, an' then I made aout tu git him hum 'thaout any more of his fluruppin' raound."

"I hain't never hed no chance o'studdyin' the nat'ral hist'ry on 'em," Solon observed, "but from what I've larnt 'oraclar, I jedge the name of fisher an' black cat don't no ways imply tu 'em. They don't ketch fish, an' consequentially they hain't fishers, an' though they be toll'able black, they don't resemblance the cat speshy no more 'n nothin' in the world. Hain't I right, Sammywell?"

"Sartinly you be," said Sam. "They don't never ketch fish—as I knows on—as mink an' auter does, but lives on squirrels an' mice an' birds an' rabbits, an' stealin' bait aouten saple traps; they're the beaters fer that. An' excep' fer their handiness in climbin' an' their hardness in dyin' the' hain't no cat abaout 'em. They're a overgrowed weasel or saple."

"They're putty scase nowerdays," Lisha said, "do' know 's they ever was plenty. Saple's gittin' scase tew, but twenty, thirty year ago they was thicker 'n spatter. A man 'at onderstood it c'ld make his dollar a day easy trappin' on 'em. Ol' Uncle Steve Hamlin uster hev his lines o' saple traps sot fer milds through the woods every fall, clear'n tu the foot o' the Hump some- times. Every little ways he'd hev a steel trap sot fer fisher that come along stealin' the bait aouten his deadfalls, an' he'd git consid'able many on 'em every year. But game 's a-gittin' scaser 'n' scaser. Samwill," he resumed, after some moments of meditative smoking, "if I luffted tu hunt an' fish as well as you du, I'd go daown tu the lake some fall 'long baout the fust o' September, tu Leetle Auter Crik, an' hunt ducks an' ketch pick'ril."

"I s'pose it's a turrible place for ducks," Sam said.

"Ducks!" cried Lisha; "good airth an' seas! I sh'ld think it was! Why, when I uster be daown that way a-whippin' the cat—an' I was a consi- d'arble sight ten year ago—they was thicker in the ma'shes—wild oats grows there, ye know—thicker in the fall 'n ever ye seen skeeters in a swamp in July. An' the' 's Gret Auter an' Dead Crik jes' as full! The' 's a lawyer daown there name o' Pairpint uster go a-shootin' on 'em, with a feller tu paddle his boat, 'n' he'd git a heapin' bushil baskit full on 'em in a day! 'N' they said 't he shot all on 'em a-flyin'! Never shot none on 'em a-sittin'!"

"Like anough," Sam assented; "I've hearn tell o' folks 'at shot patridges a-flyin', but I never was bleeged tu. I c'ld allers git shots at 'em a-sittin'."

"An' pickril!" continued Lisha, "I never seen the beat on 'em. I uster

go trollin' arter 'em wi' some on 'em, 'n' we'd hev each on us a big hook
with a pork rind an' a piece o' red flannel on 't fer bait, an' a toll'able long
line an' a short pole, 'n' we'd paddle 'long kinder easy on the aidge o' the
channel, an' I tell ye we'd yarn 'em aout! Ol' sollakers, tew; four, five, six
paounds, an' one 't I seen weighed ten paound 'n' a half."

"By gol!" exclaimed Pelatiah, wide-eyed and wide-mouthed with wonder, "ten paound' an' a half? He must ha' ben mos' 's big as one o' them
'ere whale fish 't they git lamp ile aouten on!"

"An' mushrats," said Lisha, continuing the relation of the wonders of
the lowlands, "I've seen their haousen on the ma'shes in fall an' winter
thick as ever ye seen hay cocks in a medder, 'most, an' hundreds of acres
o' ma'sh with 'em sot jes' so thick. The' was Benham an' 'mongst 'em uster
git as high as three hundred mushrat apiece, most every spring. These
'ere teamsters 'at hauls ore up here tu the forge says 'at ducks an' mushrat
an' fish is jes' as thick there naow. That 'ould be the place fer ye, Samwill!
Ducks an' fish fer fun, an' mushrat fer profit."

"Probly dey bullpawt an' eel dah, ant it, Onc' Lasha? Ah wish Ah be
dah too, me!"

"Eels! I guess the' is. Why, Ann Twine, you c'ld ketch as many o' the
dum'd snakes in a night as you c'ld eat the nex' day, an' that 's a-puttin'
on it high. Yes, an' the' 's pike an' bass, an' a gret fish 'at's got a bill like a
shellduck, on'y longer, but they hain't good fer nothin'. An' the' 's sheep-
heads an' shad, 'n' more pa'ch an' punkinseeds 'n' you could shake a stick
at in a fortnight, but nobody don't make no caount o' them, on'y boys fer
the fun o' ketchin' on 'em. An' the' 's bowfins an' suckers 'n' I d'know what
all. They hes gret times a-shootin' pickril airly in the spring, an' a-spearin'
on 'em, tew."

"Wal, suh, Onc' Lasha, Ah can shoot it dat moosrat wid spear in winter w'en he'll live in haouse."

"Ketch mushrat with a spear! Oh, naow you go tu grass, Ann Twine."

"You ant b'lieve it dat? You as' Injin if he ant git it moosrat dat way.
Bah gosh! Yas! W'en ice all be frozed up, have it spear gat on'y but one
laig baout so long as two foot, ver' sharp, wid toof on him an' woodle
handlin' tree foot, four foot prob'ly long. Den walk slow, slow, ant mak it
no nowse, to moosrat haouse. Den push him dat spear in quick! hard!
raght in middly of it. You feel it spear shake, you gat dat moosrat, mebby
one of it, two of it, sometam three of it, prob'ly. Den chawp in wid axe,
tek it off, go nudder one jus' de same. Sometam git feefty, seexty all day."

"Wal, I do' know but what ye hain't a-lyin' fer onct, Ann Twine; it saounds kinder reas'nable. You want tu git ye thirty forty traps, Samwill, an' go daown there with Ann Twine an' his spear. Then ye'd hev a French cook an' live high, duck, pea soup, an' roast mushrat three times a day."

"Bah gosh! Onc' Lasha, you ant steek you nose up dat moosrat! He pooty good for eat, Ah tole you!"

"Yes, yes; anybody 't eats snakes needn't spleen agin rats, sartin."

"Oh, Onc' Lasha," said the Canadian reproachfully, "eel don't snake, more as you was mud turkey."

"If I hed me a boat an' traps anough," Sam said, after some silent and thoughtful smoking, "I'd jes' like tu go daown there a-trappin' an' huntin' an' fishin'. An' then, arter I got a good shanty built, an' well tu goin', hev all on ye come daown a-visitin'."

"You jes' du it an' see 'f we don't, hey boys?" And there was general assent. "Yes, Samwill, we'll tackle up a two-hoss waggin an' all go. We'll go tuckernuck, kerry aour own pervision; on'y mushrat an' fish we'll expeck you tu furnish, Samwill. Wal," Lisha continued, hoisting out his porringer of a watch and consulting it by the waning firelight, "it's a-gittin' late. Why, good airth an' seas! if 't aint mos' nine o'clock! Peltier, 'f you've got that 'ere kittle licked aout, you c'n slick up a little raound, an' we'll go hum. No need o' bilin' tunight, the' hain't sap 'nough in the store trough tu draound a chipmunk. Git the baskit an' Jerushy's bowl an' come along."

Then they filed out of the sugar camp on their homeward way, while far above them in the black growth of the mountain-side the hoot of an owl and the gasping bark of a fox voiced the solemnity and wildness of the ancient woods.

Indians in Danvis

It was fairly spring; almost summer as the months go. Some patches and jagged lines of snow yet gleamed among the black growth on the northward steeps and in the gullies of the mountains, but the lower deciduous trees were in a green mist of young leaves, the woodside shade was dappled with the white moose-flowers, and the grass was green in the valley fields. The evenings had grown so short that to make anything of a visit before bedtime, Lisha's friends were obliged to come while daylight lasted. He first became aware of visitors when the forms of Joe Hill and Antoine darkened the doorway. Then came Pelatiah and the Questioner, followed by Solon Briggs, and last of all Sam Lovel came across lots from Beaver Meadow Brook, bringing a dozen fine trout strung upon a birchen twig.

"Wal, Samwill, ben a-traoutin', hey?" said Lisha. "Wal, they're neat ones, I swan! Ketched 'em in Beav' Medder Brook, did ye?" Yes, Sam caught them there. "Wal, they du say 't fishin' 's oncommon good this year; most everybody 't goes gits a good string on 'em. Oh, dear me suz! 'n' I hain't ben yit, nor tasted no fish but salt ones sen last summer."

"Bah gosh! Ah wish Ah ketch some bullpout or eel, bose of it, Ah don' care which, me," cried Antoine.

"Wal, Uncle Lisher, you sha'n't say that tu-morrer night," said Sam, seating himself on the cold stove and filling his pipe, "fer I'm goin' tu take these in tu Aunt Jerushy, an' you c'n hev your sheer on 'em fer breakfus'. Ben tu supper, I s'pose?"

"Why, Samwill, I'm a thaousan' times 'bleeged tu ye, but you'd orter keep half on 'em. You're a-robbin' yerself."

No, Sam was "cl'yed wi' traout, an' ketched these a puppus fer Aunt Jerushy 'n' you."

"Wal, thank ye a thaousan' times. Yes, I ben tu supper. I was makin' gardin tu-day, an' the smell o' the airth made me hungrier 'n a bear, so Jerushy got supper airly."

"Yes, Lisher," Solon remarked, "for a pusson of your sedimentary ock-ypations the' hain't nothin' more beneficial 'an a-gittin' aou'door;" and then, turning to Sam, "Did ye ever ketch traout with a fly, Sammywell?"

"No, I didn't never, but I hev wi' bumble-bees."

"Not a ra-al fly I don't mean," Solon explained. "That 'ere artist feller 't was raound here summer 'fore last—boarded to Joel Bartlett's a spell, 'n' fixed up a paintin' shop in his barn—'stewed Joe,' he called it—he uster go traoutin' with a whipstock of a pole 'at took tu pieces, an' hed a little brass windlass onto it tu wind up his line, an' a mess o' feathers stuck on a hook for bait, 'at he called a arterfishual fly. He'd skitter it top of the water, an' onct in a while the' 'd be a traout fool 'nough tu grab it. Then he'd wind 'im up, an' then he'd let 'im scoot, 'n' then wind 'im up agin, an' so continner on till he got 'im all fattygued aout."

"Oh, yes, I seen 'im at it!" said Sam. "I went a-fishin' with 'im tew three times. 'N' he was toll'able lucky, tew; ketched half as many 's I did. He'd tost them little feather contraptions turrible handy when the brush wa'n't tew thick. I sh'ld like tu try it if I hed the rig. He hed a hull wallet full on 'em, all on 'em named, 'green ducks,' an' 'hatchels,' an' I d' know what all. It uster tickle me tu see him when he come tu a still pond hole, or a place where the brook tumbled over the rocks, or suthin' n'uther 't he liked the looks on. He'd lay daown his pole, an' back off, an' get fust one side o' the brook an' then t'other, or like 'nough on a stun right in the middle on't, an' then aout with a lead-pencil an' a little blank 'caount book like, 'n' begin tu draw it off. He'd squint an' mark an' whistle an' mark a spell, 'n' then intu his pocket with book an' pencil an' go tu fishin' agin. A clever little creetur he was, an' took lots o' comfort bein' in the woods, an' a-fishin'. He tol' me 'at they ketched gret big salmon up Canady way wi' them feather flies."

"Bah gosh!" cried Antoine, pricking up his ears at the mention of his native province. "Yas, Ah'll see Anglish officy ketch dat so! Oh, big, big, big!"

"Oh, yes, sartinly," said Lisha. "I 'xpected you hed. Seen 'em ketched 't 'ould weigh a hundred paound, hain't ye, Ann Twine?"

"Wal, sah, Onc' Lasha, not quat so big dat. Ah don' goin' tol' lie 'f you want it Ah do. De bigges' one Ah'll see ketch dat way he'll weigh jes' 'zackly nanty-nan paoun' an' fiftin ninches, dat's all."

"Hmph! A minny, wa'n't he?" said Lisha. "Wal, we're gittin' all of a color, white folks an' Canucks, 'n' I guess we'd better hev a light," whereupon he lit the candle, which sputtered for some minutes before it made itself visible in the twilight.

"Wal, folks," said Sam, breaking the silence that prevailed while the company watched the struggles of the feeble light, "the's suthin' in these woods 'at I never seen in 'em afore."

"Why, what on airth is it, Samwill?" Lisha asked. "'Tain't a wolf, 'cause you seen one time o' the big hunt four year ago. 'Tain't a painter?"

"No, 'tain't a wolf nor a painter—I seen both—'n' 'tain't no four-legged critter—it's Injins!"

"Good airth an' seas, you don't say so!" cried Lisha; "hev ye got the' skelps in yer pockit, Samwill?"

"No," said Sam, laughing; "they've got 'em on their heads, an' hats a top on 'em, tew, for they hain't wild ones, but c'n talk English as well as

Antwine here, but not ekal to Solon quite. Raal clever, candid sort o' fellers they be, an' c'nsid'able sosherble arter you git 'quainted with 'em."

"Haow many on 'em be they? A hull tribe on 'em? He ones an' she ones, an' poppooses on boards? Where be they, an' what they drivin' at?" So Lisha strung out his questions without waiting for an answer till he finished with the demand, "Tell us all baout 'em."

"Wal," said Sam, "tu begin 't the beginnin', I was fishin' Beav' Medder Brook 't other day an' come acrost a mockersin track in the sand, 'n' thinks says I to myself, Antwine's a-fishin' ahead on me, 'n' then thinks says I, he don't wear 'em sen he got tu be sech a Yankee; 'n' a little furder long I seen tracks o' tew wearin' mockersins, an' putty soon I smelt smoke, an' then come slap on tu tew dark-complected fellers settin' by a fire a-smokin' an' watchin' a woo'chuck roastin' on a stick stuck through endways an' int' the graound, an' behind of 'em was a gret roll o' suthin' 't I thought fust sight was luther, 'n' 't they'd ben a-stealin' from you, er less was goin' to give ye a job. Then I seen 't was birch bark. I says haow de du, 'n' so 'd they, but they didn't talk none till I soddaown an' loaded my pipe an' giv' 'em some terbarker. Then one on 'em says, 'Ketch um plenty fish,' lookin' at my string, an' 'twas a putty good un, 'n' I gin 'em a dozen tu piece aout their supper. Then they begin tu git toll'able sosherble, an' we hed quite a visit."

"Wal, I'll be dum'd! Samwill Lovel visitin' 'long with Injins!" cried Lisha, holding up his hands.

"Wal, he was," said Sam, "an' got c'nsid'able thick with 'em, 'n' I don't deny it. They said haow 't they 'd come clearn up from Gret Auter Crik an tu Hawg's Back tu git bark 'at suited 'em tu make a canew, an' was goin' right back nex' day. I wanted turribly tu see 'em make a canew, 'n' tried to coax 'em to do it here, 'n' I'd git some o' the teamsters tu kerry it daown tu Vergeens for 'em when they was goin'. But they thought their fam'lies 'at was camped daown there would be wonderin' if they stayed away so long. I tol' 'em 't we'd send word by the teamsters tu their folks, 'n' it come inter my head what you was tellin' 'baout huntin' an' trappin' daown there, 'n' 't this was a gret chance fer me tu git a boat made. So I dickered with 'em tu make me a canew, an' they talked an' talked together—I tell ye, their'n 's the language tu talk in the woods. It don't make no more noise 'n a little brook a-runnin', 'n' I don't b'lieve 't 'ould skeer a fox. Wal, fin'ly they 'greed tu, an' nex' day they went at my canew."

"Shaw!" said Lisha. "Why, Samwill, them Injin canews is tottlisher 'n a board sot up aidgeways! You can't du nothin' in one on 'em, only tip over. You hain't uster no kinder boat, say nothin' 'baout them aigshell consarns. 'D ye ever see one? I hev, but never ondertook ridin' one on 'em."

"No, I never did, but I'm goin' tu in a few days. I guess I c'n navvygate it. I've crossed the Notch Pond stan'in' up on a saw lawg with my gun, more 'n onct, 'n' I guess a canew hain't much tottlisher 'n a rollin lawg. Wal, I've hed a good time watchin' on 'em make it fer three days, 'n' I tell ye it's curous tu see 'em. Furst thing they made a frame the len'th an' shape the canew 's goin' tu be on top—jes tew strips of ash fastened together tu the ends, an' bars acrost, so"—illustrating his description with a diagram drawn on the floor with a bit of coal while all gathered about him. "Then they laid it daown on a level place they'd fixed an' drove stakes clus to it agin the ends o' the cross-bars all raound, an' one tu each end o' the frame. Then they pulled up the stakes an' took the frame away, keepin' the stake-holes clear o' dirt very car'f'l, an' spread the bark daown on the place, an' then sot the frame back on jes' ezackly where it was afore, an' put some cedar strips on 't, an' big stuns top o' them. Then they slit the bark from the aidge up tu the frame every onct in a little ways, so, all raound, 'an bent up the bark an' sot the stakes back in the holes, an' tied a bark cord acrost from top to top. Then they sewed up the slits, lappin' the bark over, ye see, an' sewin' it wi' black spruce ruts peeled an' split in tew, 'n' they're jest as tough as rawhide; luther-wood bark hain't no tougher. That's as fur as they've got yit, but nex' thing, 's nigh 's I c'n make aout, they cal'late tu raise the frame tu the top an' put some raves on aoutside and fasten 'em together an' then line the hull consarn wi' flat strips o' cedar drove in tight. 'N' then when they git the seams all daubed wi' spruce gum an' taller melted together it'll be all ready fer me tu—" "tip over," said Lisha, completing the sentence for him.

"Waal, now, I guess not," Sam drawled, "but baout the fust o' nex' week you c'n all come over tu the Forge Pond an' see."

"Uncle Lisher," said Joe Hill suddenly, "is the' anything o' this story 't I hearn 'em talkin' over 't the store t'other day? Lemme see, was 't Wednesday or Thursday las' week, or was't Friday? Yes, 'twas Friday, I know, 'cause M'ri sent by me fer a codfish, an' they hedn't got none, 'n' so we didn't hev' none fer dinner Sat'day, 'n' hed t' eat traout. Wal, they was tellin', some on 'em, haow 't you was a-talkin' o' sellin' aout 'n' goin' t' the 'Hio."

The Boy Out West

The prophet of the almanac had written along the June calendar, "Now, perhaps, a spell of weather," and his prognostication was being verified. For two days the rain had come down from the leaden sky, now in drenching showers, now in drizzles slanting to the earth before the gusty north east wind, and still it came down. A robin in the apple tree where his mate shingled their nest with her half-spread wings only left off "singing for rain" to preen his wet feathers, and then began again his broken song, cheerful enough but for its import to seem unsuited to its accompaniment, the splash of the rain, the doleful sighing of the wind, and the sullen roar of the swollen streams. The beaten-down blossoms that whitened the ground beneath the apple trees, as if an unseasonable flurry of snow had fallen there, looked unlike blossoms now, but added another dreary feature to the dreary landscape; the little brown house, without light or shadow on its walls; the dripping, wind-swayed trees; the sodden fields and woods ghostly behind the gray veil of rain, bounded by the blurred, flat wall of mountains, and roofed by the low sky.

When some of Lisha's friends, troubled by a vague rumor that had floated about the valley, visited the shop that day, they found it as cheerless inside as out, chilly, damp, and fireless, and unoccupied by its owner, whose apron lay upon the shoe-bench. Sam Lovel seated himself there, and when presently Lisha entered from the "house part," and he arose to give him his accustomed seat, the old man said, "Keep your settin', Samwill; I hain't workin' none tu-day," and after pottering in an aimless way among his stock and tools, set about lighting a fire. After repeated clearing of his throat, wherein the words seemed to stick, he said as he whittled the kindling, "Wal, boys, where ye goin' tu loaf evenin's next winter?"

"Why, right here, of course, Uncle Lisher," said Sam; "you hain't goin' tu turn us aout'door, be ye?"

"No, I hain't a-goin' tu turn you aou'door; I'm a-goin' tu turn myself aou'door. The fact o' the business is, Jerushy 'n' I has baout made up aour minds tu go aout West an' live 'long wi' George."

"Wal, we heard some such talk," Sam said, "but we didn't scasely b'lieve the' was nothin' on it only talk, the' 's so much dum'd foolish gab a-goin' nowerdays. An'," he added, "I hain't heard none 'at saounded foolisher 'n this, tu me."

"Wal, naow, ye see," said Lisha, shutting the stove door, and after watching the fire a minute seating himself upon a sap tub, "me 'n' my ol' woman 's a gettin' ol' 'n' ont' the daown hill-side, 'n' 't won't be many year 'fore we can't du nothin' scasely on'y set raound, 'n' we hain't got nob'dy tu ta' keer on us then on'y aour boy. He's sol' aout in the 'Hio, an' is goin' tu Westconstant tu live, a gret ways furder 'n the 'Hio, tew, three States beyund it, I b'lieve. 'Tain't a State yit, I guess Westconstant hain't, but on'y a terry-tory. Seems 'ough we couldn't stan' it tu hev him no furder off 'n what he is naow, an' so, ye see, we've c'ncluded tu go an' live 'long wi' him. He's ben a-teasin' on us tu this ever so long, but I kinder hated tu, for I'm sorter growed in here, 'n' I hate tu naow, but I guess it's the best way."

"Wal, I guess 'tain't," said Sam, very decidedly. "You hev growed in, both on ye, an' it'll be julluk pullin' up tew ol' trees an' settin' on 'em aout agin, 'n' ye won't stan' it no better. No, Uncle Lisher, not a mite better 'n tew hemlocks took up an' sot aout. It'll be a diff'ent s'il o' land for ye, diff'ent breed o' neighbors—'f ye hev any—'n' they say 't that 'ere western country's flatter 'n a pancake, 'thaout a maountin er a big hill tu be seen, so's 't it tires a feller's eyesight clean aout a-trav'lin' so fur 'thaout nothin' tu stop it, an' no woods like aourn, they say. Haow long ye think ye can stan' it 'thaout the smell o' spruce in yer nose, er 'thaout seein' the ol' Hump er 'Tater Hill, er so much as little Hawg's Back er even Pig's Back a-stan'in' up agin the sky?"

"Sammywell's argyments is good," said Solon Briggs. "The' hain't nothin' more sartiner 'n that old, ann-cient indyviddywills hed ort tu continner tu remain in the natyve land 'at they was borned in."

"Good airth an' seas!" the old man roared, after listening with ill-concealed impatience, "what's the use o' yer talkin'? I tell ye I'm a-goin' 'f I don't live a week arter I git there!"

"Wal," said Sam, "if you're sot on it, 'n' everything 's all cut an' dried, the' *hain't* no use a-talkin'. But I sh'ld think 't you *might* ha' said suthin' tu some on us 'fore ye went so fur. 'T would ha' ben friendlier. I swear! I wish 't the dum'd torment 't invented that ere cussed Western country hedn't never ben borned! A-breakin' up fam'lies an' puttin' notions inter ol' folks's heads, blast him!" and said no more, but sat staring out at the gloomy landscape that, seen through the green and wrinkled panes of the long window, looked gloomier and more dismal than ever.

They spoke no more of Lisha's intended departure, and after a few feeble attempts at conversation, sat and smoked in silence till the day grew darker with the coming on of evening, and then the visitors departed.

Breaking Up

Though Lisha's friends continued their visits to the shop, the rainy days and the evenings spent there were cheerless and gloomy ever after he declared his intention of deserting it. The forced conversation and feeble attempts to awaken the old convivial spirit were so much like those at a gathering about the bedside of one with the certain doom of death upon him, that Lisha said, one afternoon, when the sober guests had departed, "Wal, mother, I wish 't aour fun'al was over, an' we was in Westconstant. I'll be dum'd 'f I haint 'baout sick o' bein' a live corpse! I wish't George hed 'a ben contented tu ha' stayed here! But seein' 't he wa'n't, the' don't seem 's 'ough the' was no other way only tu go. If little Jerushy 'd ha' lived, 'n' married some likely feller, as in course she would, we might ha' stayed an' lived 'long wi' her. But it wa'n't tu be so. I do' know but I feel 'baout as bad a-goin' off an' leavin' her layin' up there so fur from us's I du 'baout anything in the hull business. Poor little gal! She was a-goin' tu look julluk you."

"Oh father!" said Aunt Jerushy, with a blush mantling the wholesome old-age brown of her kindly face, as she intently scanned her purple-veined and wrinkled hands, "if she was ever tu, I do' know but it's best 'at she died when she was a baby."

"Wal, naow, Jerushy Chase, I shouldn't ha' wanted her tu looked no better 'n you did when you was a young womern, nor no better fer an' ol' womern. Folks hes got tu grow ol' 'f they live long 'nough, 'n' they can't keep all the looks no more'n they can all the feelin's o' young folks."

Uncle Lisha took a roundabout course on his way to the stove to re-light his pipe, and stopped behind Aunt Jerusha's chair a moment to caress her gray head. The sensation must have been somewhat as if a mud turtle had crawled and slid over it, but it comforted her sad heart and brought a gleam of the light of youth into her old eyes. When he bent over and shyly kissed her cheek, the long disused endearment brought back old courting days so vividly that she cried, even as she returned it—"Why, Lisher Peggs! Haint you 'shamed o' yerself?" and then glancing out of the window, "If there haint Huldy Pur'n't'n! an' if she seen ye, haow she will be a-laughin' at us!"

"Good airth an' seas!" said Lisha, as in a shamefaced flurry he raked a handful of coals onto the hearth, "'f she hain't hed bussin' 'nough tu shet her maouth sen she an' Samwill made up, I miss my guess! They've made up lost time, I bate ye! Walk!" he shouted in response to Huldah's knock, and when she entered Aunt Jerusha's surprise was simulated so well that it would have done credit to a lady of fashion.

"An' so," said Huldah, after the mutual inquiries concerning the respective families had been made and answered, "you an' Uncle Lisher is r'ally goin' tu pull up stakes an' go t' the West? You do' know haow I hate tu hev ye. Seem 's 'ough the' wa'n't nob'dy only my own folks 'at seems so near tu me 's what you du!"

"Ta' keer, Huldy!" Lisha cried.

"Wal," said Huldah, blushing as red as the peonies in the posy bed by the doorstep, "I mean—wal," with a frank look and a happy little laugh, "I mean ol' folks near! The' hain't another place in Danvis where I c'n go an' hev a raal good sed daown, only jest here! An', Uncle Lisher, one little word 't you said that day 'at Sis was lost tol' me suthin' 't I didn't know afore, 'n' 't I was feared wa'n't so. 'N' naow you're a goin' tu the end o' the airth, 'n' I sha'n't see ye 'gin, maybe never!"

"Wal, naow, Huldy," said Aunt Jerushy, as she abstractedly rapped her snuff-box and looked nowhere, "like 'nough me an' Lisher won't be c'ntented in Westconstant, an' 'll wanter come back. An' 'f things tarve as I'm a-hopesin' they will, you an' Samwill 'll be settled daown, 'n' mebby you'd take us in."

"An' you'd be most welcome allers," said Huldah. "Seems 's 'ough," she said, as over and over again she gathered in her fingers and let go the hem of her checkered apron, "'at the' wa'n't nothin' much tu hender naow, sence Samwill faound Sis. Father, he was allers kinder set agin him 'cause he's allers a-huntin' an' shoolin' raound in the woods, but ever sence he hunted tu sech good purpose that day he hain't said not one word agin him. An' mother, she hain't never sot much noways. Seem 's 'ough the' wa'n't nothin' much tu hender naow." And as Huldah looked out of the east window of the kitchen, the hilltops were glorified by the rays of the setting sun, all the rugged steeps were shining, and the shadowy ravines were hidden from her gaze; and so the way of life shone before her, smooth and unshadowed in the light of love.

By and by came the sad and painful breaking up and the auction sale of their nonportable goods, such household goods as the old clock that had marked, with its slow beats, the uneventful and comfortable course of more than half their life; the big wheel and the little wheel that had both hummed many tunes to Aunt Jerusha's touch, and were dear to her. And so to her was the churn, but Uncle Lisha saw it go to a low bidder with a feeling of relief in final separation, and a thrill of revengeful pleasure as he thought of the unhappy hours spent in pounding stubborn churnings encased in its red-painted staves. It mitigated the pangs of parting with them to know that Sam Lovel had bought the clock (with an inward resolve that it should some time resume its old place in the kitchen corner), and that the spinning wheels had gone to the Puringtons. The big wheel, Mrs. Purington said, "'ould be handy for Huldy when she went tu haousekeepin', though the flax wheel wa'n't much 'caount, sen' everyb'dy 'd gin up raisin' flax." Solon Briggs suggested that it would be "a val'able relickt of ancient past times tu Huldy's future pregenitors." Sam also bought the shoe-bench, saying that it was a "mighty comfortable seat tu set in an' smoke, with a handy place for a feller's terbacker, as well as bein' a good place tu clean a gun." He was strongly tempted to buy the favorite cow, so gentle that even Huldah might milk her, though she never should, but with the fear of his stepmother before him, he let the cow go to Joseph Hill.

"Dat damn hol' long John Dark!" said Antoine, when the giant of the turkey shoot bid off the old horse after the Canadian had gone beyond the limit of his resources in bidding.

John Dart made his way to Aunt Jerusha and said: "Mis' Peggs, I'll take good keer o' the ol' hoss, an' won't never drive 'im fast—'thaout 't is keepin' up wi' the percession tu fun'als, which I'm hopesin' won't come often, 'n' I won't never sell 'im, ner give 'im tu nob'dy only God A'mighty—I'll du that when he gits so 's 't be can't enj'y airthly life."

"Thank ye kindly, Mister ———?"

"John Dart is my name, marm," said the giant, bowing almost to the level of her sun bonnet.

"Thank ye kindly, Mister Dart, an' I'm dreffle glad 'at Bob hes fell intu sech good hands. He's ben a faithf'l creetur tu us, an' it's worried me dreffly thinkin' o' what might be become on him."

The "vandew" was over at last, and the old couple's hold on their old life was loosened with sore wrenchings of their heartstrings. Now that their hearthstone was cold and the little brown house was home no longer, they tarried with Joseph Hill during the short time of awaiting the day of departure. Lisha wandered about aimlessly, uncomfortable in idleness and continual wearing of his best clothes, taking long looks at old familiar scenes that he felt he was soon to leave forever. He went with Aunt Jerusha to the little hillside burying ground, which had grown surprisingly populous with dead since they attended the first burial there, awed then in the strange presence of death, who had now become so frequent and familiar a visitor that his coming was but briefly noted. There under the widespread canopy of the sumachs and among the rank growth of goldenrod they bade a silent farewell to the sunken graves of fathers and mothers, and the short green mound that so many years ago had hidden from their sight their baby daughter—always and forever a baby daughter to them.

"An' naow, mother," said Lisha, making frequent use of his "bendinah" as they turned away from the quiet place of everlasting rest, "we've said good-by tu them 'at's nighest tu us. Aour rhuts is putty nigh pulled up."

The Departure

Toward the end of summer Lisha and his wife were ready to begin their journey. The day of departure had come, and many of their old neighbors had gathered at Joseph Hill's to bid them farewell.

After the kindly fashion of those days, some of their neighbors accompanied them to the place where they were to embark in the canal boat that would take them the length of "Clinton's big ditch" on their way. Pelatiah drove the lumber wagon whereon was piled the "housel stuff" reserved from the "vandew." Then came a like conveyance, driven by Sam Lovel, and carrying Lisha and Jerusha, Joe Hill and his wife, Solon Briggs and Antoine, and a day's provisions for the party. They jolted over the rough road and through the little hamlet that the forge and store and tavern gave life to, and then taking the road along the bank of the noisy little river, the old people turned their backs upon the green wall of the mountains and entered on their long journey westward.

At noon they stopped to bait their teams and eat their lunch under some wayside trees and then went on. In the middle of the afternoon they entered the little city that marked the end of the first stage of the old people's journey, and the wonders of its few three-story buildings, its three churches, and the court-house perched upon the crest of a ledge, in which, Lisha told them, "the leegislatur sot onct," so dazed Pelatiah that he nearly missed finding the way to the wharf where the canal packet lay. There new wonders met his astonished gaze. A rifle shot up stream, the river almost as wide as the length of the forge pond, the largest sheet of water he had ever seen till now, foamed and thundered down a precipice forty feet high, and then its vexed waters writhed along a deep, broad reach, past the wharves, where lay the canal-boats and the little steamer that was to tow them to the lake and then to Whitehall.

Lounging about these strange immense craft were the surly or saucy canal boatmen, upon whom the young mountaineer looked with awe, for they were traveled men who must have seen nearly all of the great world, having been more than once to the end of the canal and back again, and some, it was said, had even beheld the wonders and glories of that almost fabulous city by the sea, New York.

"In an airly day," said Lisha, "some o' the Yorkers built 'em a gris' mill on them falls, an' Ethan Allen an' his Green Maountain Boys come an' drove 'em off an' hove the millstuns over the falls, or some says inter a big pot-hole nigh the top, 'n' 't they 're a layin' in the bottom on't naow. Right along here where these 'ere wharfs an' stores be, McDonner's ships was built time o' the last war; ships a gre' d'l bigger 'n them canawl boats be, Peltier. I worked here a-haulin' timber to build 'em on, an' 'twas hurryin' times, I tell ye, with the British threatenin' the hull time. We hauled a big stick here aouten the woods, for a keel, it was, wi' three yoke o' oxen, an' at it the ship carpenters went full chisel, an' in six weeks I b'lieve, it wa'n't no more, from the day 't was cud daown, the ship was all ready to go int' the water!"

With such discourse Lisha entertained his friends till nightfall, when he and Jerusha went to their berths in the packet and they to their inn, excepting Antoine, who having dug some worms, and borrowed a pole and line of a compatriot, went fishing for bullpouts.

Next morning came the sorrowful leave-taking, and after much bustle and shouting and swearing by the captains and crews of the steamboat and canal boats, wherein the bold mariners of the canal, having had the practice and experience of greater and more frequent opportunities, greatly outdid their rivals, the little flotilla got under weigh. The fussy little steamer coughed and churned its way down the beautiful river, and as it dragged the packet out of sight behind a wooded bend, the sturdy figure of the old shoemaker was seen standing in the stern beside the bowed form of his wife waving a last farewell with his red "bendina."

"There they go," said Sam Lovel, turning sadly away. "There they go, julluk tew ol' trees tore up by the ruts an' driftin' daown stream."

The Wild Bees' Swarm

One day, a little more than a year later, when the blue September sky arched the valley, and the afternoon sun shone warm into it, and the bees were busy among the asters and goldenrods in the little grave-yard that overlooked Uncle Lisha's old homestead, Sam Lovel came push-ing his way slowly through the thicket of sumachs. Under his arm he carried his bee-box, which, after looking about him a moment, he set upon the top of a little gravestone. When he had watched for a minute through the glazed lid the two or three little prisoners his box held, he carefully removed the cover and backed a few paces away. His eye caught the moss-grown inscription on the stone—"Jerusha, daughter of E. and J. Peggs; departed this life"—he had to bend down the heads of everlast-ing to read the remainder—"Sept. the 10, 18——."

He reaped away the everlastings with his knife and cleaned the moss from the letters before he took time to notice that one of his bees had climbed to the edge of the box and taken wing, circling a few feet above it, and then sailed straight toward the house; and then another and an-other arose and went off in the same course.

"Wal, naow, that's cur'ous, hain't it, Drive?" said Sam, addressing his dog, who was making himself comfortable on the grass near him, and now answered his master with a lazy beat of his tail. Sam had hardly got his pipe alight and begun to take his ease beside the dog, when back came the bees with some companions and settled into the box.

"All right," said Sam. "Le's move up," and going cautiously to it, he shut the lid, tapped the side till the bees arose from the comb in the bottom, when he shut the lower slide, took up the box and moved on in the direction the bees had taken to within a few rods of the house. Then he opened the slide and then the cover, and when the bees had filled themselves again, they sailed away with their freight as before. They soon returned and were again imprisoned till Sam had set the box on one of the posts of the garden-fence. Again he gave them their liberty, and in ten minutes a hundred bees were buzzing to and fro between the box and a knot-hole high up in the gable of the shop.

"Yes, sir," said Sam, laughing softly, "the's a swarm under the cla'b'rds o' the shop, jes' as sure 's your name 's Drive! Wal, they c'n stay there for all o' me."

He went around to the front of the house, stepping carefully lest he should tread on Aunt Jerusha's posies, uncared for now and running wild: China asters, sweet williams, and pansies struggling in a matted tangle of May-weed, posy beans and morning glories wandering away from the posts of the stoop to climb the tall pigweeds. Two squirrels stopped chasing each other over the roof and along the rattling clapboards to scoff at the intruder, and a woodchuck sounded his querulous whistle and scuttled under the shop as Sam approached it. The door was half open, and he almost expected to hear the hearty hail of his old friend; but a chance-sown poppy growing in a crack of the sill, and the fallen petals of its last flower withering undisturbed on the worn threshold, told mutely how long it had been untrodden by the foot of man. When Sam looked into the empty shop, where nothing was left to tell of its former use but a faint waft of the old familiar odor, the sconce and its mouse-nibbled candle-end, a broken last and a rubbishy heap of leather scraps, a partridge sprang from the floor and, hurtling through the open window, went sailing away to the woods.

"The fog o' the ol' stories hangs 'raound here yet," Sam soliloquized, "an' wild creeturs takes as nat'ral as tu the woods tu Uncle Lisher's shop. Come, dawg."

BOOK 2

from Sam Lovel's Camps

The Camp on the Slang

Under the Hemlocks

Beside a low-banked waterway among the reddish-gray trunks of great hemlocks, there stood, one day in the third month of a year, half a long lifetime ago, a shanty of freshly riven slabs with the upper ends slanted together in the form of an A tent. In front of it a fire smouldered, the slow smoke climbing through the branches that waved their green spray and nodded their slender-stemmed cones in the rising current of warm vapor. A few muskrat skins, stretched on osier bows, hung drying nearby on slim poles placed in the crotches of stakes, and two canoes, one a light birch, the other a dugout, lay bottom upward on the bank awaiting the day of use. The shanty was luxuriously bedded with marsh hay and fragrant twigs of hemlock, overlaid with blankets and buffalo skins, and stretching out into the light were two pairs of feet, one clad in stout boots, the other in moccasins. Four legs faded away in the dusky interior, till, beyond the knees, the eye was puzzled to follow them.

Presently the boots began to stir and then the owner became dimly visible sitting up on his couch. When he had crawled out and scraped a coal from the ashes into his pipe, and having got it satisfactorily alight, stood up and looked at the cloud-flecked sky and out on the ice-bound stream, the tall, wiry form, and quiet, good-humored, bearded and weather-browned face of Sam Lovel were fully revealed. He half turned

toward the shanty, and lightly touched one of the moccasins with his foot. "Hello Antwine!" he called, "be ye goin' to sleep all day?"

The fall after Uncle Lisha's departure to his new home in the West, Sam had taken the old man's advice into serious consideration, and finally for various reasons concluding to follow it, he bargained for the making of a lot of traps and took Antoine as partner and instructor as well, for Sam had not much experience in trapping muskrats, those fur-bearers being not at all plenty in the rapid, weedless streams of the hill country, where all his hunting and trapping had until now been done. Long before sleighing gave any sign of failing they had their boats, traps, and provisions hauled down to the trapping ground, built their rude but cosy shelter that was for some weeks to be their home, and were now waiting for the opening of small-craft navigation, when they would begin trapping in earnest.

Sam and his partner lounged about camp waiting for the opening of the water, and there was not much to break the dull monotony of those days of waiting. For the most part there was little to do but cook and eat the simple fare, and sit by the camp-fire trimming muskrat bows and tally sticks. Now and then a chopper would stop at the shanty to light his pipe, and if a Yankee, to ask no end of questions; or if a Canadian, to jabber with Antoine till Sam was driven almost wild with the incessant jargon so unintelligible to him. A mile down the creek a party of lumbermen were building a raft of logs upon the ice, and often to pass the time away Sam and Antoine would visit them, and being expert axemen, help them make "knock downs" while they chatted and joked.

One day Sam was hunting about camp for something, and Antoine asked, "What you look see, Sam?"

"I'm a-lookin' for a mushrat carkiss. I seen where a mink's ben gallopin' 'raound, an' I want some bait for a trap."

"Wal naow, seh, Sam, you goin' b'lieved what Ah'll tol' you. 'Tant no use for settlin' bait for minks to heat naow. He'll goin' sparkin' dis tam year, an' he ant cares no more for heat as you does w'en you'll goin' sparkin'. Set you trap in road where he'll goin' see hees Mamselle Hudleh, Sam, den you'll ketched it."

"Like 's not you're pretty nigh right, Antwine," Sam said, laughing, "but he might be comin' hum hungry arter his sparkin'. I've knowed of such cases"; and having found a bait of odorous muskrat flesh he hung it over a moss-covered trap in a hollow log, and next morning brought in the lithe slender fellow whose brown coat of fur became so fashionable and valuable in after years, though then worth no more than the muskrat's.

Along the winter roadway of ice, now made the most of by teamsters while it lasted, frequent loads of logs and wood or empty returning sleds came and went, crunching in and out of sight and hearing. To the eastward beyond the wide fields, from where the smoke of farm-house chimneys drifted upward, came sounds of busy life: the "jingjong" of old-fashioned "Boston" sleigh bells faring to and fro on the highway, the steady thud of flails in barns, the lowing of cows and the bawling of calves, the cackle of hens and the challenge of chanticleer; at noon the shouts of schoolboys and the mellow blasts of the conch-shells sounding for dinner. To the westward were the woods, their primeval solitude almost undisturbed, their silence only broken by the strokes of a far-off axe, followed by the dull boom of the falling tree. At night the gloomy, cryptic aisles resounded with the solemn notes of the great horned owls, and once or twice the trappers heard there the wild caterwauling of a lynx. So forty years ago the narrow Slang was the dividing line between broad fields that had long been cleared and cultivated and a thousand acres of ancient forest.

In this way the days passed, while the snow slowly melted off the fields and the ice slowly rotted. More tawny knolls cropped out in pasture and meadow, gray streaks of ice came to the surface along the creek and Slang, and in the woods the snow sunk lower and lower its winter litter of twigs, shards of bark and slender evergreen leaves, till here and there a hummock brown with last year's fallen leafage, or a mouldering log bright with ever-verdant moss, came to the checkered sunlight again.

Cold nights and cold days were not infrequent, when the saturated snow was crusted hard enough to bear a horse, and a roaring fire was needed at the shanty front to keep the trappers warmed into anything like comfort. But after each "cold snap" the south wind blew warmer than before, more crows came sagging heavily along on it from their winter exile, the woodpeckers sounded oftener their cheery roll, bluebirds and the first robin came, a phoebe called sharply for his mate and found flies enough in sunny nooks to keep him busy while he awaited her coming, and a dusky chorus of blackbirds gurgled out a medley of song from the tops of the maples, while the tardy spring drew nearer.

In these warmer days, hollow, unearthly moans and roars, rising at times almost to a yell, were heard along the lake, at first faintly from afar, then nearer, till every jagged steep of Split-Rock Mountain echoed with the wild voices, then fading away to a humming murmur in the distance. It was as if some tormented demon was fleeing over the ice, or a phantom host of the Waubanakee was rushing in swift, superhuman haste along the ancient war-path of the dead nations. It was the booming of the lake, a sound strange and almost appalling to Sam, who, till now, had never heard it.

At last a great rain came with a strong southerly wind, and the two made quick work of the snow melting, and the brooks poured down their yellow floods till the sluggish current of the Slang was stirred. The ice, for some days unsafe to venture upon, was now honey-combed, and presently was only a mass of loose, slender, upright spires of crystal, undulating when disturbed in long, smooth swells, and tinkling a faint chime as if a million fairy bells were knolling its downfall. Watery patches began to show here and there on the marshes, great flocks of geese journeying northward harrowed the gray sky, and ducks in pairs and droves came whistling down and splashed into the open water to feed and rest.

Then one morning, when Sam and his companion crawled out of the shanty, they beheld the long-wished-for sight of marshes clear of ice, and after a hasty breakfast they launched the birch and dugout and loaded them with the traps already strung on the tally sticks, and each with axe and gun they set forth to coast the low shores. The boats kept close together, the pine leading the birch, for Antoine was now to take the part of instructor. Scanning every half-submerged log they passed, he soon stopped his craft alongside a fallen limbless tree whose roots still clung to the bank, while its trunk slanted with a gentle incline into the turbid water. Abundant sign about the water-line showed that the long-imprisoned muskrats had already made the most of their newly gained liberty to swim with heads above water.

"Dah, seh, Sam, you see he been here, lot of it, an' prob'ly he'll comin' 'gin. Naow, chawp nawtch in de lawg, so," and with half a dozen strokes of his axe he cut a neat notch in the log just below the water-line, wide enough to hold a trap when set. It was a pine, well preserved, and the chips and notch were bright and fresh. "Naow you see, w'en de nawtch mek it too shone, you wan' put it on some weed, mud, sometings," and he overlaid the cut with a thin layer of sodden water weeds. "Moosrat he ant very cunny, but he lak see ting where he been look kan o' usual." Then he drove the tally pole firmly into the soft bottom, and set the trap in the notch with no covering but the two inches of muddy water that rippled over it in the light breeze.

"Dah," he said, as he resumed his paddle, "if de water ant rose or don't fell, you as' dat trap to-morrah mornin', he tol' you, moosrat!"

News from Danvis

The quiet water shone like a broad floor of silver in the early light, when the canoes left the landing next morning and began to crinkle the reflections of banks and trees and reddening sky. The few new-come robins sang their loud "Cheer up!," here and there a blackbird called "shoo-glee!" from the shores, and the loud nasal "quank! quank! quank!" of the dusky duck resounded from distant swampy coves, as Sam took his course up stream where the fewer traps were set, while Antoine coasted down stream along the flat cape that lies between the Slang and Little Otter.

Each made frequent stops to examine the traps, some of which were undisturbed; but the greater number were off the places they had been set on and out of sight under water. Such, when fished up with the trap hook, brought with them a drowned muskrat, his soft fur plastered to his body by long soaking, and his scaly tail curved like a scimitar; or a foot, the ransom a captive had paid for his freedom; or, as valuable as this to the trapper, but not so satisfying to his pride of skill, the sprung trap's jaws full of sodden weeds. In one Sam found a wood duck, his bright eyes wild with pain and fright. He eased the jaws carefully from the leg, which was not broken, and after admiring his beautiful prisoner's gay spring attire, while perhaps there was a little debate between a soft heart and a pork-surfeited stomach, he said, "Wal, I'll be darned if you ain't the harnsomest creetur 'at ever I see—too harnsome to kill in col' blood! Good-by, an' keep off 'm all lawgs this time o' year," and he tossed the bird gently aloft. As it went whistling and squeaking out of sight between tree trunks and branches with twists as dexterous as a woodcock's among the alders, Sam said after a long breath, "Wal, Sam Lovel, like 's not you're a dummed ol' chickin-hearted fool! *I* shouldn't wonder."

A little after noon he had made the rounds of his traps and was back at camp, where shortly afterward the Canadian appeared with a goodly pile of muskrats in the bow of his canoe. After dinner, as they were skinning their catch, Antoine unburdened himself, breaking out suddenly after a long silence, "Bah gosh! peekrils beegin play! Ah'll see tree, four of it! If he be good day to-morrah, we have it some fun shoot it, an' more of it heat it. You'll see any?"

"Wal," said Sam, considering, "I did see wakes of tew three fish a-skivin' away f'm the shore, but I do' know what they was."

"Dat peekrils, Ah bet you head!" and he discoursed at length on the sport of pickerel shooting, while they stretched the skins of the twenty-five or more rats their traps had yielded and hung them to dry on poles. As they lounged about the camp waiting for the evening shooting, they heard a loud call on the opposite shore a little above a cove where two brooks contributed their waters to the Slang, and the long-drawn-out call, "Sa—am—will! An—twine!" was presently followed by the dolorous howl of a dog. "If that hain't ol' Drive's hoot, I never heard it," cried Sam, his heart beats quickening at the old familiar voice, "an' I'll bate that 'ere 's Peltier a-hollerin'!" and running down to the landing he stooped and pulled the bushes aside, and peering out saw the unmistakable, lank, clothes-outgrowing form of his young neighbor, and sitting close beside him on the clayey bank Drive, with uplifted muzzle and ears drooping to his elbows, while his sonorous voice awakened lowland echoes that it had never stirred till now.

"All right, Peltier!" Sam answered, "I'll be over arter ye torights," and called back to Antoine as he set the dugout afloat, "I'll take your canew, it's stiddier 'n mine," and in five minutes the craft ran its nose up among the floating rushes at Pelatiah's feet.

"I swan! I never thought o' seein' you here yit awhile, but I'm almighty glad to," said Sam heartily, as he stepped ashore and grasped the hand that was stretched out to him a half foot beyond the shrinking coat sleeve. "An' you too, you blessed ol' cuss," as he bent down and patted the jubilant hound's hooped sides with resounding slaps, and pulled his long silken ears, while he looked into the face whose furrowed, sorrowful lines were lighted with an unwonted sunshine of joy. "What on airth brung you here? Can't you git along 'thaout me, ye durned ol' critter, hey? Come, Peltier," cutting short the hound's caresses, "git right in wi' your duds, if you've fetched any, an' we'll go over to the pallis an' git supper 'fore the roas' beef an' turkey an' things gits cold. Git in here, Drive, an' lay daown." And Pelatiah stumbled up the bank, turning toward his friend a puzzled face as he went, and returned with a great half-filled carpet bag of once gorgeous but now faded colors, which he handed to Sam, and then made another trip, bringing down this time the famous old Ore Bed. Sam's eyes shone with delight when he saw the ponderous piece, its long octagonal barrel cased to the muzzle in the "curly maple" stock, its trimmings, hooked heel plate, and patchbox of brass that glistened like gold where hand or shoulder had brightened them with wear.

"Jest ezackly what I was a-wishin' for yist'd'y. Good boy!" Sam said approvingly; "naow git right in an' squa' daown right there, an' set still, for this 'ere ol' holler lawg hain't quite so stiddy 's the scaow on the millpaund." That ancient square-built vessel, as incapable of capsizing as of speed, was the only craft Pelatiah had ever boarded till now, and he took his allotted place in the canoe with no little trepidation, the obedient hound crouching trembling and whimpering behind him. Grasping either gunwale with a firm grip he pulled lustily on the one which dipped the lower to right the long narrow boat as she backed careening from the shore. "Le' go the sides an' set still," said Sam sharply, as he headed her for the shanty, "erless ye wanter spill the hull caboodle on us int' the drink!" And Pelatiah minded, not even speaking, and scarcely breathing till he felt the land under foot again. Then regarding the Slang and letting out his pent-up breath with a great sigh of relief, "Whoofh! I swan to man, this is the goldarndest pawnd 't ever I see! I be durned 'f 'tain't wussin' the 'Tlantic Ocean!" Then turning toward the shanty he saw the array of drying muskrat skins. "Gosh all fishhooks! Where d'ye git sech a snarl o' stockin's?"

"Dat coats, Peltiet," Antoine answered, now approaching and greeting the visitor, "Moosrat coats. We'll trow 'way all hees stockin'. Haow you do pooty well, seh? Bah gosh! Ah'll glad of it! Haow pooty well all de folkses up Danvis was, hein?"

"Wal, never mind naow, Antwine, cook some o' them ma'sh rabbits, so 's 't Peltier c'n try 'em," Sam said, winking hard and covertly at the Canadian.

"Maash rrrabbeet?" he said, with staring eyes. "Ooh! yas!" as he slowly comprehended, "Ah'll got some dat all save up," and slipping behind the shanty, he soon reappeared with three pairs of small, nicely dressed hind-quarters of dark-colored meat.

Presently they were sizzling in the frying pan, and their savory odor was pleasant to Pelatiah's nostrils, as to his ears were the bubbling of the potato kettle swung on its pole over the fire and the simmer of the teapot on the outskirts of the coals. Then when the repast was spread on and about the slab that served, as far as it went, as a table, and the three seated themselves on blocks around it, Sam said as a sort of grace before meat: "The man 'at finds fault wi' this meal o' victuals is, like Uncle Lisher's customer, too durn'd p'tic'lar. A feller," he explained, as he helped himself to a potato and began to peel it with his jack-knife—for now that they could be kept in the shanty without freezing they had potatoes—"a feller come to Uncle Lisher onct for a pair o' right an' left boots. He wa'n't useter makin' nothin' but straight boots, an' when the feller come to try 'em on, lo an' behol'! they was both made for one foot! The feller begin to objeck some to takin' 'on 'em, an' Uncle Lisher he hollered so 's 't you c'ld a-heard him half a mild, 'Good airth an' seas, man, you're too durn'd p'tic'lar!'"

"Hounh!" Pelatiah snorted, "I hain't a-findin' no fault wi' your roas' beef an' turkey, by a jug full. This 'ere ma'sh rabbit is complete eatin'. I never hearn tell on 'em afore. It's darker meated and kinder juicier 'n whaot aour rabbits be. Turn white in winter, du they?"

"No," Sam said, soberly, while Antoine was choking with suppressed laughter and cursing "dat sacré bone rabbit Ah'll swaller in ma troat." "No, they're diff'ent f'm aour rabbits in c'nsid'able many ways. They're pussier 'n' clumsier, 'n' some longer tailed 'n' shorter eared 'n what aourn be, 'n' they hant turrible wet places so 's 't ye can't hunt 'em wi' dawgs, and to my notion they be better eatin', as you say;" and Sam begun on another quarter. "We'll show you haow we git 'em 'fore you go hum."

Then they sat chatting of home, trapping, and hunting, till Sam remarked, "Wal, 's Uncle Lisher uster say, it's high time all honest folks was abed."

Shooting Pickerel

When Sam, the earliest riser of the three tenants of the camp, crept abroad next morning the daylight pervaded a misty landscape. Close by the camp the silvery gray surface of the Slang was visible, then faded off into a dull white lake of fog that had for its further shore the dun upland fields and jutting capes of wooded hills. Out of it scattered trees arose with apparently unstable rootage, and roofs of barns like stranded hulks. The hemlocks dripped a slow patter of condensed mist, and the bottoms of the overturned canoes were beaded so thick with it that they looked as if sheathed with a coating of pearls. The light air from the south, so faint that it scarcely bent the columns of rising vapor, was soft with the breath of spring, and the voices of many birds uprose to welcome the beautiful day—the gurgle of blackbirds, the flicker's cackle, the robin's clear but jerky notes, the long-drawn whistle of the meadow lark away in the foggy fields, the trill of the song sparrow, and the joyous warble of the purple finch. A crow on a tree-top began to call his friends to breakfast with him on the heap of skinned muskrats that the trappers had left at proper distance from camp, and reminded Sam that it was time to make preparations for his own and his companions' breakfast. He raked a few live coals out of the heart of the ashes, and placing them beside the back-log, laid some "fat" pine shavings and slivers upon them, and after some lusty blowing got a blaze started. When he began to cut the wood to feed the fire, the noise of the axe aroused Antoine, who came out on all fours from his lair in such a half asleep and blinking condition that Sam was reminded of some hibernating animal taking its first look at awakening nature. He said nothing till

Sam hung the potato kettle over the fire, and clawing a dozen potatoes out of the grimy bag they were stored in, began to peel them. "What you goin' call dat dinny you mek it wen you git him do, suppy or breakfis, Ah dunno, me?"

"Supper, I guess, 'f you don't flax 'raound a leetle mite 'n' help. Wake up 'n' get some ma'sh rabbits ready 'fore Peltier gits his eyes open 'nough to see what kind of a critter the hindquarters growed on. 'T 'ould spile his appetite t' eat if he knowed they was mushrats when they was livin'."

"Bah gosh!" Antoine grumbled as he shuffled away to prepare the meat, "Ah'll rudder sleep as git up in a naght for heat! Ah'll jes' beegin have it some funs dreamin', you'll wek it me all up wid you hol ax— pluck! pluck!"

"High time to be a-stirrin', Antwine," Sam said cheerfully. "Traps to go 'raound to, an' then the fish shootin' you've ben a-tellin' on. It's goin' to be the neatest day 'at ever was!"

"Wal, Ah don' care for me," Antoine said, becoming reconciled to the loss of his matutinal nap as he realized what promise the morning gave. "Guess he be pooty good 'nough day—w'en he come."

Pelatiah was called when the water was drained out of the potato kettle and the frying pan was taken off the coals and set upon the slab beside it. Kneeling on the shore to wash his face and hands as the others had done already, he asked, turning his dripping visage toward them with an expression of disgust upon it, "Wha' d'ye du for suthin to drink? This 'ere water hain't fit! I hain't hed a decent drink o' water sen I come off 'm the hills. This 'ere stuff 'raound here don't hit nowheres!"

"Julluk me," Sam answered, "when I fust com' daown here. The well water an' sech didn't squench my thirst no more 'n it 'ould to open my maouth an' let the moon shine into 't. It's hard, all on 't; you can't suds a pint on 't with a barrel o' soap! But I'm a-gittin' use to 't an' the's a brook back here 'at dreens the snow aoutin the woods that you'll find toll'able satisfyin' 'f you drink tew three pailfuls on 't. Me 'n' Antwine goes over once a day reg'lar an' fills up. Draw up!" he continued, seating himself beside the slab, "draw up, Peltier, an' make yerself tu hum an' help yerself. The' might be better, an' the' is wus."

Then they fell to, and, contenting themselves with such fare as they had, were soon ready to set forth.

Sam and Antoine were to embark in the log canoe, while Pelatiah, still mistrusting the treacherous deep, was to hunt along shore, following the directions of the experienced Canadian.

The sun shone with almost summer-like fervor on the flat, wooded shore and clear, still shallows, where every sodden leaf and weed and sunken stick upon the bottom was revealed. The first frogs were sunning themselves on the fringe of floating and stranded last year's rushes that bordered the water, and on every side their crackling purr arose, as continuous, if not as loud, as the thronging blackbirds' incessant clamor, a medley of sweet and harsh notes, like the gurgle of brooks and the slow drip of water into echoing pools, with the grating and clatter and sharp click of pebbles tossed upon rocks. As Pelatiah slowly walked along the shore, at almost every step a frog startled him, scurrying over the weeds with spasmodic leaps and splashing into the water.

A slight commotion of the surface attracted his attention, and warily approaching the spot, he saw the back fin and tail of some large fish gently moving, and remembering Antoine's last injunction to shoot at a fish "way under where he was," he blazed away. Before the boil of the water had subsided he saw the white bellies of two motionless fish shining out of the bubbles and disturbed sediment, and splashing to them he plunged his arm in to the elbow and seized the largest, and tucking it under his left arm, grabbed the other. Just then he saw another that had been stunned by his shot, feebly writhing its fins and evidently gathering wits and strength for a speedy departure. How to secure it with one fish in his right hand, his gun in his left, and another fish hugged under that arm was a question that he speedily solved by seizing his right-hand fish by the tail with his teeth. But the free fish, the largest of the three, had now recovered, and as he reached for it, slipped through his fingers, and with a great surge disappeared, leaving only its slime in his grasp. After one longing, regretful look, he waded ashore with his prizes, and depositing them at a safe distance from the water, sat down upon a log and gloated over them, stretching them to their fullest length, arranging their fins, then turning them over, then "hefting" them separately and together. They were of about five pounds weight each, and most undeniably pickerel, the fish of all that the mountaineer prizes most, in spite of his intimate acquaintance with the clean, gamy, beautiful, and toothsome trout of his native streams and ponds. His admiration of this shark of the lowland fresh waters has spoiled the trout fishing in many a mountain lakelet, where the survival, not of the fittest, but of the biggest, the hungriest, and most fecund has been proved by the introduction of this alien.

In possession of the largest pickerel he had ever seen, and that of his own taking, Pelatiah had never felt more completely happy. If the day had been cold, the glow of pride and happiness would have kept the wet clothes from chilling him; in the genial sunshine of this most perfect of early spring days, he scarcely felt that his boots were full of water, that he was soaked and sodden to the waist. He heard, but only noticed as a pleasant accompaniment to his inward song of thanksgiving, the frequent roll of the partridges' muffled drums far and near in the woods; hardly wondered what unseasonable game Drive had afoot where he was making the woods resound with lazy echoes of his sonorous voice. Guns were booming all along the shores—the thin report of rifles spitting out their light charges, the bellow of muskets belching out their four fingers of powder, two wads, and "double B's," and giving one's shoulder a sympathetic twinge as he thought how the shooter's must be aching—all proclaimed that it was a sad day for the pickerel that had come on to Little Otter's marshes to spawn. Probably not one man of the fifty who were hunting them there had a thought of what the fish were there for, or would have cared if he had. There were too many pickerel, and always would be. There could be no exhaustion of the supply of them nor of any other fish. Any proposition to protect fish and game of any kind, to prescribe any method of taking, to limit the season of killing, would have been thought an attempt to introduce hated Old World laws and customs. Hunting and fishing were the privileges of every freeborn American, to use or abuse whenever, wherever, and however he was disposed. And he could not live long enough to see the end of it, for why should there not always be fish and game as innumerable in all these unnumbered acres of water and marsh and woods? Alas! why not?

So he cut the brightest blood-red osier twig he could find and strung his fish upon it, though with the feeling that a silver cord would more befit their worth and beauty. Then he reloaded his gun with a most generous charge in consideration of its recent good service, and went on in search of new conquests, his boots chuckling at every step in their lining of water, as if they, too, were rejoicing in his triumph. He soon saw where a fish was "playing" at some little distance from the shore, and working carefully toward it under cover of an insular stump, he gained that coign of vantage, and stood with unstable footing on its roots when he saw the fish within short range and fired at it. The recoil of the heavy charge pushed him a step backward, his foot caught in a root, and over he toppled at full length with a gasping grunt and a splash that drove an upward shower of water drops into the lower branches of the trees. He hardly waited to regain his feet before he scrambled to the place where he had last seen the fish. And there it was, motionless, belly up and bigger than those he had on his string! He thought as he slipped the osier through the gills and viciously toothed great jaws that he had suffered none too much for such a reward, that he would rather have been put to soak in the Slang for an hour than to have lost it.

Arrived at camp, he made a complete change of raiment, and was toasting himself in great contentment by the replenished fire when, late in the afternoon, his companions returned. He had thought of dressing his fish, but it seemed too bad to take even a scale from them before his friends had seen them in their entirety. How he wished that he might display them on the store steps at Danvis and tell the story of their capture, with judicious omissions, to the admiring audience of evening loungers. His pride was somewhat brought down when he saw the dozen or more big fellows that Sam and Antoine tossed out of the canoe, but still he felt that he had done well, for a boy, and his friends gave him generous praise.

Antoine dragged a slab to the water's edge, and seating himself a-straddle of it, slapped a large fish upon it in front of himself, which he forthwith set about cleaning, while Sam and Pelatiah squatted close by and watched the process. "You wan' scratch it, scratch it, dem peekrils great many," he instructed them out of the shower of scales he set flying. "Den w'en you'll pull off all hees shell off of it, you wan' wash heem plenty—wash an' scratch—so!" and he doused the scaled fish in the water, scraping it with his knife and washing it, over and over again, till the skin was quite white and free from a suspicion of slime. "Somebody he ant more as half scratch off peekril clean 'nough, den he cook it, an' he ant tas' good of it, den he'll said, 'dat peekrils, he don't fit for be decent!' Bah gosh! Ah show you, me!" Then he split the fish down the back, cut off the head, took out what he called the "inroads," washed it again, and cut it into convenient pieces for the frying pan. When he had tried the fat out of a couple of slices of salt pork and set the fish to hissing in the pan with the bubbling accompaniment of the potato kettle, an odor so savory pervaded the atmosphere of the camp that it made the mouths of the hungry men water, and the minutes of waiting for supper seem like slow hours of starvation. The fragrance of it was wafted to the nostrils of a wood-chopper half a mile away, and so aroused the sacred rage of hunger within him, that he was forced to shoulder his axe and go home to an early supper.

Antoine set the potato kettle on the board, and lifting the frying pan from the coals, with his hat for a holder, set it there also and announced supper. "Goo'by, M'sieu Cochon; goo'by, M'sieu Mash Rabbeet; how you was pooty well, M'sieu Peekril? Ah'll very glad for see you to-day, seh! Hoorah, boys!" The bag of dry bread was brought out, and then the three fell to work in a silence that was broken only by grunts and sighs of satisfaction, the sputtering out of fish bones, and the clatter of the few implements of onslaught. At the end of it Antoine said, as he prepared a charge for his pipe: "Wal, seh, boy, 'f Ah always feel jes' Ah was naow, Ah ant never heat no more!"

The sky had become overcast with curdly clouds except a strip along the horizon, which at sunset was a broad belt of orange-red fire glowing between the dark gray clouds and the blue-black bastions of the Adirondacks and the frayed fringe of sombre woods; and nearer than the shadows of these, the brimming expanse of unruffled water glowed with the same intense color. When the trappers crept into their nest, the night was dark and starless; a chill breath of northerly air was sighing in the hemlocks, and the great owls were hooting a dolorous warning of coming storm. Listening to them, Sam remarked as he made his final yawn under the blankets, "Not much fun nor profit for us fellers to-morrer, so the aowls sez."

Antoine's Redoubtable Victory

The next day's dawn came with slow reluctance to dimly light a dismal landscape, over which had come one of those disheartening changes so frequent in our northern latitude that it seems strange they are not expected as in the common course of nature, rather than wondered at and spiritually rebelled against. The succession of the seasons had apparently been turned backward in the gloom and mystery of one night, and where yesterday spring was jubilantly triumphant over the reconquest of her realms, winter was reigning again. Snow had been falling for an hour or more, driven by the north wind in a long slant from the leaden sky to the earth, whitening the dun fields and turning the brown and green woodlands to spectral gray, till the trees looked like ghosts of the slain embodiment of spring. The sluggish waves of the Slang beat with a sullen wash on the wind-swept shores, but in the sheltered coves a seal of leaden ice was set upon them. The wild ducks, happy and content in any weather that gave them open water, were splashing and diving and breasting the black flood, but the land birds were in sorry plight. They huddled in the thickets for shelter, and if one attempted to pipe a song, its thin, half-frozen notes added no cheer to the day, but rather made it the more dreary.

When Sam awoke with a dull sense of changed weather in his bones, and sat up in his bed to look abroad, the picture set in the triangular frame of the shanty front, a pointed bit of gray sky above white fields and black water, with a foreground of snow-laden bushes, the blackened stakes, cross pole and brands of the dead camp-fire, was so utterly cheerless, that only the desire of companionship, ever craved by misery, impelled him to arouse his comrades. The hound came stretching and yawning forth, and after a sorrowful look abroad and a sniff of the damp air, gave a dolorous whine, and crept back to his dark corner to comfort himself with forgetfulness of the outside world. While Pelatiah suffered in silence, with unworded wishes for the comfortable warmth of the kitchen stove at home, Antoine loudly denounced the meteorological change. "Ah'll never see so many kin' wedder in litly while all ma life tam! What for he ant jus' well be sprim wen he'll get all ready, jus' well as jomp raght back in midlin of winters? Bah gosh, Ah dunno, me! Wal, Ah don' care, Ah s'pose we'll got have it some fire on aour stofe, ant it?" and getting himself together he began a search, axe in hand, for some dry kindling. Chipping away the weather-beaten outside of an old stump, he soon got at its yellow heart, and with shavings and splinters of it presently had a cheerful blaze lapping the snow and dampness off the back-log. Breakfast was hardly in preparation when the snow turned to more dreary rain, that came pelting down with a dull patter, freezing as it fell. All hands turned cooks and made frequent rapid dashes from the shanty's shelter to the sputtering fire, one encouraging its feeble efforts with a punch or a morsel of dry fuel, another giving the frying fish a turn or a shake, another snatching out of the veil of smoke a hurried glance at the pot that was fully possessed of the proverbial perverseness of watched pots, and stood long on the order of its boiling.

When at last patience was exhausted and hunger would no longer be temporized with, they made a sally and brought in the half-cooked rations. The potatoes seemed to be suffering an epidemic ossification of the heart, for every one had a "bone in it," and the fish, except the outside and thinner parts, was raw. Antoine's onions did strong and excellent service in helping out the sorry meal, and when it was got through with the little party settled down to making the best of the discomforts of a rainy day in camp. They related the events of yesterday; what befell Pelatiah he told to his companions with but few eliminations, for he felt no unwillingness now to let them enjoy the fun of his mishaps.

Sam and Antoine had not gone far on their cruise the day before when, as they rounded the point between the Slang and the creek and floated slowly over the sunny, wooded shallows, a party of "playing" pickerel was sighted by the Canadian, who was paddling. Two or three lusty fellows had the upper tips of their tails and dorsal fins above water, now gently moving them, now splashing about in a spasmodic flurry, then disappearing for a minute, then breaking the surface in another place near by. Antoine got the canoe close to them without alarming them, and Sam fired into the thick of the group. The Ore Bed's big bullet made the water boil and set half a dozen swift, arrowy wakes flying off in different directions; but that was all. Not one silvery, upturned belly gleamed out of the settling sediment. "Oh, sacré ton sac! Oh, bah gosh! da's too bad. Oh, you'll shoot all over it! Ant Ah tol' you more as fo' honded tousan tam, wen you'll shot at peekril you ant want shot at it, hein? You'll want shot at it where he'll ant look so 'f he was! Way onder where you'll see it! You don't can't rembler dat, hein? Bah gosh! wen Ah'll rip-proach you up to some more of it, 'f you ant did more better as you was dat tam, Ah'll goin' shoot masef!"

"Wal, Antwine," Sam said with a shamefaced little laugh, "I never shot at one afore, 'n 'f I don't du better next time you 'reproach' me up tu some fish, you shell du the shootin'. Re-proach! Oh, golly! wal, I'll be durn'd 'f I s'posed you'd lugged any o' Solon Briggs's big words all the way daown here!" and moistening a patch he rammed a bullet down the long barrel, making the grimaces that one who drives home the ball in a muzzle-loading rifle always does, as if his own interior was suffering the leaden invasion.

"Wal, Ah don't care, Sam, Ah'll hit dat words 'baout so close you'll hit dat peekrils, ant it?"

"Cluster, Antwine, cluster, you knocked the head right off on 't!"

And so with restored good-humor they went on till another bunch of fish was sighted and got near to, when Sam, aiming well under, "on-hitched." Four good-sized pickerel, some hit, some only stunned, rolled bellies up and were got in board before they had thought of moving a fin. In such murderous fashion, approved by custom like many another quite as bad, they got all the fish they cared for, and met with no mischance worse than one or two misfires.

Antoine proposed to concoct a chowder, which he promised them should furnish a dinner so good as to make amends for the badness of their breakfast.

"Dey ant on'y but jes' one ting was better as feesh, an' dat was be feesh wen he be cook in chowdy, 'cep' mud turkey." So putting on a heavy coat he took the kettle to the shore and spent so much time there in washing it that he came back with a shell of frozen rain upon his garments, such as loaded all the branches with its dull glitter, cracking and clattering with every sway of the wind, and crunching under foot on the iced mat of last year's herbage. Pork, fish, potatoes, crackers, and onions furnished all the requisites for a chowder, a dinner all in one pot, and one that needed no constant tending, therefore well suited to the conditions of a roofless kitchen in a stormy day. When it was set to seething over the now well-established fire, they sat in the shelter of the shanty front, the elders smoking frequent pipes, Pelatiah solacing himself with spruce gum.

"Samwill," he said after much speechless if not quite silent rumination, and a long look out into the cheerless, icy woods, with no sign of life in them but one red squirrel chipping a cone on a hemlock limb, and too much depressed in spirit to utter one saucy snicker or defiant chir, "Samwill, I sh'ld think the' 'ld be bears, an' painters, an'—an' annymills in these 'ere woods. They're big 'nough, seems 's 'ough."

"Don't 'pear to be much in 'em bigger 'n coons," Sam answered; "we thought we heard a lynk oncte or twicte, but mebby 't wa'n't nothin'. Like 's not the's a painter a-travelin' through 'em oncte 'n a while praowlin' back an' to, but I ha'n't seen no signs on 'em."

"Tell us 'baout that painter 't you killed, Samwill," said Pelatiah, starting up with a sudden interest; "I never heard ye, though I've kinder hearn tell on 't."

"Oh, the' wa'n't nothin' 'baout it, only I happened to shoot him."

"Wal, Samwill, tell 'baout it, won't ye?"

"Wal," Sam said, looking abstractedly into the fire while he slowly

filled his pipe out of a nearly-spent blue paper of Greer's or Lorillard's
"Long smoking," "the' wa'n't no painter huntin' 'baout it, only a happen-
so. I was a bee huntin', in September it was, 'n' his hide wa'n't wuth fo'-
pence only to look at, 'n' I'd got some bees to workin' in a little lunsome
clearin' 'way up 'n under Tater Hill, 'n' lined 'em int' the woods, 'n' reck-
oned I'd got putty nigh the tree, 'n' I was saunderin' 'long lookin' caref'l
at every tree 'at hed a sign of a hole in it, when I seen a shake of a big
limb of a great maple, 'n' then I seen the critter scrouched onto it clus to
the body 'n' a lookin' right at me. I'd left the Ore Bed back in the clearin'
much as ten rods off 'long wi' my bee box, 'n' my hat sot mighty light on
top o' my head as I backed off, slower, I guess, 'n' I'll go to my own fun'al.
Soon as I got him aout o' my sight—though I don't s'pose I was aout o'
his'n—I made durn few tracks to the ol' gun, I tell ye, 'n' then come back
slow 'n' caref'l. There he sot scrouched daown jest where I left him, an'
his durned yaller eyes right on me 's if he hedn't never took 'em off, 'n'
mebby he hedn't. When I got in 'baout six rods, I drawed a bead right
betwixt 'em 'n' onhitched. He didn't jump, but kinder sagged daown ont'
the limb 'n' turned under it 'n' le' go fust one foot 'n' then 'nother, 'n' arter
hanging' by the last bunch o' claws for a minute, come daown, kerflop.
He clawed 'n' flurupped 'n' graowled julluk any durned waounded cat,
'n' I stood back 'n' gin him the floor. But his senses was all knocked
aouten on him, an' he didn't know 'nough to git to me 'f he wanted tu.
I hussled 'nother charge int' the Ore Bed tol'able spry, but 't wa'n't
needed—he was deader 'n hay 'fore I got the cap on. An'," said Sam, after
a pause in which he refilled his pipe, "I faound the bee tree not tew rods
furder on, an' tew weeks arter I took it up an' got a hund'ed paounds o'
the neatest honey 't I ever see." And he seemed to feel quite as much
satisfaction in the recollection of finding the bountiful supply of wild
honey as in the killing of the great cat.

"By gol!" said Pelatiah, letting out his long-held breath in a great sigh,
"I sh'd thought you'd a ben scairt!"

"Wal, no," Sam said, still thinking of the bees, "I hain't feared o' bees;
they never sting me none tu speak on."

"Dat mek me tink," said Antoine, coming in from a brief inspection of
the chowder, and nursing a coal that he had scooped out of the ashes in
his pipe bowl, "mek me tink one tam me ma brudder-law keel one dat
panter in Canada. We was go huntin' for deer. Ah guess so, an' da was
leetly mite snow on de graoun'. Wal seh, we'll see it track, we ant know

what he was be, an' we'll folla dat, oh, long, long tam. Bamby he'll go in hole in rock, leetly laidge, you know, 'baout tree, fo', prob'ly seex tam big dis shantee was. Wal, seh, boy, Ah'll left it ma brudder-law for watch dat holes, an' Ah'll go 'raoun' back side laidge see all what Ah'll see. Ah'll look veree caffly, an' what you tink Ah'll fin' it? Leetly crack in rock 'baout so wide ma tree finger of it, an' dat panter hees tail steek off of it 'baout so long ma arm, prob'ly, where he'll push hind fust in dat holes. An' he'll weegly hees tail so," waving his forefinger slowly. "Wal, Ah'll tink for spell what Ah do. Den Ah'll go cut off strong steek so big half ma wris' and two foots long. Den Ah'll tek hol' dat tails an' tied knot in him, veree caffly, den Ah'll run steek t'rough an' pull knot hard! Oh, bah gosh! you'll oughty hear dat panters yaller an' holla! Wus as fo' honded tousan' cat! Yes, seh! Oh, he'll hugly, Ah tol' you! but he can't help it, he can' gat it loose 'less he pull up hees tails off. Wal, seh, Ah'll lafft at it, Ah can' help it, mos' Ah'll split off ma side. Den Ah'll go 'raoun' ma brudder-law, an' he'll be scare mos' dead, an' goin' runned way, Ah'll tol' heem, Ah goin' in dat holes shoot dat panters. 'Oh, gosh!' he'll ax me, 'he tore you dead more as forty piece!' Ah'll say, 'Ah so good man Ah'll don' 'fraid me.' Den Ah'll crawl in dat holes an' Ah'll shoot it, boom! right 'tween hees head! An' bamby pooty soon he ant yaller some more, be all still as mices. Den Ah'll come off de holes an' Ah'll tol' ma brudder-law he'll crawl in an' pull off dat panters. He'll pooty 'fraid for go, but bamby he go. He touch hol' of it, he can' pull it cause hees tail tie, but he ant know. 'Bah gosh!' he say, 'dat panters more heavy as two ton! Ah can' pull it!' Den Ah'll go 'raoun' an' taked off dat steek, an' holla 'pull!' an' ma brudder-law pull more harder he can—boom! he go tumbly on hees back, dat panters on top of it! Oh! 'f he ant scare, ma brudder-law. Yas seh! Wal, seh, boy," after a pause during which no one spoke, "'f you ant mek b'lieve dat stories you go Canada 'long to me Ah show you de steek. Ma brudder-law he'll saved it. Ah ant never tol' you stories so true lak dat, seh!"

"I ha' no daoubt o' that, Antwine; you couldn't tell a lie big 'nough to choke ye. Hain't that 'ere mux o' yourn 'baout done? I'm a-gittin' wolfish."

After due examination the French cook pronounced the chowder ready to be served up, and it proved so toothsome that of the whole kettleful there was hardly enough left for Drive's supper.

Then with smoking and more story-telling they wore out the dreary day, and at nightfall the sky was brightening with the promise of a more cheerful morrow.

Pelatiah Goes Visiting

The bright and cloudless morning had a sharp chill in its breath, and the Slang was frozen from shore to shore, its waters smooth with ice of the regulation thickness of the first and last cold mornings of a year—namely, "as thick as window glass." Even in the wide expanse of Little Otter there was no open water but in streaks along the channel, marked by shimmering wavelets in their lines of blue and gold when the first rays of the sun shot across the landscape. All the hills and mountain ranges were hoary as they had been in midwinter, for snow had fallen on them while rain had fallen on the lowlands of the Champlain Valley. There could be no visiting of the traps before noon, for though the stout dugout—a shapelier craft, be it said, than Uncle Lisha had prophesied could be turned out by its builder's hand—might make its way unharmed through the ice, it would cost hard work, and the frail birch would be cut in shreds in making a passage through it. And so, when breakfast was cooked and eaten, and the slight task of washing the few dishes performed, there seemed not much but loafing to fill the forenoon with.

"We can't eat half o' them 'ere fish afore they spile," Sam remarked, after a long look at the hanging row of dressed pickerel; "I wish 't some o' the folks up to Danvis had t' other half. Say, Peltier, don't ye wanter take a walk an' see the country?"

"Honh! I swan, I'd know 'baout it," with a blank stare toward the far-off hills of his birthplace; "I do' know 's I raly wanter hoof it clearn ov' to Danvis t'day!"

"Danvis! Shaw! nob'dy wants ye tu. I was a-thinkin' mebby 't 'ould be a pious idee to take three four pickril up t' ol' Mister Bartlett, 'at gin us leave to camp here. A dreffle clever ol' gentleman he is, a forty-leventh cousin of Joel's, an' a Quaker too, but t'other kind, Hicksite. He lives up there in that tew-story white haouse. 'Tain't more 'n a mild, 'n' we c'n set ye crost in Antwine's canew, er you c'n go 'raound 'f you'd druther. 'Tain't fur t' the head o' the Slang, er tu where you c'n cross on some lawgs. 'F you'd jes' livs not go an' take him a mess o' them fish, I'd be 'bleeged tu ye. 'N' Antwine, we're e'en a most aouten terbarker 'n' crackers. S'posin' you set Peltier acrost, 'n' go 'long up t' the store 'n' git the staffs o' life? 'N' say, Peltier, the's an al-killin' slick gal up t' Mr. Bartlett's!"

Pelatiah's blushes shone through the sunburn of his honest face. "Oh, you git aout, Samwill!" with a bashful guffaw; "I don't care nothin' 'baout no gals!" Then, with quick forgetfulness of his denial of such weakness, as he looked down upon his worn and outgrown raiment, turning his arms this way and that to inspect their covering, "I do' wanter go a-lookin' 's I du, where the's any—any young folks!"

"Wal, Ah don' care for me," Antoine said, getting promptly to his feet, "Ah guess Ah'll lookin' well 'nough 's Ah do, an' Ah'll gat ma close all preffume for go see de gal. Ah'll carry dat feesh, an' Peltiet go store for de *pro*-vizhin. Ah ant see homan so long ago Ah'll freegit what kan close he wore. Come, hoorah boy!" He cut a forked twig from a water maple, and stringing four of the nicest fish upon it led the way to the landing, whither Pelatiah presently followed after hatcheling his towy locks with the sparsely toothed and only comb the camp afforded, and vainly attempting to pull his trousers down into neighborliness with his boots. They launched the dugout, and boarding it, ploughed and broke their slow way to the farther shore, the ice crashing and tinkling and jingling along their course, and hissing in long fissures on either side. When they had landed, Sam noted that after keeping together through the first field, Antoine diverged to the right in the direction of the store at the Corners, and Pelatiah to the left toward the big white house that shone among its gray locusts and against its dusky background of orchard. With his pleased half laugh and muttered "jes' 's I 'xpected," came a faint sigh as he turned his eyes toward the white dome of Tater Hill, in whose morning shadow dwelt his buxom sweetheart. There was some comforting promise in the ranks of drying muskrat skins that brought a contented expression to his face after he had cast a slow calculating glance upon them. Then he gathered some turpentine from half a dozen boxed pines, and melting it with grease in a bullet ladle, set about salving his canoe, which had got a grievous wound from a hemlock snag. He had the camp all to himself, for Drive had gone off hunting on his own account, and his earnest baying could be heard away upstream, mixed with the querulous whistle of the woodchuck he was besieging. But Sam was never weighted with any feeling of loneliness in the companionship of the woods. If, when among the patriarchal trees and their tribes of tenants and dependents, any sense of isolation made itself apparent, it was what he called "a good lonesome," and he enjoyed it today. Out of the woods came only its own voice and the voices of the wood folk: the sigh of the pines and hemlocks; the thud of the partridges' drum-beat, beginning with measured strokes and ending in an ecstatic roll; the soft cluck and whistle of the jay's love-song, intermitting with his more discordant cries; the woodpecker's note of mating time, as if he was sharpening his bill with a steel for the battles love might cause; and from far away, like the jingle of many discordant bells made almost melodious by distance, came the clamor of a convention of crows gathered to denounce some detested hawk or owl or fox. Near by a chipmunk clucked incessantly over his recent discovery of a new world wherein were sunlight and fresh air; and Sam's neighbor, the red squirrel, was in high spirits with such sunshine after storm, and flung at him a shower of derisive jeers and snickers from the trunk of the great hemlock, where he clung with spasmodic jerks of feet and tail.

"You sassy little cuss!" said Sam, "what sorter names be them you're a-callin' on me? I'm a dum'd good min' ter stop your chittereein' with a pill aouten the Ore Bed! You'll be a suckin' aigs an' killin' young birds wus'n a weasel in less 'n a month, you little pirut! But you're hevin' lots o' fun livin', 'n' I d' know 's they're my aigs 'n' birds, so jaw away." And Sam lit his pipe with a coal and continued the application of the plaster to the canoe bottom.

Now and then the ice fell along shore with sudden jingling crashes to the level of the falling water, and as the forenoon wore away and the shadows shortened it melted apace where the sunshine fell full upon it, and open water began to ripple and shimmer in the breeze, and there was a prospect of making the round of the traps in the afternoon if Antoine returned in time. The rent in the canoe was mended, and Sam lay taking a lazy smoke beside the ashes, casting an occasional glance across the Slang for his companions, when a slight wake attracted his attention, and he saw a small, dark object swimming past. "Naow, Mister Mushrat," he said, as he crawled into the shanty and brought forth the Ore Bed, "don't ye know 't ain't healthy for none o' your fam'ly 'raound here?" but as he crept to the shore with his rifle cocked and at a ready, he saw that the lithe, snake-like movements of the swimmer were not those of the muskrat. "Ah, Mister Mink, beg pardon an' make my manners," he said, speaking with the spiteful crack of the rifle. The silent wake ended with the spat of the ball, but before the first wavelet set the ice to tinkling along the shore, the mink slid to the surface feebly making the last struggles for his tenaciously held life. "That trouble in yer head is too much for ye," Sam said, as, after launching the birch, he picked up the yet writhing animal and gave it a finishing whack on the gunwale of the canoe, "you tough little cuss. What a hard-lifed critter an auter must be; julluk you, only cut tu a bigger partern. By the gret horn spoon! I wish 't I could git a crack at one on 'em jes' onct! 'N' the' hain't one left in the hull o' these tew cricks they give the' names tu, I s'pose. Ho, hum! Haow many year afore the' won't be nothin' left, I wonder? Not till arter I'm a-sleepin' under a blankit o' sods, I hope." As he sighed and cast the vague yet scrutinizing glance of a hunter over water and banks, and it was caught by something larger than mink or muskrat swimming toward him, nothing was further from his thoughts than the old adage, "The devil is nighest when you're speakin' on him." "What's that 'ere ol' fool of a haoun' dawg comin' hum by water for? An' it col' 'nough to—Drive, you cussed ol' fool," beginning under his breath to formulate a rebuke; then as it became apparent that the swimmer was not Drive nor any other dog, quite holding his breath, he reached cautiously forward for the gun, which he was too experienced a woodsman to let long accompany him uncharged. His nerves vibrated with a slight tremor when the stock touched his cheek, but at the right moment the long barrel hung firm in his grip and the Ore Bed snapped out its sharp little voice. "'F that hain't an auter the' hain't none!" said Sam, looking anxiously over the vacant water as he arose and began to reload the rifle. "An' I'll be dum'd 'f I hain't missed him! Hev I forgot haow to shoot jes' the minute in my hull life 'at I'd orter shot the clustest?" But now, a rod or more from where the beast had disappeared, it broke to the surface again in a wild, writhing, flur-rying struggle, like a great fish in its death throes; and Sam, having hastily but steadily finished the loading of his gun, fired with instantaneous aim at the dark center of the widening circles of waves; then, laying hold of his paddle, with a few strokes sent his craft thither, and dealt the strug-gling otter a downright blow with the paddle's edge that took all the fight and nearly all the life out of him. When he lifted his prize inboard—the last otter ever killed in these waters—Sam was as full of happiness as Pelatiah had been over the capture of his big pickerel, but he raised no shout of triumph; he only heaved a great sigh of intense satisfaction and said, "Well, there ye be!"

Not long after Sam had gone ashore Pelatiah appeared on the east-ern bank.

"You needn't git nothin' for me t' eat," Pelatiah said, as Sam began preparations for a late dinner, "for they made me eat dinner with 'em. Oh, my gol! a heap bigger 'n I c'ld see over, they piled ont' my plate! They hedn't hed a fish this year, 'n' they was turrible 'bleeged tu you, 'n' made me bring a hull ha' bushel o' apples, signofiders an' gillflaowers, they be. I'm goin' to take the bag hum sometime. An' they thee'd an' thaou'd me jes' 'f I was a member 'mong Friends 's they say. 'N' old Mister Bartlett he wanter know 'f I knowed any stiddy feller 't wanter hire aout for six or eight mont's, an' fin'ly sez he, 'does thee wanter?' S'pose aour folks 'ould let me, Samwill, bein' 't I hain't come o' age, an' haow much 'd I orter ast him? Say," without waiting for an answer, "that gal hain't their darter, she's their hired gal, but she's harnsome 'nough to be the Pres'dent's darter. She's neater 'n any schoolmarm! Oh! 'f I wa'n't 'shamed o' my darn'd ol' ragged duds, an' me a-stickin' tew foot aouten both ends on 'em. Shouldn't s'pose she'd ha' spoke tu me, but she ast me a hull lot o' questions 'baout my folks, an' kep' a-smilin' jes' 's clever! S'pose she wouldn't look at me agin, would she, Samwill?"

"Can't tell ye, Peltier; she's no tellin' nothin' 'baout what women folks 'll du or won't du," Sam answered, rising and brushing from his tawny beard the crumbs of the crackers wherewith he had made his dinner. "Wal, I must be off an' tend to what traps I can."

The sun had gone down behind the woods and twilight was creeping over the landscape, and the evening air was vibrating with the ceaseless purr of the toads and the shrill chime of the Hyla's vesper bells, before the light dip of Sam's returning paddle was heard, followed presently by the swish of the canoe bottom on the matted drift of rushes. He had as little to show for his voyage as was to be expected after such an unpropitious night for trapping as the last had been.

Breaking Camp

After the cold snap came a week of soft-breathed days and dark, still, frostless nights, wherein the traps waylaid many a nightly wandering muskrat, and the trappers' harvest was rich.

Some of the earliest comers of birds were beginning nest-building; the wood-ducks had chosen their homes, and dusky ducks in pairs sought the remotest coves, while great flocks of their companions went on their way northward. The crows scorned now the once prized heap of muskrat carcasses, for they had entered into full possession of their ancient rights, and swaggered about the fields with an air of absolute ownership, and were evidently somewhat impatient that their tenants, the farmers, were so slow in beginning corn-planting.

More birds came from the south: reinforcements of the dusky army of blackbirds, with flashing troops of redwings; the main body of the robins joined the advance guard, and the thickets were more populous with slate-colored snow-birds, and noisy with their sharp metallic chirping; and there were many arrivals of later comers. The highhole cackled and hammered again on his lofty perch; the white-throated sparrow called all day long for the ever-absent Mr. Peabody, and the wailing cry of the grass plover arose from meadows and upland pastures. Out of nooks of the marshes the booming of the bittern resounded over the watery level, a sound so strange to Pelatiah's ears that he asked, "Who be them fellers a-drivin' stakes in the ma'sh, an' what be they a-duin' on it for?" and was greatly astonished when told that it was only the voice of a bird, and entertained an uncomfortable suspicion that Sam was fooling him till one day when he stealthily stalked the sound and saw a "gob gudgeon" standing on a mass of marsh drift diligently pumping out his dolorous love-song. "Golly blue!" Pelatiah remarked, as, when he disclosed himself, the startled fowl sprang upon his awkward flight with a contemptuous parting salute, "his ol' pump needs primin' 'f that's all he's got for so much fuss!" By day and by night stranger outcries came from the marshes, weird laughter and wild yells, the voices of unknown waterfowl that were never seen.

"Darn it all! I s'pose I'd ort t' be t' hum a-helpin' aour folks, but I snum, I'd druther stay here!" and Pelatiah's gaze wandered across lots to the white house.

"Wal, we'll all go to rights, Peltier," said Sam; "the trappin' 's 'baout done up—hain't got sca'sely nuthin' these tew three nights—'n' I expec' the'll be a team arter us 'fore the end o' the week, 'n' then we'll pull up 'n' clear aout."

"Bah gosh!" cried Antoine, "we'll ant go 'fore the bull pawt was bit an' we'll ketch lot of it! No sah! De evelin was be gittin' warm, an' Ah'll know he was bit pooty soon, prob'ly to-naght, prob'ly to-morreh naght, Ah dun-no. Ah'll gat some hook an' lahne w'en Ah was go store. Where Ah'll put dat? Hoorah, here he was! Naow, Sam, give me some bullet for mek sinkit an' Ah'll feex up for try to-naght, 'f Ah can fin' som' wum. Ah'll gat some pole-feesh more as week 'go. Oh, Ah can ketch it if anyboddy can ketch," he bragged as he half hitched a hook on to the coarse line. "Ah was preffick freeshymans." Then he split one of the Ore Bed's big balls half in two and closed it on the line, which he then rigged upon a pole that had had more labor bestowed upon it in trimming and peeling than its original worth seemed to have warranted, for it was top-heavy and as crooked as an eel. Perhaps its owner considered this a virtue rather than a fault, and hoped that the reflection of the contorted "hard hack" might entice some lonely eel to its companionship; and the eel was to him what the trout and salmon are to the scientific angler. Having his outfit arranged to his satisfaction he crossed the Slang in the dugout to the cultivated fields beyond in quest of earth worms, and Pelatiah accompanied him on his way to return the borrowed bag, while the camp was left to the keeping of Sam and his hound.

Sam busied himself with bundling up the dried peltry, and Drive was as busy with ineffectual digging in the nearest muskrat burrow, which he did not abandon till long after the beleaguered rat had ploughed his way to safety toward the channel of the Slang with a sluggish, heavy, underwater wake faintly marking his furrow; then, shaking and wiping some of the dirt from his long ears and sorrowful face, he sought more congenial pastime in chasing and being chased by a vixen who had begun housekeeping and the rearing of a family not far away. Once, rating this ancient enemy of her race with angry, gasping barks, she followed him so close to camp that Sam got a full view of her in her sorry and tattered faded-yellow garb of vulpine maternity, not twenty yards behind the slinking, shamefaced hound. "Good-arternoon, marm!" he said; "'f 'twas in the fall o' the year, naow, yer tail 'ould be pintin' tow-wards that 'ere sneakin' ol' bundle o' kag hoops, an' the'd be a diff'ent style o' music in fashion! Good-by, marm," as the vixen vanished behind the veil of hazy undergrowth; "I wish ye good luck a-raisin' yer fam'ly, an' 'ould like to make the hull of yer 'quaintances come November, an' ye git yer good close on. Oh, Drive! hain't you a spunky dawg, a skulkin' hum with yer tail atween yer laigs afore a nasty little bitch fox not quarter 's big as you be!" as the hound came up to him and endeavored to explain the peculiarities of the situation with whimpers and more deeply corrugated brow, and quick, low-swung tail beats that shook all his lean anatomy. "A spunky ol' haoun' dawg you be! But yer julluk me, an' I guess the most o' tew-legged he humerns. Lord! I'd druther wrastle with a mad painter 'an to face a jawin' womern, I be durn'd if I hedn't! If they won't take the spunk aouten a feller, he's tougher 'n a biled aowl!"

Late in the afternoon, a team of horses came in sight hauling a lumbering wagon slowly across the fields toward the farther shore of the Slang.

"Hello!" cried Sam, "there comes aour baggidge waggin. Who is 't a-drivin'? Jozeff Hill, I guess, b' the dumplin' shape on him, an' the way he jounces 'raound on the seat, toes jes' techin' the waggin bottom. Yes, that's Jozeff."

Sam went over in the dugout to meet him and helped him to unharness the horses and shelter and feed them in the shed of an untenanted barn that stood in the middle of the field. Arriving at camp Joseph was cordially welcomed by the others, and soon began to unladen himself of his burden of neighborhood news, to hear which now would remind one of the items of a country paper of today. While his late dinner was cooking, and while he ate with full enjoyment the fried pickerel, he told them that it had been "a good sugarin' year—fust chop—wal, more 'n midellin, anyway."

The sun was down, and the reflected gold of the western sky lay unbroken on the quiet water save where a skimming bank swallow touched it with the light dip of his wing, or a fish lazily rose to an insect that dimpled it as it fell exhausted in its too adventurous flight, before the returning dugout vexed the Slang into a thousand distortions of mirrored sky and shores.

Antoine's bait hunting had been successful, and he had an old teapot half full of angle-worms—an encouraging sign of future luck, he thought.

As evening drew on they all began to gather a pile of wood to illuminate that night's bullpout fishing, which was to be the great final event of this spring's camp life. Antoine had provided plenty of bait and the angling outfit for his friends after the approved fashion of his own, except that possibly some of the poles were straighter than his; and at dusk they lighted their fire and began fishing. The fish were plenty, and blessed or cursed with good appetites, and one after another, with a sluggish, stubborn, downright pull for life and freedom, was torn from its watery hold and came walloping and creaking to land. To Sam, Joseph, and Pelatiah the unhooking of one was at first a rather perilous feat, and Pelatiah gave a bellow of pain when his finger was impaled by the horn of his first fish. "You wa'n't caffle, Peltiet," said Antoine, as the young fellow came to the fire, by turns sucking and inspecting the injured finger; "dem bullpawt he's bit pooty hard wid hees horn, Ah tol' you! Touch hol' of it jus' sam' lak Ah do, you t'umb an' fingler 'hind hees side horn, you palm you hand of it 'fore hees top horn—so. Den squeezle heem, haard!" and they all soon got the knack of it after the added lesson of some sorely punctured hands.

The generously fed fire sent up great tongues of flame licking at the gloom, and showered an upward rain of sparks into the branches that waved and tossed in the rising currents of warmed air. Across its dusky-edged circle of light, as the fishermen went to and fro, fell elongated shadows of legs, here joined to the gloom as if that was some enormous beast of undefined ponderous form noiselessly circling about the fire, there stretched from where the distorted, shadowy bodies flitted like gigantic goblins among the spectral boles of great trees. On the water side the poles and lines were defined against the darkness with seeming unreality, as if they were the angling gear of piscatorial ghosts; and when a plunging bait and sinker or a writhing outdrawn fish broke the water, and wavering shimmers of reflected light started forth and vanished in the blank silence, it was as if they had broken on the intangible shores of the land of ghosts. But by the cheerful, living fire there was life enough, and such sport as satisfied these jolly but most unscientific anglers. By midnight they had sport and bullheads enough to have satisfied greedier men than they were.

Next morning the sleepy occupants of the shanty awoke late, and even while Antoine was cooking the appetizing breakfast of fish, the others bestirred themselves in making ready for departure. And when the breakfast had been made speedy way with, the canoes began to pass across the Slang with cargoes of peltry and camp gear. By the middle of the forenoon the boats had made their last trips, and, with the baggage, were snugly stowed on board the wagon, the horses were hitched on, and the homeward journey began. All but Joseph Hill, who drove, trudged beside and behind the load through the greening fields that lay between the Slang and the highway. They were not very jolly as they set their faces toward their native hills, for who ever left a camp where few or many happy hours have been spent without a touch of regretful sadness? Even the hound seemed touched with this feeling, and sent wistful glances backward as he ranged the fields and snuffed the faint odors of last night's fox trails. As Sam cast a last look on the spot that had been his home for a month, a bittern's booming and the lazy quack of a dusky duck came from afar across the hazy marshes like friendly farewells, and the camp squirrel chattered from his favorite hemlock a not unkindly adieu. A wreath of smoke fluttered away from the dying campfire like a gauzy flag lowered and trailing on the ground.

Not many days passed before mink and skunk and woodchuck began boldly to visit the deserted shanty, and mouse and chipmunk took up their abode in it. Moss and lichens began to grow on the slowly rotting roof, blades of grass and weeds sprang up among the brands and ashes of the fireplace, and growth and decay began to obliterate the traces of human occupancy.

A Letter from Uncle Lisha

The trappers tarried in Vergennes to dispose of their peltry, and succeeded in doing so on terms satisfactory to all concerned, after some lengthy bargaining with the hatter, whose shop was made conspicuous by a stuffed lynx set in its window.

After brief sightseeing and the purchase of a few articles not to be found in the Danvis store, they resumed their homeward way. The road was long and rough, but almanac and sky promised them a moonlit night for what should remain of their journey after daylight had gone. Their shadows in the setting sun were moving far before them along the road in a grotesque silhouette when Joseph Hill gave the reins to Sam while he donned his "s'tout." When he had thrust himself, with a series of jerks, into that close-fitting, many-caped garment, he began his customary, uncertain search for pipe and tobacco.

"What in Sam Hill!" he ejaculated, as he brought up from the recesses of a pocket of his "gret cut" a soiled and travel-worn letter, and held it at half arm's length before his staring eyes. "What in Sam Hill! Oh, Samwill Lovel! 'f I hain't kerried this 'ere letter fur you all the way f'm Danvis an' so fur back, an' never thought tu give it tu ye! My sakes! I'm shameder 'n a licked dawg! But the's one comfort, Huldy never writ it; it's a furrin letter, f'm way off."

Sam turned it over and over, studying the ill-written address and postmark and the dauby seal, puzzling himself to guess from whence it had come a long while before he thought of solving the riddle by the easiest way. Then he sniffed a familiar odor.

"By the gret horn spoon, boys, it's sealed wi' shoemaker's wax, an' it's f'm Uncle Lisher!" Reading to himself, while his companions waited for what he should give them thereof, it ran in this wise:

Hegalgan, Hegalgan Co.,
Wis. Feb. the 4th.

S. lovil respected frend.

I take my pen in hand to seet myself to rite thees fu lines to let you no that i am wel whitch i hope this may find you the saim. i do not like the westconstant so mutch as i ekspekt i shud and Jerusha my wif is not ruggid. we are lonesum for the mowntins whicht this countray is flattern a pancake. nor no woods to call woods nigh to smel of a balsum a spruce a hemlok whitch our ize miss the site and my noze whitch you no not small the smel now my frend i want you to see joel bartlit and see if he will take what he giv for the ole plase if he will bargin for it as if youself byin i hav got anuff to pay up i will let you hav it on sheers me and Jerusha to liv with you and hulda til we dy and you tacare of us til we dy and you shal hav the plase then anser as soon as you can and not say nuthing of this to noboddy but hulda whitch i hope you are marrid most happy your frend til deth

Elisha Peggs, p s

Visions of a cosy home of his own arose before Sam as he read the letter to himself, and still as he read to his companions such portions as he might, there floated before his mind pleasant pictures of the future—the "house part" of the old couple's domicile again warmed to life, and a brighter life than it had ever known, the shop, with Uncle Lisha on his bench hammering merrily on his lap-stone, and the old visitors in their chosen places. For a moment it seemed almost a reality, then vanished like smoke in the wind, as he remembered how seldom happy dreams are realized.

The pale half moon grew silver bright in the darkening blue, high above clouds aflame with the sun's afterglow, and the clouds faded to pearly gray, and gray shadows grew black across the moonlit road and fields as the little party journeyed slowly homeward, still discoursing of the old friend so freshly brought to mind.

The Home Reception

When they came to the house of Sam's father, the men aroused themselves to unload his canoe and other effects and bade him good night, "or mebby good mornin'," Joseph said, unwilling to commit himself even in a parting salutation.

They went their way, and left him "on the chips," which were the only garniture of the untidy yard. Sam sighed as he turned from watching the departure of the wagon and cast a look over the house he called his home. Its nakedness and unthrift were as drearily apparent in the faint light of the clouded moon as in the glare of day. It had never looked homelike since his mother died, for the kindly touches of her brave but feeble hand had been quickly effaced by the shrew who, with unseemly haste, was installed in her place.

"If she'd lived," Sam said to himself, pitying his uncared-for childhood, "mebby I'd ha' been suthin' better'n a loafin', shifless, huntin', fishin' creetur. 'F I'd hed her an' a hum 'at was a hum! But mebby it's better for her as 'tis; the' wa'n't much comfort for her here, I guess," and he pitied her hard life more than his own. "Mebby a womern c'n du suthin' for me yit." He must see Joel Bartlett tomorrow and learn if there was any chance of buying back the old place.

He raised the latch of the unfastened door and pushed it open as quickly as its creaking hinges and sagged condition would let even him, who had learned so well its telltale tricks. When he had closed it he listened a moment, but heard no sound that betokened the awakening of the inmates. There were only the slow and squeaky ticking of the tall clock, the purring of the cat under the cold stove, the gnawing of a mouse somewhere in the woodwork, as mice had always been gnawing since he could remember sounds, and the gasping, intermittent snoring of his father, that used years ago to make his heart stand still as he lay listening in his lonely bed, wondering if the last explosive expiration was not final and he the most forlorn of orphans.

Taking from its box on the mantelpiece a homemade brimstone match, and lighting it with a coal raked from the ashes, he lighted the slender dip candle which he found in its accustomed place by the matchbox, and as its feeble light illumined the kitchen's tidy discomfort, the bare walls, newly whitewashed, the few well scrubbed wooden-seated chairs, the big table, Sam comprehended at a glance, as he hung the Ore Bed on its hooks, that house-cleaning was over, and was thankful that his return was so well timed.

The slight sounds of his entrance had not awakened his stepmother; perhaps it was the light that aroused her, perhaps it was the clatter of Drive's toe nails as he sniffed an inventory of the room's contents, perhaps the rattle of her cherished crockery, when Sam explored the pantry shelves in search of something for himself and Drive to eat, but just then her voice flashed out sharply:

"Who's that?"

"It's me," he answered, and asked, "haow be ye all?"

"Me! yis, an' high time 'at 'me' come hum, I sh'd think!" she snarled in a sleepy voice; "but I do' know 's the' was any p'tic'lar need o' sneakin' in in the dead o' night, when the's jes' 's many days 's the's nights; awakin' up folks 'at hevs tu work stiddy, instid of shoolin' 'raound a-trappin', an' a-huntin', an' a-thisin' an' a-thatin', so 's 'tain't work. Make thet 'ere pleggid haoun' dawg lay daown, a-trompoosin' over my clean kitchin floor 'at I've scrubbed and scaoured half a day."

"Here, Drive," Sam said, as if he had not heard her tirade, "here's a col' johnny-cake, an' I'll d'vide wi' ye."

"O dear me, suz!" groaned Mrs. Lovel, "I wish 't the' wa'n't none o' them pleggid men in this livin' worl', erless I wish 't I was dead."

"Seein' 't the's so many more on 'em 'an the' is o' you, I'd take the cheapest way tu git clear on 'em 'f I was you, marm," said Sam, taking a mouthful of johnnycake and dropping as generous a piece into Drive's alert jaws.

"I won't die tu please you," she snapped, smothering the last word in the blankets as she settled herself in the bed, whose sudden spiteful creak proclaimed that she would vouchsafe no further speech.

"She sartinly never done much tu," Sam said to himself, as he gave his dog the last morsel of their frugal supper.

His father, who had not deemed it prudent to appear earlier, now came forth, very quietly, a queer figure in a short red flannel shirt astilt on long bare legs, bringing to mind the old simile of a "shirt on a bean-pole." While he scratched his side with a scant handful of flannel, he welcomed his son with a pleasant smile and a whispered,

"Wal, Samwill, haow air ye? Hed good luck, an' kep' well, hev ye?"

"Yes; an' be you well, father?" Sam answered and asked in a whisper, scanning the old man's weak, kindly face.

"Find suthin' t' eat? The's some pork an' beans in there some'eres," indicating the pantry by a sidewise nod. "Do' know where she put 'em. Hey, Drive, good ol' feller!" he whispered, stooping to pat the hound very softly. "You better keep middlin' still, ol' feller!" as Drive's friendly tail-beats smote chairs and wall. "Wal, I guess I'll be crawlin' back. She's putty nigh beat aout a-haouse-cleanin' an' so be I."

Sam took Drive to his bed in the barn, and then sought his own in the cheerless kitchen chamber. Home was home after all, and he settled himself to sleep under the sloped ceiling with a sense of usage, if not of perfect content, in which there was a degree of comfort. In his dreams he was a boy again, and his mother's toilworn hand caressed his weary head with the kindly, unforgotten touch of the nights of long ago.

As soon as might be next day he sought an interview with Joel Bartlett, and after much roundabout talk concerning weather and crop prospects broached the real object of his visit. He was not disappointed when Joel refused to dispose of the Uncle Lisher place at the price he had given for it, for that was not the thrifty saint's way of doing business. But when he offered an advance of fifty dollars, then of seventy-five, and finally of a hundred dollars, and each offer was promptly refused with a declaration that Joel "did not feel clear tu sell at no price likely tu be gi'n him, bein' it come in so well with his own farm, which it was onct a part on, the original tew-hunderd acre pitch drawed tu the right o' Hezekier Varney, which he in sóme ways foolishly got red on," Sam turned away, his heart heavy with hope deferred. Not yet, as he had permitted himself to hope, was the door of a real home opening to Huldah and him.

That night the lovers built nothing so grand as a castle in the air, only a snug log-house up among the cheaply valued acres of woodland that Sam's small savings would buy. Better that, they said, than going to the West, far from kindred and old friends and the beloved Green Mountains.

The neighbors remarked that "Sam Lovel hedn't never took a holt so afore as he did in this spring's work."

But when the slack came after planting, the old wild spirit laid hold of him. "I got tu go daown there a-fishin' jest oncte," was his answer to his sweetheart's opposing arguments.

❈ The Camp on the Lake ❈

Voyage Down Little Otter

Following out a plan conceived during his spring campaign on the Slang, when he had been amazed at the numbers, size, and variety of fishes inhabiting Champlain waters, Sam Lovel and some of his friends with a wagonload of camping outfit were one day slowly jolting down the steep, winding road to the landing below the first falls on Little Otter.

It was one of those lazy afternoons in June when all nature basks in the new warmth and nothing seems better to all things than to be still and enjoy laziness. The bullfrogs sitting on the rafted logs at the mill tail only winked their enjoyment of sunshine as they dozed beside their voiceless brothers, the little turtles. A kingfisher sat motionless on a fishing stake, apparently regardless of the swarm of minnows poised beneath him. A big fish, finding himself floating too near the glassy surface, broke it with a languid flap of his tail as he sought cooler depths, the slow wavelets just stirring the young water weeds and lapsing softly on the shores. High overhead a hen hawk swung in a wide circle as slowly as swept the lazy drift of silver clouds above him, and almost at rest upon the wing. The voices of the birds were hushed; the merry bobolinks jangled only occasional snatches of song in the meadows, where loitering strawberry pickers lounged in the long shadows of trees, and a wood pewee in the great elm over the mill was the only one of the thousand singers that sang continuously, and his sweet, pensive notes seemed like the fragrance of flowers, more exhaled than sung. The pervading spirit of indolence had fallen upon mankind as well. The miller lounged in the doorway of his mill with no sign of his vocation but the dust on his garments. Women lolled in doorways with elbows on knees looking intently at nothing, while children, too young to be at school, were taking their afternoon nap. But the curiosity of these good people was awakened and unwontedly stirred by the arrival of Sam's party, for a camping outfit was an unusual sight in those days, when camping was not in fashion with those who were considered quite respectable. Only white vagabonds and bands of Canadian Indians who had not much better shelter at home were supposed to live in shanties and tents for the pleasure of it, even in the pleasantest weather. Perhaps the memory of the hardships of the pioneers, some of the younger of whom were yet living, was not enough obliterated for such primitive ways of life to seem at all desirable to their descendants. At any rate, the folks about the falls wondered to see such decent-looking men as these coming of their own free will to take boat here to go to the lake for some days of vagabondizing. This they signified their intention of doing when the miller and the sawyer with moderate haste drew near.

Sam inquired for the owner of a roomy boat to take their effects to the mouth of the creek, and the miller, looking at the sawyer, said, "Wal, there's ol' Uncle Tyler, he's got a tollable big scaow boat, an' hain't nothin' much t' du. Mebby he'd take ye daown t' the san'bar. S'pose he would, Sargent?"

"Yaas, I sh' think like 'nough he would."

"Yes, he'll du it," the miller said very confidently now.

"Goin' fishin'? Thought most likely ye was. Uncle Tyler lives up yunder in that leetle haouse wi' the linter on the west side on 't—that leetle heater piece is his'n, an' there he is a-pokin' raound in his garding. There, he's comin' daown t' see what's a-goin' on—thought he would—hain't nothin' else t' du. Most on us putty busy this time o' year; ha' no time tu be foolin' raound daytimes."

"So I see," Sam said. "C'n we git someb'dy t' keep aour hosses a week er so?"

"Wal, Sargent's got a parstur handy," the miller replied, questioning the sawyer with his eyes.

"Jump?" Sargent asked.

"No, sir," Sam answered; "do' wantu, an' can't," which statement the subdued mien of the ancient and clumsy animals seemed to verify. So a bargain was made with the sawyer for their keep, and Uncle Tyler being now present, bestowing a slow, senile, lop-jawed stare impartially on each of the newcomers, negotiations were entered into with him. "They wantu hire yer boat tu take 'em daown tu the san'bar," the miller shouted with great distinctness, "Your boat! san'bar!" yet louder and pointing to the scow drawn up among the willows, and then down the creek.

"Ooo-h!" said Uncle Tyler, slowly looking them over again. "Where'd ye say ye come from?"

"Hain't said," Sam answered.

"Stanstead? Why, that's way up beyund Canerdy line! Hoss thieves up there!" Uncle Tyler said severely, turning the focus of his dull stare on to the horses.

"We-live-up-tu-Danvis," Sam proclaimed with slow and loud distinctness.

"Ooo-h! Danby!" said Uncle Tyler, "'way saouth o' here—Quaker taown. Haow come ye t' come way up here? Hain't Quakers, be ye?"

"Dan-vis," Sam roared.

"Oh, ooo-h, yis! Danvis, yis, yis, over here," and the old man pointed vaguely eastward. Sam nodded assent. "Yis, yis, Danvis."

Arrangements were made with Uncle Tyler to take the most cumbersome of their baggage to the lake in his scow next morning, and accommodations for the night were found for the party at the miller's house. The remainder of the day was passed by them in comfortable lounging about the neighborhood of the mills, watching the boys catching rock bass at the foot of the rapids, themselves taking a hand occasionally in the sport of capturing these vigorous biters, and in informing themselves concerning a desirable camping ground, and the best places for fishing.

Uncle Tyler's appointed hour of departure, "arter breakfus," came in good time, and the party was afloat not long after sunrise. Sam and Antoine led the flotilla in the birch and dugout, which had been transported from Danvis on their wagon, and Uncle Tyler, Solon, and Joseph were captain and crew of the scow. The old man steered with a paddle, and struggled with his latest borrowed pipeful of damp plug tobacco, while each of the others manned an oar and wrestled desperately with it, for rowing was a new and painful experience for them. Now they "caught crabs," and now they dug the bottom with the oar blades, bringing up on them specimens of aquatic plants that would have rejoiced the heart of a botanist; and they bumped their noses and their knees with the handles, while the splashing of the water, the creaking and thumping of the clumsy oars, and the grunting and puffing of the rowers, intermingled with the directions of the helmsman, delivered in the loud, unmodulated tone that deaf persons are apt to use, made a confusion of sounds most wonderful to hear. If the ancient mariner laid aside his paddle for a moment to give his pipe its often-needed lighting, Solon's oar was sure to be midway in or at the beginning of a stroke, while Joseph's blade was pointing at some quarter of the heavens between the zenith and the horizon, and presently the scow was headed for the shore, her bottom brushing over the young rushes and sedges of the marsh. "For massy's sake! didn't nary one on ye never have a holt of a noar afore?" he would shout, as with lateral sweeps of his paddle he got the boat upon her course again. "Don't dip so deep! Keep the blades o' yer oars jest onderneath the water—but ye got tu stick 'em in the water! ye can't row in the air!" as one of them skinned the surface with his blade. "Oh, for massy's sake! can't ye hear nothin', er can't ye onderstan' nothin'? Gimme a holt o' them oars, an' git aout o' that mighty quick!" crawling over the baggage toward them. "Lay daown—er git aout an' go afoot! I don't keer a dum mite which! Ketch me a-goin' a-bwutin' agin along o' a passel o' idjits 'at do' know a noar f'm a pudd'n' stick! Ye can't row a bwut no more'n a goose c'n gobble!"

One bestowed himself in the bow, the other in the stern, while the old man, as speechless with wrath as they were with mortification, sent the boat forward with long, even strokes that made the water surge under her broad bow. The young lily pads danced madly on the waves of her wake, and the little whirlpools that spun away from the oars twisted into tangles the slender new leaves of wild rice and engulfed fleets of water beetles.

The commotion on board the larger craft had caused Sam and Antoine to cease paddling and wait to ascertain the cause.

"What hail dat hol' can' hear not'ing man?" Antoine asked as they looked back. "He'll don't goin' t'row Solem an' Zhozeff board over, ant it? Oh, bah gosh! Ah'll bet you head Ah'll know what was de matter be! Dey'll can't roar!"

"Wal, by the gret horn spoon! I sh'd think by the saound 'at he c'ld roar 'nough for the hull three on 'em!" said Sam, as the steady rumble of Uncle Tyler's angry bawling came over the water.

"Oh, Ah'll ant meant roar, a nowse! Ah'll meant r-r-roar dat hol' boats wid r-roar! Ant you'll on'stan', hein? Ah'll ant never see langwizhe lak Angleesh, me!"

"Wal, Antwine, I never did nuther—not as you speak it." The scow seemed to be making fair progress now, and they went on their way.

When the two canoes came to where the tributary East Slang somewhat widened the slow current of Little Otter, Sam pointed with his paddle to the low cape, now green with water maples in full leaf, even now standing ankledeep in the still brown water, whose weedy surface dully reflected their greenness and graceful ramage and the flash of the starlings' wings that flitted among them. "Up there, Antwine, is where we camped last spring, an' hed fun. I wonder haow it looks naow 'at summer's come, if the shanty 's standin', an' whether that 'ere little squirrel sets there a-chitterreein' on that hemlock yit? Dum'd 'f I don't gwup an' see haow it looks some day; lunsomer 'an it did then, I guess."

The scow having now drawn near, they passed on together toward the lake. "I was a-cal'latin'," Uncle Tyler said, addressing the fleet in general, but particularly his crew, "for ter troll some comin' 'long, but you be so okkerd! I got a rig there an' posserbly you might hang on to 't so 's t' snag a pickril," and reaching before him he took up a short pole with many crooks in it for its length whereon was wound a stout line which had a hook baited with a piece of pork rind and a strip of red flannel. While he kept the boat slowly moving he unwound thirty feet or so of the line, and handing the pole to Joseph went on at a leisurely stroke. "The' hain't no better trollin' graound in the hull crik 'an the' is atwixt the tew Slangs," he said, and as they neared the mouth of the South Slang Joseph returned jerk for jerk on the trailing line with a grunt thrown in. "What be I a-goin' t' du naow?" he asked in dire perplexity, though he set his teeth and held to the bending pole with a will; "I can't get him 'thin twenty foot on us wi' this dum'd little short pole."

"Gim me a holt on 't!" said Uncle Tyler, dropping his oars and rising to the occasion. Laying hold of the pole he drew the tip far behind him, and grasping the line hauled it in hand over hand with deliberate celerity, till the wide-mouthed pickerel came gaping alongside and was lifted on board by the hook, forgetting to resent his injuries till he dropped on the bottom of the scow, which he then belabored with strokes of his tail, while he snapped his ugly jaws. He was a slab-sided fellow, whose six pounds of weight were spanned by two feet and a half of length, but he was admired as a beautiful monster by Solon and Joseph, and almost as much by Sam and Antoine, who came alongside to look at him.

"Massy sake!" cried Uncle Tyler in wondering pity, "It does beat all natur' haow you folks does vally these 'ere goo'-for-nothin' pickril! I'd a gre' deal druther have a neel. Wait till ye git aholt of a fo' fi' paound pike, an' then you have a fish 'at's wuth a-havin'! Pickril!"

Now they were on the last reach of the channel, bending here in a long curve through the "wide ma'sh," as Uncle Tyler informed them this portion of the stream was called. Through the willowy gateway of the creek's mouth they could see the lake, the "Bay of the Vessels," with Garden Island, green and white with leaves and blossoms, set like a nosegay on its shining bosom, clasped in the rocky arm of Thompson's Point. They soon passed the "Slab Hole," a great drift of flood wood lying along the western shore, and presently landed.

The pickerel was dressed and fried for dinner, and even Uncle Tyler, despite his unfavorable opinion of pickerel, made way with a generous portion of it. The old man was paid for his services, and made preparations for his homeward voyage. He pushed his craft afloat and embarked.

They had not finished pitching the tent before they were assailed by swarms of hungry mosquitoes, the constant warfare with which left them little time for peaceable labor, and soon made it apparent that there was no comfort nor rest for them in this place. Sam and Antoine made their way to the top of the rocky bluff, and finding their persecutors much less numerous, the tent and camp equipments were carried thither and their temporary home established among the cedars. Northerly winds from the lake and southerly winds from the cleared fields landward swept their winged enemies away and filled the air with balsamic fragrance that reminded them of Danvis woods, and through the green masses of cedar boughs and meshes of trunks and branches they caught glimpses of the blue lake crinkled with gold and silver waves. The thin soil and the rocks were spread with a soft carpet and cushions of fallen cedar leaves and moss set in various patterns of russet and green, and about the bases of the rocks were springing the young shoots of mountain fringe, ready to overrun them with a graceful invasion of vine and flower.

"Ah'll tol' you, boy!" cried Antoine, looking with admiration on the carpeting of the tent floor, just finished with his last armful of cedar twigs, "'f he ant mek you felt sleepy for jes' look at dat beds! Oh, 'f we ant took comfor' here! An' don't dat neat fireplaces you'll buil' dar?" inspecting the result of the others' labors—a broad fireplace built of flat ledge stones. "Jes' as handle as stofe was; yas, seh, more handle, 'cause you'll don't got for hopen no door for put hwood, an' you'll don't got for took off no gribble for brile you pot of it! Dat mek it all de hwomans in Danvit cry 'f he'll see it!"

Then they set about spending the day in accordance with the chief purpose of the expedition. Sam fitted up a trolling rig after the approved pattern of Uncle Tyler's, a bit of his flannel shirt furnishing the red rag unprovided by their kit, and trolled up and down the creek in the bark canoe. Antoine made a rude spear of a cedar pole and sharpened nails and prowled along the low shore of the creek in quest of spawning fish, while Solon and Joseph, unwilling to trust themselves in birch and dugout, wandered westward along the safe and stable shore of the bay.

Explorations

Solon and Joseph fished off the rocks when they came to eligible places, and caught a few perch and rock bass, while they continually feasted their eyes with the wonderful sight of the lake, so immense a body of water that, it seemed to them, it gave a fair idea of the immensity of the ocean. This was more impressed upon them when they had strolled to Bluff Point, and looking beyond the promontory of Thompson's Point, saw the blue lake and the blue sky meet far to the northward, with bluer dots of distant islands hung between them, and the white wings of sloops whose hulls were beyond the horizon. And there was the tall white tower of Split Rock Lighthouse, newly built, and now a pillar of cloud by day, a star by night to warn mariners off its perilous rocks, and giving these mountaineers a vivid realization of the dangers besetting those who go down to the sea in ships: perils and dangers that the waves seemed always whispering of as they hungrily lapped the rocks and chuckled wickedly in the water-worn caverns. By and by they saw a smoke arising from the watery horizon, and after it a speck, which at last grew till it became a steamboat, a leviathan which soon wallowed ponderously past, close to the farther shore, its gay flags and pennons flaunting bravely against the shadowed steeps of Split Rock Mountain, a wake of foam following the roaring paddle wheels. Some time after the majestic apparition had vanished behind the promontories to the west of them, the waves of its wake came in, beating the rocky shore with slow, sullen surges, like baffled foes retreating from the path of a conqueror. Strange woods set afloat far away came tossing ashore to the windrow of wave-worn logs, slabs, chips, and bits of painted boats that lined the shores. An old shoe suggested thoughts of drowned men, and white-winged gulls hovered like spirits over the distant waves. It was all very new, and strange, and mysterious. These two anglers bore back to camp but few visible trophies, when in the afternoon they followed thither their shadows, elusive guides that were now distinctly seen leading the way across broad patches of clean forest floor, now dancing in vague outline and confused dismemberment on tree trunks and low branches, and now disappearing in a throng of other shadows or a mass of shade. But the sights they had seen better repaid the time and travel spent than much bigger strings of fish than they carried would have done, and they were content.

Antoine prowled along the shore from the Slab Hole to the South Slang and to the rotting and displaced abutment of the old bridge that had just given up the weary task of spanning so much marsh and so little channel. He transfixed many unlucky bullpouts wriggling slowly in and out of their spawning holes, and transferred them with great satisfaction from his rude spear to his string of elm bark: battle-scarred amazons, torn and stabbed by the horns of other amazons, and lean fathers of the race of bullpouts, as scarred and wounded as their war-like wives. To the Canadian a bullpout was a bullpout, to be taken at any time, by any means, and without regard to its condition. If he ever thought, as doubtless he never did, how the continuation of his most prized fish depended on procreation, doubtless he would not care, for what Canuck ever did? Apparently it is their belief that fish were created solely for them, and belong to them alone, and that they have a right to take in any manner, as they will if they can, the last one today, though there should be no fish for any one forever after.

As Sam with noiseless strokes paddled his canoe up the great bow of the channel where it winds through the lower end of the "wide ma'sh" and slowly trailed his lure of pork rind and red flannel along the border, marked by purple young lily pads, unwittingly he crossed it, and a grating succession of tugs at his hook reminded him that he had been too contemplative in his recreation and had gone astray into the shallow and weedy false channel that runs straight lakeward from near the mouth of the South Slang. He hauled in his line, cleaned his hook of its burden of weeds, and retraced his way to the true channel, which having regained, he paid more attention to his course, and was presently rewarded by a sturdy tug that had in it the unmistakable viciousness of a pickerel's bite. Yet as he hauled in the line, hand over hand, the resistance was so sullen and sluggish that he was half-inclined to think he was drawing in only another raft of weeds, till he saw the gaping jaws splitting the surface. He soon had a lusty pickerel boated who, beginning his fight too late to avail aught but annoyance of his captor, hammered the cedar lining of the canoe and snapped his jaws wickedly till he was knocked in the head with the paddle.

A little later the trolling bait was nibbled and then seized by a fish that proved to be of nobler metal. Swimming deep, he fought every inch of his unwilling way to the canoe, which when brought to he attempted to run under, but Sam foiled this device, got him alongside, and skillfully lifted and swung him aboard. He was of handsome form, and his small, firm-set scales were golden green on his sides and silver white on his belly. In every way he looked gamy and good, a fish created to afford both sport and toothsome food. Sam had never seen his like, but rightly guessed him to be the "pike," whose excellence Uncle Tyler had extolled.

He had fish enough now, and paddled or drifted anywhere, hearing and seeing many things of interest to such a simple lover of nature. From far and near in the green expanse of marsh came strange outcries, laughter, yells, and more subdued jargon, converse of unseen waterfowl, strange voices of birds who were strangers to him. He recognized the voices of some old acquaintances when occasionally a bittern boomed, and the blackbirds grated and gurgled out their notes, and when some old choir leader of the bullfrogs sang his short prelude and his brethren struck in and bellowed a grand chorus that made all the wooded shores resound. Once an old wood-duck convoyed her newly launched fleet of callow ducklings out of the rushes into the channel just before him, and then in sudden panic at sight of his larger craft took wing for cover of the woods, flying low and followed almost as swiftly by her brood, simulating flight with ineffectual plumeless wings, but actually making their way by running like water sprites over the water after her. Now and then a dusky duck would splash out of the weeds with a loud alarm of quacking, but her young always kept out of sight if they had yet ventured so far as the channel's edge from their birthplace. There were no signs of Sam's last spring's dear enemies, the muskrats, but the floating crumbs of their midnight feast, chips of the water-lily roots, and shreds of aquatic weeds. Their winter huts had all been swept away by the high water of spring, and only shapeless rafts of rubbish grounded here and there among the rushes were left to show how industriously these little water folk had builded but a few months ago. Their homes were now in burrows in the banks, the occupancy of which was seldom indicated in daytime but by the roiling of the watery entrance or the sluggish underwater wake of a silent incomer or outgoer.

Great blue herons sentineled the shallows, or fanned their slow way from one to another, and now and then a bittern made a startled, ungainly flight from the densest beds of rushes, while kingfishers scolded and clattered along their jerky course or hung over minnow-haunted shoals as if suspended by invisible threads, which presently were severed and let them fall into the brown water with a splashing upburst of spray. The scraggy tangles of button bushes were noisy and flashing with innumerable nesting redwings, sunfish and perch were incessantly snapping at the various insects resting on or hovering about the water plants, and great fish surged through the rushes in pursuit of prey or in swift retreat from the boat. The marshes were busy with the life of their thronging tenants in the happy summers of those days. Alas, that now they are so silent and deserted!

Over the tops of the rushes Sam caught occasional glimpses of Antoine stealing along the shore in his nefarious bullpout prodding, and mildly "dum'd him" in soliloquy "for a wus'n half Injin." In the afternoon he paddled to the mouth of the creek, and after looking at the dancing waves of the sunlit bay clasped in the arms of the green-clad June shores, and watching the majestic sweep of an eagle wheeling above the cliffs, he beached his canoe on the rushy shore of the landing and took his fare of fish to camp, whither his companions soon came. At nightfall they had their bountiful supper of fish, and then as they smoked their pipes about the dying embers each told the story of his day's outing.

Next morning, directly after an early breakfast, Antoine, with Solon and Joseph, set out; meanwhile Sam kept camp for an hour or two, and then went out for a little trip on the bay, cruising across the shallow water of the northeast shore to the mouth of Lewis Creek, which till now he had not seen. Its beauty invited him upstream, and when at the first bend he turned and looked forth upon the lake, through the noble colonnade of ancient water maples and buttonwoods to the grim, unshorn steeps of Split Rock Mountain, beyond the broad expanse of water without a craft in sight upon it or any sign of human presence anywhere, he fancied that he felt something of the sense of complete isolation from all his fellows that the first white voyagers here must have experienced. But in those old days one could not have been so sure of having it safely to himself, as Sam was reminded by the sight of a flint arrowhead on a mud bank among the rushes. For many years after his visit to it this part of Sungah-netuk retained its primitive character, and was a place where one might easily imagine himself set back a couple of centuries to the times when New England was indeed new, when Petowbowk was the warpath of sav-age and civilized nations, and knew not the peaceful keel of commerce.

Across the sunny blue sky drifted only silver shreds of clouds, too thin to cast a shadow on the sunlit marshes and shores and quiet waters; through the rushy level the marsh wrens discordantly rejoiced over the building of their cunning nests; in the woods the wood and hermit thrushes rang silver bells and breathed celestial flute notes, and the jangle of a thousand bobolinks came from the meadows.

Pelatiah's Life in the Lowlands

Soon after his visit to Sam and Antoine at their trapping camp, Pelatiah had returned to Lakefield and taken service for the season with Friend Bartlett. The smiles of the pretty hired girl, the memory of which had almost as great a share as the wages offered in luring him from his moun-tain home, had thus far continued to brighten his life and make his faith-ful toil light, since it was rewarded morning, noon, and night by the sight of the face that had become to him the most beautiful, by the sound of the voice that was the sweetest in all the world.

One Sunday morning in June the peace and quietness of the day seemed to have reached their fullness in and about the Quaker home-stead. Pelatiah sat whittling on the platform of the well with his back against the pump, just breathing "Old Hundred" through his puckered lips. Near him stood the fat and sedate old horse which he had just har-nessed to the "shay," and by his side lay the fat old dog, who, in sem-blance of sleep, was waiting to accompany his master and mistress to meeting. He could hear hardly a sound coming from the open doors and windows of the house. The buzz of a bumblebee imprisoned by the raised sash of the kitchen window was loud enough to well-nigh drown the almost noiseless footsteps of Friend Rebecca Bartlett as she moved to and fro in preparation for departure, though occasionally above these was heard the cautious, long-drawn clearing of Friend John Bartlett's throat, accomplished with care that it should be thoroughly though not too loudly done, partly as practice for the same performance during the stillness of meeting, and partly as a reminder to his wife that he was waiting for her. The hens in the dooryard clucked and crated in subdued tones, and the old red rooster, though his gay feathers were sadly "out of plainness," kept as decorously "in the quiet" as if he was a member of his owner's sect. Two or three frivolous swallows twittered and swooped in pursuit of floating feathers, but the great body of the tenants of the eaves were holding a silent meeting on the barn roof. The bobolinks in the meadow, beyond the influence of the First Day atmosphere of the staid homestead, withheld not a note of their merry songs, meant, perhaps, only for world's people and naughty strawberry pickers, but the robins in the apple trees were as voiceless as the unstirred leaves, and the catbird skulked in silence along the row of currant bushes. Pelatiah wondered if the pump would utter its usual discordant shriek, and was almost tempted to raise the handle. Then through forgetfulness or impatience he whistled aloud a few notes of the old Psalm tune, and Rebecca came to the door tying the strings of her "sugar scoop" bonnet.

"Peltiah," she said in a mildly severe tone, "thee needn't whistle for Bose, he's right there by thee! Thee may bring up the horse now."

While Pelatiah pocketed his knife and arose, brushing the shavings from his trousers, she went back to free the bumblebee from its glass prison, brushing it down the lowered sash with a folded handkerchief which exhaled the faint odor of dried rose leaves. "Now, get off with thee, thee foolish thing!" she said, as the bee blundered away into its regained paradise of outdoor June.

The chaise lumbered up to the horse block, and the good couple got on board, Bose soberly wagging his tail as he superintended their embarkation.

"Don't thee think thee'd better go to meeting, Peltiah?" Rebecca asked, getting the young man within the narrow range of her deep bonnet. She asked him this question every First Day morning, and was regularly answered, "Wal, no, marm, I guess not this mornin'."

They slowly got under way, and when they were out of earshot of the hired man, Rebecca remarked: "Peltiah seems like a steady young man, but it is a pity he isn't more seriously inclined."

"He's a master hand with a hoe," her husband said, looking down the even rows of his young corn, where not a weed was to be seen among the green sprouts that regularly dotted the mellow soil, "and I do' know as I ever see a better milker."

Pelatiah was anticipating a day of perfect happiness, for the girl, whose name was spelled Louisa and pronounced Lowizy, had as good as asked him to go to the woods with her for young wintergreens. That morning when he brought in the milk and they were alone in the cheese room, she had said there were "lots of 'em up in the maounting"—the rocky hill which Lakefield folk honored with that name, for a mountain they must have, and this of all the hills in town came nearest being one— "lots an' sacks of 'em, an' anybody might git a snag of 'em if they was to go up there naow. She wish't she had some, but she dasn't go alone, for she knew she should git lost, an' th' was an ugly toro in Austin's pastur'." Pelatiah felt that he would brave all the bulls in Lakefield to gather a handful of aromatic leaves for her, but he had not the courage to tell her so, and only said he would get them for her if he knew where to find them. Whereupon she giggled and said that she would go and show him where they grew, and that then, if there was time enough and she could "stan' it," they might go to the Pinnacle, where they "could see all creation an' part o' York State." So it seemed settled that when chores were done and the old folks had gone to meeting, they should go "a-browsin'," as Pelatiah inelegantly termed it.

Now he was waiting for her, while he conned gallant phrases and neat compliments, and thought just how he would tell her that he "liked" her. How easy it all was now, as he rehearsed it to his heart, but he knew that opportunity would frighten away all utterance, and he reviled himself for a bashful booby. Yet he felt himself brave enough in the face of real danger, and if the terrible bull that kept all the berry pickers out of Austin's pasture would but attack them he would show his devotion, how he would defend her even at the cost of his life. If the bull was put to flight then she would faint, as in such cases young ladies always did in the stories he read, and he would bear her in his arms to the nearest brook and bathe her face till he brought her out of her swoon. He had never carried a young lady in his arms; Lowizy was a buxom maiden, no light weight certainly, but he thought he could manage such a precious burden, though it would be more easily done if she could be induced to ride pickaback, which, however, would not be in accordance with the established usage of the stories. When she was restored to consciousness, opened her eyes and saw him bending over her, what if he could not help pressing his lips to her pale cheek? He blushed to think of it, and wondered if she would ever forgive him. If he should be badly hurt, who but she would nurse him; and if he died how could she help but grieve for him? The thought of it almost made him shed a tear for himself. But then it was very likely that the bull was a harmless bugbear whose viciousness was an invention of the owner of the field, and would give Pelatiah no chance of heroic deeds. So he drifted back to imaginary commonplace opportunities, till Lowizy came to the door more bewitching than ever, in a pink calico dress and a white apron with two little pockets stuck upon it like swallows' nests made of snow, useless but pretty.

Just then a young fellow, seated in a square-boxed wagon of amazing height, drove up at a pace which seemed reckless, considering how far above the ground he was perched; and as recklessly he sprang down to the ground, endangering the straps of his trousers, the long swallow tails of his blue coat streaming upward and the brass buttons flashing. He drew near to Lowizy, who greeted him too warmly and with too great a display of her best manners, Pelatiah thought, as he stood aloof glowering at the new-comer, while the two conversed earnestly, though in a tone too low for any word to reach his ear. Then she ran into the house; and Pelatiah's heart grew sick with a foreboding of disappointment. He tried to whistle in token of indifference, but his sullen pout wouldn't be utilized as a pucker, and though defiant and attempting to fortify himself with the inward assurance that he was as good as the finest dandy of the lowlands, he could not help feeling mean and awkward as he contrasted his suit of sheep's gray, new though it was, and as much too long for him as all former clothes had been too short, with the gay and fashionable apparel of his till now unsuspected rival. It was exasperating to see the fellow take out a cigar, and having decided which end to light, begin to puff it; and then with his thumbs in the arm-holes of his waistcoat strut back and forth beside the wagon. "Tew high an' mighty tu take a noticte on me, hain't ye? For all, the top o' your plegged shiny hat hain't so high as the seat o' yer wagon box!" Pelatiah inwardly addressed him. "Oh! you're a gol buster, hain't ye? I'll bate a cooky I c'ld heave ye ov' the top o' yer dum'd ol' waggin!"

All unconscious of such disparagement and of everything but the fine figure he must be making, the rustic little dandy strutted in his pride till Lowizy reappeared with some new finery added to her attire and a useless little parasol in her hand. When he had gallantly assisted her to scale the steps of the wagon and the "boost," as Pelatiah to himself termed the feat, had been accomplished, he climbed in. Not till the fine equipage began to turn in perilous haste did Lowizy bestow a word or glance on Pelatiah. Then as she spread her parasol she looked back, and said: "Mr. Gove, when the folks return, tell 'em that my maw is quite sick an' I've got to go hum—ahem—go home an' see her."

"I guess her maw hain't turrible bad off," Pelatiah said bitterly, when a few moments later he heard her laugh ringing down the road as merry and carefree as the song of the bobolinks. So sick at heart that his knees were weak, he leaned on the door-yard fence and watched them out of sight. So the stories he had read of the fickleness of women were not fictions, but simple truth, were they? It was hard to learn it by actual experience, hard to lose the simple faith that all things are as they seem, that affection may be no more than an outward show, and kind words have no meaning. His honest heart was so sorely hurt that the counter-irritant of anger could not cure it now; there was no present cure for it, but he bethought him that there might be a balm for it in the sanctuary of the woods, to which he had often fled when assailed by lesser ills. He would not go to that contemptible little mountain of Lakefield, to be continually reminded there of the happy hours he had been cheated of, but to the great woods westward, deep and dark enough to hide him from the false, hateful, wicked world.

He cast the unaccustomed summer burden of his thick sheep's gray coat on the nearest plum tree of the dooryard, and in the regained freedom of shirt-sleeves felt his heart somewhat lighter as he pushed toward the Slang. On a fallen tree he crossed its narrow upper channel where the border of the green marsh was gay with the purple blossoms of flags, where a lonely heron stalked in fancied seclusion, and where a bittern, perhaps his last spring's acquaintance, startled him almost off his balanced foothold, with her affrighted squawk and sudden uprising to her labored flight.

Breasting the undergrowth of the bank, he was soon in the midday twilight of the ancient forest, where brooded a solemnity greater than within any temple built by hands, a silence deepened rather than broken by the summer note of a chickadee, the chimes of a woodthrush, and the sigh of the unfelt breeze in the tops of the great pines and hemlocks.

Pelatiah took his way along an old lumber road, where sled tracks and footprints of oxen, made in the latest of last spring's sledding, were almost overgrown with forest herbage, and every mossy cradle knoll was starred with the white flowers of dwarf cornel or glowed with the blood-red drops of the partridge berry.

It made his recent wound twinge again when he came upon a patch of wintergreen, the "young-come-ups" showing the tender tints of the first unfolded leaves among the rusty and dark-green leaves and plump crimson berries of the old plants. What happy moments he had thought to spend gathering the freshest and tenderest for the girl who had so cruelly forsaken him. He could not taste nor touch one now, and was sure he never could again, for even the sight of them made him sick.

On either side of the way stood old friends to welcome him—great hemlocks, maples, whose sweets only the Indians and squirrels had tasted, poplars shivering with the memory of a century's winters, towering elms and bass-woods, and all the graceful birches. He saw also a few great pines which had thus far escaped the lumberman, hickories with sharded trunks, and noble white oaks, all strangers to him in the woods of Danvis; but he missed his familiars, the spruce and balsam firs, their songs and the odor of their breath. A shrewish jay came to scold him, a squirrel to scoff at him, a shy wood bird, some constant dweller in the forest's heart, flitted near and watched him with timid curiosity; a mother partridge made a fluttering pother almost at his feet, while her callow brood dispersed like a sudden spatter of fluffy yellow balls and magically disappeared.

With no purpose of reaching any particular point he wandered on, holding his way along the dim woodland aisle till it led where sunlight and blue sky shone from the outer world through the green-gold leaves and netted branches of the marsh's palisade of water maples.

Passing under these he saw the creek, the bold bluff at its mouth, and beyond a broad blue strip of the lake. When his eyes became used to the sunshine he saw figures moving beneath the bluff on the farther shore, and heard voices that somehow seemed familiar. There was no mistaking Sam Lovel's voice when presently he loudly called Antoine's name, nor the Canadian's when he answered.

Pelatiah hastily mounted a huge fallen tree that reached well out into the marsh, and shouted lustily, "Hello, Sam! Antwine! whoop! Come over here. It's me, Peltier."

The figures became motionless in attention, then drew together in brief consultation, then one detached itself from the group, a paddle banged against a boat's side, a canoe drew out from the landing, came swiftly up the channel and swished into the wide marsh in front of him.

"I never was so glad tu see anybody in all this everlastin' world," said the heartsick and homesick big boy as his friend Sam stepped on shore and shook hands with him. "Of all folks I never hed no thought o' seein' you, an' me on'y shoolin' 'raound in the woods jest tu kill time."

"Wal, Peltier, haow be you gittin' along? Like your place?" Sam asked, seating himself on a log and making ready for a smoke, deferred since he left the camp landing.

"Wal, yes," Pelatiah said, slowly considering his answer, "yes, I hev liked it fustrate."

"Hev liked it? You hain't hed no fallin' aout wi' the folks, I hope."

"No, not no fallin' aout wi' them. Do' know haow 't I could, for they're the cleverest folks in all creation."

"Wal, that pretty gal hain't gigged back on ye?"

No answer but a look of woebegone sheepishness.

"Oh, shaw, Peltier, nev' mind a gal's tantrums. You an' her 'll be thicker 'n tew hands in a mitten, t' rights."

"No, sir! not never no more!" Pelatiah replied with spirit. "I won't stan' bein' fooled by nob'ddy, if they be harnsome."

"My!" said Sam, "she was harnsome as a pictur!" and then, doubtful whether he was quite loyal to Huldah in such admiration of another, qualified it by adding, "but the's them 'ats jist as harnsome."

"If she's harnsome as a pictur, she's decaitful as a snake, an' I won't stan' bein' fooled!"

"Oh, yes, you will, Peltier! They'll fool a feller agin an' agin till he gits so's 'at he likes bein' fooled. She's jest begun on you an' you hain't got use to 't, but you will, see 'f you don't. But come, le's go over an' see the rest on 'em. They ben a-talkin' an' surmisin' baout you all the mornin'. Come, I'll git you 'raound by kyow time." And Sam, leading the way to the canoe, shoved it afloat and stepped in.

Pelatiah took his place and was surprised at the little trepidation he felt on finding himself fairly embarked on the broad channel.

"Why, Peltier, you keep the tarve o' the canew lots better'n you did last spring," Sam said, approvingly. "Guess you ben a-practizin', hain't ye?"

"Hain't ben in a boat sence," Pelatiah said. "Guess it's 'cause I don't care 'f I be draounded."

"Oh, shaw, Peltier! 'F you was tu git spilt aout you'd claw for shore an' holler like a loon. Folks 'at's got your ail is allus a-wantin' tu die, but they enj'y dyin' so much 'at they hain't in no hurry tu hev the job finished up. You'll wanter live forever when you git t' eatin' the fish Antwine's a-cookin'. Pike an' pick'ril 'at 'ould make a man's maouth water tu see, though the's more fun for me in the ketchin' 'an in the eatin'. But I du eat 'em to make a good excuse fur ketchin' more."

Pelatiah was warmly welcomed by his friends, and almost forgot his misery while he listened to the news they told of folks and affairs at Danvis. The fish were as good as freshly caught and nicely cooked fish could be. When they had eaten he was taken along the bluff to see something of the wonders and beauty of the lake, which impressed him even more than they had Solon and Joseph.

Antoine, with the air of its chief proprietor, expatiated on the immensity of its waters and its commerce, but more on the numbers, variety, and excellence of its fish.

"More as t'ree honded tousan of it, prob'ly, an' all de kan dat ever was hear of it, 'cep' whale an' dry codfeesh, Ah guess. Ah'll lak dat lake, me, 'cause he'll gat so much feesh, an' 'cause one en' of it steek raght in Canada! Yes, sah! wen nort' win' blow he'll breeng wave from Canada, where Ah'll was baun, w'en Ah'll was leetly boy, where Ah'll married my Ursule an' where Ah'll faght w'en Ah'll growed up for be hugly!"

They urged Pelatiah to get a day off during their stay and spend it with them, which he promised to do, if possible, even though it cost him the glories of the Fourth of July at Vergennes.

In good season to get him home by chore time, Sam embarked with him in the log canoe and paddled up stream and into the East Slang. Such a change had summer wrought here that he hardly recognized the scene of last spring's exploits. Where then the wide water stretched from shore to shore, was now a green, rushy level, divided only by a narrow channel that crept with many turns on its sluggish way to the creek as if any other course or none at all might as well be taken. The scraggy clumps of button bushes were now green islands in the marsh and populous with gay and noisy communities of redwings. The western shore bristling with naked branches when he last had seen it, now was softly rounded with all the luxuriant leafage June could give it, and the old camp was just discernible embowered in leaves and shadows. A narrow boat path leading to it and a clumsy log canoe drawn ashore there showed that the landing was yet in use.

Pelatiah was set on shore farther up stream on the east bank at an open place to which he guided Sam, informing him that it was known as the "John Clark place," and was a famous resort for bullpout fishing in May. Here it was agreed that Sam should meet him next morning, if the hoped-for day's leave of absence were obtained, and then he went his way and was soon heard "whaying" the cows home.

On his return voyage, Sam ran in at the landing, from which he noticed that a well-trodden path led away into the woods. Though the place showed disuse and wore the changes wrought by the season, the greenness and bloom of early summer where so lately had been the brown and naked gray of early spring, there was much to remind him of the pleasant weeks he had spent there. There were whitened piles of muskrat bones, picked clean by many a big and little scavenger of the woods, cast-away stretchers and tally sticks, scales, and mummied heads of fish, and Antoine's old fish poles. There were sticks of leftover firewood close by the ashes and brands of the last campfire. The shanty kept its form, though the slabs were losing the fresh hue of newly rifted wood. The bedding of straw had grown musty and was pierced with pale sprouts of such unthreshed kernels of grain as its latest tenantry of wood mice had spared.

While Sam sat smoking a meditative pipe, his old acquaintance, the squirrel, became aware of his presence and gave him a characteristic welcome, snickering and jeering and making such an ado that his wife and children came to learn the cause of it.

"Hain't ye 'shamed to be sassin' your better afore your young uns?" Sam addressed the bright-eyed native, "but I d'know 's I be your better, an' I'm glad to see ye fur all your sass."

Then he pushed off in his canoe and went his way homeward. Night was falling. The channel was strangely widened in the uncertain light; its marshy borders far away vague and mysterious among the brooding shadows of the wooded shores, and the reflection of the first eastern star danced along his wake before he reached the landing.

Garden Island

The camp was astir early next morning, and Sam was glad to find Pelatiah waiting at the "John Clark place," his unhappiness somewhat lessened by the prospect of a day's outing. Sam had had the forethought to bring trolling tackle along, and as they fared slowly down stream Pelatiah trailed the lure along the border of lily pads.

He struck a large pickerel, and had the luck, in spite of his flurried awkwardness, to get it safely into the dugout, and rejoiced exceedingly in its capture and in Sam's praise of his skill, as well as in anticipation of the display of such a trophy on his return to Friend Bartlett's. He would like, he thought, to see that little dandy spark of Lowizy's struggling with such a fish, almost as big as he, and as likely to haul him overboard as to be hauled inboard. Was it possible that Lowizy might feel a sympathetic pride in his achievement? He had fancied that his heart was steeled against her blandishments, some of which had been vainly expended on him last evening, succeeded by an air of injured innocence that proved as ineffectual. But now he began to feel a forgiving softness and some twinges of remorse. He began to frame excuses for her conduct, and accused himself of cruelty in answering her in monosyllables, and for not having filled the washboiler for her before he came away. Sam dispelled this silent mood by proposing plans for the spending of the day. "I ben kinder wantin' tu go aout tu Gardin' Islan' ever sen we ben here," he said as he sent the canoe on her way with slow strokes of the paddle, never changed from side to side, but steadily delivered on one side without a perceptible deviation of the bow from its direct course.

"The bay's as still as a mill-pawnd tu-day, an' s'posin' you 'n' me take a v'yage aout there? We c'n git back afore noon an' then fish 'long wi' Sole an' Joe till it's time for you tu go hum."

The prospect of voyaging more than half a mile out into the immensity of the lake was rather appalling to Pelatiah, but his faith in Sam was unbounded, and the prospect of setting foot on a real solid island was as alluring as an adventure of discovery, and so after a little deliberation he fell in with the proposal.

Arriving at camp, the plan was broached to Solon and Joseph, who at once declared that they had no inclination for so perilous a voyage.

"It's still 'nough naow," said Joseph after a careful inspection of the cloudless sky, "but the's time 'nough for it tu up an' blow like all git aout 'fore we c'ld git aout there and back agin."

Solon advised keeping to the shore or near it, and gave it as his opinion that the contemplated visit to the island was "an attemptin' of improvidence."

While Pelatiah tethered his precious pickerel safely in the shallow water, Sam got a lunch of bread and pork, some poles, lines, and bait from camp, and the two set forth.

While they were on the shallows, frequent touches of the paddle on the sandy bottom, assurances that connection with the solid earth was not yet severed, had given Pelatiah a feeling of safety. But now that the paddle could not touch the bottom, the clams and their slowly traced tracks faded out of sight in the deeper water, the ripples of sunshine no longer crinkled the sands with gold, and there was nothing but water to be seen beneath the boat save where some great rock dimly showed in the green depths, like an ugly monster lying in wait for a victim, he wished himself on land, and was glad enough when they grated on the rocky slant of the island's southern shore. He could hardly tell whether such isolation was quite pleasant, but it was a new and strange sensation to have this little patch of rock and scant soil all to himself and Sam, but for its few inhabitants, the birds and reptiles, mice and perhaps a family of minks, for they saw one gliding along the shore, as lithe and silent as a snake.

They made the round of all its borders, the sheer wall of the north shore, where storm-bent cedars and birches clung along the brink, and the long incline of rock on the south shore, where thickets of flowering shrubs made a breastwork of bloom just behind the line of driftwood and pebbles thrown up by the high water of spring. They explored the interior, where a goodly growth of almost all the deciduous trees of the region was unaccountably nourished in the thin red soil. They carved their names and the date of their visit on the largest white birch in characters which some later comer might possibly decipher. Then they fished off the eastern and western points of the island, catching perch whose armor of green and gold was darker and brighter than those of their brethren of the creek.

Once when Pelatiah cast his bait into a wide fissure of the submerged rocks it was seized in a sudden onset that reminded him of the biting of his familiars, the trout. But this was a lustier fellow than any denizen of Danvis' brooks, one that would not be jerked out overhead at the first stroke, but clung to the water tenaciously till, the line's length away, he broke the surface and sprang thrice his length above it, then regained his watery grasp almost as soon as the parted wavelets closed above his bristling dorsal fin. It was no exercise of skill, but only stout tackle and a strong pull that overcame him, yet Pelatiah was none the less exultant when at last he hauled his prize out on to the rocks and pounced sprawling upon him, as Sam said, "Julluk a boy ketchin' a frog."

"This must be a 'Swago, as they call 'em," he said when its captor ventured to quit hovering over the goodly three-pound bass, and gave him a chance to examine it.

After a while, when both had tired of trying to catch another bass, the pulsing rumble of a steamer's paddles was heard, and they hurried to the west point to see her pass.

So intently did he and his companion regard the steamer that it was not till she had passed out of sight and the waves of her wake began to beat the rocks at their feet with sullen surges that they noticed what a change had come upon the sky, how silvery domes of thunder heads had reared themselves above the mountains, shadowing some in a blue black as somber as the bases of the great cloud temples had become, till mountain and cloud were an undistinguishable, looming mass of blackness. The south wind which had risen from a scarcely perceptible waft of soft air to a breeze that ruffled the lake and briskly stirred the leaves was now hushed, and no sound was heard but the slow wash of the steamer's wake and some voices of shore life, faint, occasional, and far away. It was as if nature was holding her breath in expectation of some outburst of her elements, presently voiced by a threatening growl of distant thunder, rolling along the western horizon.

From the dark clouds a veil of rain had fallen, completely hiding the distant mountains and the farthest western shore, while it had begun to flatten the nearer crags of Split Rock into a sheer wall whose even tint of dull gray was broken only by the white shaft of the lighthouse and the dull flash of the waves which the coming wind hurled against the point of the rugged promontory. Beyond the advancing veil, whitecaps gleamed out of the obscurity, and out of it scudded a sloop with close-reefed sails and anchored in the shelter of Thompson's Point.

When the frequent flashes of lightning quivered down from the sky, it was as if the veil was torn with jagged rents that for an instant revealed a conflagration of the universe. Incessant peals of thunder rolled in repeated bursts and muttering growls, swelling, and dying in echoes from cloud, mountain, and headland, with a continuous undertone of the roar of wind and waves on distant woods and rock-bound shores. The wind, yet unfelt by the castaways, sent the hurrying clouds in a wide, majestic sweep across the sky till all the sunlit blue was blotted out and the landscape was overspread with a gloom more awful than the darkness of night, flashing into instants of distinctness when wind-swept waves, and clouds, and trees, for a pulse beat, stood still in the white fire of the lightning. Then cat's-paws ruffled the black, still waters near them, a brief patter of big drops fell like leaden plummets on water, rocks, and leaves, and then all at once the lake seethed at their feet, the lithe branches of the birches streamed to leeward of their bending trunks, and the sturdy cedars tossed in brief resistance as the long-driven slant of the storm burst upon them.

Sam and Pelatiah were drenched before they could reach the partial shelter of the nearest clump of cedars, which only broke the force of the wind, while every branch and twig seemed to become a conduit to pour, dribble, and drip down their backs and upon their knees, every raindrop the tree caught.

"I don't s'pose it's nothin' tu what they hed time o' the flood," said Sam, wiping his wet face with a wetter coat-sleeve, "but I du feel mor'n I ever did afore for the poor creeturs 'at was aouten the ark."

Through the loopholes of their poor shelter they could see nothing but the blown and pelted trees and rocky bounds of their island, and a little beyond these the seething, angry sweep of the waves, whose white crests and black furrows faded into the gray downpour and fleeting drift of the rain, and it was as if this patch of rocks and earth was all that was left to them of the stable world whose blue mountains, green woods and fields and sunlit waters an hour ago had shone about them. Then the fury of the wind abated somewhat, the rain hissed less angrily upon the hurrying waves, the torn clots of black clouds swept more slowly across the sky, grew more infrequent, then had all passed by; the nearest head-land was dimly revealed, vaguely defined shores reappeared and again clasped the bay, a distant field was lighted by a gleam of sunshine and shone through the vapor in golden green, the leaden hue of the waves turned to living blue and green, and as the last growl of the retreating storm was muttered among the eastern mountains, the sunlight came sweeping over all the landscape.

Sam and his companion crept from under their roof of dripping branches and stretched their cramped limbs in the genial warmth of the rekindled sunlight.

Sam comforted himself with a pipe, a solace which was denied Pelatiah, as was also the rumination of his cud, for which he vainly searched his pockets, remembering at last that he had given his only remaining piece of gum to the faithless Louisa. Far better, he thought, than if he had it, if she was now chewing it and was reminded by it of him. Would she feel any anxiety concerning him if he did not return that night, as it

now seemed probable he could not, and be sorry that she had been un-
kind? Or would she and all of them think that he was careless of his
word or had deliberately broken it?

"Wal, naow," said Sam, "I guess we'd better be pickin' up an' pullin'
foot for camp." And gathering their tackle and fish, they hastened to
where they had landed.

When Sam and Pelatiah reached the mainland, Solon and Joseph were
waiting to welcome their friends, undemonstratively, but heartily, and to
comfort them with that balm which we are ever ready to give but never
to receive—"I told you so."

The day was now too far spent for Pelatiah to get back to his evening
chores, so he was easily persuaded to wait for the supper for which some
hours of Crusoe life had given him a sharp appetite.

While Sam was making ready to transport Pelatiah on his homeward
way, Pelatiah proposed to cross the stream to that point with Sam and
make his way thence through the woods, thus saving his friend the long
voyage up the creek and Slang. Sam thought this inhospitable and a non-
fulfillment of his promise, but Pelatiah insisted that he had had quite
enough of boating for one day, and would much rather feel the solid
earth under his feet. So he went his way into the gathering twilight of
the woods.

Reconciliation

Pelatiah had not been brought up in the woods to be scared by owls,
as he more than once assured himself as he stumbled along the darkening wood road, half-carrying, half-trailing his big pickerel and
bass, but he fancied that their hollow hoots had never sounded so like
derisive laughter, "Ho! ho! ho! Ho! ho!—ho! ho!" repeated by one another till the echoes joined in the dolorous mirth. A whippoorwill, far
away on the border of the forest, was not insisting on the summary chas-
tisement of poor Will, but repeating this new culprit's name with sharp
reproachful reiteration, "Pel-a-tier, Pel-a-tier, Pel-a-tier!" The trill of a toad
rang in his ears like a long-drawn jeer, and the bellowing of the bull-

frogs along the Slang was shaped by his fancy into solemn words of rebuke, advice, and warning, "Didn't go hum! No, no! Go hum! Go hum!
Don't du it agin, agin, never agin!" Not a word of comfort for the poor
fellow among all these voices of the night, that followed him out of the
gloom of the woods, and, looking up to the sky, he saw the stars blinking
at him with unpitying eyes.

Shellhouse Mountain, which but yesterday he had despised as a hillock that would be but a pimple on the face of old Tater Hill, now uplifted
on a vague foundation of shadows and asserting itself as a bound of the
visible world, stood before him and frowned upon him like a dark,
scowling brow. The lights that dotted the highway went out one by one,
as the farm folks went to bed but a little later than their poultry. The
living world was forgetting him, or cared nothing for him, the good-for-
nothing fellow who had broken his word, and Bose was barking as if he
scented a stranger. Yet it heartened him a little when, prompted by his
faint shadow, he looked over his right shoulder and saw the thin crescent
of the new moon. In confirmation of this lucky sign, he presently discovered a light shining from an upper window of the big white house, Lowizy's window, he was sure, and, perhaps too anxious to sleep, she was
waiting for him. Yes, now he saw her form, a lovely silhouette set in the
frame of the casement. She was looking for him, and he was only restrained from calling to her for fear of arousing the household. He would
have ventured to whistle just once if his tremulous lips had not refused
to pucker. Then the silhouette faded to a shadow and the light was put
out. As he entered the dooryard Bose ceased barking and came whining
and panting to welcome him, and assure him that he had, at least, one
friend there, one who, following close at his heels, superintended the
hanging of the precious fish in the cool, safe corner of the woodshed. In
those happy times when tramps were unknown, farmhouse doors were
never fastened at night, and in summer were often left open, as Friend
Bartlett's kitchen door was now. So pulling off his boots at the threshold,
Pelatiah silently went in and made his way to his bed in the kitchen
chamber.

The blithe chorus of the robins had not long been ringing in the dewy
freshness of the early morning when Pelatiah was astir, an hour before
any other member of the family. First he cleaned the fish so nicely that
Antoine could have found no fault, and then he drove up the cows from
the night pasture. He was milking his second cow when Friend Bartlett
appeared with his pail and stool, and he was glad to see no shadow of

displeasure on his employer's kindly face, to detect no tone of reproof in his cheery voice when he addressed him.

"Well, Peltier, thee didn't get back quite so airly as thee expected, did thee? I didn't hardly think thee would, for when I was a boy an' uster go a-fishin', if they bit, I hated ter go off an' leave 'em, an' if they didn't bite, I wanted ter wait till they did."

"Oh, I'm awf'l sorry, Mr. Bartlett, an' shameder'n I c'n live, but I couldn't help it!" and he went on explaining his mischance, forgetting to milk old Spot till she thought he had done with her and moved on. When he went to the cheese-room with two filled pails, by some lucky chance, Lowizy was there, blushing like a June rose and never handsomer than now.

"O, Peltier!" she cried, coming toward him, radiant with a pleasure that surely could not be feigned, and so shone upon him that the last icy corner of his heart melted at once. "O, Peltier! I'm dreffle glad ter see ye! I was afeard 'at you was draownded an' I never slep' one wink all night a-thinkin' on't!"

"Would you ha' cared 'f I was draownded, Lowizy?" he asked, trembling so that his unsteady hands poured half the milk outside the strainer and a little on the floor.

"Don't ye slop!" she said, sharply, and then in a tenderer tone, "Don't ye think I would? But you never thought o' me onct a-worryin' while you was hevin' high jinks wi' your frien's!"

"I swan tu man!" swore Pelatiah, as he set down his last-emptied pail, "the' wa'n't a minute 'at I wa'n't a thinkin' 'baout you while I was a-fishin', an' when we was on a deserlate islan', an' a-wishin' 'at I hedn't ben cross an' 'at I'd filled the wash biler for ye. O, Lowizy, I was mean, an' I'm sorry, an' I won't never du so agin, an' I wish't you c'ld forgive me, but I don't s'pose you ever can."

She could not withhold forgiveness so humbly asked. She rushed to him with upturned face and put her arms astride his neck, one cream-bedaubed hand holding the dripping skimmer, the other the half-filled basin, and as the tins clashed behind his head he held her in his arms and kissed her.

"Peltier! Hey, Peltier! Bring back them pails!" Friend Bartlett shouted from the cowyard gate.

As the heavenward-soaring lark, pierced by the cruel shot of the gunner, falls fluttering down to earth, so at Friend Bartlett's impatient call Pelatiah dropped from the rose-tinted clouds whereunto in delicious affright he had been upborne, and went stumbling through the dooryard knot-grass, while a still, small voice repeated Sam's words, "They'll fool a feller agin an' agin." But his heart whispered that this could not be fooling, and then, as he sat down to his cow, sang inwardly to him this sweet assurance, while the dancing streams of milk kept rhythmic time to the song that no one else in all the wide world could hear.

At breakfast, Rebecca Bartlett's placid face beamed kindly upon him as she said: "Thank thee, for the nice mess o' fish thee brought, Peltier, but I'm sorry thee had such a tryin' time. We see it stormin' on the lake and felt a good deal concerned about thee, thinkin' thee might be out in a boat, and more so when thee didn't come back, for we knew thee would if thee could."

The gloom of night was gone, its dolorous voices hushed. Sunlight flooded the earth, and the soft air was full of the joyous songs of birds. Could this world, now so full of light and joy, and warm with love and kindness, be the same that so lately frowned upon him? He would never doubt the signs of the moon again, and never Lowizy.

When the next Sunday came, Pelatiah again declined to follow Rebecca Bartlett's suggestion that he should attend Friends' meeting. Yet he heard something of the simple service, for he was wandering with Lowizy along the western rocky slopes of Shellhouse, where, hidden by the leafy screen of the woodside, they could look forth across the pasture to the gray and brown shingled sides of the old meeting house, through whose open doors and windows came the voice of the preacher, whose spirit was moved most audibly. Today, certainly, the green and flowery aisles of the woods were pleasanter than that barren interior, and distance softened to tunefulness the doleful cadence of the sermon.

The "young-come-ups," though a week older, had lost nothing of their pungent sweetness. In fact he, who, a week ago had thought he never could touch one again, now was sure they never tasted so good. If at times the low song of the pines seemed to voice solemnly the words, "They'll fool a feller agin an' agin," he shut his ears to it, it was not sung for him.

Sungahneetuk

The day after Pelatiah left was to be their last day, for tomorrow they were to break camp and go at least as far as the Falls on their homeward way. For their credit as fishermen and for the pleasure of their friends at home, they must take with them fish enough to give each neighbor a mess. Danvis would expect every man of them to do his duty and bring it—a pickerel.

As Sam looked eastward from the top of the bluff beyond the broad creek, a kingfisher hung steadfast for a moment on vibrant wings above the shallows, then dropping like a plummet, arose almost with the up-bursting splash of his plunge, and presently proclaimed his good luck with a metallic clatter of his castanets. A fishhawk, cruising vigilantly above the channel, suddenly swooped and tore from the water a prize so heavy that, in labored retreat, he barely gained the cover of the woods in time to escape the swift onslaught of an eagle, lord paramount of all air, water, and earth hereabout.

Sam accepted these omens as auspicious of a good day's fishing, verifying what he had already felt in his bones, and he departed in his canoe, paddling up the lower reaches of the stream, where the dipping willow tips scarcely bent to or rippled the slow current, and the reflections of trunks and leaves stood motionless on the glassy stream till the boat's wake set them a-quiver, as its slanted bars of golden light climbed rushes, ferny shores, and gray tree trunks and then dissolved in green and gold among the sunlit leaves; or a gar-pike, watching with wicked eyes the advancing prow, stirred them with the slow ripple of his sullen retreat. Then a muskrat voyaged from one shore with a freight of weeds trailing from his jaws and undulating with his wake, then sank with it to the underwater doorway of his home and left his wake fading in slow pulsations above him. A green heron, startled from an overhanging branch, went flapping awkwardly along the narrow lane of sky while his distorted double flapped more awkwardly along the lane of water.

There was no sign nor sight of the outer world but the frayed stripe of blue sky overhead, one glimpse of Camel's Hump set in darker blue against it, and, seen for an instant through a break in the green and gray wall of trees, Mt. Philo's crown of pines and shorn sunlit slopes.

The solitude was very pleasant to this simple lover of nature who in certain moods was happiest when alone, yet not alone, for he felt a perfect companionship with the woods and their inhabitants close about him. There were other fishers than he but for whose busier plying of their craft he might have forgotten why he had come, so satisfied was he with the lazy voyaging. A heron stood with poised spear in an outlet of the marsh waiting for luck with an angler's patience. An alert mink slid from the bank, cleaving the water with an almost noiseless plunge as if he were a brown arrow shot into it. Not so a kingfisher, who proclaimed from afar his coming, just swerved from his jerky course for the boat, then hung for a moment in quivering poise and dashed down so close that the spray of his noisy plunge fell in splashing drops not twice the canoe's length from her prow, then flew to a raft of driftwood and perching upon its topmost stick bragged as loudly of his minnow as Antoine might of an eel.

Sam had passed one landing which showed in its forked rests for poles, brands, and ashes of fires, heads and scales of fish, much use as a fishing place. Now he came to another where the stream bent from north to west, just above a little islet, whose willows, great elms, water maples, and one noble buttonwood were bound in a tangled cordage of grape vines. Here were the same signs of frequent fishing. An old boat that had long since made its last fishing and trapping trips lay rotting at the bank, with fish at home under its sunken stern and remnants of muskrats' recent feasts on its mossy thwarts. Landing here he fished from the shore, and having no bait but worms, for a while caught only perch. These bit vigorously enough to raise high expectations, sadly disappointed when the brief spurt of resistance was over and the fish came swinging ashore. But when such trivial warfare ceased for a while and there came at last, after a brief toying with the bait, a downright tug and then a strong upstream sweep of the line that made it sing and the cedar pole trembled to the shrill song as it bent in his grasp, Sam felt assured that he was contending with a bass without the proof presently given. The water was smitten underneath, shivered into crystal drops as the gallant fish shot thrice its length above the surface, raining crystals from every fin till the circling wavelets of upburst and plunge met. Though Sam's weapons were of clumsy strength, he fought his antagonist fairly as he often had large trout with lighter tackle, not heaving him out overhead as boys do sunfish, but tiring him out with the long, uncertain struggle which, if we are to believe the only testimony that we ever hear, is as much enjoyed by the fish as by the scientific angler.

"There," said he, when he had gently lifted the exhausted bass ashore, "you didn't git away, did ye? It mos' seems as if you'd orter, but I guess I'm glad you didn't. By the gre't horn spoon! You're harnsome as a pictur' an' you fit like a coon!" If there were other bass here they scorned such humble fare as worms, and after offering in vain the finest in his box, Sam reembarked and voyaged farther up stream. There was a stronger current to make way against, running between higher banks, overhanging in a fringed network of roots of old trees that shaded them, elms with great buttressed trunks, water maples so nearly like them in form that it needed a second glance to assure one that they were not elms; oaks that had showered down mast to feed woodducks in a hundred autumns, clumps of basswood, lusty sons of the dead giant whose mouldering stump they stood around, and here and there towering buttonwoods, shining specter-like among the shadows, more like ghosts of other departed giants of the forest than like living trees.

Stream and banks beautified each other with shadow, with mirrored greenness of leaves, graceful bend of trunks and limbs, with quivering rebound of sunbeams from ripples again and again repeated till they flickered out in the translucence of pools or the gilded green of leaves. Every reach disclosed new beauty and promised more beyond when the glitter of the stream flashed forth from the shadows of a bend.

One who sees it now for the first time can hardly imagine how beautiful Sungahneetuk was then. One who saw it then and now beholds its abomination of desolation, the shrunken current crawling between banks avariciously shorn of all their trees, of their last green fleece of willows, worthless dead, but priceless, living, to him who loves the beauty that the hand of God has wrought, can but wonder why some awful retribution has not fallen upon the spoilers, nor can he withhold his own feeble curse, wishing that he had the power of God to enforce it.

A railroad in Vermont was almost undreamed of then, and there was no shadow of coming destruction brooding over the peaceful woods and waters, nor did the thought enter Sam's mind to mar his enjoyment of the sylvan scene, that it ever would be changed but by growing older, nor lose anything but by the natural decay that in some way compensates for all it takes.

Now and then, where the bottom faded out of sight in a swirl of dull green under tangled threads of sunshine, he invited the bass to taste his worms, but they would not, though he frequently saw them hanging near his bait on waving fins, then moving away in leisurely disdain.

Presently he descried on the bank above him another angler who was just slipping a fine bass on to the withe that already held a dozen or more. When he had again tethered them in the edge of the stream, he took up his pole and stole cautiously along, carefully scanning the water. Sam landed and followed, watching him in the hope of learning something from one so successful, if he were not so by sheer luck. As Sam drew near the man saluted him with a nod given over his shoulder, showing a face beaming with good humor, for how could a man who had caught a dozen bass wear a sour visage?

"I kinder wanter see haow you du it," Sam said in a low voice. "I never ketched but one 'Swago in my life."

The fisherman looked at him in pitying wonder, then laughed a little and beckoned him nearer. He pointed to a little basin scooped in the sandy bottom and cleared of every large pebble and water-logged weed and stick. A bass hovered always near it and sometimes over it, and now charged furiously upon a perch that had intruded on the sacred precincts, pursued it out of sight, and in an instant returned. When a sodden water weed drifted into the precious basin, she seized it before it could lodge there, and, carrying it beyond the downstream rim, dropped it where it was borne away by the current.

"That ere 's a bed," said Sam's new acquaintance. "Naow, see here," and sheathing his hook with an unlooped worm, he dropped it quietly a little above the bed and let it drift down on it. The fish rushed at it, seized it, and darted away with it, but before she had time to drop it the angler struck sharply, and almost in the same instant landed her on the grass behind him.

"Thet's the way tu du it," the fisherman said, as he unhooked the fish.

"Wal, it does take the rag off'm the bush for quick work," said Sam; "but I don't ezackly git a holt on 't. Does these here 'Swagos live in them places all the time?"

"Laws a massy, no! Them's the spawnin' beds, where they lays the' aigs. Don't you see this one's just ready tu lay her'n?" and Sam now noticed that the bass was profusely voiding spawn in her struggles.

"She'd stick tu it like teazles till they was hatched an' a spell arter, an' not 'low nothin' on 't. Then they clear aout, an' arter the middle o' July you won't see a 'Swago bass in the crik till 'long airly in the fall. Then the' 'll be some little fellers not bigger'n rock bass."

"Wal," said Sam, with a sigh of disappointment, "I allers thought it was a pleggid mean trick tu ketch traout on the' beds, an' I guess this hain't no better."

"But it ketches 'em, an' that's what a feller wants," argued his companion. "Come along an' we'll find another bed, an' you try it once, jest for greens."

"Wal, I do' know but I will jest once to see 'f I can," and they went slowly along the bank till another bed and its guardian were discovered.

Sam did exactly as he had seen his instructor do, and soon was fast to a good three-pounder. This, however, was not torn from the water as the other had been—though the guide shouted, "Slat 'er aout! You got 'er hooked good. Slat 'er aout!"—but was vanquished in a fair fight and then drawn gently to the shore. Sam unhooked her tenderly without taking her from the water, then watched her as, lying on her side, she feebly waved her fins, then stood still a moment as if dazed by the recovery of freedom, and then, as she surged away and vanished in a flash, he addressed her:

"Good-by, marm. Nex' time you see a worm in your nest you poke it aout wi' your nose."

"What in thunder d'd ye let 'er go for?" his companion demanded in a vexed tone, when his astonishment found other expression than a blank stare.

"That's the way t' du it," Sam answered quietly; "I jist wanted tu show you haow."

"Wal, I swan! you mus' be a dum'd fool!"

"That's what I've tol' myself a hundred times," Sam replied rather sadly, but with good nature, "but I can't help it, an' so I hain't tu blame for it. Wal, I guess I'll be goin'. I'm 'bleeged tu ye for what you've showed me an' tol' me. Good-by."

Past landing, island, and quite shores the canoe slid down stream in greater solitude than it had voyaged upward. The kingfisher had ceased his clatter, the full-fed mink fished no more, the heron had flown to his mate in the tall pines, and the muskrat was asleep in his burrow. There was a sluggish stir of life when the turtles slid off the logs with a clump and an unctuous splash, and in the lazy float of myriad insects drifting against the sunlight like a veil of gauze in the unfelt wafts—a suggestion of life somewhere in the boom of a bittern far away in the marshes, in bird songs sung in distant meadows.

Breaking Camp

The cobwebs of mist on the marshes had not caught a sunbeam when the camp was astir next morning, for the smoke of its fire arose earlier than the sun, that had only gilded the treetops above it when breakfast was ready. The meal was eaten in unwonted silence. There were no plans proposed for the day's sport, for there was to be no sport, and no one attempted to joke, for though the prospect of getting home was pleasant to men who had seldom been so long away from it, there was some heaviness of spirit attending the last of these days of carefree life, days without beginnings and endings of chores, nor filled with worry nor weary toil, days of hand-to-mouth living and such primitive unthought-of tomorrow as the heart of the best-tamed man loves and yearns for when its last drop of old, wild blood awakes, as it sometimes will, and tingles through his civilized veins. This uneliminated atom still holds us to kinship with nature, and though it may not be the best part of us, without it we should be worse than we are. He who loses all love for our common mother is, indeed, a wretched being, poorer than the beasts.

When breakfast was eaten, the frying pan, kettle, and tin plates were cleaned as they had not been before since leaving the home cupboards, for they were soon to undergo the inspection of housewifely eyes, which the glamor of a hundred pickerel would not blind to the imperfections of man's careless or unskillful scullionry.

"I tell ye what," said Joseph Hill, as he scraped away with a clam shell at the bottom layer of a week's accumulation of burned grease, "I'm a-goin' tu tell M'ri 'at we hedn't got no soap, an' the water here is hard, 'nough on't an' tew much, but it's hard an' won't take a holt o' grease, no mor'n it does yer stomerk."

"The way 'at oliogernous grease conjoles in a dish when it ketches it away f'm hum is suthin' beyond my misapprehension," said Solon, while he swabbed a plate with a stick of firewood. "It's suthin' 'at nothin' but the female mind o' womern c'n rassle with. Consarn the dishes! Let's sink 'em in the crik, accidental."

"Then we'd ketch it wus," said Joseph, as he began scouring his frying pan with a stone. "I druther send this an' stay myself, 'an tu go hum wi'eout it. M'ri's allers tellin' how 't her gran'ther, I don't know but 't was her gran'mother, fetched it from C'nnect'cut an' cooked basswood leaves in 't in the scase year.* Sam Hill, you take it, grease an' sut an' all, an' leave me here!'"

Antoine, on his knees scouring knives and forks by thrusting them into the earth, said:

"Wal, Ah don' care for me, 'cause you see, boy, Ah'll was be de cook an' Ah'll ant risponsibilitee for de clean, hein, Solem, ant it?'"

"Wal," said Sam, wiping out the kettle with a handful of leaves and packing a dirty shirt and a pair of socks in it, "I hain't responsible tu nob'd'y."

"But your time's a-comin', young man, an' you wanter be gittin' ready for 't. H. P. is the fust letters of her name, an' she hain't thick under the nail an' won't be when the's a L. sot tu 'em. You'll see!" said Joseph, and his words had a portentous ring as he delivered them into the frying pan held close before his face while he anxiously inspected its interior. "I r'aly du b'lieve 'at I c'n see iron, leastways I've got daown tu signs o' the fust breakfus. If folks only hed sense 'nough tu du the cookin' on sticks an' coals an' hot stuns an' eat off'm chips an' birch bark, they 'ld take more comfort in livin', seems 'ough they would. If they didn't hev quite so much present enj'yment, they wouldn't hev so much dread o' the futur'. Anyways, I wish't this dum'd ol' fryin' pan hed stayed in C'nnect'cut if M'ri's gran'ther an' gran'mother'd hed tu eat the' browse raw. Seems 'ough I did, most."

To Sam occurred the happy thought of taking the dishes down to the lake shore. There, with the abundance of sand and water, the labor of cleansing went on more satisfactorily to the men, but greatly to the discomfort of as many sandpipers. These flitted back and forth past them on down-curved wings or stood astilt in the shallow verge, jerking out cries of alarm with every beat of their wings or tilt of their slender bodies.

About the middle of the forenoon, Sam looking upstream from the camp, where he was busy packing blankets and outfit and more odds and ends than he remembered bringing, descried a boat in the farthest bend. At first it seemed stationary, with oars rising and falling in purposeless strokes, like a great waterbug waving its antennæ for the mere sake of motion. But it was drawing nearer; the red flannel back of the rower's vest could now be made out, and the rise and fall of his straw

---

*A season when all crops failed, and the early settlers of Vermont were reduced to pitiable straits, was long remembered as the Scarce year.

hat, and the thump, squeak, and splash of his oars could be heard, and the surge of the water before the broad bow of the scow. And then forsaking the long curve of the channel and striking right across the marshy cape, that is half water and half weeds, it headed for the mouth of the creek. Sam was certain enough of the rower's identity to shout to his comrades that Uncle Tyler was coming.

They went to meet him at the landing, when gaping with his deaf stare at his course, though he who is known as Time was steering for him, he sent the scow ashore with a final stroke. Time's salutation shouted at the top of his voice was, "Any of you fellers got any terbarker fer this ol' critter? He begged the last mossel 't I hed an hour ago."

Uncle Tyler took his pipe from the seat beside him, knocked the ashes out on the gunwale, and came rheumatically ashore with his left hand extended.

"Massy sakes alive! I sent up tu the store for some by Sargent's boy, but he forgot it! That tarnal boy can't never remember nothin', an' I'd orter knowed better'n tu sent by him."

"I'm glad it wa'n't you 'at forgot for oncte," said Joseph, who by a lucky chance had at the first attempt hit upon the right pocket and handed over his last depleted paper of long-cut. Uncle Tyler was soon comforting himself with what most mitigated his chronic unhappiness, a pipeful of what it pleased him to call "borrered terbarker."

"Naow hurry up an' be spry," he said, "for I'd orter be tu hum a-workin' in my gardin."

Brother Foot's camp-meeting tent had been taken down and packed, and, with all their other effects and the box of salted fish put on board the scow, they were ready to depart; but Sam had forgotten something, which obliged him to revisit the site of the camp. He was ashamed to tell it was only for a last look.

The downfall of noontide sunlight splashed the floor of the woods with gold around silhouettes of branches, twigs, and leaves, bent over the rocks and crinkled along the last year's leaves they were laid upon. Between leaves, branches, and tree trunks, were shown, in fantastic shapes, patches of sky and lake, and all the sunlit outer world. Birds sang blithely of their happy life and, mingled with their songs, came from far away, sounds of the life and stir of the world, and yet this place seemed lifeless.

How lonesome and forsaken it was! The carpet of old brown leaves worn by frequent footsteps down to the black mould of dead years, strewn with tobacco paper, broken pipes, and fishbones, the castaway ridgepole of the tent lying like a fallen rooftree athwart the matted bed of cedar twigs whereon they had dreamed dreams pleasanter than life, so deserted now that a chipmunk ventured to explore it. It seemed to Sam almost like the ruins of a house wherein he had dwelt for years.

For old acquaintance' sake he tried to light his pipe in the ashes of the fireplace, but the last ember was dead and only exhaled a faintly pungent odor of smoke.

"But I'm comin' agin!" he said, and as he hurried down the steep footpath, a vireo sang behind him as if to call him back.

Rest

On the afternoon of the next day, the wagon bearing the fishermen and their camping outfit made its lumbering entry into the street of the straggling hamlet known to all Danvis folk as The Village. Such an interest was aroused by this arrival that everyone within sight who might on any pretext leave his affairs did so and drew near.

"Wal! If these 'ere men folks don't beat all natur'!" said one goodwife to another, to whose gate she had come for companionship and ease of mind. "Jest a runnin' crazy arter some fellers 'at's ben tu the lake a-fishin'."

"Has he heard what's happened tu his haouse?" the other woman asked, when, after admiring the fish her husband had brought her, her thoughts reverted to what had been uppermost in the minds of the gossips.

"My goodness gracious!" the good man ejaculated, and his face grew blank with the shock of suddenly remembered propriety and neglected opportunity.

"I don't b'lieve nob'dy ever thought tu tell him! Here, 'Lizy, take a holt o' this fish, an' I'll go an' tell him."

"Oh, say, Lovel," he said, returning and putting one hand on Sam's arm, "hev you heard f'm hum to day? Hev you met Tom Hamlin 'tween here an' V'gennes?"

"Heard f'm hum? Met Tom Hamlin?" Sam repeated with a puzzled air.

"We hain't heard nothin', nor met nob'dy"; and then anxiously, "the' hain't nothin' happened tu father, hes the'?"

"Wal," said Clapham, considering, "the' hain't tu your father, an' then, agin, the' hes—not egzakly tu him, but to his wife." Then after a little pause, "Not to break the sad news tew suddingly, she died and departed this life at twenty minutes arter nine this mornin'."

Sam drew near his home; its outward discomfort never more impressing him than now, as, coming across lots, he approached the rear of the house where litter and makeshifts were most displayed. There was a clutter of broken crockery and useless tinware pitched from the back door into the vigorous growth of weeds; a cartwheel with half its felloes gone, set upon a sagging post and bearing some dishcloths and a couple of milk-pails; two or three barrels laid upon their sides with pales driven in front served as hen-coops, wherein as many unhappy hens were in a constant worry concerning their wandering chicks, a worry intensified when a cat prowled past toward the house with so much more than ordinary uncanny feline stealth that Sam's flesh crept as he watched her creeping, halting, listening, always intent on something unseen within the house. When he hurled half a broken earthen milk pan at her, she crouched and glared wickedly at him an instant before she scurried away through the weedy cover.

Going to the front of the house, Sam found his father, where he was almost sure he should, leaning forlornly on the sagging gate post, gazing abstractedly at nothing when not casting a casual glance up or down the road.

"Wal, father, haow be ye?" he asked, putting his hand on the old man's shoulder.

"Why, Samwil!" turning with a little start, and taking his son's hand, "I wa'n't 'spectin' on ye so soon. I'm awf'l glad you've come, for this 'ere's knocked me gally west. You never liked her none too well, I know, an' I know 't the' wa'n't no love lost, but won't ye go in an' see her? She looks turrible peaceable—more so'n I most ever seen her."

Sam could not refuse this common mark of respect expected of all who came to the house of mourning, and followed his father into the house, stopping on his way through the kitchen to greet the women whose tongues had been busy with the gossip which was the chief compensation of their labors.

When he saw into what serenity the hand of death had molded the face that he had always seen so fretfully unrestful, he marveled at the undreamed-of-kindly possibilities of the harsh features, and all resentment of past injuries was swept out of his heart. He forgave her and wished he might ask her to forgive him for hard and angry words that now could never be recalled. It came upon him suddenly how repentance may come too late for the soul's perfect comfort.

New Life in the Old Home

The Lovel house, which for many years had not been a very cheerful one, was now more lonesome than ever. The two men, the hound, and the cat were its sole inmates for many weeks, except when a neighborly housewife came to wash, iron, and bake for them, and Sam realized as never before how different were the "good lonesome" of a solitary campfire and the dreariness of a womanless hearthstone.

When the good people of Danvis had been for some time expecting it, it happened of a Sunday that the intended marriage of Samuel Lovel and Huldah Purington was "published" at the town house, in which, for lack of a church, all religious meetings but those of the Quakers were held.

A week later there was a quiet wedding at the Purington homestead.

Much pains had been taken that an invitation should reach Pelatiah Gove, and he had taken no less to be present. As he went home from the wedding with his mother, he stammered out a confession that he was engaged to a "gal as harnsome as a pictur' an' smartern a steel-trap, an' her name was Lowizy."

"Why, Peltier!" cried the good woman, stopping short and facing him in almost breathless amazement. "Why, my sakes! You're tew young tu think o' sech a thing! Y'r father an' me was much as ten years older'n you be when we was married."

"Wal, what on't? You tew lost ten year o' good times 'at you'd ha' hed, an' we hain't a-goin' tu be fools 'cause you was—not by a jugfull, maw."

Wedding journeys were not the fashion in Danvis in those days, and that of Sam and Huldah was only from her father's house to that of his, and was quite uneventful.

Huldah was duly installed as mistress of her new home, and now Timothy Lovel could smoke his pipe in peace in his own kitchen, or in the square room if he chose, and Drive might take his ease undisturbed in the best patch of sunlight that fell upon the floor.

A great deal of the Purington thrift seemed to have been transplanted with its new mistress to the tumbledown place, which outdoors as well as in began to brighten into a pleasanter home than its old inmates had known for many a year.

Huldah was intently counting the stitches on her needle, held close to the candle that faintly illumined the close of the short summer evening. Sam had succeeded in the discovery of a sheet of foolscap whereon the flies of more than one season had recorded their summer's sojourn, and he was now rummaging the top shelf of the cupboard in quest of a pen.

"I'm a-goin' tu set ri' daown an' write a letter tu Uncle Lisher tu come. Him an' Aunt Jerushy c'n hev the back bedr'm as we talked, an' he c'n hev the linter for a shop."

"An' they'll be most welcom 's fur 's I c'n make 'em," said his wife.

With a sigh of satisfaction, Sam pictured to himself a renewal in the "lean to" of the old comradeship that had existed in Uncle Lisha's shop. For he was too young to know that old times can never return in all their fullness, and that the happy, carefree days of youth, once spent, are gone forever.

BOOK 3

from Danvis Folks

Two Returning Pilgrims

A homesickness, that time could not cure nor alleviate, became so insufferable to Elisha Peggs and Jerusha his wife that, after enduring it for three years, they bade farewell to their son and daughter-in-law and to the grandchildren who had been the strongest tie to hold them to their uncongenial Western home, and set forth on the long journey to their native town of Danvis.

At first they voyaged on the Great Lakes, then with greater comfort on the Erie and Champlain Canals. Now a lively and industrious little steamer that never gave sign of weariness was towing their long, narrow canal packet out of the marshy windings of Lake Champlain's upper channel into widening waters. A restful home feeling began to come upon them with a sense of proprietorship in the landscape. For here on their right hand lay their own beloved Vermont, with its eternal mountains and its homesteads grown gray in the possession of generations of one name.

The tide of travel was setting westward, and in its feeble backflow this old couple found themselves with but few companions, and these not very congenial ones. Most of their fellow passengers were returning from spying out the land of promise, to sell their gear at any price and remove their families to the region of unlimited possibilities, which they were continually vaunting, while the impossibilities, except in the direction of poverty, of their New England birthright were as continually set forth, to the disgust of Uncle Lisha's loyal Yankee soul.

"It's a dirty bird 'at faouls his own nest," was his reply, to their disparagement of his beloved stony soil. "I druther hev the leetle chunk o' V'mont sile 'at's goin' tu kiver my ol' bones 'n tu hev the hull splatteration o' yer West."

"There ain't room enough 'mongst your hills to lay you down level," said a dapper little man who was the acknowledged wit of the company.

"Wal, then, let 'em stan' me up in a post-hole."

There was also a land speculator, in shabby clothes and a pervading uncleanliness, with a portfolio of plans of unbuilt cities, which he persistently spread before every eye that would follow his dirty, talon-like forefinger as it pointed out the most desirable lots and traced the lines of traffic that were surely to be established. "I'll guarantee to make any man rich, yes, sir, forty men rich, if they'll follow my advice and buy as I tell 'em."

"Good airth an' seas," cried Uncle Lisha, returning his spectacles to their steel case and shutting it with a spiteful snap after a brief inspection of the maps. "Ef I hed sech a chance tu make other folks rich, I'd try it on myself fust, an' ef it worked, I'd buy me some store clo's an' a hunk o' soap;" and thereafter the land speculator was silent in the old man's presence.

Presently the hoary ruins of Ticonderoga confronted them on the western shore, and it was as if its self-vaunted hero, Gran'ther Hill, had come to welcome them to the dismantled fortress. Then Chimney Point and Fort St. Frederic's shattered walls swung apart before them, and they passed into the broad expanse of calm blue water that between pleasant shores stretched far away into the pearly haze, where rock-anchored, purple islets and white sails of laggard craft hung alike moveless on the undefined verge of lake and sky. Then far away to the northeast, silently welcoming them, in ghostly grandeur the landmarks of their state, Mansfield and Camel's Hump, towered through the film of haze; and what warmed their hearts still more, the lesser peak of their own Danvis mountain, in whose shadow they had dwelt so many years. How impatient they were to be there again, yet dreading the changes that time, in a little space, might have wrought.

It was with devout thankfulness that Uncle Lisha and his wife found that the time which had seemed so long to them had wrought few changes among old friends and familiar scenes. If they could but have taken up the broken thread of their far-spent life in their old brown house and shop, the measure of present contentment would have been full. Yet they inherited, in some measure, the adaptability to change which has come, through restless generations of pioneers, to the Yankee race, and they were content to be the welcome inmates of the Lovels' hospitable home.

It was pleasant to be so near the old home, and it comforted them to know that human life had quite gone out of it when they forsook it. The capricious November weather having fallen into an unexpected mood of mildness on the day after their arrival, they walked down to the old place and found it little changed since they had last seen it, except by the air of complete desertion that pervaded it.

They pushed open the unlatched door and entered with an awed sense of being the ghosts of their former selves, yet apparitions that would affright no one, nor scarcely disturb the squirrels that hoarded their stores in the garret, nor interrupt the woodpecker's tattoo on the gable clapboards, nor awaken the woodchuck from his long nap under the flooring of the shop. Upon this floor, that was indented with his own and innumerable other heel-marks, the old cobbler saw the rubbish of leather scraps almost as he had left it, but for the blue mould that had gathered on it, quite overpowering with mustiness the odor of tannin and wax that once pervaded the dingy little den.

Thence the two went into the house part, in which their married life had begun, where children had been born to them, where they had toiled and grown weary and rested, whose low-browed rooms were hallowed by days and years of happiness and sorrow and the slow healing of bereavement.

In the kitchen, from the blank fireplace, with its ashes of the last fire they had kindled there, already showing a green film of moss, the crane stretched out to them its naked, sooty arm, whether interrogating or supplicating, seemed not clear to them. Out of the smoky ceiling the empty iron hooks reached toward them as if asking the old burdens of crooknecks and dried apples. Amid them, the empty stovepipe hole stared down at the unworn patch of floor the winter stove had covered, in silent reproach. Their own hushed voices sounded hollow and unnatural.

In vain they strove to rehabilitate the rooms in imagination with their old furniture; they could not make them homelike nor bring any warmth of their old life to dispel the pervading smell of unused, unpainted wood, except once when Aunt Jerusha opened the kitchen cupboard and there came out of it a faint, embalmed odor of loaf cake and gingerbread that made them both hungry.

Groping in the furthest corner of the upper shelf for some forgotten relic of the old life, her fingers touched some soft, yielding fabric, and then drew forth a rudely fashioned little rag doll, whose ink-marked features had almost faded into the dingy hue of the homespun linen face. With fond, speechless wonder they looked upon it for a moment, and with one accord went over to the east window, where, with eyes dimmed with something more than age, through the haze of the calm autumnal day, they saw the scarlet sumach bobs shining out of the wilderness of the little hillside graveyard where they buried their only daughter, in the long ago of her childhood. For a brief space the deserted house seemed again to be their home, and the scurry of the squirrels overhead, the patter of a little child's feet. Thankful to leave it with the impression of such a presence, they went out, closing the door reverently behind them.

They went down the tangled, untrodden path to the little gate that was still held shut with a chain weighted with a rusty plow-point.

The Country Post Office

Thanksgiving festivities were over, and Uncle Lisha had been several days among his old neighbors, yet in deference to them, as in turn they were his entertainers and guests, and to himself as a returned traveler, he continued to wear his best clothes with heroic endurance of discomfort.

"I ben dressed up so long I begin to feel like a minister," he said, as he rapped the ashes from his pipe on Sam's stove hearth one morning when he had finished his after-breakfast smoke. "Ef I don't shuck myself aouten my t'other clo'es pooty soon, I shall be a-preachin' er duin' suthin' onbecomin', but fust of all I got tu seddaown an' write George a letter. Hev you got s'm ink an' a sheet o' writin' paper an' a pen, Huldy?"

Envelopes were not known in Danvis, and the letter needed the united endeavors of the old couple and Huldah to properly fold it and to tuck it into itself. Then Uncle Lisha laid the letter into the crown of his beaver hat, wadded it in place with his bandanna, put the hat on his head, struggled into his high-collared, tight-sleeved blue coat, and set forth toward the post office with the dignity due to his important mission.

Though his feet were encased in his tight best boots, the familiar path was pleasant to him as to his eyes were all the wayside objects, the old wall parting with its gray lines the sumach thickets, now stripped of all their autumnal glory but the enduring scarlet of the bobs, the rail fence zigzagging among rank goldenrods whose riches were taking flight on white wings. A red squirrel tacked along the top rails in alternate nearer and further attendance upon him, yet keeping continually abreast till he came to a great butternut-tree, and, scrambling up its grooved bark, began jeering at his wayfaring comrade as impudently as his forebears had in bygone years. His gibes did not disturb the old man's equanimity as they might have ruffled the boy's. He smiled up at him amusedly, and turned the squirrel's mockery to anger by picking up a brown nut and cracking it on the big rock that stood, as such are sure to do, the convenient adjunct of the butternut tree, and, having cracked it, ate it under the very eyes of the self-assumed owner of all the nuts in Danvis.

There was a well-remembered beech, whose unshed golden-brown leaves were beginning to bleach to a pale tint, wherein a flock of silently industrious jays displayed brief glimpses of bright color. The spread of its wide branches and the girth of its huge trunk seemed scarcely increased by the many years of lusty growth since he carved the letters "E. P." and "J. C." entwined in a love knot on the smooth bark, yet initials and emblem and date of the dead old year were moss-grown scars. The old man smiled in kindly pity on the half-forgotten folly of the youthful lover, and then, looking about to see that no one saw him, got out his knife and scraped the moss from the letters and love knot.

Then he stumped briskly forward, brushing the frost-blackened Mayweeds with hasty footsteps till he was startled by a vagrant partridge that burst from a clump of weeds close beside him and sailed on set wings away to the woods.

"Good airth an' seas," he exclaimed, as he watched the bird's arrowy flight, curving down to cover at the woodside, "ye might's well kill me as skeer me tu death. Oh, if you'd sot still an' I'd seen you an' hed me a gun, I'd ha' got you. An' I druther hev you 'n tew perairie chickens."

Crossing a little bridge, he presently came to the homestead of the Goves, on whom he called and found a warm welcome. After Mrs. Gove had bustled about to seat the visitor in the most comfortable chair and to send the youngest girl to call her father from the barn, she sat down opposite her old neighbor and devoted a few moments to a careful consideration of his appearance.

"Wal, Uncle Lisher," she said, with an exhalation of satisfaction, "lookin' at you, an' not lookin' back, it don't seem's 'ough you'd ben gone six mont's. You hain't altered a mite. An' is Aunt Jerushy as chirk as you be? I wanter know! Well, the Western kentry has agreed wi' you, oncommon."

"It 'greed wi' aour health better 'n what it did wi' aour feelin's. We toughed it aout 's long 's we could stan' it an' back we come tu bother aour ol' neighbors endurin' the rest o' aour days." His eyes came down from roving along the limp skeins of pumpkin hung to dry upon poles above the stove and settled with an inquiring look upon her face.

"You hain't never bothered nob'dy an' you won't never," she said heartily, and then bustling toward the door. "I wonder what's a-keepin' Levi; finishin' a bundle, proberbly, but I'll go an' git him."

"No, don't ye. I can't stop but a minute, an' I'll jest g'waout an' say haow de du. Fact on 't is," he said impressively, "I ben writin' a letter 'n I'm a-kerryin' of it tu the pos' office. But where's Peltier?" he turned at the door to ask.

A troubled look overcast Mrs. Gove's cheerful face. "I do' know where Peltier is. Mebby he's gone lookin' at his mink traps, an' mebby he's over tu—tu—the village. Peltier 's in a mis'able, mopin' way, Uncle Lisher. He's ben dis'p'inted. Expectin' tu marry a gal, even so fur's tu go tu git merried, an' she was gone wi' another feller, an' it's nigh abaout ondone him. He mopes an' he goes tu Hamner's, an' I'm afeared he drinks. I wish 't you 'd talk tu him, Uncle Lisher, he allers sot so much by ye, mebby your talkin' 'ould 'mount tu suthin'. Me 'n' his father an' Sam's don't take no holt on him."

"Peltier was allus one o' my boys," the old man said; "I made him his fust boots an' showed him haow tu ketch his fust traout, an' he'd hear to me. I will talk tu him, Mis' Gove."

Levi Gove was too industriously inclined to quit labor for visiting, and after a brief but loud interchange of greetings, carried on amid the rustle of cornstalks, the old man went on his way to the store.

There he found the merchant and postmaster, as lank, alert, and clean shaven as ever, and as constantly saying "Yes" in varied inflections of assent or query, and effusive in the cordialty of his welcome.

"There's a letter," handing it to the postmaster, "I wanter hev go tu my son, George Peggs, in Westconstant. I suppose it will go all right, won't it, Mr. Clapham?"

The postmaster held it at arm's length above the level of his eyes and scrutinized it from that point for a while, then laid it on the counter, and, leaning over it on his elbows, as intently scrutinized it from above.

"Yes, Mr. Peggs," he said confidently, "that letter 'll go tu its deestination, without a daoubt. Yes, wonderful tu think on, hain't it," as he slowly wrote the postmark on the corner of the letter, "haow a message can go from here to the far distant West in ten days or a fortnit? Yes, eighteen and three-quarter cents is the postige your son 'll hafter pay, which he won't begretch it, for hearin' from his ven'able parents."

"It's a dumbd sight more 'n it's wuth to read, but I wouldn't ha' writ it for that. I'd ruther tap tew pair o' boots."

When the letter was safely deposited in the drawer devoted to outgoing mail matter, Uncle Lisha readjusted his spectacles and inspected the contents of the showcase that stood on the end of the counter.

"See anything you'd like to purchase, Mr. Peggs?" and Clapham sidled behind the counter and examined the contents of the showcase as interestedly as if he had just discovered it.

"What's these 'ere sugar hearts wuth?" Uncle Lisha asked, tapping the glass above them with his forefinger.

"Them 's a cent apiece; haow many shall I put ye up?"

"I guess I'll git one on 'em fer Samwill's new boy, an' I guess I'll git a cent's wuth o' snuff fer Jerushy, an', lemme see, a snuff bean, she lost hern a comin' hum."

Uncle Lisha withdrew quietly and took his way homeward. As he plodded past the Gove homestead the wandering thoughts that bore him company turned toward his young friend Pelatiah. He cast a searching glance about the premises, half hoping and yet half fearing that he might discover him, for he shrank from the duty to which he was committed.

"I s'pose I'd ort tu stop an' find the boy an' give him a talkin' tu, tu rights," he soliloquized, "but I guess I'd better wait an' ketch him kinder accidental. This 'ere cornerin' a feller up an' rammin' advice intu him somehaow don't make it set so well as it does to kinder coax it intu him julluk a pill in a spo'ful of apple sass."

He quickened his pace till he had passed the house and come to the little bridge that spanned Stony Brook. As he lingered there idly watching the flow of the stream whose every bend and purling rapid and trout-haunted pool he knew as well as the corners of his old shop, and listening to its changing babble, familiar to his ear as the thud of the hammer on his own lapstone, he distinguished amid its liquid tones the sharp, metallic clink of a trap chain, coming, as a moment's listening assured him, from directly beneath the bridge.

"Someb'dy's ketched a mink er a mushrat," said he to himself, "'n' I'm goin' tu meddle wi' other folkses business tu the extent o' puttin' the poor creetur aouten his misery."

He descended to the bank, picking up a convenient cudgel as he went. When he peered into the dark shadow of the bridge he was not a little startled to discover the figure of a man sharply defined against the light. He was kneeling on the gravel between the abutment and the stream, so intently engaged in setting a trap that he was not aware of an intruder till Uncle Lisha tossed a pebble at his feet. The old man felt pretty sure of the trapper's identity, and was not surprised when Pelatiah's face was suddenly turned toward him with an expression of wonder overbearing its now habitual ruefulness.

His own silhouette, foreshortened as he stooped beneath the low bridge, bracing his hands upon his knees, was not recognized at first, but there was no mistaking his hearty hail, "Good airth an' seas! Peltier, don't ye know yer Uncle Lisher?" resounding with exaggerated volume through the narrow passage.

Pelatiah left the half-set trap and came crouching forth, brushing his soiled palm on his thigh in preparation for the vigorous hand-shaking that awaited him. When greetings were exchanged the two seated themselves on projections of the abutment and surveyed each other with kindly scrutiny.

"You hain't growed old a mite," said Pelatiah.

"I've ben a-growin' young sen' I come back makin' up what I lost in three year."

"An' Aunt Jerushy, is she tollable well?"

"Jest as smart as a cricket, an' tickled tu death tu git back hum again. An' haow 's things goin' wi' you, Peltier; well, I s'pose?"

"My health 's good 'nough," said Pelatiah, sighing as if that were an affliction, but Uncle Lisha did not heed it.

"Trappin' some, be ye?"

"Some; got a few traps sot fer mink an' mushrat. The' 's a mink a-ha'ntin' raound this 'ere bridge."

"I heerd your trap a-jinglin' an' thinks, says I, the' 's suthin' er 'nother sufferin' intu a trap an' I'm a-goin' tu be marciful an' kill it, ef 'tain't a skunk. My marcy don't extend tu skunks, erless I've got a gun. It's tough for any creetur tu be in a trap, whether no he 's humern or a dumb critter. Both git intu 'em, an', more times 'an not, the' hain't no gittin' aout, on'y by death er takin' off a laig. Most any dumb critter 'd ruther git free at the price of a laig er foot 'an tu stay an' die er be knocked in the head, an' they 're sensibler 'an lots o' folks which they'll jest hump theirselves an' grunt an' squall er flummix permisc'us till they git t' other foot an' like 's not both han's intu another trap, an' there they be. The grip o' the trap gits sorer and sorer, an' they quit a-pullin' an' give clean up, which hain't no way fer a man tu du." The old man beamed a kindly smile upon his companion, who sat with downcast eyes, slowly grinding the gravel beneath the heel of his cowhide boot, upon which Uncle Lisha's eyes finally fell, to note with displeasure that it was ripped and red for lack of grease.

"An' you've goddaown tu buyin' store boots. Goo' fer nothin' things, made aouten split luther an' stuck tugether wi' short paigs. An' the idee of a feller 'at ketches mushrat, an' hes their ile, lettin' his boots git as red as a fox's tail." He evidently thought Pelatiah in a desperate strait and spoke with such sudden sharpness that the young man was startled from his listless attitude. "But you come up," he said with less asperity, "an' lemme take the measure o' yer hommels an' I'll make ye suthin' 'at you 'll know you 've got on when you wear 'em, an' that 'll be wuth spendin' a leetle ile on." Then, almost without pause, he said, irrelevantly, "Why, Peltier, from what I heerd I 'spected tu find you married an' settled daown, stiddy." Pelatiah flushed and made a quick, impatient movement, "Wa'n't you expectin' tu, one spell?"

"Ef I was, I hain't naow, nor never shall ag'in," the young man said in a low voice.

"Why, what's the motter ails ye? Merryin' 's a good thing when ye find the right one."

"Haow in tunket 's a feller goin' tu tell when he hes?" Pelatiah asked, rising in such excitement that he bumped his head against the planks and sat down as suddenly as he had risen.

"Hurt yer head much?"

"Wisht I'd knocked the dumb thing off 'n my shoulders," he replied savagely. "Haow 's a feller goin' tu tell? That 's what I'd like tu know. I thought I'd faound the right one, an' I thought more on her 'an all the hull world. I worshiped the airth she walked on. She might ha' walked on me—she did pooty nigh, an' I was praoud tu hev her. An' I, dumb fool, thought she liked me jest as much. Mebby she did, fer a spell, an' thought she 'd faound her mate,—it's hopesin she wa'n't foolin' me the hull endurin' time,—an' then 'at she had n't. She promised tu hev me an' we was a-goin' tu be married, an' the time was sot, an' then at the last minute she went off wi' another feller an'—an' I s'pose they' re married, but I can't seem tu think on her as belongin' tu nob'dy else. She 'd ort tu suffer some, but I hope she 's happier 'n what I be. She might be, an' yit be in hell."

"You hed bad luck, Peltier, but all women hain't alike."

"The' hain't none no better 'n she was," Pelatiah said vehemently. "The' wa'n't never one harnsomer, an' haow could there be one better other-ways? They 're all fickleder 'n the wind that blows, an' lighter 'an the blubbers on this brook."

"'T ain't no sech a thing," said Uncle Lisha, emphasizing each word with a downward jerk of his head. "I've roosted wi' one womern goin' on tow-ards forty year that 's ben faithful an' true all them years, an' ther 's lots more o' the same sort, fer I don't cal'late I'm the on'y lucky man on the livin' airth. You got intu a trap nat'rally 'nough, bein' 't was baited wi' a pooty face, an' it kinder leggo, an' naow ye c'n shake a loose foot which you 'd ort tu be thankful it did n't take a laig, so tu speak, er mebby yer life."

"It might 's well. I wisht it hed," said Pelatiah, grinding the gravel away savagely with his heel.

"Sho, no, you don't, nuther. Say, Peltier, what d' ye du wi' yer fur? Sell it tu Clapham, du ye?

"No, Hamner 's hed most on 't."

"Hamner? He don't pay cash?"

"No"; but Pelatiah did not look up.

"Look a-here, Peltier Gove," said the old man impressively, you 're a-flummuxin' intu a wus trap 'n the fust one was, a-tryin' tu draowned yer trouble wi' rum, 'specially Hamner's pizen. Rum may cure a bellyache, but not never a heartache, not tu stay cured. It 'll numb it fer a spell, but it 'll make it come on wus 'n ever, an' need heftier dostin' every time tu numb it ag'in. I do' know haow long you ben a-tryin' on 't, but I du know 'at you 've faound it jest 's I tell ye. An' you 've got tu stop it right stret off er you 're a gone sucker. Right stret off. Not no foolin' wi' one more drink, ner no tu-morrers, ner birthdays, ner New Years, ner leavin' off gradwil. It 'll be a tough job, but you c'n du it. Shet your maouth as tight as if 't was sewed up wi' a waxed eend, an' don't ye onrip it fer no coaxin', inside er aout. You 've got tu du the job yerself, not but what God A'mighty 'll help ye, but you 've got tu boost, tew. I cal'-late 'f the' 's goin' tu be any prayin' done, a feller hed better du it fer himself. It'll 'maount tu more 'n all the ministers this side o' kingdom come, a-prayin' for him. An' naow I've said my say, an' you c'n go on settin' your mink trap. Bait it wi' mush-rat 'f you 've got it, it's better 'n fish. Don't forgit what I 've said tu ye, an' come an' see Aunt Jerushy soon 's you can. I shall git settled daown tu work in tew, three days, an' I want all on ye tu come in, jest as ye uster in th' ol' shop. Good-by."

He stooped his way out with due care for his head and its precious covering, and clambering to the roadway resumed his homeward course.

"There," he said, with a sigh of relief, "I've gi'n the boy his pill. I d' know but I forgot the apple sass, but it 's hopesin it won't set bad an' 'll du him good."

Pelatiah sat long after his old friend left him, with his chin upon his hands, staring abstractedly on the swift current of the brook, in whose voice he seemed to hear the kindly words of advice repeated again and again. When he arose and resumed the setting of his trap his face wore a stronger and more hopeful expression.

In the Linter

Next morning Uncle Lisha laid aside his holiday attire with a sense of great relief from the constraint and care which their wearing had imposed upon him, and put on his ordinary garb with the comfortable feeling of being rehabilitated in his real self. Making such haste with his breakfast that Aunt Jerusha said he was "in a bigger hurry 'n a boy a-

goin' a-fishin'," he put on his leather apron and set about the odd jobs of
mending for the family.

Sam and his father went out to their husking, and the door between
the kitchen and the shop being opened, that the old man might have the
companionship of the women folks, the house presently rang with the
merry thud of the hammer on his lap-stone.

Huldah was paring apples with a worn-out shoe knife discarded from
Uncle Lisha's kit, and Aunt Jerusha quartered and cored them with frugal
care that the least possible share should go to the pigs, while Sam and
Huldah's new baby made frequent excursions on all fours between the
two great objects of interest presented by the two industries.

Now he brought a chubby fistful of stolen shoe pegs to his mother's
knee, then made restitution to the owner with a slice of apple, begrimed
by repeated contact with the floor during its transportation.

"Why, yes, bub," said the old man, beaming down a kindly glance
through his round glasses upon the upturned baby face as he took the
proffered gift and laid it on the bench beside him, "it's turrible nice, but
Uncle Lisher don't 'pear tu feel like eatin' on 't jest naow. He hain't apple
hungry; guess he eat tew much breakfus' er suthin'. Ta' keer. Don't put
his leetle hanny ont' the lapstun. Git it smashed finer 'n a barn. No,
bubby, couldn't hev the wax. Gaum him all up so 't mammy 'd hafter
nigh abaout skin him tu git him clean ag'in; an' haow she would scold
both on us, an' haow we would cry, would n't we? Here, take a pooty paig
to Aunt Jerushy an' ask her 'f she ever see sech a cur'osity. Clipper, naow."

"Thank ye, a thaousan' times, you darlin' creetur," cried Aunt Jerusha,
when the child had scrambled to her with his gift. "I never see a neater
paig an' I'm a-goin' tu keep it tu hev me a shoe made."

Several neighbors dropped in at the shop in the Linter the evening of
the following day to learn of any news of the ravager of Joel Bartlett's
flock. Solon Briggs took his seat behind the stove, Joseph Hill seated
himself with laborious care on the chair of most doubtful stability, Antoine sat on the floor with legs crossed after the fashion of Turks and
tailors, and Pelatiah perched uncomfortably, as became his state of mind,
on the corner of the shoe bench. With the autocrat of the little realm
on his leathern throne, the social pipes alight, Pelatiah ruminating his
innocuous cud, they could hardly realize that the old familiar intercourse
had suffered a three years' hiatus.

"I should raly like to know what specie of savagarous beast has been
a-deevastatin' Joel's sheep."

"Proberbly," said Joseph, venturing to tilt his chair on its front legs to enable him to spit at the stove hearth, "it's a wolf er suthin'." The chair gave a creak ominous of collapse, and he carefully readjusted it to its complete if precarious support of his weight. "Seem 's 'ough this 'ere chair was a leetle mite more weewaw 'an it uster be," and he leaned cautiously to one side and the other to inspect the spreading legs, "but I don't know as it is," slowly bending forward for a general survey of them, between his spread knees; "I guess it 'll stan' a spell."

"I wish 't you 'd bust the tarnal ol' thing, Jozeff," said Uncle Lisha, with nervous impatience. "It's squeaked an' it 's squoke till I am sick an' tired of it."

"It best was, you 'll seet where Ah 'll was, Zhoseff, den it ant be danger for fall off or broke up you sit, ant it?"

"Judgin' f'm what I hearn," said Uncle Lisha, after watching the chair with a hope of the fulfillment of his wish, "I s'pect it's a wolf. It's ben a good spell sen' there's ben one on 'em raound these parts. It's a massy the varmints ain't so thick as they used to be. When I was a boy you c'd hear 'em a-yowlin' up on the maountain, most any night, 'nough tu make yer back freeze. Naow an' ag'in, they used tu kill folks, I s'pose. I never knowed o' their killin' anybody fer sartain, but some on 'em 'lowed they killed Cephas Worth an' eat him clean up, an' then ag'in, some cal'lated they did n't."

The noise of stamping feet was heard on the doorstep, and Samuel entered. All eyes were turned inquiringly upon him, for he wore the triumphant air of one who bears important tidings.

"Wal?" Uncle Lisha laconically voiced the impatience of the audience.

"Arter a good deal o' searchin', I faound the track an' follered it tu a spreuce cobble a mild east o' Joel's, an' I cal'late he 'll lay up there till he gits hungry ag'in. I've tol' ev'ybody 'long my way hum, an' naow you fellers want to start right straight aout an' pass raound word to ev'ybody to rally in the mornin' an' meet at Joel Bartlett's. S'posin' Solon an' Jozeff notify the folks up their way an' Antwine them up his 'n, an' Peltier daown west, an' as soon 's I get a bite o' suthin' tu eat, I 'll go over to the store where there 'll be a lot a-loafin' raound so 't I can send word to heaps o' folks. It's airly in the evenin' an' the' 's time tu raoust aout a party 'at 'll make it lively for the ol' wolf. Turn 'em aout, Uncle Lisher."

The Hunting of the Wolf

The morning sunlight had not touched the treetops of the crest of the western Danvis hills, when half of the arms-bearing population of the township were arriving at, or tending toward, the appointed gathering place, some in sleighs, some on foot, each bearing some sort of firearm. The morning was not far spent, when a formidable force had gathered about the premises of Joel Bartlett, a strangely warlike array to be mustered in those peaceful precincts, yet Joel beheld it with a kindly and approving eye as he stood in the doorway, with Jemima peering timidly out behind him.

"It's a heavy weight on my mind to see so many men bearin' carnal weapons," she said with a very audible sigh; "it seems too much like the marshalin' of the hosts for battle."

"But thee sees, Jemimy, it hain't for no puppus of sheddin' humern blood ner even for larnin' an' practysein' the weeked art o' war, but jest tu quell the ravenous beasts of the wilderness, which can't be wrought upon by the Word nor by returnin' good for evil."

"Yes, I s'pose thee's right, Joel; but I can't help my mind a-dwellin' on what guns was mostly made for, in times formerly. Ah, me! But, Joel, won 't thee tell these good folks to come in an' get some nut cakes and cheese if any on 'em has occasion. Some must have eat breakfast uncommon airly this mornin'."

Joel loosened the pucker of his lips, and loudly proclaimed the "invite," which was accepted with great alacrity by many who stood in no need of refreshment, and with more diffidence by some who already were reminded they had breakfasted at an unwonted hour.

"Wal, I guess abaout ev'ybody's got here 'at's comin'," Sam Lovel said, after a careful survey of the roads and cross-lot bypaths, "an' we 'd better choose a captain an' be a-moggin'. I move we hev Captain Peck for aour captain. Half his comp'ny 's here an' 'll foller his orders nat'rally."

"If they don't du better 'n they du tu trainin', it 'll take a corp'ral tu ev'ry private tu keep 'em in line," said John Dart, struggling with a dry mouthful of doughnuts and cheese. "Then, ag'in, he hain't no hunter. We want you, Lovel."

"No, it'll look better tu hev Captain Peck," Sam insisted; "you secont him, Dart."

"Wal, I don't care. I secont Cap'n Peck, wi' Sam Lovel for leftenant."

"You hear the nommernation," Solon Briggs said, taking upon himself the office of moderator. "As'el Peck for capting of this hunt, wi' Samwill Lovel for leftenant, sort of aidycong to give advices and et cetery. You that's in favor, say 'aye,' contrary minded, say 'no.' The ayes have it, an' you chose the above-mentioned to serve you, as heretobefore stated."

Captain Peck, a brisk little man, somewhat swelled up with the importance of his dual offices, held a brief consultation with Sam, and then in his biggest military voice, usually reserved for trainings, gave the order, "Fall in, men," and, presently, "Forrid, march," and the motley company, numbering a hundred or more, went forward in disorderly ranks toward the objective point.

"You must stop your gab, men," Sam continually insisted, as he passed along the talkative line, 'erless you'll skeer that aire wolf clean tu N' Hampshire. You hain't got nothin' to say but what 'll keep till we git a line araound the cobble, an' then you c'n shoot off your maouths as much as you're a min' ter."

A half hour's march brought them to the foot of a rocky hill densely clad with a black growth of spruce and fir, whose blue shadows deepened into a twilight obscurity that the infrequent shafts of sunlight pierced but to make the deeper. Three sides abutted on partially cleared fields, the other swept up with a long curve to the steeper declivities of the mountain.

The triple column, now separated in two single files, one led by Captain Peck, the other by Sam, began to inclose the hillock. When the leaders met on the further side, without discovering the outgoing track of the wolf, word was passed that the circuit was completed, and the order given for the men to take proper distances and move toward the centre. Gradually the circle narrowed. The gloomy depths of thicket after thicket were invaded and passed. Each moment, the more excitable hunters grew nervous with expectation, the cooler, more steadily alert. To some, every moving shadow took on a wolfish semblance; steadfast rocks and stumps became endowed with grim, alert life; now a gun was leveled to an unsteady aim and its useless discharge forestalled by the sharp, peremptory caution of some clear-eyed and cool-headed veteran, till at last the word came too late to prevent one careless shot, which was the signal for a scattered fusilade from various posts of the encircling line.

The random firing aroused the wolf from his lair and sent him sneaking from one border of his constricted limits to find another as effectually guarded against his passage. Then he swept around the circle, searching with eager eyes for some vulnerable point, disclosing fleeting glimpses of himself that drew upon him occasional shots, which increased his long, regular lopes to a wild, scurrying flight, now bounding from side to side of the cordon, now skirting it in an agony of fear, whimpering as he ran, now halting, half cowering, while he looked in vain for some loophole of escape.

Once, as he thus crouched for an instant, Sam's quick eye caught sight of him, and, taking an instantaneous aim, he saw the sight shining in bright relief against the dark gray fur of the wolf's side. As he felt the trigger yielding to the pressure of his finger, his heart filled with anticipated success, but, with the dull click that was the only response to the fall of the striker, it collapsed and sank like a plummet.

"Cuss them caps o' Clapham's," he groaned wrathfully, "if one on 'em ever does go, I wish he might be shot with it."

A shot from Captain Peck's gun cut loose a shower of evergreen twigs above the wolf, who cringed beneath their light downfall and then sprang away, vanishing like the shadow of a wind-tossed branch in the gloom of the thicket.

Pelatiah's post was on the valley side of the hill where he had caught sight of the wolf several times, and once had taken a hasty and ineffectual shot. It had all happened in a flash, and he was confusedly trying to remember whether he fired at the wolf or into the treetops, and to formulate an excuse for his miss that should be satisfactory to himself as well as to others, when he was startled by a sudden crash of dry twigs on the crest of the ledge just above him, and almost at the same instant he saw the animal flying at full speed down the sharp declivity directly behind him, so close upon him that he could only think to shout lustily and brandish his gun to scare the brute back into the woods, but it only swerved a little from its course and rushed madly on.

Not many paces to Pelatiah's left stood Beri Burton, as gaunt and grim as the wolf himself, and so transfixed with surprise at the sudden apparition that he stood stock still, his large jaws agape, till the wolf was within his gun's length of him, and he stepped backward to make way. His heel caught a fallen branch, and he fell sprawling on his back. The wolf, snapping and gnashing his white fangs, swept over his prostrate form, and, clear at last of the perilous cordon, sped away toward the hills.

Pelatiah vainly attempted to cover him with a pottering aim for a moment, then took the track, and presently disappeared among the blue shadows and gray tree trunks.

Beri Burton slowly got upon his feet, sputtering and mumbling, till, having come to as intelligible speech as was possible to him, he shouted loudly:—

"Wolf gone. Wolf gone ter Jerooslum. Gol dumb sech er wolf." Then as one and another of the party came hastening up, he related again and again the incidents of the wolf's escape. "Gol dumb sech er wolf. Run kerchug right ergin me an' knocked me over, kerwollopp. Flopped one foot int' my maouth. Wisht I'd bit foot off. Yes, sir, flopped dumb foot right square in my maouth."

"Can't blame him as I knows on," said John Dart. "He'd got tu put his foot somewheres."

"By the gre't horn spoon! we're a smart lot o' men," said Sam, joining the gathering group, "to let that wolf git away from us in that way. All Adams an' Pocock 'll be pokin' fun at us fer a year to come."

"Why didn't some o' you smartins shoot him, then?" Beri growled; "hed chances 'nough, I reckon, by the bang-whangin'. Gol dumb sech shootin'."

"Don't seem's 'ough Adams an' Pocock hed no 'casion to laugh," said Joseph Hill. "It wa'n't their wolf, leastways it hain't got the earmark er brand o' ary one o' the towns, fer 's I c'n see."

"'T ain't aour wolf nuther, fer's appears," said Sam. "But what way did he head? Where's Peltier? Someb'dy said he seen him last."

"Dumb fool's chasin' on him," Beri mumbled. "'Spec he's goin' tu ketch him, prob'ble."

"Peltier was mos' crazy in hees head," Antoine explained. "He was kanna he-widder, cos hees gal goin' leff him, 'fore he 'll got marree togedder."

"His head's straighter 'n aourn on this business," said Sam, "an' we might as well mog along arter him. The hunt is up for tu-day. But the critter may lay up on Hawg's Back to-night an' give us a chance to-morrer."

And so the dejected and disappointed wolf hunters made their way into the clearing, each one loudly blaming every one else, and himself silently and less satisfactorily, for the barren result of the hunt.

On the morning of the great hunt there were at least two nonparticipants, who through being such were quite as heavy-hearted as were now any of the baffled hunters. Uncle Lisha sighed heavily as he returned to the shop after the last of several tours of observation which he made into the back yard, where he could look across the fields to the rendezvous and see the men already clustering in knots in Joel Bartlett's yard, and hear the subdued jangle of arriving bells.

"Ho, hum, I'm tew short-winded and stiff-j'inted tu keep within hollerin' distance of the oldest an' laziest on 'em, an' I might jest as well seddaown an' go tu work, but I wisht a feller's laigs wouldn't grow ol' no faster 'n his speerits. Ho, hum!" and settling himself into his seat, he picked up his board, leather, and knife, and endeavored to lose sight of age and infirmities in the intricacies of his craft.

Aunt Jerusha looked in through the open kitchen door, and seeing his hands resting idly on the board, and his eyes staring abstractedly out of the window, she said in a coaxing voice:—

"What makes ye try to work, Lisher? I wouldn't ef I was you. The' hain't no men folks workin' to-day. Put on yer kwut an' hat an' mittens an' go over to Joel's. You c'n see 'em start an' git the fust news when they come back. Wouldn't you, Huldy?"

"Sartainly. It'll do you good an' I sh'd like to go myself," Huldah said encouragingly, as she looked in over Aunt Jerusha's shoulder, and the baby, pushing between their skirts, scrambled over to the old man, bearing one of his mittens in his milk teeth.

"Wal, I swan, ef Bubby an' the hull kit on ye are sot on gittin' red on me, I guess I'll hafter." And so smiling down upon the crowing child, as he donned his outdoor gear, he trudged forth across the fields.

Desertion by its men folks had not brought complete quiet to the Lovel homestead, any more than to others that day similarly deserted in Danvis, for the women's tongues enjoyed unrestrained freedom to wag at will.

Aunt Jerusha fully realized the privilege, when, after stopping at the shop window to watch her husband's slow progress across the fields, she reentered the kitchen, and, seating herself restfully in her favorite chair, she took out her snuffbox and regaled herself with a long-inhaled pinch of the fragrant powder, to which she in turn invited each nostril with impartial twists of her mouth from side to side. When she had returned the box to the deep pocket and fumbled forth her copperas-checked, homespun handkerchief, she settled back in her chair and made declaration:—

"I will say, Huldy, 'twixt you an' me an' the whippin' pos', 'at it's a raal comfort oncte in a while to be clean red o' men folks. Not tu say but what I set store by well-behaved men folks, sech as aourn' be, an' consider 'em a necessary blessin', but you do git cl'yed o' the best o' things arter tew long spells."

Huldah picked up the baby from the floor, seated him on her lap, wiped his chubby cheeks with a moistened corner of her apron, and kissed them with long inhalations of their subtle fragrance that only a mother can catch, before she answered.

"I 'spect 'at th' was a time when you couldn't hev tew much of Uncle Lisher, an' begun to hanker arter him the minute he was out of sight."

The russet of the wrinkled cheeks was tinged with a faint blush that kindled a responsive glow in Huldah's conscious face, and both laughed an acknowledgment of the touch of nature that makes youth and age akin.

"I hain't denyin' young folkses' foolishness, but that don't signify. What I du say is, 'at when folks gits settled daown to the tussle o' livin', there be times when it's restin' tu hev men folks aouten the way. Women wants a chance tu talk about their consarns, an' argy their own way. Somehaow men can't argy, but keep a-givin' their reasons an' their whys an' wherefores. Women know a thing is so, an' jest stick tu it, an' that's argyin' 'at gin'ally fetches men araound er shets 'em up, which answers the puppus."

"Yes," Huldah concluded, as she trotted her boy at arm's length and looked at him in absorbed admiration, "I s'pose the common run o' men folks is sot an' onreasonable, but it does n't seem 's 'ough Sam was, on'y mebby a leetle grain 'baout goin' huntin' an' sech."

"Wal, I can't say 'at father is nuther, not in a gin'ral way, ner yet yer father Lovel. Semanthy argy'd him aouten that. But all men folks ain't like aourn, an' I like tu git shet of even them oncte in a while, an' have a raal ri' daown womern's talk. I do' know as I enj'yed it much wi' George's wife, 'cause she was everlastin'ly blamin' George, which went ag'in' my gizzard; fer if there ever was a 'commerdatin', clever man, George is, if he is my son, an' she'd orter know it. But with you, Huldy, I enj'y talkin'." So they fell into comforting discourse.

And at Joseph Hill's house: "It's a mighty pooty idee 'at I hain't a goin' tu turn aout along wi' the rest on 'em. Tew ol'? Hain't so spry 's I useter be? I'm younger an' spryer 'an you be, Joe Hill, ef I be risin' eighty-seben." So Gran'ther Hill growled and roared as he stamped to and fro across the kitchen in his stocking feet, glowering at his son's abashed face, as at each turn it was brought within range of his angry eyes.

"Don't seem 's 'ough it 'ould be noways best, father," Joseph feebly argued, "it 's tew exposin'; you 'd get rheumatiz an' neurology."

"Rheumatiz an' ol' rology more like. Ef I got 'em they wouldn't hurt me none. A man 'at's marched tu Canady in the winter hain't agoin' tu be skeered aouten a wolf hunt by a pain in his laigs er a toothache, 'specially when he hain't got no teeth. Naow, look a-here, Jozeff," turning before his son and assuming a less aggressive tone, "I've got to go an' show 'em haow. The' hain't a man jack on 'em 'at knows beans about wolf huntin', never see a wolf an' would n't know one if they did see him. 'T ain't no ways likely the' is a wolf, but ef the' is, he'd orter be hunted as he'd ortu be."

"Jes' so, father," said Joseph, catching hopefully at the veteran's skepticism, "I don't b'lieve the' is no wolf, an' the' hain't no need o' you er nob'dy else's goin'; 't ain't nothin' on'y dawgs."

"You must be a idjit, Jozeff Hill, tu think 'at dawgs 'ould kill sheep in the way them was killed. I tell ye it's a wolf, an' by the Lord Harry I'm goin' tu help kill the cussed varmint. Gi' me that aire gun."

"The' hain't a ball er a spoo'ful o' shot in the haouse, father."

"That's almighty pooty haousekeepin'; no shot ner ball? You'd a tarnal sight better be ketched wi'out tea an' sugar, yes, or rum, 'an wi'out am-mernition. Bub, where's yer fish lines? Fetch me ev'y sinker you got."

The younger Josiah obeyed the order with an alacrity stimulated by a desire to further his grandfather's purposes, which, if carried out, might make him his necessary attendant.

"I wouldn't go if I was you, father," pleaded his daughter-in-law, "it's tew hard fer you, an' then ag'in, I want you tu stay an' ta' care o' me."

"You don 't need nob'dy. The wolf hain 't a-goin' tu come in the haouse an' eat you. Jozeff c'n stay."

"But you see, father, I sorter promised tu go, an' I've got tu."

"So hev I got tu. Gimme my boots."

"Father," said the son, playing his last card, with an air of deep dejection, "I'm turrible sorry, but I took 'em over to Uncle Lisher's las' night tu git 'em mended;" and he breathed a silent prayer, "The Lord forgive me fer lyin' an' keep me from gittin' ketched at it."

"You etarnal, infarnal, meddlin' idjit," his father roared, his voice shaken with anger, "haow dast ye send my boots to git mended? Haow'd you know I wanted 'em mended, say? It does beat hell amazin'ly, what tarnal luck I did hev, a bringin' on ye up. I don't wisht you was dead, but I swear, I wisht I hadn't never hed ye. Clear aout. Go an' hunt yer tarnal wolf, but ye shan't take my gun. Not a step aouten this haouse does that aire gun go, 'thout me a kerryin' on 't. You c'n take Bub's bow-arrer, it's good 'nough fer you. Er borry Joel Bartlett's ol' britch-burnt, hang-fire, Quaker gun. Yeou shoot a wolf, Lordermighty!"

Joseph fled in dismay from the rattling volley of his father's wrath, nor stayed his steps till they brought him to the meeting place, while his wife, with all the children but the eldest boy, retreated into the fastnesses of the pantry. Little Josiah, secure in his position as his grandfather's favorite, remained, the sole and undismayed spectator of the old man's rage.

"Blast 'em. Kerryin' off my boots," the veteran fumed, still pacing the rounds of the kitchen. "I'm a good minter go in my stockin' feet, jes tu spite 'em. I hope the Lord it hain't nothin' but a dawg. The idjits wouldn't know the diffunce."

The boy held out two plummets of hammered lead and one half bullet. "What was you goin' to do wi' 'em?"

"Load this 'ere gun wi' 'em," was the hoarsely whispered reply. "I 've made killin' shots at two-legged and four-legged varmints wi' wus slugs 'an these. Gimme me a holt on 'em an' I'll load her jest fer the fun on 't." He took the big gun from its hooks and carefully measured in his palm a charge of powder from the great oxhorn, poured it into the barrel and wadded it with tow, dropped the sinkers in one by one, wadded them and primed the piece, while the boy's eyes closely followed every movement.

Maria heard the clang and thud of the iron ramrod and peered anxiously through the pantry door.

"Why, father, what be you a-duin'?"

"I'm gittin' ready tu ta' keer on ye ag'in' the wolf tackles ye, M'rier," he chuckled scornfully. "Shet the door, M'rier, an' 'tend tu yer cookin'; me an' Bub's stan'in' guard." He fondled the gun and wiped the dust from the barrel with his coat sleeve, and aimed at the clock.

"Du ye wanter go awfle, Gran'ther?" whispered Josiah.

The old man nodded his head repeatedly without withdrawing his aim from the centre of the clock face.

"Sh-h-h, I know where your boots be. In the paoundin' berrel in the back shed. I'll fetch 'em when ma goes down suller arter the 'taters."

The grandsire's slow, senile stare gradually gave way to a look of intelligence, and the two conspirators, in pantomime, enjoined secrecy.

Wondering at the sudden silence, Maria peeped through a cranny of the door and saw the old man quietly seated in his chair, and called to him as she bustled about her work:—

"I'm turrible glad you gin it up so sensible, father."

"Sho, I hedn't no idee a-goin'. I was jest a-foolin' Jozeff. Ketch me a-goin' dawg huntin' along wi' that mess o' idjits," and he winked hard at his grandson, who, under cover of the stove, was growing red with smothered mirth.

"My sakes," said Maria, coming out and looking at the clock, "I mus' git the pertaters and put that fish a-fresh'nin'."

As her step was heard on the last cellar stair, Josiah stole out to the back shed and presently appeared with the boots, which his grandfather drew on in tremulous haste, while the boy, after driving the small children back into the pantry and closing the door upon them, brought the old man's hat and cane.

"Hurry up, Gran'ther. Ma'll be up in a minute," he whispered as he hovered about the ancestral chair in a fever of excitement. Then he opened the door and the old man passed out as noiselessly as his stiff joints would let him, with his long gun trailed in careful avoidance of lintel and posts, just as the muffled thud of the last potato announced the filling of the pan.

"Can 't I go with you, Gran'ther?" Josiah asked eagerly; but his heart sank as he read refusal written in the stern yet half-regretful face bent upon him.

"Could n't nohaow, Sonny; 't would n't du any good an' might du hurt. Them idjits 'll shoot awful keerless an' might hit you. You gwup an' look aouten the saouth garret winder, an' you c'n see Haidge Hawg Cobble where they say the wolf 's lyin' up. Naow go an' tell 'em I 've gone aout tu the barn, an' so I hev, an' mebby a leetle beyend." He gave the boy an approving pat on the head that gave some comfort, though it drove the coarse sealskin cap over his eyes.

The veteran's departure was covered by the barn from the observation of the inmates of the house. As he plodded across the snowy fields his thoughts went back to the old days of humble, unrequited heroism, when he marched with Warner and his Green Mountain boys to Canada. In a misty daydream he saw the frozen level of Champlain stretching in lifeless loneliness behind the rangers' march, the wintry gloom and desolation of the forest opening to them the only path beyond. He heard again the click and swish of snowshoes, the low, cautious word of command drifting back along the triple files. For a little space it quickened his pulse and pace, and for a moment he was young again, till, tired by climbing a high rail fence, he leaned against the nearest stump to rest, and realized that he was but a feeble old man, the superannuated, sole survivor of the band, to follow whom, he lingered a little on the verge of the eternal mystery.

"A goo' for nothin' ol' critter as orter stay tu hum wi' women an' young uns," he sighed, half minded to turn back, when his eye was caught by a moving speck far away toward Hedge Hog Cobble. Something familiar in the movements of the distant object drew upon it the veteran's closest scrutiny.

"That hain't no dawg, it's tew big fer a fox. By the Lord Harry, it's a wolf, an' he's a-comin' stret tu me."

He sank stiffly behind the stump and cocked his gun while he steadfastly watched the beast's swift approach. Now he could see the wild, cunning eyes, now the red tongue hanging slavering from the white-fanged jaws, and now he aimed, with all the skill that eye and nerve could command, just before the pointed nose, and with a prayer as devout as he ever uttered, pulled the trigger, as with swift, long lopes the wolf ran past, fifty yards away. With a snarling yelp, a long, floundering fall, and a quicker recovery of his feet, with a broken foreleg helplessly dangling, the wolf charged wildly at the fence, clung a moment to the top rail, fell back, and then plunged at the nearest but too narrow interstice between the rails. The impetus of the leap drove him halfway through, but there he was caught at the hips. He pushed desperately with the uninjured foreleg and clawed vainly with his hind feet for a hold on the nether rail, and was slowly worming his way through, when Gran'ther Hill pounced upon him, seizing him by both hindlegs, and, bracing his own feet against the fence, he held on and shouted lustily for help at the top of his high-pitched, cracked voice.

The wolf writhed from side to side, and snapped his wicked jaws within two feet of his captor's hands, without being able to harm him, but his struggles were fast exhausting the strength of the old man, who, almost in despair, saw the prize slipping, inch by inch, through the fence.

Then he heard rapid steps, and turning his head he saw Pelatiah's lank figure close beside him.

"Ketch a holt here, quick," he gasped.

Pelatiah lent one strong hand to his relief, and the old man loosed his hold. Snatching the gun from Pelatiah, he staggered to the fence, and, with a cruelly deliberate aim at three feet range, bored the wolf's skull with the heavy charge of buckshot. "There," he panted, as with a grim smile he regarded the last struggles of his victim when Pelatiah had drawn it forth from the fence, "he knows naow what he gits by runnin' ag'in' a real ol'-fashioned hunter. S'pose he cal'lated the' wa'n't none left, an' the' hain't on'y one. But I'm almighty glad you come, young Gove, fer I was nigh abaout tuckered, an' ef I hed tu let go, the critter might ha' flummixed along a good piece afore I c'ld ha' loaded up. Good Lord," he gasped, aghast at the sudden recollection that he had no ammunition, "I hed n't another charge. Wal, I be glad you come, young Gove. Where's the rest of the idjits? Git up on ter the fence an' holler like a loon."

Pelatiah's triumphant shouts soon brought in the foremost of the straggling pursuers, who, as they beheld the dead wolf and heard the story of his death, were variously moved with admiration of his slayer's prowess and chagrin for their own lack of it.

"By the gret horn spoon!" cried Sam, stroking the wolf's gaunt side almost tenderly and looking up at the old man's serenely happy face, "I'd ha' gi'n the ol' Ore Bed tu ha' shot the critter myself, but I do' know but I'm gladder you done it, Cap'n Hill."

"I reckon 'at my chances is gittin' a leetle sca'cer 'n yourn, Sammy. But you might profit more by them 'at you git, ef I'd hed the bringin' on you up. I consait you hed the makin's of a hunter in ye ef ye'd on'y hed me er even Peleg Sunderlan' tu eddicate your nat'ral gifts."

"Hooray for Danvis!" roared John Dart as he came upon the scene. "Adams, ner Pocock, ner nary other town can twit us o' losin' aour wolf naow, Lovel. I was growin' shameder an' shameder tu meet any on 'em, an' was studyin' more lies tu tell 'em 'an I c'ld ever ben forgive fer under any circumstances. You 've saved the credit of your taown, Cap'n Hill, an' mebby my soul."

"Gol dumb sech savin'," Beri Burton growled. "Danvis hain't got much tu brag on when it's got tu ressureck the dead a'most, tu kill a wolf."

"Shet yer head," Dart growled savagely.

"An' call aout the infants," Beri persisted. "He wouldn't er shot er wolf if that aire shimble-shanked Gove boy hedn't er hel' his laigs."

"He'd waounded him, so 't he couldn't but jest go, an' he'd got him eenamost killed when I come up," Pelatiah magnanimously protested.

"Wal, le' 's stop our gab an' start aour caravan," said Dart. "We've got tu show tu the village this arternoon. Where's Cap'n Peck?"

"Skinned it fer hum, half an hour ago," some one answered.

"Wal, let him go. I was goin' tu propose 'at we fired a s'lute, but nev' mind. Who 's got a gun 's long 's Cap'n Hill's? Fetch it here. Lay it daown 'longside o' his'n. Naow, lay the wolf top on 'em. Naow, Cap'n Hill, you set top o' the wolf."

"Yis, du! Yis, du!" other voices shouted with Dart. The hero of the day rather reluctantly complied.

"Ketch a holt o' the muzzles, Lovel, an' I'll take the butts. Up he goes," and the veteran hunter and his grim quarry were lifted aloft and borne forward, amid the cheers of the party.

"What's up?" Joseph Hill panted, breathless with his exertions to overtake his comrades.

"Your superannual, ancient sire is, Jozeff," said Solon, "him an' the wolf. Hain't you hearn how he slewed him?"

"Good Lord," Joseph groaned; recognizing the elevated countenance of his father, his eyes anxiously sought his feet.

Catching sight of him the old man bent upon him a frown, the severity of which was somewhat softened by the pride of his achievement, and laughed down at him scornfully, "You ondutiful leetle cuss, you hid my boots, did you? Did you s'pose a man 'at had took Ticonderogue an' fit tu Ben'n't'n an' went tu Canady 'long wi' Seth Warner an' hunted Tories wi' Peleg Sunderlan', couldn't smell aout his own boots? You must be a almighty smart boy."

Though conscious that his artifice was justified by his headstrong father's infirmities, Joseph fell to the rear in confusion, and the procession continued its triumphal progress to Joel Bartlett's.

Uncle Lisha had waddled forth to meet it, roaring a welcome that was heard at every house in the neighborhood. When Joel beheld the grim trophy he was startled from his accustomed propriety, by the whistle that escaped unwittingly from the long-puckered lips.

"Friends," he said, chanting in the monotonous tune to which his sermons were set, "I feel to thank you, one an' all, for a-girdin' on your swords an' a-goin' forth tu battle against the beasts of the field which they ravage aour folds, an', as it ware, spile our barnyards. I thank you, friends, fer a-stretchin' forth your carnal weepons in behalf of a man whose ways has ben more led untu the plowshare an' the prunin' hook 'an tu the sword an' the spear. There's suthin' due more 'n thanks tu mortal man, an' I feel it bore in on me tu ask you, one an' all, tu enter my haouse" (as he paused and ran his eye over the company, as if making a mental computation of its numbers and capacity, more than one hungry stomach yearned for the anticipated offering of doughnuts and cheese), "an' git intu the quiet an' render silent thanks tu Him 'at has been pleased to reward your indivors with victory. Arter which," Joel continued after a solemn pause, "Jemimy, my wife, will pervide some sustenance for your carnal bodies, tu which you will be most welcome."

Few were inclined to accept the invitation to a repast, the first course whereof was likely to be long and unsatisfying to their present need, and so with thanks and excuses almost all hastened to avail themselves of the more exhilarating and substantial refreshments that were to be found at the tavern and store.

Gran'ther Hill's crown of laurels was further weighted with fresh contributions, some sprigs of which he generously permitted to adorn the youthful brow of Pelatiah, and was more content to enrobe himself in the misty glories of the past alone than to share these present, flimsy honors with another.

The First Fox

Sam, moving about cautiously in his stockings, was attempting the impossible feat of building a fire in the stove without making a noise, for it was early and he hoped that he might not disturb any of the family.

The wood tumbled about in the box as if endowed with perverse life. The griddles would slip and clatter and the doors bang as if they were made for no other purpose. Uncle Lisha, being a light sleeper, was aroused and came forth to learn the cause of the unseasonable disturbance, with his waistcoat in one hand and buttoning his suspenders fumblingly with the other.

"What on airth is the motter, Samwill? Baby hain't got the croup er nuthin', has he?" he whispered anxiously.

"No," was answered in a hollow whisper; "goin' huntin'. Thought I'd hev me a baked 'tater and cup o' tea tu start on, 'f I c'd git 'em 'thaout wakin' the hull neighborhood, but this consarned stove's ben dancin' a jig sence I fust touched it an' the wood turnin' summersets. But I've got the 'taters in. Sorry I waked ye, Uncle Lisher. Drive, you ol' fool, quit yer whinin' an' caperin'. We hain 't goin' yit."

"I'd slep' a plenty," and Uncle Lisha drew a chair to the stove and toasted his feet comfortably on the hearth. "Where be you goin', Samwill?"

"Well," said Sam, carefully filling a powderhorn while Drive watched the operation with intense interest, whining and treading the floor with his front feet, "I'm a-goin' tu take Peltier a fox huntin'. I b'lieve 'f I c'n git him int'rested in 't an' hev him kill a fox er tew, it'll git him over mopin' and honin' himself to death arter that misible gal. The' hain't nothin' like huntin' tu take a feller's mind off'm trouble."

"Wal," said the old man in a draughty whisper that set the candle flaring, "I d' know but what it 'll help some, but I shall reckon more on fishin'. But I tell ye, I b'lieve he 's kinder taken a shine tu that aire Varney gal, an' that's a-goin' tu cure him."

"'T won't 'mount tu shucks. Peltier hain't that kind o' chap tu shift his likes sudden. I don 't b'lieve he 'll ever keer a row o' pins for any other gal. The best 'at can be done for him is tu git him from dwellin' on his trouble, an' I don 't know o' nothin' better 'n huntin'. The quiet of the woods an' the noises, which is nigh about the same thing, is mighty soothin', an' the smell o' dead leaves an' the spreuce an' balsam is stren'- thenin' tu the narves, an' when you git raly woke up with the hootin' o' the haound a-drawin' nigher an' you hear the fox a-rustlin' the dry leaves an' snappin' the dry twigs, it sets your heart afire an' burns aout all the foolishness an' trouble."

"Mebby," said the other, "but fishin' is turrible soothin'. I'd ruther chance it on fishin' an' that Varney gal. She 's a strornary nice gal."

Sam opened the oven door and tested his cookery with a pinch. "My 'taters is done. Set by an' ha' some, Uncle Lisher?"

But the old man chose to wait for a more elaborate meal, and Sam hastily swallowing his tea, potatoes, and cold meat, and assuming his equipment, was ready to depart just as Pelatiah appeared, and the two held forth in the growing whiteness of the winter dawn with the old hound, sobering down to the business of his life, ranging steadily be- fore them.

There had been a hoar frost in the night, and every fence and tree was turned to misty silver and pearl, and the mountain arose before them against the paling azure like a great cloud of pearl, unstable, ethereal, as if the lightest breeze might waft it away. There was a haziness in the atmosphere giving it an apparent softness that seemed to belong to another season, and make one almost expect to hear the songs of birds coming from the silver foliage and see the stir of insect life among the feathery herbage of the frost, grown in a night upon the snow.

But the few sounds that scarcely broke the silence were all of winter. The smothered chuckle of the ice-bound brook, the resonant crack of a frozen tree, the muffled crow of a housed cock, and the discordant cries and flicker of the gay plumage of a jay early faring abroad were the only signs of life astir save the hunters and their hound.

Old Drive soon found the warm trail of a fox that had been mousing among the snow-covered aftermath, and he presently set the mountain-side and the hills to bandying melodious echoes that awoke all the valley from its slumbers.

A dozen house dogs burst into vociferous baying at the distracting multitude of airy voices, and as many cocks sent forth their ringing challenges, and one by one the farmhouse chimneys began to lift their slanted pillars of smoke against the pearl-gray hills and blue sky.

There began to be signs of choring, the creaking and slamming of barn doors, the lowing of cattle, and men calling them to partake of their brown loaves, the stacks. Then were heard the mellow notes of horns and conchs, presently followed by a cessation of the sounds of labor. These, after a time, began again, with the clear, woody ring of axe strokes, the muffled thud of flails, the shouts of ox-teamsters and the drawling creak of their sleds.

The hunters gave heed to none of them. Only to the voice of the hound were their ears attentive as it tended toward the hills that buttressed the mountainside, letting here an echo fall asleep, here awakening another to wild mimicry.

"Ef he hain't got him up, he will in less 'n five minutes," said Sam after a moment of breathless listening to the hound's eager baying. "You pull foot for the saouth end o' Pa'tridge Hill. The' 's a big hemlock in the aidge of a leetle clearin'. Stan' there. If he gits past ye goin', he 'll come back that way. Stick to 't as long as the dawg stays on the hill. I'll go to the north end."

He struck off at a swinging gait, and Pelatiah in a divergent course made his way to the point indicated. He reached it much out of breath with climbing and excitement, his heart beating such a tumultuous accompaniment to the notes of the hound, drawing nearer and nearer, that he could scarcely hear their music.

He cocked his gun, and strove to settle his trembling nerves while he strained his eyes to catch a glimpse of the fox, for he could hear the hound crashing through the brush and whining and panting as he puzzled over a double of the trail. Then his heart stood still at a sudden flash of ruddy fur among the brush, his gun was at his shoulder, his finger feeling the trigger, but with a qualm of disgust he saw a red squirrel scampering along a log.

The music of the hound swept past, and Pelatiah's heart sank with the sense of lost opportunity. But he remembered Sam's assurance that the fox would come back, and took hope again. He backed into a comfortable position against the hemlock and listened half dreamily to the pulsing diminuendo of the hound's bugle notes and to the minor voices of the woods. A party of inquisitive chickadees sounded their cheery call close about him, a nuthatch piped nasally as he crept in a downward spiral along the branching trunk above. A woodpecker industriously tapped a dead tree, the squirrel dropped a slow shower of cone chips, and a company of jays attuned their voices to unwonted softness as they discoursed together.

Yet he was continually aware of the hound's mellow notes overbearing all these sounds, though faint and far away, till suddenly there broke above them all the short, thin report of a rifle, and almost with the fading out of the brief echo the baying of the hound ceased.

"Wal," said Pelatiah, letting his hopes down to the earth with a sigh. "The fox 's dead, that 's sartain, but I should n't ha' thought Sam would ha' cut in ahead on me an' shot him. That wa'n't the Ol' Ore Bed! 'T wa'n't laoud enough! It 's some skunk that 's sneaked in an' stole aour fox, an' by gol, he 'll haftu hump hisself ef I don't ketch him er run him in."

He pushed rapidly forward in the direction that he heard the shot. His course was lengthwise of the ledge, with so few obstacles that a half hour's walk brought him to the end of the fox's track, marked with a great blood-stained wallow in the snow. Leading straight away from it toward the little valley behind the hill went the tracks of a big pair of boots with a disproportionate stride.

"A short-laiged critter," Pelatiah remarked, as he settled himself upon the trail, "an' I guess my shanks' hosses 'll fetch him."

The trail presently led him to a narrow clearing and a little gray house that stood in forlorn nakedness of shade-trees and outhouses, close to an untraveled highway. The big boot tracks held straight across the poor little garden with its feeble array of bean poles bearing their withered garlands of rustling vines, passed the starved woodpile and its dull axe, to the neatly swept doorstep.

"Consarn his pictur'," and Pelatiah waxed hot with wrath as the trail grew warmer, "he 's sneaked intu Widder Wigginses'. But he need n't cal'late petticuts 'll save him. I'll skin 'im if the 's a dozen women standin' raound. The blasted thief."

He stepped softly upon the plank doorstep, and was about to enter, when he heard the excited voice of a boy and stopped to listen. He also heard the sibilant rush of air from the nipple of a gun and the soft pop of a withdrawn patch mingling with disconnected words and knew that the speaker was cleaning a rifle.

"Oh, ma," cried a voice with a grunt that indicated the pushing down of a patch. "I tell ye, it was fun. I popped him right plum through the head, an', sir, I dropped him right in his tracks. An' hain't he a neat one! An' naow I'm goin' to skin him an' stretch him an' take him daown to Clapham's an' sell him an' git you some tea an' sugar."

"It 'll be turrible good tu hev some ag'in, 'specially when a body is feelin' so peakéd," said a feeble voice. "An' haow did you happen tu kill a fox, Billy? That's men's game."

"Oh, I was up on the hill tryin' tu git a pa'tridge, an' I heard a haoun'-dawg a-comin' an' I jes' stood still as a post, an' fust I knew it, I seen the fox come bobbin' along an' I up an' let him hev', an' daown he flopped, an', sir, I could n't b'lieve 't was treue, an' when I r'aly got a holt on't I got dizzy an' all of a tremble, an' the nex' thing I thought on was the tea an' sugar fer you. An' then the haoun'-dawg come up and chawed him a spell, an' then I slung him on my back an' p'inted fer hum."

All the fire of Pelatiah's wrath was quenched and he was about to retire as silently as he had come, when he was arrested by the voice of the woman pitched to a tone of earnest reproof.

"Oh, Billy, you hed n't ever ortu done that. You'd orter waited an' gi'n the hunters the fox. It 's jest stealin'. Father allus said so. Oh, Billy, they 'll be arter you, an' nob'dy knows what they won't du tu ye. Whose haoun'-dawg was it, Billy?"

"It was Sam Lovel's ol' Drive. It 's the fust fox 'at ever I shot," Billy whimpered, "an' haow be I ever goin' tu git yer tea an' sugar?"

"It don't make no diffunce; you mus' take that aire fox right stret tu Samwill Lovel. You 've got tu take it tu them it belongs tu. Mebby the

Lord 'll pervide; but I d' know, it's long a-waitin'. Hang up the gun an' start right stret off. Take the fox an' start right off like an' hones' man."

Pelatiah broke in unceremoniously upon poor Billy's mournful preparations for departure, his unannounced appearance startling alike the boy and his sick mother, who stared at him half frightened, half indignant, from her uncomfortable support of scant pillows.

"The' don't nob'dy want no fox, Mis' Wiggins," he burst out impetuously. "Samwill an' me don't want him, ner won't hev him, nuther. Bub c'n take him right daown tu Clapham's an' git all he can fer him. Dollar an' a half, I shouldn't wonder. We won 't have it, I tell ye. We would n't tech tu take the fust fox 'at a boy ever shot. We know how he feels, me an' Samwill."

Certainly not by experience did Pelatiah know; but by sympathy, perhaps he did, today.

"Be ye much sick, Mis' Wiggins? Bub had better git Darktor Stun tu come up. I'll hev mother come over. Good-day."

He hurried to go, in as great confusion as that in which he left the widow and her son, who found not words but only grateful looks to thank him.

He stopped at the meager woodpile and plied the dull axe with sturdy strokes till three or four armfuls of wood were ready for the stove, and then hurried away up the long eastern slope of the hill. He laughed at himself as he recalled his recent small adventure. "Poor leetle shaver, a-floppin' 'raoun in his dead father's boots an' me a-bilin' myself up to lick someb'dy. Gol!"

Then through the stillness of the woods the mellow cadence of the old hound's bugle notes stole upon his ears, and all his thoughts were turned to the day's purpose. Listening to get the direction, he became assured that the earnest, insistent baying was almost confined to a fixed point.

"By golly, he 's started another, an' holed him, I guess. But I'll hyper over and git the dawg."

As he neared the place, the steep western side of the hill, he found that the hound was moving in small circles and felt renewed hope, and his heart gave a great choking bound as he caught a glimpse of the fox dodging among the rocks and brush of the steep hillside. So steep and slippery was the footing that Pelatiah was obliged to slip his arm around a sapling to hold his position, and so standing, he cocked his gun and

waited, his heart rising and sinking as Drive's notes approached and re-
ceded.

Suddenly, like a ruddy blossom that had burst from the wintry hillside, the fox appeared on the top of the rock and turned to look back at
the dog. The sight was drawn against the arched side, the trigger was
pulled, there was a kick of reassuring force, a responsive roar and a
wreathing, slowly-lifting cloud of smoke that for one moment of sick-
ening doubt Pelatiah tried to peer through, and then he was filled with
unspeakable joy at sight of the fox lying beside the rock, gasping spas-
modically, while his magnificent brush was moved with tremulous undulations. And then he knew how Billy Wiggins had felt. Not till he had
laid hold of his prize did he find voice to halloo to Sam, but then he did
it with such repeated vociferations that there was danger of alarming all
the valley.

Sam soon appeared on the scene, imperturbable but congratulatory.

"You done almighty well, Peltier, but where 's your t'other fox? I hearn
a shot an' the dawg come tu me."

"Wal," said Pelatiah, hesitating a little, "Widder Wigginses' boy shot
him an' I hed n't the heart tu take it away from him. An' she 's sick an'
they 're poorer 'n snakes. No tea nor no nothin'."

"An' ye done almighty well, Peltier," Sam said, after attentive consideration of the case. "Huldy an' me 'll go over there to-morrer an' see tu 'em.
An' naow le' 's skin that aire fox. By the gret horn spoon, he's a buster!"

Going Fishing

If the medicine administered by Sam for Pelatiah's wounded heart did
not cure that member, it eased its pain and was taken with a relish.
Every propitious hunting morning found him afoot betimes with Sam
and their trusty comrade, Drive, breasting the snow-drifted steeps, ranging the windswept ridges, and guarding the likeliest runways, while their
hearts beat fast or slow to the swelling and dying cadence of the hound's
melodious voice.

Then at nightfall, when the valley lay in blue shadows, with stars of houselights beginning to twinkle from its depths, and the last touch of the departing sun painted the great mountaintop with pulsing, nacreous tints against the rising shadow of the world, while beneath crept up the devouring monochrome of pearly gray, they fared homeward, often proud with a burden of trophies, always content with intangible ones or the comfort of deferred hope.

Uncle Lisha watched the treatment doubtfully.

"Huntin' may du it, but fishin' is soothin'er, an' I cal'late more on 't;" and he waited with impatience for the opening of the waters and the coming of his own opportunity to become a mediciner.

It seemed as if winter would never relinquish its sway even when the allotted period of its reign had expired. There were lapses, when the air came soft from the south, and the crows took heart of grace to return to the inhospitable land, and a solitary song sparrow to sing in the garden cherry-trees. Then the bitter winter wind came howling down from the north, and beat back the vernal tide, driving the crows in wind-tossed flight to the woods, and freezing out the sparrow's song, and making the sugar-makers idle but in anathematizing the untoward season.

At last there came a mild warmth into the atmosphere and up out of the earth, thawing the snow from beneath, till tawny hillocks and ridges cropped out. Warm showers poured down from clouds that parted to give glimpses of heavenly blue and drop squadrons of sunshine to charge across the fields, where changing sky and steadfast mountain swam inverted in the pools. The brooks were full to the brim of their snowy banks, and the rush of their yellow currents filled the air with a soft, changing murmur, like the song of the wind in pine woods. There was a busy hum of bees about the fresh sawdust and sappy logs of the wood-pile, and the idle buzz of flies warmed to life on the sunny side of buildings. Out of the maple woods still drifted the pungent smoke of the sugar camp and the fragrance of boiling sap.

Uncle Lisha opened the shop door to let in the pleasant outer warmth and sounds. He heard the sharp, imperative note of the first phoebe-bird, and saw her swooping among the swarms of flies, and as he drove the pegs and trimmed the tap, he counted the days till he could go a-fishing.

So the spring drew slowly but surely on. Fields and highways became dry and pleasant to feet that were weary of snowy and icy paths. The snow that endured but in grimy drifts was not like snow, so coarse-grained was it, and besmirched with litter and the débris of ploughed fields.

The purple mist of swelling buds enfolded the woods; the yellow windrows of pussywillows were piled along the brooks, where arose the crackling clatter of the first frogs, the shrill chime of the hylas, and the incessant trill of the toads.

The robins came, querulously yelping at first, then joyously celebrating their arrival; and the bluebird and his song floated down from the sky together. The voice of the brooks had fallen to a soberer cadence, that seemed to sing of fishing, and so, one morning, Uncle Lisha resolved to rouse Pelatiah and learn the condition of the water.

At an early hour the two anglers were behind the woodshed, Pelatiah turning the moist soil, dotted with green tufts of young motherwort and catnip, while Uncle Lisha stooped before him, turning the clods with his fingers and picking up the lusty worms as they were disclosed.

"The' 's sati'faction in fishin' from the fust start," he said as he dropped a worm into the battered teapot between his feet. "More 'n there is in huntin'. You don't see nothin' afore you when you 're puttin' paowder int' your horn an' shot int' your bag. But when you grab holt of a worm's head an' feel him a-lettin' go of the airth, slow an' reluctin', you c'n eenamost feel a traout snatchin' at him. An' there bein' worms goes to show the' must be fish, bein' that they was made for one 'nother. There, Peltier, I b'lieve we 've got 'nough," and he arose, straightening his spine with the backs of both grimy hands which he then brushed on his trousers, and the two set forth.

A dappled sky, filtering soft streams of sunshine, and a constant waft of south wind, invited them; the long whistle of meadowlarks called them, and a high-hole on a dry stub drummed a rapid, ringing roll to accelerate their steps.

Presently they came to a thicket that bordered the brook, where gray stumps of departed trees stood half disclosed among the misty ramage of saplings and the dark pyramids of young evergreens, and where yellow beds of adder-tongue mimicked sunlight, while spears of bloodroot pierced their own green shields and the first moose flowers splashed the shadows with their white blossoms.

As they entered it a partridge uttered a note of alarm and went hurtling away out of a flurry of dead leaves, and a woodchuck smothered his own querulous whistle as he retreated into his newly opened hole.

Uncle Lisha feeling in his pocket for his knife, slowly searched for a proper rod.

"An' the' 's consid'able enj'yment gittin' a pole," he continued, as if his discourse had suffered no interruption. "You don't wanter be tew fast, er you 'll be lierble tu run away f'm good uns, an' git desput an' take up wi' a mean un, jest as lots o' folks du in this world, 'goin' through the woods an' takin' up wi' a crooked stick,' at last. Then ag'in, you don 't want tu be tew slow an' pertic'lar er you won't never git tu fishin'. An' arter all, there will be disapp'intments, Peltier," he went on, bending down a sapling and slashing it from the stump. "You pick you aout one 'at looks all right, but when you come to trim it, it 's crookeder 'an a snarled waxed eend, erless it 's top-heavy, er suthin', an' that 's the way o' the world ag'in. But you don't want tu give up fer that, an' say the' haint no decent gals,— fishpoles, I mean,—an' say you 'll be dumbed if you try tu go a-fishin', fer the' 's jest as good fishpoles stan'in' as ever was cut, an' the' 's lots o' fun waitin' fer you tu git your sheer."

"When you've got a holt o' the best-lookin' one the' is an' it turns out tu be brittler 'n dry popple, what's the use o' tryin' to pick aout another?" Pelatiah asked as he carelessly trimmed a young birch.

"It wa'n't nothin' but dry popple an' you misjudged," Uncle Lisha answered as he neatly trimmed the branches and knots from his pole, "an' you wanter try ag'in, not seddaown an' mump."

He put the finishing touches to his work, snapped his knife shut against his hip and began to tie on his line.

"I don' cal'late the' 's as much fun gittin' ready fer huntin' as the' is fishin'. You buy your gun er borry it an' you do' know what it 's goin' t' du, mebby kick you like all possess' an' kill nothin'. If it's one you 've hed, you know all abaout it, an' haint no expectations one way ner t' other. An' you don' make it er fin' it, on'y feed it so much paowder an' tow an' shot. I don' cal'late these fellers 'at hes 'em a j'inted pole, wi' a leetle brass windlass on 't, gits half the enj'yment we du. They must feel allers afeer'd o' breakin' on 'em, er suthin', an' they must feel almighty mean to be a-foolin' fish wi' them feather contraptions. Fishes' feelin's orter be considered some. We give 'em the chance o' gittin' suthin' good. They offer 'em nothin' more 'n dry hus's. But le' 's git tu fishin'."

The trout were plenty and hungry and gave these simple anglers all the sport they desired, wherein, if no fine art of the craft was exercised, much good judgment and knowledge of the habits of the shy trout were displayed.

Making their slow way down the stream, they crept stealthily up to every promising place, taking here, a wary old trout from his log-roofed stronghold or root-netted hiding place, and there, three or four from beneath a circling raft of foam bells that slowly wheeled and undulated at the foot of a tiny waterfall, reinforced with new bubbles as others burst, and keeping ever the same.

They came to an alder-arched bit of water that looked promising, but there was no chance to make a cast. Uncle Lisha hunted the bank for a chip, which being found, he coiled his line upon it and set it afloat. It went tossing and whirling downstream among the shadows and the sparkle of rapids, uncoiling the line as it went, till it was all out and the baited hook was drawn overboard, and with a wavering plunge went out of sight.

There was a sharp tug, responded to by a too vigorous strike, and a fine trout came flying out of the water with a long, upward curve that hung him on an alder bush six feet above the brook.

Uncle Lisha waded down stream to secure him, beginning to discourse again as he splashed cautiously along the slippery bottom.

"As I was sayin', I cal'late fishin' is better 'n huntin' most any way you take it. You 're more sartain o' gittin' suthin' as a gin'l thing, an' ef you don 't you don 't feel no wuss ner nigh so tired. An' what you git, you git, an' what you waound, goes off an' gits well, stiddy a-lingerin' an' suff'rin' an' dyin' mis'able. Then ag'in"—he was reaching up for the dangling fish, rising on his toes,—"it 's soothin'er"; both feet slipped, and with a great splash he sat down, half damming the current that swirled and gurgled about his hips.

"Yes," he reiterated stoutly, as Pelatiah helped him to arise and regain the bank, "it 's soothin'er, but I won't say I like it quite so dumbed soothin'. But I don't keer a darn, I've got the fish."

His clothes were wrung out and they fared forward, the old man still enjoying the sport while his trousers slowly dried in the genial air.

The brook babbled its endless story to them. From distant meadows came the songs of meadowlarks, the cackle of flickers, and the long wail of a plover. On the soft breath of the south wind were wafted past them in wavering flight the first butterflies, purposeless of aught but mere enjoyment.

"It 's soothin'er," he repeated, "on accaount o' huntin' bein' excitin'er. You git more time tu set an' think abaout nothin' an' look araound an' listen an' git tu feelin' peaceable, when the luck hain 't tew almighty bad. But that don 't make a feller so grumpy an' rantankerous as onlucky huntin'. When I ben a-humpin' over ol' boots and shoes till I do' know myself by smell or feelin' f'm a side o' so'luther, the' hain't nothin ' 'at fetches me tu myself ag'in' like goin' a-fishin'. I'd livser git a mess 'an tu not, feelin' better carryin' hum a respectible string an' hevin' more pluck tu go ag'in' female opposition nex' time the fit takes me, but ef I don't git enough tu raise a smell in the pan, I 've hed me my fishin'. I 've seen the brook an' heard it a-talkin' tu itself an' mebby to me, I do' know, an' like 'nough seen some odd capers o' birds er animils, an' got the kinks aouten my j'ints, an' so don 't caount I 've lost the day. S-s-h-h. See that pleggid mink."

He pointed out the lithe, alert, dusky form poised on the verge of a brookside boulder, intently scanning the eddying current beneath, and the two watched him make a noiseless, arrowy plunge, and emerge with his writhing prey and bear it into the net-barred fastnesses of the bank.

"An' he 's a-hevin' his leetle fishin' tu, which I don 't begretch it tu him, seein' he does it so slick an' handy. An' naow, Peltier, I guess we might as well call it we've got 'nough. We might git more, but we do' wanter be hawgs. You 've got a string o' fish 'at ought tu make a man happy an' contented an' fergit lots o' trouble, an' I hope it does, better 'n all Hamner's pizen, which it 's hopesin' you 've forsook. Naow, whenever you git daown-hearted, go a-fishin'." He felt an almost painful heart twinge that reminded him of long bygone boyish anticipation.

"It can't quite tech the ol' spot," he thought to himself, "but thinkin' o' fishin' an' goin' a-fishin' comes nigher fetchin' on 't 'an most anythin'." Then speaking aloud:—

"It 's a-hopesin' 'at I won 't never git so I can 't go a-fishin' whilst I 've got sense tu enj'y it. Lord, haow many times I think o' ol' Kit Jarvis a-tryin' tu go a-traoutin' arter he got blind as a bat. He was a master hand for huntin' an' fishin' an' a mate o' yer father, Jozeff, when I was a boy.

"But whilst he was a tough, hearty man, he begin tu git blind. It wa'n't fellums on his eyes, for they looked jest as nat'ral 's ever they did, on'y when he was a-talkin' tu you, they would n't hit you, but p'int off tu one side mebby an' be shut when he was a-listenin' tu ye. But he would go a-huntin' arter he got so 's 't he could n't tell a barn from a haystack, an' they said he shot a pa'tridge by the saound of her quit-quittin', an' he 'd go kerwack ag'in' a tree afore he see it, an' cuss a spell an' then laugh an' make fun of hisself.

"But he gin up huntin' arter he 'd shot your gran'ther's yullin' fer a deer. 'Never knowed my gun tu cut up sech a caper as that afore,' says he, 'an' I won't trust it no furder.'

"But yit he would go a-traoutin', an' us boys, the Lord forgive us, useter laugh tu see him a-pawin' wi' one hand fer suthin' 'at wa'n't there, an' a-pokin' his stick julluk a pismire feelin' its way 'mongst strange things, an' stan'in' harkin' fer saounds julluk a hawg in a cornfiel' an' mebby tost his hook ontu a lawg or rock, an' wait an' wait fer a bite. I wonder the Lord did n't strike us mis'able leetle torments blind, but mebby 't was 'cause we useter onsnag his hook fer him an' onsnarl his line, an' led him tu the best holes, an' mebby 't was cause He don 't take much 'caount o' sech leetle, onsignificant critters' duin's.

"Arter a spell he gin it up, jest oncte in a while tu set by the mill pawnd an' fish for chubs an' dace. 'I c'n feel 'em bite an' pull, an' hear 'em floppin' in the grass, an' they smell like fish, an' it's better 'n nothin' ef 't ain't much fun,' says he, 'an I 'spect it 'muses the minnies tu see sech a ol' dodunk a-tryin' to ketch 'em.'

"When it come his turn to die I guess he was glad on 't. 'I ben the same as dead this ten year,' says he, 'the world a-rattlin' raound me 'thaout no more 'caount on me 'an if I wa'n't in 't, my own flesh an' blood grown up 'thaout my knowin' haow they look, er seein' my ol' womern's face er my nighest friend, er seein' the grass an' the trees leaf aout er shed the' leaves, er ever p'intin' a gun er hookin' a traout, an' jest a-settin' an' harkin' in the everlastin' dark! It's lunsome, I tell ye. A blind man 's uselesser 'n a dead man, an' you can't bury him aout'n the way an' be perlite.'

"Wal, it's hopesin' the dark won't overtake none o' us afore it's time tu go tu sleep fer good."

So they took their way homeward in the gathering twilight, with the vibrant purr of the toads ringing all about them, and now and then a startled bird scurrying out of the dead grass before them.

"See the pooty pooties, Bubby," said Uncle Lisha, dangling his string of fish before the delighted eyes and reaching hands of Sam's baby. "No, could n't hev 'em naow, Bubby, but when he gits big an' wears trouses he shell go 'long wi' Uncle Lisher an' ketch snags on 'em, an' mammy 'll cook 'em an' tell us tu go ag'in."

A Rainy Day

It was a May day with April weather. The rain had poured down in intermittent showers during the night. In the morning the rising sun transmuted the gray mist to floating gold, and turned the tremulous strings of sundrops on every bending twig to resplendent jewels.

The sheep began to scatter over the pastures, mumbling out calls to their lambs as they cropped the wet grass.

But the robins sang vociferously for more rain; the sun veiled itself with a drifting cloud, bordering it with gold, and shooting from behind it broad, divergent, watery bolts; a film of shower was trailed along the mountainside; the blotches of sunlight narrowed and faded into the universal somber gray, and, after a brief pattering prelude, the rain poured down again, and swept across the blurred landscape in majestic columns, that fled along the earth while they upheld the narrow sky.

Then it stopped as suddenly as it began, the sun shone out and revived the drowned splendor of the earth, the bedraggled robins sang again, and the murmur of the swollen brooks rose and fell more distinctly with the puffs and lulls of the inconstant wind. Then the sky would darken and blot out the patches of blue and the half-built arch of a rainbow, and the new showers chase away the straggling sunbeams, and the pour of the downfall overbear all other sounds.

Thus it was pouring, when Uncle Lisha came into the shop from the house and put on his apron, stooping low as he tied the strings to look out through the blurred panes upon the narrow landscape. He saw the innumerable jets of the puddles leaping up to meet the rain, the pelted, dodging leaves of the plum and cherry trees bending over their fallen blossoms, that like untimely snow, lay beneath them, where a group of fowls stood, bedraggled and forlorn, with shortened necks and slanted tails.

Beyond, all objects became flattened and more indistinct till, in the gray background, mountain and sky met and dissolved in each other.

An umbrella was coming up the road, dodging from side to side as the bearer avoided puddles and sprang across rivulets. The misty fabric materialized into blue cotton, and presently entered the shop, closed, with its depressed point streaming like a conduit, followed by Pelatiah, who set it to dribble in a corner as he said, "Haow de do," and then "Gosh," as a sufficient comment on the weather.

"I'm turrible glad you 've come, Peltier," said Uncle Lisha, searching among his tools for his pipe, "fer it's a lunsome kinder day, an' I wa'n't expectin' nob'dy. It 's kinder chilly, an' I don't b'lieve but what you 'd better whittle up some kindlin' an' start a fire in the stove."

Nothing loath, Pelatiah got some wood from the box, and, kneeling before the stove, whittled some kindling, laid and lighted it, and, still kneeling, intently watched the slow progress of the flame.

"Wal," said the old man, looking at him with kindly anxiety, "haow be ye gittin' 'long? Feelin' any comf'tabler in yer mind?"

"It aches contin'al," Pelatiah answered.

"You don't go tu Hamner's no more?"

Pelatiah shook his head as he got on all fours to blow the reluctant fire, and answered, "Not sence you gin me a talkin' tu 'n under the bridge."

"You done almighty well, boy, an' you jest stick to 't. When you hain't tu work, you go a-fishin' as often 's ye can, an' when it gits so 't there hain't no fishin', go a-huntin', an' 'twixt 'em they 'll fetch ye aout."

The two doors opened almost at the same moment, and Sam entered from the kitchen leading his now toddling boy, followed by his father, bringing in an ox-bow to whittle and scrape where litter offered no offence, while Solon and Antoine came in from the rainy outer world.

"Hoddy do, all de company?" Antoine saluted. "What you 'll said 'bout fishin's? Ah s'pose prob'ly you an Peltiet tink you felt pooty plump for ketch so many feesh, ant it?" He got beside the stove, steaming in the growing warmth, and preparing also to smoke. "Wal, seh, Onc' Lasha, dat ant not'ing, not'ing for wat Ah 'll do wen Ah leeve in Canada."

"Naow lie, dum ye," Uncle Lisha growled.

"Haow many tam," Antoine demanded with grieved impressiveness, "Ah 'll gat for tol' you Ah ant never lie? M'sieu Mumpson, he 'll read me 'baout George Washin's son chawp a happle-tree wid hees new saw, an' tol' hees fader he 'll do it 'cause he 'll can' lie. Ah 'll chawp more as forty happle, prob'ly feefty tree 'fore Ah 'll lie, me. Yas, sah. But Ah 'll goin' tol' you. Great many tam, but one teekly tam Ah 'll go feeshins an' Ah 'll trow mah hook wid nice waum on it an' de traout was so hongry in hees belly an' so crazy in hees head dey 'll go after it so fas', de fus one git it, de nex' one touch hol' hees mouf of dat one's tail an' de nex' de sem way till dey was twenty prob'ly 'f dey ant fifteen all in string, an' Ah 'll pull it mos' so hard Ah 'll can't, an' seh, Ah 'll gat all of it honly de middlin' one was kan o' slimber, an' broke off, so Ah 'll loss de hine en' of de row. Hol' on," as Uncle Lisha began to open his mouth, "Ah 'll ant fineesh. W'en de traout in de water see where Ah 'll sot mah deesh of waum on de bank, he 'll beegin jomp on de bank for gat it, an' tumble top of herself for gat it. Den, seh, Onc' Lasha, Ah'll peek up mah deesh an' shook it, an' holly 'caday, caday,' an' dat traouts folla me home so fas' Ah 'll had to run an' shut de door for keep it from feel up de haouse."

"Ann Twine," said Uncle Lisha, heaving a sigh of relief and sinking back into his seat till the leathern bottom creaked, "I was raly afeared you was a-goin' tu tell one o' your lies."

The End of a Journey

The uneventful summer passed, marking its almost imperceptible changes by the withering of one flower and the blooming of another; the growth of grain and grass, their ripening and cutting down, the slow stoop of fruitful branches under their increasing burden, the song and silence of birds, and the stealthy southward march of sunrise and sunset along the mountain crests. And lo, it was fall with no bloom but the goldenrod and asters, with the red flame of the sumach kindled in mimicry of bloom.

Bobolinks, swallows, and orioles were gone, and but now and then some remaining singer remembered or sang his summer song, and the crickets chirped with fainter monotony in the chill evenings.

The calls of migrant birds came out of the gloom from afar and near, and afar again, while the listener wondered what they were. After a day portentous of storm, with gathering clouds and steadily increasing wind, there came a wild night.

Afar among the desolate mountain peaks, the wind roared with sullen, incessant anger, intermittently heard between the surging blasts that swooped upon the valley and drove the rain in a fierce, assaulting slant, with attending wraiths of flying scud.

The jaded horses of the mail wagon splashed wearily through the puddles whose agitated surfaces glittered dimly in the light of the mud-bespattered lantern, and halted in front of the post office. A wind-tossed shout of the mail driver, and the thud and clank of the mail bag on the wet platform, at once brought forth the alert, bareheaded postmaster, to whom was vaguely revealed by the bolt of light shot through the open door a forlorn, bedraggled figure crouching beside the driver. Clapham strove to make it more distinct with a shading hand, but could not guess even at the sex of the muffled form until a wet ribbon fluttered and snapped about the head. Then the wagon moved on with its feeble light struggling through the storm and darkness.

"Jim 's got him a passenger," he announced to the only visitor whom the arrival of the semi-weekly mail had yet tempted forth in such weather. "An' it's a womern. I can't e-magine," he pondered with hovering hands arrested over the fastenings of the mail bag and eyes staring into space, "what womern is a-traveling sech a night. I'll bet a cent I know. It's that Meeker gal that 's ben tu work in a fact'ry 'way daown in Massachusetts. Yis, sir, that 's jest exactly who 't is;" and chuckling over his sagacity he began to undo the straps, and his visitor, waiting for his paper, thought "like 'nough" as he lounged over to witness the always interesting operation.

The changes of the season were but dully noted by Pelatiah. He was sorry when the fishing days were ended, for they had brought him some consolation for a bereavement crueller than death, if not forgetfulness of his faithless sweetheart, the gleam of whose bright eyes flashed up at him from the evanescent bubbles, now mocking, now piteously pleading, and whose voice called to him, far and elusive, in the many voices of the woods. He had come to think without resentment of the girl who had won his heart but to rend it, remembering faults but to study apologies for them, and cherishing with fondest memory all that was best in her, the best, he was sure, that was possessed by any woman. Yes, she was dead to him, and he could never be fooled or happy again.

He found some solace in dogged, steady work, yet while his hands mechanically dug potatoes, husked corn, held the plough, or wielded the axe, his thoughts were continually straying back into the old wearisome paths.

The early fall had brought its ordinary sport. There had already been coon-hunting in the cornfields, but the shouting rabble of men and boys, the yelping pack of dogs of all breeds, and the wild uproar of the closing scene when the dislodged coon fought to the last gasp against the relentless host of enemies, constituted sport little to his liking. There were plenty of squirrels barking and squalling in the nut trees, and wild pigeons gleaning the grain fields; and partridges were well grown. That very afternoon, as he drove the cows up from the back side of the pasture and passed a clump of elder, the berry-laden tops were rent apart as by a sudden explosion, and half a dozen strong-winged birds burst forth and shot in long curves toward the woods.

Such sports seemed trivial, but better was at hand when in the frost-silvered dawn he and Sam would be afield waiting for Drive's whimpered prelude to burst into melody, signaling them to make all speed to their runways.

He was thinking of this as he moved uneasily about the kitchen, waiting for a lull in the wild weather that he might go up to Sam's and plan a fox hunt for the quiet day which was sure to follow the storm. Now he let in a rainy gust at the narrowly opened door, now he peered into the blankness through the beaten panes. He watched with dull interest the flickering lantern of the mail wagon struggling against the wind and rain. With as little interest, though it reached out toward him in shivering reflections across the ruffled, rain-pelted pools of the road, he saw it stop at Clapham's to drop the mail bag that brought him no more letters.

He turned wearily away, and said to his mother:—

"I b'lieve I'll gwup tu Samwill's a spell"; and took his hat and coat from their peg.

"Why Peltier Gove," she exclaimed, dropping her hands and the stocking she was darning into her lap together, while the ball of yarn fell unnoticed to become the plaything of the kitten. "You 'll git soppin' wet an' ketch your death cold, an' it 's darker 'n Egypt."

"It don't rain sca'cely a mite naow, an' I wanter see Samwill pertic'ler."

His mother arose and went to him, laying a gentle hand on his arm as she said in a low, beseeching voice:—

"You hain't a-goin' tu Hamner's, be ye, Peltier?"

"No, marm, I hain't. I don't go there no more," he answered, with a decision that was convincing.

"Anyb'dy 'at's got a ruff over 'em an' do' know 'nough tu stay 'n under it sech a night, ortu be put in the 'Sylum," his father said, shutting the stove hearth with a spiteful kick of his stockinged feet.

His sister, casting a scornful glance at him from her hemstitching, said witheringly, "Lordy! I hope tu goodness I shan't never git in love ef it's got tu make fools o' folks!"

Pelatiah looked reproachfully at her and went out, only saying to himself, "I hope tu the Lord you never will, Alviry."

More than a lack of sympathy and the impatience with his melancholy

evinced by all the family save his mother, a desire to be out in the wildness of the night impelled him to go forth. The raging elements gave him
something to fight against, and he felt a kind of purposeless heroism in
breasting the fierce buffets of the wind and the pelting rain.

As he struggled forward toward the road, bending against the furious
blasts, he ran against some one, and both were brought to a sudden
stand.

"Ooogh," gasped a boyish voice. "Is that you, Peltier? I was a-comin'
arter you. The' 's someb'dy tu Hamner's wants to see ye, right off. My! Ef
you did n't skeer me!"

The words were whisked away by the wind, but not till Pelatiah had
caught them all.

"Someb'dy wants tu see me tu Hamner's? Well, they won't, thet's all! I
hain't a-goin' nigh Hamner's fer nob'dy, Billy Wiggins."

"But ye got tu," the boy shouted up to him. "They said you must,
Hamner an' ol' Kezier."

"But I won't," persisted Pelatiah stoutly. "Who is 't? That feller 'at
buys fur?"

"No, I do' know who 't is, but you got tu come. Both on 'em said so.
It 's life er death, they said, both on 'em, Kezier in partic'ler. I would n't
go back alone fer one dollar!" and Billy clutched at Pelatiah's fluttering
coat skirts and tugged toward the road.

A strange presentiment flashed upon Pelatiah's brain and his heart
choked. Life or death! He remembered his promise to his mother and
was ready to break it, and, taking the boy's hand in his, they went down
the road, struggling against the surges of the wind.

Their way was less obscure when the lights of the stores and tavern
fell across the ruts and puddles, quivering as if the feeble rays trembled
in the wind. Beyond, the broader, ruddier glow of the forge banded the
road, pulsing with every throb of the hammer whose thundering beats
were always heard, now rising above the lulls of gusty uproar, now dully
accentuating the fiercer blasts.

"Haow come you daown tu the village sech a night?" Pelatiah asked
suddenly.

"Why, hain't you heard? I 've hired aout tu Hamner," Billy asked, re-
sentful of such ignorance.

"You hed n't orter. 'T ain't no place fer a boy, an' your mother needs ye
tu hum."

"She was willin'. An' I c'n be airnin' suthin'. She's got real tough, naow,
an' I go hum oncte a week an' chop wood an' tinker up."

At Hamner's they entered a dark passage through a side door and groped their way up a flight of stairs. Beaconed by the light shed through cracked and shrunken panels, they came to the poorest chamber in the tavern. Hamner had evidently shrewdly classified the quality of his guest. The door was opened by a bent old woman, who, after assuring herself of Pelatiah's identity by a brief, keen glance, admitted him, but unceremoniously excluded Billy, to the disappointment of his boyish curiosity.

"She 'pears tu be asleep naow," the old woman whispered, peering over the candle that she shaded with her hand at the motionless form on the bed. "She's a dreffle sick gal. Hamner was afeerd she was a-goin' tu die right on his hands, an' he hustled right off arter the darkter, an' he come an' gin her suthin' that sot her tu sleep. I don't b'lieve he thinks she 's goin' tu live, fer he did n't say nothin', only sythed arter he 'd pulted her, an' ast tew three questions, an' said her fowlks had orter be sent fer, an' she said she did n't want tu see nob'dy, on'y you."

The old woman cautiously uncovered the candle and let its light fall for a moment on the haggard, fevered face that lay among a confusion of tangled golden hair on the lank pillow. Pelatiah's presentiment was verified, and it was not the surprise of recognition that made him start, but the woeful change grief and despair and sickness had wrought in the face.

"Is she some o' your fowlks? I sh'ld a'mos' thought yer mother 'd ha' come ef she was," the old woman whispered in a hoarse, monotonous buzz.

Pelatiah shook his head and she leered at him with a ghastly grin that revealed one yellow tooth, the sole survivor of the white rows that youthful smiles long ago disclosed. There was a terrible revelation in that wrinkled visage of the old age that a sinful life brings one to, and he was thankful it was in the power of death to forestall it.

"Ooh, yer gal, eh? Wal, Jake's goin' tu see the s'lec'men, er the poormaster, an' hev her took keer on."

Pelatiah started. "You go an' tell him the' hain't no need on 't. I'll take keer on her. She hain't goin' tu be no taown charge!"

"I never hed no idee you was sech a lively young feller," said Keziah, leering at him with an admiration that filled him with disgust.

"Go quick! I 'll stay with her."

He placed a chair softly beside the bed and sat down, as the old woman left the room. The girl moaned, moved uneasily, and opened her eyes, looking wildly about till they rested on Pelatiah, and then a look of gratitude lighted them.

"I was 'feared you wouldn't come. I hed n't no right to ask you, but I could n't help it," she said, in a thin, weak voice. "I hain't got a friend on airth—not one, not one," and her piteous voice broke with a sob before she answered his questioning, puzzled gaze. "No, he never married me. He went off an' lef' me. I must tell ye quick, fer it seems as though I was goin' away somewheres, right off; an' when I went hum my folks turned me aou' door, an' I went tu work aout, where they did n't know me, an' I took sick, an' they would n't keep me no longer, an' I come here. It seemed as 'ough I'd got tu see ye once more, an' tell ye I'm sorry I was so mean to ye. You can't never forgive me, but I wish 't you would n't hate me."

"I never hated ye one minute, Lowizy," he spoke in a choked voice, and then, after a conscientious questioning of his heart, "an' I du forgive ye. Mebby you 've bore more 'n I hev."

"Thank ye, Pelatiah. Be ye willin' tu take a holt o' my hand?" she asked timidly, and for answer he clasped tenderly in his rough palm the thin, hot hand that was feebly stretched out to him. She closed her eyes and sighed restfully, then, after a while, asked:—

"Why, it ain't June, is it? Seems 'ough I heard the birds singin' and smelt the young come-ups. It 's time I was a-goin'. Good-by, Peltier." The feeble tension of the little hand relaxed in his, her last breath fluttered out upon his cheek, and the poor fickle heart grew still forever.

"Is she sleepin' yit?" old Keziah whispered, entering on tiptoe and exhaling an odor of strong waters.

"You need n't be afeered o' wakin' her no more," Pelatiah answered solemnly.

"Good land o' livin'!" she gasped in an awed voice. "You don't say she 's dead?" and then, after assuring herself by a look and touch, "Poor little creetur! It 's turrible to be took so young."

"I don't b'lieve 't is, not allers. Is Jake up? I wanter see him." As he groped his way down the narrow stairs, it seemed as if years had passed since he climbed them.

The storm spent itself in the night, and the morning broke on a peaceful world. As peaceful under the white veil of the dread mystery into which she had passed after the storm of life was the face of the dead girl. It was as if she had gone forth into the unfathomed hereafter, as well assured of forgiveness there as here.

Attended by a few sympathizing friends, Pelatiah laid his dead, now wholly his, to rest in the shadow of the flaming sumachs in the old graveyard on the hillside. There was no service but the brief testimony of Joel Bartlett, who felt moved to say:—

"Inasmuch as we hev ben told by One formerly that aour Heavenly Father does temper the wind tu the shorn lamb, I feel it bore in upon me that this poor leetle lamb, which may hev strayed fur f'm the flock, is gethered tu the fold by the Good Shepherd."

Unseen by any but Pelatiah, Huldah covertly dropped a spray of pale asters into the open grave. As the careless clods began to fall with muffled thuds on the straw-covered coffin, the little company silently dispersed.

"It kinder seems 'ough Peltier felt wus 'n the' was any need o' his feelin', considerin', but mebby he don't, I d' know," Joseph Hill remarked to Antoine as they lingered last at the graveyard gate.

"If you 'll seen dat gal w'en she was 'live an' fat an' jes' good as anybody gal, you 'll ant blem Peltiet fer cried."

A Gathering Cloud

The continual roar of the November wind on the mountains was at times overborne by the nearer uproar of blasts that swooped upon the valley, screeching through the withered herbage, clashing the naked branches and driving the fallen leaves in sudden scurries against the low window of the lean-to.

But if the outer world was cheerless the shop was cosy, and Uncle Lisha and Sam were enjoying its comfort over their pipes and the affairs of their absent friends. At times the draughty little stove ceased its fluttering monotone, as if holding its breath to listen to the conversation. Then it resumed its roar as if the subject was too trivial for its attention.

"Yes," said Sam, "Peltier 's pooty sober, but he 'pears tu be kinder settled daown, an' not narvous ner off in a dream as he was. Why he 'd hev spells last year 'at he 'd stan' a-gawpin' off int' the air, at nothin' anybody else could see, an' let a fox go skippin' by him wi'aout seein' the critter ner takin' no notice till Drive come on his track an' looked wonderin' as if askin', 'Why in time did n't you shoot?' Oncte he let a silver gray go by him jest that way. That r'aly tried my patience, fer it seemed as if it would ha' cured a feller of most anythin' tu ha' shot that fox. Then ag'in, he 'd be all in a whew, an' blaze away wi'aout takin' no sight at nothin'. But he 's carm as a eight-day clock this fall, an' hain't let a fox go by yet, ner missed ary one."

"I cal'late he 'll be all right when fishin' time comes raound ag'in," said Uncle Lisha, splashing an obdurate tap in the tub and then bending it back and forth with impatient jerks. "Good airth an' seas. I b'lieve that aire so'luther must ha' come off 'm an off ox, it 's so dumbd cont'ry."

"It jes' as likel' he come off caow, prob'ly," said Antoine, catching the last remark as he entered the shop and took his favorite seat. "Ah 'll have see caow was more wus fer do he 'll man' to, as hoxens, jes' sem' as hwomans was," and he crowded the tobacco down in his pipe and drew his crossed legs closer under him.

"Hwomans was funny kan o' peoples, an' so was mans, prob'ly. Ah 'll b'lieve more as half de tam de fun ant pay fer de troublesome fer get marry. Folkses had more good tam fer be hol' bachely an' hol' gal. Ah do' know if Peltiet ant lucky for ant gat marry, prob'ly."

"Sho, Ann Twine, you 've took twicte as much geniwine comfort as ye would ef you'd ben a-shoolin' 'raound julluk a lunsome garnder all yer days, an' so hev I, along wi' my ol' goose, an' so 's Sam, tew, a-hevin'. One tech o' that leetle goslin' o' hisen, a-snugglin' up tu him, is wuth more 'n ten year o' his ol' wil' goosin'. Hain't it, Samwill?"

Sam nodded a hearty affirmative. He could hear the slow rock of a cradle in the next room above the subdued voices of the old wife and the young, and the occasional responses of his father, who preferred the amiable converse of these two women to the babble of the men.

"The trouble is," Uncle Lisha went on, "folks gits married tew young, 'fore they r'aly know what they want, an' bimeby wake up an' fin' they got what they don't want, an' then they jest set the' sharp aidges tow-ards one 'nother the hull endurin' time."

"It ant gat no diffrunce," Antoine protested. "W'en Ah 'll was marree, Ah 'll was heighteen, an' Ursule was feefteen, an' we 'll ant quarrly honly fer made up ag'in. Mebby some tam Ah 'll had fer slap it leetly mite, but we 'll be all raght pooty quick. Wal, seh, Onc' Lasha, der was hol' man an' hol' hwomans in Canada gat marree togedder w'en dey was hol' an' in t'ree day dey was set heat dinny, an' leetly maouse run on de haouse, an' hol' hwomans say, 'See dat maouse.' Hol' mans say, 'It was rats,' an' hol' hwomans say, 'No, it was maouse.' 'Ah tol' you it was rats,' he 'll said. 'Maouse,' she 'll said, an' dey holler 'Rat,' 'Maouse,' an' get so mad he 'll go 'way an' stay t'ree year. Den he 'll come back, an' she 'll was veree glad fer see it. 'It was too bad you 'll go 'way so, jes' for leetly maouse.' 'Ant Ah 'll tol' you it was rats?' he 'll holler, and he 'll go, an' never come some more. What you tink fer hol' folkses naow, One' Lisha?"

"Yis, the' 's ol' fools as well as young fools, an' it 's hard tellin' which is the biggest. But I've hearn tell o' tew ol' critters 'at got sot aidgeways an' come aout better 'n you tell on. They'd lived together thirty year, but bimeby they fell aout, an' they 'd mump raound all day 'thaout speakin', an' when it come night they 'd turn the' backs tow-ards one 'nother an' snore, an' purtend tu be asleep, each one wishin' 't t' other 'd speak, but nary one would n't fust. An' so it run on till one night in the fall o' the year they heerd a turrible rumpus 'mongst the sheep in the yard, an' he ups an' dresses him an' goes aout. Arter quite a spell, an' he did n't come back, she slips on her gaownd an' shoes an' aout she goes tu see what 's the matter ailded him, an' lo an' behol', he was clinched in with an almighty great bear, the bear a-chawin' at him an' him a-huggin' as hard as the bear tu keep him f'm gittin' his hind claws intu his in'ards, which is onpleasant. 'Go it, ol' man, go it, bear,' says she, 'it's the fust fight ever I see 'at I did n't keer which licked.'

"She stood lookin' on a leetle spell, with her fists on her hips, till she see the ol' man was a-gittin' tuckered, an' the bear a-hevin' the best on 't, an' then she up with a sled stake an' gin the bear a wollop on the head 't knocked him stiffer 'n a last, and then they hed a huggin' match over the carkis of the bear, an' lived tugether as folks ortu, tu the eend of the' days."

With a briefly admitted blast of the wind, Solon and Pelatiah entered the shop. After the usual comments on the weather had been exchanged, Pelatiah asked, "Has any on ye seen them fellers 'ats ben puttin' up tu Hamner's these tew three days?" All ears were pricked up, for it was a rare event for Hamner to have guests of such long standing.

"T'ree four day?" cried Antoine in interrogative incredulity; "what kan o' folks you 'll s'pose dey was put uppin' so long for heat hees codfeesh an' cookhover pettetoe?"

"Why, no; I hain't heerd on 'em," Uncle Lisha confessed, listening attentively, though he made a show of attending to his work while he awaited an answer to the question, "Who be they, Peltier?"

"That 's more'n I c'n tell ye fer all I 've seen 'em more 'n oncte. One on 'em 's a kinder starved lookin', dreamin' ol' critter 'at wears specs an' black clo's,—wal, looks like a minister 'at's lost his sheep an' hed n't got so much as the tag-locks fer tendin' on 'em afore he did lose 'em. An' the'

's another feller 'at looks nigh abaout as hungry, but not so pious. Seem
's 'ough I'd seen him 'raoun' afore a diggin' gingshang rhut. But t' other
one 's a all-fired cute lookin' chap, look 's if he lived off 'm the top shelf
ev'ry day an' wears han'some clo's off intu the woods an' a gold chain tu
his watch an' don't smoke nothin' but seegars. I heard Hamner call him
Colonel Ketchum."

"Good airth an' seas, ef he 's 'raoun', there 's some speckerlatin' goin'
on some'rs."

"It wouldn't s'prise me none ef they was accomplishes o' that aire Bascom, a-connivin' in his nufarious tricks," Solon said.

"Why they hain't been a-nigh him as anybody knows on," said Pelatiah.

"Wal," Uncle Lisha said, applying himself more diligently to his
work, "whatever they 're up tu, I don't s'pose they 'll du none on us no
good."

"What ail dat Bascoms? He 'll borry money of ev'ree bodee, an' dey
say dey can' anybody gat hees pay, honly promise, promise, nex' week,
nex' week."

"I'm glad he 's in the same fix I be," said the old man. "He hain't got
none o' my money, ner I hain't nuther."

"An dey say folks was hear loaded team goin' 'way from de store in de
naght, an' dey t'ink he 'll carry hees good."

"Sho! You don't say? Wal, I'm afeered he 's a tough cud fer someb'dy
to chaw, I r'aly be, an' a turrible nice-spoken, candid-appearin' feller he
is, tew."

Sam arose, went to the door, and looked out into the gusty night, and
retired to the kitchen. He bent for a long time over his boy sleeping in
the cradle where Huldah, sitting sewing at the table corner, could jog it
with her foot. Then he cast a troubled glance upon his wife and Aunt
Jerusha at her knitting, and at his father nodding over the braided husks
coiled in many convolutions about his legs and on the floor. Then he sat
down in moody silence to whittle the morning's kindlings.

"You'll ant s'pose prob'ly Sam was lend it money, ant it?" Antoine
whispered.

"Good airth an' seas, no," said Uncle Lisha, in a voice as guarded as
its emphasis would allow. "Samwill hain't no money tu lend, but he allers
took onaccountable tu that aire Bascom, an' he can't abear tu hear a word
ag'in him." And rising, he began to untie his apron, a hint that hastened
the departure of his guests.

Dark Days

S am's chores were done betimes next morning and his breakfast was hardly eaten, when he announced an abrupt departure by saying that he had an errand at the village.

"What be you in sech a tew for?" Huldah asked. "You hain't aout o' terbacker, I know, fer the' 's nigh a paper full in the sullerway, an' it hain't a week sence you got a paound o' paowder an' four paounds o' shot." She could think of no possible errands that demanded such immediate attention. She followed Sam to the door and laid a hand on his arm. "What is 't, Sam? The' 's suthin' a-pesterin' on ye, I know by your looks. Why don't you tell what 't is? Hain't your wife the one you 'd orter tell your troubles tu?"

"No man ever had a better one," he said earnestly. "It hain't nothin' much. Don't you cross no bridges till ye come tu 'em, Huldy," and he hurried away at as swift a pace as ever took him to a runway, barring the exigencies that demanded running. He wished it was night that he might run now, but it would not do, for every old woman on his route would sally forth to know if he was going for the doctor, and delay him with no end of questions.

When he entered Bascom's store, he was startled to see how bare it had become since he saw it last. Half the shelves were empty, and the tempting display of the counters had shrunk to a forlorn array of odds and ends. A sharp-eyed stranger was prowling softly about with a note-book and pencil in hand and Bascom was lounging near, in apparently careless attendance.

"Why, good morning, Lovel. Glad to see you. Mr. Whitney, Mr. Lovel. My friend Mr. Whitney is helping me take account of stock. Lovel's a particular friend of mine, Whitney. Greatest fox-hunter in the country."

Mr. Whitney nodded, looked suspiciously at Sam, and went on noting down his memoranda.

"Say, Lovel," Bascom continued hurriedly, "I want to go fox-hunting with you, or rabbit-hunting. That suits me better. What do you say to going some day next week?"

"I don't never hunt rabbits," Sam answered with a preoccupied air. "Break my dogs never tu foller 'em. I 'd like tu see you a minute, Mr. Bascom."

"Certainly, certainly, step this way. Well, then, call it foxes, though I never could kill a fox. I ain't sharp enough for them"; and he led the way to the dingy little counting-room whither the lynx eyes of Whitney followed them till the door closed upon them.

"What can I do for you, Lovel?" Bascom asked with solicitous good humor.

"Look a here, Mr. Bascom," said Sam in a low, restrained voice and dashing at his subject as a bashful man does when he dare not hesitate. "I want you tu gi' me some s'curity fer what I 've signed wi' ye, on them bank notes. It 's run up tu nine hundred dollars an' up'ards, an' ef anything should happen, it 'ould knock me gally west."

"Why, certainly, Lovel, I'll be glad to secure you. What do you say to a lien on the stock in the store?"

"Why, seem 's 'ough it looks kinder slim," Sam said doubtfully.

"Well, perhaps; I've had a big trade lately, but it's worth a good deal more 'n nine hundred. I shall be getting in my winter's stock next week, though, an' I can fix you then, so you'll feel easy enough."

Sam shook his head. "I guess I'll take a lien on what you 've got, an' you c'n give me another, when you git your new goods in."

"All right, Lovel. I'll attend to it right off, to-morrow." Sam's countenance fell. "You see I can't attend to it to-day, on account of helping Whitney. Tomorrow will do just as well, won't it, Lovel?"

"I 'd a good deal druther hev it made aout to-day."

"Then, again," continued Bascom, "the town clerk and the 'Square have both gone to V'gennes. Went by early this morning, an' we could n't get the papers made out."

"Wal, I s'pose I'll hafter wait," said Sam, turning to go. "You don't blame me none, Mr. Bascom? I hain't got nothin' but the farm an' a wood-lot an' the stock an' the' 's three ol' folks dependin' on me, an' it 'ould be awf'l tough if anything should happen."

"Why, of course, but you need n't be uneasy. But say, if you are," and he sank his voice to a whisper, "why don't you deed the farm back to your father?"

"No, sir," and Sam's face flushed; "I hain't no slink ef I be a dumb fool."

"Oh, there 's no harm in your doing that if it would make you feel any easier. That's all it would be for, anyway. But do as you like. Come down in the morning and we 'll fix the lien."

He followed Sam to the outer door and looked after him with something of concern in his restless eyes; then saying to himself, "If he will be a blasted fool, he must take his chances with the rest," he returned to his uneasy lounging.

That night he was speeding behind Hamner's best horse, toward the lake, on his way to Canada, a fugitive from Danvis, where he was never seen again.

On his way to the village, the next morning, Sam was met by the ill tidings, already running like wild fire along the quiet roads, that Bascom's store was closed, everything in it attached by distant creditors, and he gone, no one knew whither. Sam went on to receive complete assurance of the rumor, and then returned to his home, bearing the burden of a heavy heart. His white, set face frightened Huldah when he entered the kitchen.

"Be you sick?" she asked anxiously, but he did not answer till she had followed him into the bedroom. Then seating himself on the bed, he drew her to his knee and with desperate rapidity told her the whole story of his wretched entanglement with the unscrupulous adventurer. She listened to the end without speaking, and then, holding his face with both hands close to hers, she said:—

"Sam, why did n't you tell me afore? I don't blame you fer nothin' but that. You hed orter ha' tol' me, an' mebby I would n't ha' let ye, fer I allers mistrusted that Bascom. He was tew clever an' tew false-eyed."

"Yis," said Sam, "tew dumb clever an' cute fer sech a do-dunk as I be. He kep' me a-thinkin' it 'ould be all right, tu-morrer, tu-morrer, wi' his promises. On'y yistiddy he promised faithful, tu gi' me s'curity, an' naow all he hed is 'taiched up an' he gone an' lef' me tu face the music alone. Ev'ything we 've got is jes' the same as gone. Them bank fellers tu V'gennes don't show no marcy.

"The sheriff 'll be here tu rights," said Sam, "fer them bank fellers is sharper on the scent of a dollar 'an Drive on the track of a fresh-started fox. I'd ruther take a wus lickin' 'an ever I got yit 'an tu see him a-levyin' on the stuff, an' the lan' that Gran'ther cleared on the fust pitch 'at was made in Danvis. He could ha' settled at the lake ef he hed n't ben so afeared o' the fever 'n' aig. Mebby ef he hed, an' I 'd ha' been raised there, I should n't ha' ben such a tarnal fool. But then ag'in, mebby I would n't ha' faound you."

"What a caoward I be!" Sam exclaimed. "Lord, I wish 't I c'ld run off int' the woods an' hide, er lay daown an' sleep an' never wake up tu remember nothin'."

"Oh, no, you don't nuther! You wanter live an' see what kin' of a hunter the baby 's goin' tu be," said his wife.

At length, facing the irksome duty of inflicting pain, Sam called his father into the shop, and, in the fewest possible words, unsparing of self-condemnation as a penitent of his own scourge, he told the ill tidings to the two old men.

His first look abroad revealed the well-known figure of the constable rocking and swaying up the road in his thorough-brace sulky, a species of carriage used by no other person in the community save by the doctor.

The officer hitched his well-known white horse much too conspicuously in front of the house, and then began to levy on the personal property in a disagreeably calm and business-like manner. Sam had always liked Constable Beers, and had voted for him at every March meeting for years, but he hated him now, and swore never to give him his vote again. He, however, relented when the constable, having made the rounds, turned to him and said with a sigh of regret:—

"Darn it all, Lovel! the' hain't pus'nal prop'ty 'nough tu half satisfy the claim, an' I 've got tu 'tach the land. I 'm tormented sorry, but I 've got tu du my duty. You must n't lay up no hard feelin's ag'in' me, as 'twixt man an' man."

"I did n't know but—you lufted tu, same as butchers lufster kill critters," said Sam. "They hain 't nothin' ag'in the critters, but they like the business."

"Wal, then, I don't," said the constable; and then, in a loud whisper, though no one was in earshot, "why, if you had any idee this was a-comin', why in tunket did n't you deed the lan' back tu yer father?"

"Proberbly, 'cordin' tu most folkses' idee, 'cause I was a dumbd fool."

Friends in Adversity

Sam wandered uneasily about in pursuit of work that had no purpose but to keep him from thinking. At last, he shouldered the ox-yoke and started for the meadow. As he passed the hog pen, he fairly resented the indifference with which the hogs were taking on fat for another man's benefit, and begrudgingly threw them their accustomed largesse of nubbins, though they grunted lazy recognition of his familiar footstep. It put him more out of humor to see the contentment with which the cows and oxen grazed, jowl deep in the aftermath, and the sheep nibbling the pasture knolls, all indifferent to impending change of ownership, though they had so long been his daily companions. The old hound alone seemed sympathetic, walking at heel, spiritless and dejected, scarcely noticing the last night's fox trail that the reeking herbage still exhaled, and meeting his occasional glances with a wistful face more troubled than his master's.

The mood of nature was as little in accord with his as was that of his flock and herds. The sun shone out of the soft sky with genial warmth on woods and fields not yet quite stripped of painted leaves and green grass by the final desolating blasts of late autumn. There was a full measure of hearty cheer in the notes of migrant crows and other birds that delayed departure or stayed to brave the stress of winter weather; only the trisyllabic plaint of the thistle bird, gleaning the ripe weed seeds, had a cadence of sadness and farewell.

"It's all the same tu the airth an' the dumb critters, who goes or who comes! All but you, Drive," he said as he slipped the oxbow on old Bright's burly neck and fastened it in the yoke and called Broad to take his place. "But I hope whoever gits a holt o' you ol' fellers 'll be good tu ye, an' the caows an' the ol' mare. I don't want you 'bused ner the farm nuther."

He yoked the oxen to the cart and drove them out to the field for the last shocks of unhusked corn. The plough stood in an unfinished furrow among the stubble and frost-blackened pumpkin vines. Sam drew it out and heaved it upon the cart with spiteful energy.

"By the gre't horn spoon, I won't plough another furrer fer the Lord knows who," he soliloquized in a tone that accorded with the action; and with a long look, as if bidding the familiar field farewell, he hauled home the last load and turned the oxen loose.

He watched them wander off in search of the choicest feed and then set himself to husking, while his vagrant thoughts wandered in futile quest of a way of escape from the troubles that beset him. His eyes went over and over the familiar interior. It was hard to think that the old barn was passing out of his ownership. Every nook and corner of scaffold, bay, and stable recalled some incident of childish sport or freak of fancy, linked with the thoughts of youth and manhood so intimately that their years seemed but as days, childhood and youth but parts of dawning manhood. The rudely carved initials and figures were translated again in their old significance; the scars, the knots, the contortions of grain took on again the semblance of men, beasts, and birds, that had been realities to his childish imagination. All the familiar surroundings seemed too much a part of himself to go out of his life while he yet lived.

"Consarn it!" he cried out impatiently, as he tossed aside a bundle of stalks, "my idees runs wilder 'n a haoun' pup on a back track, an' never gits nowheres. I'll tell ye what, ol' dawg," addressing the hound curled up in the comfortable warmth of the sunshine falling on the barn floor, "we 'll go off int' the woods a day, jest you an' me, an' see if we can 't git 'em straightened aout."

Drive's tail beat a rustling response on the cornstalks, and his sad brow was lifted in new corrugations of inquiry.

The shadow of a figure debased the gold of the floating motes and crept along the floor till it fell upon the bundle rustling on Sam's lap, and Pelatiah's lank figure materialized behind it. Drive wagged recognition, and Sam turned a surprised face over his shoulder to welcome their comrade.

The simple greetings, "Why, Peltier," "Wal, Samwill," expressed a deal of friendliness, but no more was said till Pelatiah, after the custom of such visitors, seated himself, drew a bundle of corn across his knee, and began husking. For a while there was a continuous rustling of husks, leaves, and stalks, punctuated by the snapping off of ears and their sharp click upon the growing pile; then, as the two huskers finished their bundles together, Pelatiah said, after much embarrassed clearing of his throat:—

"I s'pose it 's true what I hearn abaout that aire Bascom 's gittin' you intu sech a mess?"

Sam nodded assent, and Pelatiah continued, "I 'm turrible sorry, Samwill, an' I wish 't I hed the means tu help ye more 'n what I hev; but I hev got some, which I want you tu take an' use it."

He leaned far back, straightened his left leg, went down into the depths of his trousers' pocket, and brought up therefrom a wallet, from which he took a small roll of bank notes, and carefully counted them upon his knee with a frequently moistened forefinger.

"I hed consid'able more 'n forty dollars 'at I 'd saved up one way an' 'nother," he said apologetically, as he completed the counting, "but the fun'al, an' the darkter's bill an' Hamner's took above half on 't. But I want ye tu take this an' not trouble tu pay it back ontil things eases up on ye."

He stretched it out toward Sam with an awkward bashful eagerness glowing in his honest face.

"Oh, Peltier, I couldn't!" Sam protested, his voice choking and his eyes moistening. "I'm a thaousan' times obleeged tu ye but I could n't take it."

"But I want ye tu, Samwill. 'T ain 't much, I know, but it 'll help over the pitches some, maybe," Pelatiah urged.

"I'm as 'bleeged tu ye as if 't was a thaousan' dollars, but I could n't take it. I do' know when I c'ld pay you, an' I hain't a thing tu s'cure you, an' ev'rythin' here 's 'taiched up."

"I don't care when you pay me, I want you tu take it an' use it jest 's if 't was yourn." Pelatiah thrust the money further toward Sam's withdrawn hand. "I did n't s'pose you 'd spleen ag'in' takin' a leetle favor f'm me, Samwill, sen' I've took so many f'm you," Pelatiah said, in a grieved tone, and still holding out the proffered loan.

Sam looked steadily into the earnest, kindly blue eyes and took the hand and money in a warm, firm grasp.

"Ef you'r goin' tu feel that way 'baout it, I shall hafter take it, but I hed n't ortu."

"You hed n't ortu? You 've gottu," said Pelatiah joyfully. "It 'ould burn my pocket tu kerry it an' you a-needin' on 't, so there!"

"Wal, ef you will hev it so, you will, but you got to take a note 't any rate. Come int' the haouse an' I'll write one."

Pelatiah protested, but Sam was inexorable, and, after counting the money carefully, pocketed it and led the way into the house.

"Bad luck is good luck when it shows a feller who his frien's is," Sam said, laying a gentle hand on his young comrade's shoulder as they entered the door.

Long before the constable posted the notice of the sale in Hamner's bar-room and in Clapham's store, the news of Sam's disaster was spread through half the township.

Luck of the Woods

"They say the Widder Needham wants tu let her place on sheers," said Sam to his wife the next morning, when they, the baby, and the hound were the only occupants of the kitchen, "an' I 've thought o' tryin' fer that, but I do' know, I can't git a holt o' nothin'. I b'lieve I shall hafter go off int' the woods by myself a spell," and he cast a casual glance up at his gun that was gathering the dust of disuse. "Then ag'in, I kinder want tu look over aour maountain lot. That hain't ben 'taiched, an' it seems 's 'ough it might be turned tu some accaount. The' 's a slew o' timber on 't, an' I c'ld build us a turrible neat lawg haouse aouten them spreuce."

"Oh, I allers thought a lawg haouse wus jest as cute as could be an' allers wanted tu live in one," Huldah said with enthusiasm.

"Mebby you 'll git the chance. An' if I c'ld hit the forge folks on a coalin' job, I might make well on 't. If 't was cleared up, I s'pose we might git a livin' off on 't. It 's c'nsid'able uphill an' I don't s'pose the sile o' land is fust chop, but I guess it 'ould raise white beans an' buckwheat an' both on 'em is fillin'."

"Good land, Sam," cried Huldah. "Don 't fer lan 's sake say buckwheat afore Mother. She 'd hev a conniption fit an' hev aour ears all cracked off 'm aour heads afore the buckwheat was in blow."

"I don 't set no gret store by it myself," Sam conceded, "but it 's better 'n a snow bank, an' high duck folks is gittin' tu think buckwheat pancakes is some punkins. But the' can't no Green Maountain Boy go ag'in' beans. They was victuals an' drink tu the ol' settlers, an' ammernition, tew, fer I 've heard Gran'ther Hill tell haow 'at they shot Yorkers with 'em. I guess I'll go up an' look the lot over an' see. An' I s'pose I might as well take my gun along an' Drive 'ould feel bad if I left him."

"No, you mus' n't hurt Drive's feelin's," said Huldah, smiling, as she roused the hound from the heavy sleep that linked one hunting bout with another.

"I allers feel better in the woods an' c'n think better in 'em, an' mebby c'n git my idees straightened aout."

The breeze touched him softly as the breath of June, nor scarcely stirred the drifted windrows of fallen leaves, nor tossed alee the gray ashes of the goldenrod's burned-out flame, nor bore from the veiled mountain the low song of the evergreens. The tranquil babble of unswollen brooks rose and fell with the light wafts, the bluebirds' carol floated down through the haze that was spun from sky to earth, the meadow-larks sang their long-drawn summer songs again, the lazy caw of lingering crows came from their latest woodland camp among the evergreens, and a partridge's April drum call throbbed through the filmy copses. It was as if nature were solacing herself in this autumnal truce for all turbulence of her forces, past, or henceforth possible.

With scarcely a thought of his course, Sam entered the woods and heard as in a dream the old hound's rustling footsteps as he ranged about him. And hardly more did he notice the impatient whine that told of a puzzling scent, half exhaled since Reynard fared homeward from his early mousing, nor yet the first clear note that announced a more exhilarating savor with assured direction. But when the melody became exultant and continuous with competing echoes he awoke to a realization that the fox was afoot, and he instinctively made for a favorite runway.

Sam listened in vexation of spirit to the receding notes of the hound and the answering echoes growing fainter and fainter, till they were scarcely distinguishable above the fitful stir of dry leaves in the vagrant wafts of air, and the constant monotone of the evergreens on the wind-loved heights.

At last they faded beyond the scope of intentest listening, and, dismissing with them all thought of sport, he went on over ledges and through depressions toward the mountain lot. His woodsman's eye soon discovered the faint marks of one boundary which he traced to an ancient corner-tree, encircled by its axe-scarred "witnesses" and bearing the moss-grown initials of the colonial surveyor and the numbers of the four lots whose common corner it had established, when Governor Benning Wentworth held disputed sway over the New Hampshire grants. Thence he carefully followed the eastern line through the forest whose autumnal silence was as unbroken as the dead stillness of winter, save for the occasional rustle of fallen leaves and the liquid tinkle of a rivulet ringing its course with a chime of foam bells.

The iterant clamor of a log-cock on his accustomed beat, the patient tapping of his lesser brethren, a squirrel's rasping of a nut, the petulant squalling of the jays, were sounds common to both seasons, but as Sam, with the habitual caution of a hunter, went noiselessly onward, he became aware of sounds that seemed strange and at variance with these.

It was the noise of delving with spade and pick in stony soil. He moved cautiously in its direction till he came to the brink of ledge overlooking a level plateau or terrace, whereon he saw, almost beneath him, three men whom he at once recognized from Pelatiah's description as Hamner's mysterious guests. The one who was steadily wielding a pick he recognized as a trapper and root digger from a neighboring town.

The ministerial looking gentleman in seedy black clothes was carefully examining the upturned earth and stones. The third, who was evidently first in the order of their worldly standing, was intently watching the proceedings, while nervously puffing a cigar of such fragrance that when it reached Sam's nostrils it gave him a desire to smoke, and he instinctively put his hand in his pocket for pipe and tobacco. But denying himself, he quietly stretched out in a comfortable position to peer over the edge of the cliff to see what kind of work was being done on his property.

"Well, Professor," he heard the smoker saying, "what's your opinion of it?"

The professor chucked some specimens thoughtfully from hand to hand and answered in measured precision:—

"It is apparently an ore of good quality, but that can of course only be ascertained by smelting it in sufficient quantity for a practical test of its quality."

"Worth buying, do you think?"

"Certainly," was answered with a decision that was presently qualified by, "at a reasonable figure, Colonel."

"Of course," the colonel answered impatiently; "it isn't likely any one will ask a steep price for a mountain woodlot. But suppose they should get their ideas up, how much will it do to pay?"

"It is very convenient to the forge," the professor pondered. "Hematite is apt to be hard, but it can be mixed with a softer ore to advantage,— the bed appears to be quite extensive,—I should consider it safe to pay a thousand dollars."

Sam's heart was beating so loudly that he mistook it for the ponderous throb of the forgehammer two miles away, and prognosticated a storm from what he called the "hollerness o' the air."

"Pooh, a thousand dollars! Any of these people would jump at half that. It's more money than they ever saw, and it's nothing but a woodlot anyway." The colonel threw down the stump of his cigar and stamped it out.

"And that would leave you five hundred to buy another race horse, another 'Cock of the Rock,' or to divide between me and our friend Trask here who is the real discoverer of the bed."

"Oh, William is going to be well paid for his time and trouble," said the colonel.

"Wal, I cal'late I ortu hev suthin' more 'n day's wages, seein' 'at I diskivered this 'ere ore bed," the person referred to remarked, squatting on his haunches so that his knees were on a line with his ears, his arms outstretched between them while he meditatively poked the earth with the point of the pick. "Yis, an' more 'n I c'ld ha' airned diggin' jinshang, or trappin'. Sssh, hear that aire haoun' dawg? He's comin' right stret here. Gawlly bleue, I wisht I'd fetched my gun."

He suddenly uncoiled his long legs and sprang up like an attenuated jack-in-the-box, bending an attentive ear as he stretched out a wide-spread hand to enjoin silence.

Sam was giving such close attention to this conversation that his ear did not catch the voice of the returning hound until drawn to it by the words and attitude of Trask. Almost in the same instant he saw the fox a long gunshot off on the brink of a ledge, picking his way along the naked rock, intent on the strategy of a puzzling trail, yet with nose and ears alert for any lurking enemy. Sam took in at a glance that most perfect picture of cunning that nature gives, the cunning which it was his chief delight to foil, and the hunter's instinct rose above all other thought or plan.

His gun was aimed with deliberate celerity and in the same instant spat forth its deadly charge, and in the midst of a requiem of echoing report and resounding bugle-notes, poor Reynard tumbled down the cliff, almost at the feet of the prospectors, who were more startled by the sudden apparition than was he by the stroke that ended his life with its first shock.

The secret of his presence being disclosed, Sam descended to secure his quarry, which he did with well simulated surprise at the discovery of witnesses of his shot.

"By the gret horn spoon!" he declared, coming to a sudden halt before the group, with the fox lying yet untouched at his feet. "You folks scairt me aouten a year's growth, a-comin' ontu ye so onexpected. I 'd jes' as soon ha' thought o' runnin' ontu a camp-meetin' up here, for I s'posed Drive an' me an' the wil' critters hed the woods all tu aourselves. Hain't strayed off an' got lost ner nothin', hev ye?"

The colonel hesitated a moment, considering whether it were not best to accept this as an explanation of their presence, but at once dismissed it as not a plausible one.

"Why, no, I can't say we 're lost, for our friend Trask here seems to know the lay of the land. But I'd like to see the owner of this lot. There 's some timber on it I 'd like to get. This yellow birch is just what I want. There are some pretty good trees here. That tree and that," indicating with his forefinger a couple of shaggy giants that reared their rustling manes just beside him,—"don 't you think they 'd do, Professor?"

The professor ran a critical eye over them and nodded a dubious affirmative.

"The' 's slews o' yaller birch all through here, fer two mild, jest as thick as 't is on this lot," Sam said.

"Yes, I know, but I want the pick of it all, and I'd as soon begin here as anywhere."

"I don't see what on airth anybody wants o' yaller birch," said Sam; "ef 't was cherry birch for furniter, naow, but yaller birch, good land, what du ye want o' that?"

"Never mind what I want of it," said the colonel, with the air of one impatient of questioning, "I want it. I 've been informed this part of the mountain belongs to a man by the name of Lovel. Do you know him?"

"Yes, I know him."

"Do you think he 'd be likely to sell it? For a reasonable price, of course, you understand."

"Yes, I know him. He 'll sell," Sam said, and then continued with apparent irrelevance, as he stirred the upturned velvet-black earth with his toe, "This 'ere is a kinder cur'ous lookin' sile o' land. Some on 't looks as 'ough it hed got rusty a-lyin' raoun' useless so long. Guess like 's not the' 's iron in 't."

The colonel deigned to notice it with a sidewise glance.

"Ah, yes, it does look a little odd. Trask has been digging some of his wonderful roots here. The owner's name is Lovel; I believe I'll call and see him."

Sam straightened his fox upon a convenient log preparatory to skinning it, seated himself astride it, and began whetting his knife on his boot.

"You need n't bother tu. He 's right here all ready fer a trade. I 'm him. Naow, haow much be you goin' tu offer?"

"You!" cried the colonel quite taken by surprise; and then, advancing toward him with his right hand cordially outstretched, "Why, Mr. Lovel, I'm delighted to see you, sir. Delighted. You are just the man I want to see, and meeting you here saves lots of bother. My name 's Ketchum; they call me Colonel sometimes."

Sam stuck his knife in the log, and not without a flattered sense of receiving distinguished consideration took the proffered hand of the most celebrated speculator and fast man of the county.

"And this is my friend, Professor Stillman, and Mr. Trask. You may have met Trask, for he 's a hunter," the colonel said, introducing his companions. "That was a capital shot, Mr. Lovel. If I 'd made it, I sh'd be proud as a peacock. I never could shoot a fox. They 're too smart for me. Have a cigar, Mr. Lovel?"

Sam was nothing loath to accept the proffered Havana, already recommended by the fragrance of its predecessor beyond all need of words. The colonel obligingly lighted a new-fangled match in a little vial of liquid and held it for him till the cigar was properly fired. He had never tasted anything with so delicious a flavor before; yet it only made him hungrier for his more satisfying pipe. Having his own cigar well lighted, the colonel took it from his lips to say, while he regarded Sam with a shrewd downward glance, "Now, about this woodlot,"—he emphasized wood,—"What are you going to ask for it? Cash on the nail, the minute the deed is signed?"

"What 'll you give?" Sam asked, feeling the edge of his knife with a critical touch.

"Oh, I don't want to put a price on another man's property,"—encouraging his cigar with a few rapid whiffs. "Name your price and I'll tell you whether I can pay it."

Sam nerved himself to a supreme effrontery and made his offer in a voice so steady he wondered if it was his own.

"Wal, then, I'll take fifteen hundred dollars fer 't;" and was so appalled by the extravagance of the price he had named that he did not venture to look up, but began carefully ripping the hind leg of the fox.

"Wheeew," the colonel blew out a mouthful of smoke in a long whistle of surprise. "Fifteen hundred dollars! Good Lord, man, are you crazy? Why that's more than a thousand acres of this mountain land would bring. You 're joking, Mr. Lovel. Let's quit this fooling and talk business."

"I mean just what I say. Fifteen hundred is my price," Sam said, gathering confidence he knew not how.

"Oh, well then, it 's no use talking," the colonel declared, with assumed indifference that scarcely concealed his vexation. "I don't want the birch bad enough to give that, or half of that. Some other lot will do as well. Come, Professor, we might as well be off. Come, Trask, show the way out."

Trask shouldered his pick and spade and led the way with long strides, followed with slower steps by his companions, who presently halted and conferred together in low tones. The colonel returned a little to ask:—

"You really mean to say that fifteen hundred is your price?"

"Sartainly," said Sam, stripping a leg of the fox.

"It's ridiculous. Fifteen hundred dollars for a patch of mountain land only worth the wood and lumber that 's on it."

Sam suddenly faced toward him: "Look a here, Colonel, what's the use o' yer foolin'? 'T ain 't the wood you want. It 's this 'ere iron ore." He picked up a handful of the black and rusty fragments and held them out in his open palm. "I do' know what it 's wuth, mebby four times what I ask fer it, but you c'n hev it fer that, hit er miss."

It had seldom befallen Colonel Ketchum's brazen face to be surprised into such blank astonishment as now overspread it.

"Who the devil told you there was ore here?" he blurted out.

"Oh, I've known it fer quite a spell," Sam said with a coolness that was amazing to himself, considering he had known it but half an hour.

"Well, if there is, it may not be worth a thing."

"I 've hearn there was them 'at 'ould pay a thaousan' dollars fer 't. It 's consid'able handy tu the forge. I guess the Comp'ny 'ould give suthin' fer 't."

The colonel retired to confer with the professor, then came back: "Well, I've concluded to take the chances and give you a thousand." Sam shook his head. "Well, let 's split the difference and call it twelve fifty."

"No," said Sam, completing the stripping of the fox of its beauty and tossing the carcass aside, "I guess I 'll give the Comp'ny a chance fust."

The colonel chewed his cigar, forgetting to nurse its languishing fire, and after some moments of silence said, "Well, I 'm going to be a confounded fool and give you your price."

"I p'sume tu say I'm the fool," said Sam, with a nervous laugh.

"Mr. Lovel," the other said, regarding him with growing admiration, "I'm not surprised that you take in the foxes."

"I can't help knockin' 'em over when they blunder right ontu me."

"Well, Mr. Lovel, I'll pay you cash down, when we get the papers made out, tomorrow."

"All right. An' naow I s'pose we might as well hyper aout o' this," Sam said, carefully shaking the fur of the fox skin into comely fluffiness. "Be you folks goin' my way? Come, ol' dawg."

Drive reluctantly arose from the bed he had made in the leaves, refreshed himself with a sniff of the fox tail dangling from his master's pocket, and limped with gingerly, footsore steps in the rear of the party, as it took its way down the rough descent. The colonel discoursed with as continual volubility as the uncertain footing would permit, and seemed in excellent spirits for a man who had just made a bad bargain, as he continually averred he had done. After appointing a meeting at Joel Bartlett's for "drawin' writin's" for the next morning, Sam parted from his new acquaintances where their ways and his diverged, and held across the fields homeward, with a light heart.

"I 've allus faoun' my luck in the woods," he thought. "It fetched me Huldy. And naow it 's saved me a hum fer her an' Bub an' the ol' folks."

When Sam saw his own house light shining through the early autumnal gloaming, chimney and roof taking form against the hazy sky and nebulous glimmer of relighted stars, and traced the dusky slopes and swells of meadow and pasture, they had never seemed so dear as now, with the sense of reestablished possession.

Now he could see Huldah appear at one of the kitchen windows whose welcoming light he had seen on the hill; he knew she was looking out for him as she had doubtless done for countless times since the shadows began to blend with the hazy twilight, and the crickets, warmed to life in the soft air, chirped faintly in farewell concert.

Huldah's face, sadly sobered of late, brightened at the sight of her husband, and its brightness was mingled with surprise when she noted his unexpected cheerfulness.

"Why, Sam, you must ha' had 'stror'nary luck a-huntin' erless you faoun' a better farm 'an you expected tu, up in the maountain."

"I hev hed a streak o' luck in the woods ag'in, Huldy," he said; and when he had hung up his gun and kissed his boy, he beckoned her to the bedroom and told her the whole of his story.

Aunt Jerusha's face, sober almost to sadness, yet calm with the peace conquered in many trials, met his in questioning surprise and caught a reflection of its renewed cheerfulness as he passed her, saying, "I 've fetched hum good news, Aunt Jerushy, an' Huldy 'll tell ye," and going into the shop he imparted it to his father and Uncle Lisha.

BOOK 4

from Uncle Lisha's Outing

A Rekindled Campfire

The company in Uncle Lisha's shop, after discoursing of hunting and lamenting the decrease of game, lapsed into a meditative silence, which was broken at last by Sam Lovel's deep-toned, deliberate voice.

"I tell ye what, I 'm jest a-hankerin' tu go daown tu Leetle Otter Crik, a-duck-huntin'. Don't ye remember, Antwine, what a mess on 'em the' was, a-hengin' raound, that spring we was a-trappin'? The' must be sights on 'em there in the fall, when the wild oats is ripe."

The Canadian grunted emphatic assent without interrupting his energetic pulls at a pipeful of damp tobacco till it was in full blast; then he gave further testimony.

"Yas, seh, dey was great many dauk dat tam, but naow dey was two dauk quarrly for every wil' hoat, an' dey was more as honded taousan' bushil wil' hoat."

"That 's ruther more 'n I should ha' sot 'em at," said Uncle Lisha, punching a hole in a patch with a crooked awl and inserting the bristle of a waxed end. "But I 've seen slews on 'em on the ma'shes, an' I do' know 's you 're lyin' much, for you, Ann Twine. Why don't ye go, Samwil, you an' Solen an' Jozeff an' Peltier an' 'mongst ye? Ye might jest as well as not, right arter ye git y'r corn cut up, an' stay a good spell, 'fore tater diggin'."

"Bah gosh! Ah 'll go, me," cried Antoine. "Ah 'll can show you haow for shot de dauk! Ah 'll was be preffick mans for kill dauk, me."

"Me an' yer father an' the women folks c'ld git along wi' the chores, julluck rollin' off 'm a lawg," Uncle Lisha continued without noticing the Canadian's self-invitation, "an' I don't see as there 's nothin' tu hender ye goin'."

Sam pondered the proposition for a considerable time before he replied with a question.

"Why won't you go, Uncle Lisher? The chores hain't no gret, an' I c'ld git Billy Wiggins tu help du 'em."

"Me go?" said Uncle Lisha, casting a quick glance on Sam to see if he meant what he was saying. "Good airth an' seas! I 'm tew ol' tu go skylarkin' raound wi' a passel o' boys! I should jest sp'ile the rest on ye's fun. Better take yer father, Samwil."

"You couldn't snaike him daown there wi' a yoke o' oxen. He 'd a sight druther stay 'long wi' the women folks. You would n't spile no fun, an' if we settle on goin' you got tu go tew."

"Yas, seh, you jes' good leetly boy as we was, Onc' Lasha," Antoine declared for his further encouragement.

The old man sat meditating for some time with idle hands upon his knees before he answered:—

"Wal, the' hain't no denyin' but what I 'd luf tu. I use tu squirmish raound them ma'shes consid'able when I was 'a-whip-pin' the cat' daown there thirty year ago. An' I sh'ld luf tu see the folks. I p'sume tu say the 's some 'at hain't fergot me yit. But I guess I 'd ortu stay tu hum an' help yer father an' the women folks." He heaved a sigh of resignation and gave the patch a resolute punch with the awl.

"You need n't let that hender ye," said Pelatiah Gove, "for I c'n turn tu an' help 'm if the 's any extry job."

"Why, you 'll go 'long wi' us, Peltier," said Sam.

Pelatiah shook his head in slow but determined negation. "No, I don't want to go—not down there," and they all knew why.

The household divinities proved kind, and when Sam's cornfield had lost its semblance to a miniature tropical jungle and had taken on the likeness of a village of aboriginal wigwams, he and his friends set forth for the lowlands in the chill, vaporous stillness of a September dawn.

The sun was low in the west and cows were coming home through goldenrod- and aster-bordered lanes and dusty highways when the travelers jolted over the ruinous Slang bridge. Half an hour later they were at the old campground on the rocky bluff, its place still marked by a russet mat of decaying cedar twigs and the stone fireplace, which Antoine was delighted to find in serviceable condition. He at once got the necessary provisions and utensils from the wagon and set about getting supper while the others unloaded the wagon and pitched the tent.

Sam drove away to the nearest farmhouse to find keeping for the horses, and after a while came stumbling out of the gathering gloom into the light of the campfire, to which his nose guided him as well as his eyes, for Antoine's cookery diffused a far-reaching savory odor to direct and hasten the steps of a hungry man.

The camp had already taken on the cheerful aspect of an established abiding place, blankets and boxes having been stowed inside the tent. In front of it Uncle Lisha and Joseph sat, comfortably smoking their pipes as they quietly watched Antoine prancing around the frying-pan and potato kettle, while his shadow sprawled along the ground and leaped from trunk to branch in ever-varying grotesqueness of form and motion.

As they smoked their after-supper pipes and planned the morrow's campaign, in every lull of conversation they could hear the quacking and splashing of the host of ducks feeding in the marsh, and now and then the pulsing whistle of swift wings as a belated flock came in from the lake, and then the restful sounding splash as the newcomers settled upon the water to join the feasting horde.

Then, while the dying fire snapped itself out and the dancing shadows sank into the universal gloom, the tired hunters were lulled to sleep by the slow wash of waves and the low song of the cedars.

The Ducks of the Little Otter

The campers were astir betimes in the silver dawn that they counted of greater worth for their use than a golden day. After a hasty breakfast, Sam and Antoine embarked in the canoe at the landing above the Slab Hole, where the boats were unloaded the night before; but Uncle Lisha and Joseph preferred the stable land to the fickle waters, and prowled westward along the lake shore as slowly and almost as stealthily as a couple of aged mud turtles might have gone over the same ground.

When Sam and Antoine paddled out from the landing a thick film of fog lay upon marsh and channel, undulating in the almost imperceptible breath of the morning breeze, but disclosing the dun and green rushes and glassy water the canoe's length away, beyond which color and substance dissolved and vanished in the pearl gray mist. Now a vague form loomed up in the marsh's edge till it shrunk to the solid reality of a muskrat house, then again became unreal in the veil of vapor. To the voyagers' eyes there was nothing substantial but themselves and their canoe and the little circle of glassy water sliding smoothly into the fog before, rippling a widening wake into the fog behind.

Now and then the raucous quack of dusky ducks was heard calling to their befogged mates, and the rustle and splash of some unseen life occasionally stirred in the marsh; but far or near there was no sound telling of human presence save the tinkling drip of the paddles or the scratching of a weed along the canoe's side, or a few whispered words of consultation.

So for half an hour they drove the arrow of their wake through the fog till at a turn of the channel Sam saw the ripple of another wake ruffling the water before him, and following it toward its point discovered five dark objects appearing as if hung in the mist. In two cautious noiseless motions he laid down the paddle and took up his gun, then aimed and fired just as the ducks, now suspicious and restless, were pivoting, on the point of taking flight. As the smoke slowly lifted it disclosed two ducks killed outright and one fluttering toward the marsh with a broken wing, while two drove away into the fog, uttering wild quacks of terror. Antoine stopped the cripple with a timely shot, and then sent the canoe forward with a few dexterous strokes of his paddle till Sam could recover the dead birds.

The report of the guns was followed so quickly by the roar of myriad wings, as a mighty host of waterfowl uprose from the marshes, that it seemed a part of the echo which rebounded from along the wooded shores and far away among the distant hills, and then for a few moments the air was filled with the whistle of wings as the disturbed flocks circled above the almost invisible intruders or set forth in flight toward the lake.

"Wal, there!" said Sam, after listening till the confusion of sounds subsided to a faint whisper of retreating flight and the splashing flutter of laggards suddenly alarmed at finding themselves alone, "I guess we started aout the last duck in the hull crik, an' might as well go back tu camp. The' can't be no more, the' hain't no room for 'em."

"Oh, Ah 'll tol' you, Sam, dey was roos' top one 'nudder, an' dey ant honly top one flewed off yet," Antoine answered in a low voice. "Naow we go in de ma'sh for load off aour gaun."

With a few strokes they sent the canoe her length among the wild rice stalks to insure greater steadiness while they stood up to reload their guns. The sun was rising, and the first level beams paved a gilded path and pillared and spanned it with resplendent columns and arches of mist as it lifted and wreathed in the light wafts of the uncertain air, and now through and beneath the rising vapor a stretch of the channel shone in a curving line of silver, still barred with fading ripples of the canoe's wake. Sam's eyes were following it as he capped his gun, when suddenly he crouched upon his knees, whispering hurriedly:—

"Scrooch daown, Antwine, th' 's su'thin' comin'; I 'm goin' tu try 'em if they don't light."

Antoine bent his head low as a flock of teal came stringing down the channel in arrowy flight, and Sam, aiming a little ahead of the leading bird, pulled trigger. The hindmost teal in the line slanted downward, and, striking the water with a resounding splash, lay motionless when the impetus of its fall was spent.

"Wal, if that don't beat all natur'," Sam said with a gasp of surprise. "That 'ere duck was ten foot ahind o' the one I shot at. What sort o' ducks du ye call 'em, Antwine?"

"He come 'fore you call it dis tam, but w'en he ant, you call heem steal dawk in Angleesh, Ah b'lieved so. He was plumpy leetle feller," Antoine remarked as he picked up the bird, when Sam had reloaded and the canoe was again in mid-channel.

"An' a lively breed they be, tu shoot a-flyin'," Sam commented, as he examined this victim of chance. "'T aint no use a-shootin' at 'em. You got to shoot 'way off int' the air ahead on 'em, an' let 'em run ag'in your shot. Naow be we goin' tu poke along er lay low for 'em?"

"Wal, seh, it bes' was dis tam o' day, we go 'long kan o' slowry. 'Long mos' to evelin' was de bes' tam for hide in de ma'sh, w'en de dauk come for hees suppy. Naow, you be ready for shoot an' Ah 'll paddle de cannoe, me."

They had not gone far up the channel when the canoe in its stealthy progress came close upon a dusky duck sitting among the wild rice, where she might have remained unseen and unsuspected but for her alarm. As she sprang with a startling splash and flutter clear of the rank marsh growth, Sam thought to profit by his experience with the teal and fired too far ahead of his mark, making a clean miss. He stared at the escaping duck and Antoine offered the consoling comment: "Dat feller ant run ag'in you shot, prob'ly."

Sam repeated his mistake with two or three more rising birds, but got two more in a sitting shot at a flock of wood duck discovered in a nook of the marsh, and then to Antoine's great disgust easily knocked over a coot that stupidly permitted them to paddle within short range.

"Dat feller ant worse you' paouder, Sam. You see he gat mout' mos' lak' hen was, an' hees foots some lak' hen, some lak' dauk, an' he 'll ant t' oddur t'ing or one. Ah 'll 'spec' prob'ly it was hens try for be dauk, or dauk try for be hens, an' he 'll ant mek' up very good. He mek' some good fedder for Zhozeff. Hello, Sam, you 'll know dis place, ant it?" he asked with eager interest as he came to a narrow tributary channel with fishing stakes set on either side.

"Wal, if it hain't the East Slang, sure as guns," said Sam in joyful recognition of their old trapping ground. "I tell ye what, Antwine, we mus' go an' take a look at aour ol' hum'stead," and Antoine turned the canoe's prow into the narrower waterway and followed its lazy meandering among the broad level of the marsh to where the sluggish current creeps between narrower margins of wild rice, rushes, and sedges flanked by open fields on the east and, at that time, by almost unbroken forest on the west.

At the nearest point of this shore they found an opening to their old landing and pushed the canoe to a berth alongside a clumsy dugout which gave evidence of recent use in a fishpole and line and a basin of earth in which a few angleworms were crawling and reaching vainly for a way of escape over the edges of rusty tin. A well-worn footpath led away through the bushy border and under the hemlocks.

"Le' 's gwup tu the ol' shanty," and Sam led the way to the familiar spot.

It was not hard to find, for the moss-grown slabs were lying in a crushed heap upon the broken ridgepole, and in front a patch of ashes filmed with moss, nourishing fireweed whose silver-winged seeds were now drifting alee on the light breeze, marked the place of the old campfire. Beside it was the log seat, softer than it used to be with decay and a cushion of lichens. They seated themselves upon it, looking around upon the desolation with half melancholy interest while they slowly filled their pipes.

"It looks so as if de folks was all dead gre't many year 'go, an' it seem so we was de folks," said Antoine ruefully. "It mek' me feel lonesick."

"Yes, it does make a feller sort er lunsome, a mournin' for the feller that was himself oncte."

"Dat true as you livin', Sam. Bah gosh, seh, it ant seem if Ah was me, w'en Ah 'll re'mbler dat leetly boy in Canada wid hees fader an' mudder, young folks dat dance all naght, an' Ah 'll gat honly one brudder-law, an' de summer las' mos' all de year an' de winter ant never too long 'cause Ah 'll happy every day. Oh, Ah 'll ant dat leetly feller. Den w'en Ah 'll growed big mans Ah be naow Ah 'll ant know much an' can' spik Angleesh more as frawg; dat ant de sem' feller Ah was naow, for know much anybody an' spik jus' lak' Yankee. Den Ah 'll faght in de Papineau war more hugly as dev', naow Ah 'll was peaceably mans, honly w'en Ah 'll was get mad, den dey want for look aout, everybody but you, Sam. Oh, Ah 'll was been great many feller, me."

"We're gen'ally tew folks all the time," said Sam, following a climbing wreath of tobacco smoke with meditative eyes. "One is the feller 'at we know an' t' other 's the feller 'at other folks knows, an' most on us is almighty shy o' showin' the one 'at we know tu other folks. By the great horn spoon! I das n't hardly look at my Sam, myself, he's got so many mean streaks in him. Hello, there 's aour ol' squirrel, er one 'at looks jus' like him, a-snickerin' at your Antwine or my Sam this minute." He pointed with his pipe at a red squirrel that was jerking himself into a frenzy of derision on the trunk of a hemlock.

The sun and the breeze had burned and blown the mist away and the day was bright with the beauty of late September, the clear blue sky, the first autumnal tints of the unthinned foliage bordered with the lesser glory of woodside goldenrod and aster, the marshes with their broad masses of bronze and russet and gold, unbroken, save where the scarlet flame of an outstanding dwarfed maple blazed among the colder tints, and the verdure of the grass lands, as green as in June.

Such sounds as were heard were distinctive of the season and some were conspicuously absent. The flute of the hermit and the bells of the wood thrushes were silent. The booming of the bittern and the chorus of the frogs no longer sounded over the expanse of marshes. Birds that rejoiced melodiously over the earth's fresh luxuriance in June uttered now only brief notes of farewell to the kindling glory of her ripeness. Only the bluebird sang, and with a mournful cadence. The crows cawed lazily, jays squalled apart or in united vociferation, chickadees repeated their own name, nuthatches piped their nasal call, woodpeckers hammered with voiceless industry and never a rattling drum-call; these and the squirrels were the only tenants of the woods who gave audible evidence of their presence.

Across the fields from distant farmsteads came the regular thud of flails, and from one barn the clatter and roar of a new-fangled threshing machine; and there was also the rumble and clatter of farm wagons and the bawling of plowmen, shouting as if their oxen were deaf or a mile from their driver. Piercing through these larger sounds there could be heard the shrill voice of cockerels practicing their yet unlearned challenge, and the yelping of wandering flocks of turkeys harvesting the half torpid grasshoppers and gleaning the grain fields.

Every sound that came to the ears of Sam and his companion, as they unconsciously listened, was as indicative of the season as the visible signs of the year's ripening which met their abstracted eyes.

"Wal, Antwine," said Sam, arousing himself and knocking the ashes of his pipe upon the grave of the old campfire, "Le' 's go," and Antoine followed with him the path into the shadow of the hemlocks.

A Way Station

Tangles of hobble bush sprawled over the russet carpet of hemlock leaves, gayly flecked with variegated rattlesnake plantain, overtopped by yellowing sarsaparilla; and a crowded cluster of scarlet berries, still upheld on their withered stalk, marked the place where the fiery bulb of the Indian turnip was hidden. There were moss-covered cradle-knolls and moldering trunks of the old trees whose uprooting had formed them, with trees already old growing upon them. Great mats of sphagnum were in the hollows between, and all were the characteristics of the undisturbed floor of the ancient forest.

For all these Sam had a keen eye, noting the difference of forest growth here from that of his own hill country and speaking of it to his companion, but never of the beauties of nature, for, with the deep and tender feeling of the true lover, he could not prate of the charms of his mistress to the common ear.

Antoine enjoyed them with an undefined touch of the same feeling, but more than the symmetry or majesty of a tree he saw the axe helves in the hickory, the baskets in the ash, the plank in the hemlock and pine, and the medicinal virtues of the prettiest plant were more to him than its beauty.

Ten minutes' leisurely walking brought them to a clearing of a few acres where some young cattle were pastured. They left off grazing on the approach of the strangers, whom they curiously regarded for a moment and then scampered into the woods in a flurry of alarm. A small log house stood in the middle of the clearing with a pole-fenced garden patch in front wherein some cabbages flourished in the virgin soil in spite of poor tending. A few beanstalks drooped their frostbitten leaves over the clattering remnant of dry pods, and the withered cucumber vines, linking together the dropsical overlooked fruit, showed with what rampant growth and how riotously they had gadded abroad under the summer sun and showers.

A thin wreath of smoke trailed upward from the low chimney, diffusing a pitchy, pungent odor even to windward in the light breeze, and the merry notes of a fiddle, accompanied by the sound of jigging feet, came through the open door.

"Bah gosh, de smell an' de nowse was kan' o' Frenchy, don't it?" Antoine remarked as they drew nearer; but he started backward with an exclamation of astonishment when, still unperceived by the inmates, he cautiously peered in at the door. "Oh, dey was too da'ks color mos' for mah rellashin," he whispered, as he fell back to Sam's side, "Dey was nigger!"

Sam stole forward and looked inside. Sitting with his back toward the door was a lithe-figured and very black negro, energetically playing a fiddle, which divided his attention with a taller and more strongly built man of the same race, who was putting his whole soul into the elaborate execution of a jig, occasionally exhaling his breath in a gusty puff that was almost a deep-toned whistle, while the fiddler expressed his delight in the performance by frequent squawks of laughter.

Presently the dancer finished with a grand flourish and a final bump of his quivering heels, and slouched across the room to refresh himself with a draught of water from a pail that stood in the corner, while his comrade hugged his instrument under his arm and rocked to and fro in a spasm of delighted laughter.

"Oh, ah, oh, Lord," he gasped, "if that don't knock the spots out 'n all the dancin' ever I ever did see. Oh, oh, yah, yah! oh, Lord!"

"Wal, yas, honey," said the other modestly, as he dropped heavily into a creaking splint-bottomed old chair, "'at 's er de way dey wu 'ks de heel an' toe down in Ol' Firginny. Now, I 'se gwine for to sing ye dat ar' li'l' song ag'in, so 's you can ketch de chune wid you wiolin," and he began to sing in a deep sonorous voice, beating time with his palms upon his knees, while the other felt for the air with uncertain touches of the fiddlestrings.

"De coon fas' 'sleep in de holler ob de gum,
    'Who dar? Who dar?'
Brer Fox come a-scratchin' 'roun' de do' ob his home,
    'Who dar knockin' at de do'?'
De coon cock he eye an' he listen wid he ear,
    'Who dar? Who dar?
Who dat a-wantin' ob somebody hyar?
    Who dar? Who dar a-knockin' at de do'?'
'Dat's me, Brer Coon, so prepar' for to die.'
    'Who dar? Who dar?'

"Coon squirt 'bacca juice plum in he eye,
    'Who dar? Who dar knockin' at de do'?
'Taters in de ashes, cawn b'ilin' hot,
    'Who dar? Who dar?
Come ter yer supper, table all sot,
    Who dar? Who dar knockin' at de do'?'
Brer Fox run blin', smash he head 'g'in de tree,
    'Who dar? Who dar?'
'Oh, you ain't de man I 'se wantin' for to see,
    'T ain't me, 't ain't me, knockin' at de do'.'"

"Yas, sah," the tall negro remarked, when the song was ended and cordially applauded by his friend, "w'en dey is 'bout fawty niggahs jes' a-shoutin' dar ar, yer could jes' set an' listen at 'em all night."

Unwilling longer to play the eavesdropper, and loath to leave such entertaining company, Sam stepped forward and knocked on the doorpost.

"Good mornin'," he said. "'Scuse me for interruptin', but me an' my friend stopped tu see 'f we c'ld git a drink o' water. This 'ere crik water 's p'isen, I b'lieve."

Both negroes had arisen suddenly when Sam knocked, the taller with an alarmed, alert look, as if in quick consideration of a way of escape, the other with an abashed yet half-defiant air. The first seemed assured of no evil intention by a glance at the visitor's quiet, good-humored face, and stepped backward with a questioning smile on his own no less good-humored visage.

"Water? Course you can hev' some water. My stars! haow you did scare me," said the violinist, emphasizing each sentence with a chuckle and a jerk of the head. "Didn't s'pose anybody was in a mild o' here. No, sir. An' me an' my cousin was sort o' keepin' house whilst the ol' woman an' the coon 's gone. My brother hain't been tu see me afore, I do' know the time when, an' we allus hev' to hev' a little fun when he does come. Oh, I forgot you wanted some water. 'T ain't the best water in the world," he apologized, as he brought a brimming dipper of milky looking water, "but it 's some wet."

Sam sipped with gingerly lips, but found it better than the clearer, weedy-tasting creek water, and gave it as cordial approval as one could who had been accustomed to the crystal springs of the mountains.

"Ha' some, Antwine? It's pooty good water fer the time o' year," but Antoine would not be prevailed on to help him with this excuse for their call.

Another person now quietly appeared at the door, a placid-faced middle-aged man in red flannel shirt-sleeves that contrasted oddly with his broad-brimmed hat and sober-hued waistcoat of unmistakable Quaker cut. His sudden appearance did not seem to surprise the negroes, whom he accosted pleasantly, while he saluted Sam and his companion with more reserve, regarding them with some wonder.

"Well, James," he said to the master of the house, "so thee 's got company, has thee? And who might thy friends be?"

"That's more 'n I c'n tell ye, Mr. Bartlett."

"I guess you don't remember us, Mr. Bartlett," Sam said, rising from his broken-backed chair and extending his hand as he smiled on the puzzled face of the Quaker. "Me an' this man shantied on your land here one spring, four, five year ago. We was a-trappin' mushrat. Peltier Gove come tu see us an' hired aout tu you. My name 's Samwil Lovel, an' this 'ere 's Antwine."

"Why, dear me, yes," said Friend Bartlett, his face brightening with recognition as he shook Sam's hand. "I thought I 'd seen thee somewhere. And this man too. And Peltier, how 's he? He an' Lowizy are married, I s'pose."

"Wal, Peltier 's abaout so," Sam answered soberly, "but he hain't merried. Lowizy 's dead."

"Thee don't say. Wal, that 's sad, to be sure," Friend Bartlett said in a grieved voice. "Poor child, poor child. It will grieve my wife to hear it, for she set great store by Lowizy. And Peltier was a stiddy, clever young man, poor boy. He must be greatly cast down."

After some further conversation with Sam he turned to the negroes and his eyes fell upon the fiddle. "Well, James, thee has been entertaining thy visitors with music, has thee?" He bent over the instrument curiously and touched the strings with one cautious finger, withdrawing it with a start and an abashed face as they gave forth a resonant chord. "Well, it 's rather a pleasant sound to worldly ears, I dare say," he remarked, and then in a low voice to the man whom he called James, but who was Jim to the world's people, "thee should be careful about attracting strangers to thy house, James, while Robert is with thee."

"I had n't no idee the' was a livin' soul within a mild o' here, Mr. Bartlett; no, sir, I had n't," Jim protested, with many an emphatic jerk of the head. "They popped right on tu us as if they 'd riz right aout o' the airth. I hain't none afeared o' the tall feller, but I do' know 'bout that gabbin' Frenchman," and he cast a suspicious glance at Antoine, who, unconscious of unfriendly scrutiny, was leisurely whittling a charge of tobacco for the waiting pipe between his teeth.

"I come down to fix up the fence a little and look at the young cattle," Friend Bartlett explained to the company, as he went to the door and picked up his axe which he had set down there.

"Friend Samwel, I 'd like to speak with thee a little about Peltier," hesitating over the untruth of the pretext. "I feel clear to trust thee," he said in a guarded voice when Sam had followed him apart to a comfortable leaning-place on the fence, "but I ain't quite so clear in my mind about thy companion." He paused a little, abstractedly hewing the withered leaves off a sunflower stalk. "The fact is, that tall colored man is a fugitive from slavery, and might be in danger if some folks knew he was here."

"I 'spected where the critter come from," said Sam, "but ye need n't be afeared o' me tellin' on him, Mr. Bartlett, an' I don't b'lieve Antwine would either, not tu mean no harm. All 'at ails him is he 's tew full o' his gab."

"Well, Samwel, thee must caution him. It would be sad if anything should happen to hinder this poor man's getting to Canada."

"I guess the' hain't no danger o' that, Mr. Bartlett."

"More than thee thinks, perhaps." Friend Bartlett glanced cautiously toward the house before he added, "I feel free to tell thee that strangers have been seen not many miles off that we mistrust are looking for him."

"Du you b'lieve it?" Sam asked in surprise. The Quaker nodded. "Wal," Sam drawled out, "I ruther guess they won't ketch none o' their stray black sheep up this way—not if I c'n help it."

"Thank thee, Samwel; but I think if nobody lets out the secret they won't be apt to discover his hiding place. Try to keep thy companion's tongue bridled for a few days. Now, I won't hinder thee any longer," and the Quaker moved slowly toward the house.

"Come, Antwine," Sam called, "le' 's be a-moggin'," and Antoine coming forth, the two began to retrace their way to the landing.

"Farewell," Friend Bartlett called after them, "thee tell Peltier what I told thee and remember me in kindness to him, will thee?"

Visitors in Camp

At the edge of the woods Sam turned and took a careful observation of the clearing.

"I s'pose the 's a landin' daown there on the crik 'baout as nigh as the one on the Slang, hain't the'?" he asked.

"Wal, Ah do' know, prob'ly. Yas, Ah guess yas. What you wan' know, hein?" Antoine answered and asked.

"Oh, nothin', on'y I was a-thinkin' if the canew was there we c'ld git tu camp quicker. My stomerk's cryin' cupberd if that feller's water is victuals an' drink. Haow is 't wi' your 'n, Antwine? You hain't hed even water tu stay it."

"Bah gosh!" cried the Canadian with hungry zest, "Ah 'll can heat one of dat dauk raw an' hees fedder."

"That 'ould hurt Joe's feelin's; he wants all the feathers for a peace offerin' tu M'ri," said Sam, lengthening his strides till a glimpse of the open sky beyond the landing was seen, when he slackened his pace and peered cautiously out upon the open marsh.

"Hssh," he whispered, drawing back and slowly sinking upon his haunches, "the' 's a hull snag o' ducks a-squaddlin' raound not four rod f'm the canew. We c'n crawl up an' git a crack at 'em."

Crawling side by side, they wormed their way within short range of at least a dozen wood ducks that were swimming, diving, and bickering over choice morsels in the narrow pathway of water that made from the channel to the landing. Then taking deliberate aim at the thick of the flock, they fired at the word given by Sam. Above the rolling cloud of smoke they saw but five terrified survivors scurrying away in scattered flight, and beneath it when it lifted seven dead and wounded unto death, all of which they speedily secured, even to one poor cripple that skulked among the weeds and was mercifully dispatched by a stroke of a paddle.

"There, Antwine," said Sam, as the canoe floated out upon the channel, "you set for'ad; I done all the shootin' I want tu."

Thus disposed, they paddled down the Slang. As they passed the trim newly built muskrat houses, almost every one of them had a tally stick stuck beside it marked rather conspicuously by a bit of birch bark inserted in a cleft at the top.

"Dat was Injin fashi'n," Antoine commented, "an' Ah bet you head dere was some of it trappin' raound' here."

"Jest their shifflin' way, ketchin' lots o' half-growed ones. But the' 's plenty o' white folks 'at 's jest as bad. I wonder where the creatur's is campin'. I sh'd like tu run on tu 'em."

"Oh, Sam, you 'll want great many t'ing, ant it? You 'll fan' two nigger an' one Quakers to-day already, an' naow you 'll want Injin. Say, Sam, what kan o' nigger you call dat beeg one, hein?"

"I do' know 's anything more 'n a tol'lable black one. Why?"

"Wal, seh, he 'll gat diff'nt of aour kan' o' nigger. He 'll ant spick Angleesh sem' lak' you was an' me an' dat odder nigger. Oh, Ah tol' you, Sam," he said impressively, and looking over his shoulder at his companion, "Ah 'll b'lieved he was slave runaways nigger from Souse 'Mericay."

"Sho', Antwine, you du git cur'us ideas int' your noodle."

"Wal, Ah 'll b'lieved dat, me," said Antoine decidedly.

"Wal, s'posin' he is," said Sam carelessly, "let him run; I shan't stop him."

"Prob'ly de mans dat hown it was willin' for give feefteen, prob'ly twanty-fav' dollar. Haow many you s'pose, prob'ly?"

"I s'pose," said Sam with impressive earnestness, "if a man was mean 'nough tu du sech a sneakin' job he 'd ortu be sunk in this 'ere crik, an' I cal'late that 's as mis'able a death as a fellow could die. If you want tu keep friends wi' me, Antwine, don't you tell nob'dy 'at we seen sech a man—not nob'dy."

"No, no—no, Ah 'll won't tol' mah waf', no, sah;" adding after some reflection, "honly Onc' Lasha an' Zhozeff, prob'ly."

"Wal, if you must tell someb'dy er bu'st, I s'pose they 'd be as safe as anyb'dy. But don't ye open your head tu no strangers. Naow, remember."

"Dat all Ah want. But Ah 'll tol' you, Sam, it mek me felt kan o' mean for keep all Ah 'll know for mahsef."

"Hol' on," said Sam, steering the canoe close to the marsh where a muskrat house stood in a narrow environment of open water, "there 's a poor leetle mushrat not so big as a haouse rat, all wopsed up in a mess o' weeds where he can't draown ner git away."

As the canoe ran alongside, he reached out and carefully disengaged the trap and its struggling captive from the entanglement of marsh weeds, and after a brief inspection pressed the spring till the jaws opened. When the little prisoner found himself free he made off with scrambling splash into the marsh as Sam gave him a parting admonition.

"There, you poor little devil, go your ways an' grow bigger. Naow, Antwine, would n't a feller be meaner 'n pusley tu put that leetle chap back int' the trap ag'in?"

"Yas, prob'ly," said Antoine; "but Ah 'll ant spec' de Injin t'ank you much, prob'ly, ant it?"

"Wal, I wan't ezackly considerin' the Injin's feelin's."

Their way down the Slang and creek was unmarked by even an unsuccessful shot, for the few ducks they saw arose too far out of range to tempt them to the trial of the uncertain chance. Now and then they were startled by the sudden uprising of a heron beating upward with labored strokes of his broad vans in a long slant to level flight over the marshes, or the frightened squawk of a bittern jerking himself into the air and stumbling through it on awkward wings to a safer retreat. A countless dusky swarm of blackbirds rose up from their busy feeding among the rice in a sudden cloud and with a dull roar of innumerable wings, as if a mine had exploded beneath the flock.

When they rounded the last great bend and came in sight of the bay, they saw a large craft with a single square sail coming in toward the mouth of Lewis Creek.

"Hurra' for Canada," cried Antoine joyfully, after regarding it intently for a moment. "Look, Sam, dat was Canada boats."

"What makes you think so?"

"Oh, Ah 'll know it by hees sail jes' easy as you can tol' nigger by hees skin. Yankee boat ant got square sail lak' dat more as he wore botte sauvage or heat pea soup. Prob'ly, he brought some salt for sol' it or come for bought some happle, prob'ly, bose of it, Ah d' know 'f he ant. Ah 'll gat brudder-law was be captain for one of it. Mebby dat was be mah brudder-law, mos' likel'. Ah 'll go see to-naght 'f Ah 'll ant in de morny, me."

"Wal, I 'll go with ye. It 's turrible interestin' tu look at furrin shippin', an' that looks like an ol' buster, nigh 's big 's a canawl boat."

"Oh, dey was beauty boats," said Antoine proudly. "Ah 'll tol' you, dey was mek de water roar lak' Onc' Lasha w'en he sleep."

Presently they were at the landing among the willows under the bluff, a place made familiar to them in their summer fishing trip of a previous year. Thence, laden with guns and game, they climbed the steep to the camp, where they were loudly welcomed by Uncle Lisha and Joseph, who generously congratulated them on their success, though it abated the pride of their own achievements.

"Wal done, boys." Uncle Lisha slowly counted the ducks, carefully inspecting and observing each and inquiring its kind. "You did du fust rate, sartain. But what sort o' critter 's this 'ere?" he asked, picking up the coot and minutely examining it. "Ann Twine, hev you be'n a-robbin' someb'dy er nuther's henrwust?"

"No, Onc' Lasha," said the Canadian, one hand busy with the potato kettle and frying-pan, while from the other he snatched hasty mouthfuls of bread to appease the cravings of his fasting stomach, "dat was you good boy Sam, an' Ah 'll tol' it he don't ought for do so weeked. But he want for pracsit for shoot, so he 'll shot de folkses' hen. What you t'ink for dat, hein?"

"No, 't ain't a hen nuther," the old man decided, "but it looks more like one 'an some o' these 'ere patent new-fashion Chinee faowls does. Clapham's got a rwuster 'at come f'm Boston 'at he calls a High-shang er Hang-shy er some sech a name, 'at don't look no more like a civilized barndoor faowl 'an you du, Ann Twine, an' when he does what Clapham calls crowin', it scares child'en. I never heard sech a' on'arthly yollopin'."

"Wal, Onc' Lasha, dis t'ing was kan' o' fool dauk. Dat hees nem of it. We jus' brought it home for de fedders for Zhozeff."

"Wal, me and Jozey hes picked 'em all off'm them lettle baby ducks 'at we got, an' don't you b'lieve both on ye 'at he was so savin' 'at he pulled the pinfeathers aout with his teeth, an' we got pooty nigh a piller case full, an' the ducks is dressed, complete. Haow be ye goin' tu cook 'em, Ann Twine? Rwust 'em, er bile 'em, er fry 'em? I 'm kinder hankerin' for some hot victuals."

"Wal, Ah 'll b'lieve Ah 'll goin' for fry it, for be quickes' way for our hongry," said Antoine, laying the split teal in the frying-pan with a generous lump of Danvis butter from the Lovel dairy. "Come, Sam, ponch de fire. Zhozeff, pull up you stump an' chaup off some hwood. Hoorah."

The fire was properly replenished, the potatoes boiled merrily, the frying pan screeched, and Antoine pranced around them fully impressed with the importance of his office, while the others sat on the fireside log hungrily watching him with their backs to the world.

"I do' know as ary one on us told ye 'at we hed comp'ny whilst you was gone," Joseph said. Antoine held an attentive ear above the crackling of the fire and the turmoil of cookery, upon which he kept his intent eyes, shielded by one protecting hand, while the other, armed with a fork, urged the process of cooking with frequent prods and shakes of the contents of the pan.

"Wal, sorter comp'ny er vis'ters er callers, mebby you might call 'em. Tew fellers they was 'at come a-saunderin' up an' sod daown an' smoked a spell an' peared turrible sociable. Hed guns, they did, kinder huntin', but was inquirin' if the' was colored man livin' anywher's raound here, o' the name o' Jeems suthin' er nuther. What was 't, Uncle Lisha?"

"I do' know," Uncle Lisha replied, "I tol' 'em 'at we hed n't had time tu git 'quainted wi' the white folks, let alone the niggers."

"Color' man," cried Antoine, lifting his voice above the roar and crackle of the fire, the walloping of the pot and the sizzle of the pan, and making it very audible though his back was turned to his hearers. "Bah gosh, me an' Sam was visit some black color' mans an' hear of some red color' mans. An' seh, de black color' mans leeve raght over dere behin' de hwood, pooty clos' neighbor of us, seh. He gat for stay wid heem one slave nigger dat was run 'way wid hese'f all de ways from Sous 'Meriky, an' oh, he would dance you never see to beat it w'en t'udder nigger was fi'le. An' dat beeg slave run'way nigger was sing jus' lak' black yallerbird, sem as de gros riche lady gat in leetly wire coop. Oh, Ah 'll tol' you 'f Ah 'll hown dat nigger, Ah 'll ant took more 's feefty dollar for it, no, seh."

As Antoine ceased, Joseph slowly turned in his seat to reach a stick of wood and was confronted by two men standing close behind the unconscious group.

"Sam Hill!" he ejaculated. "Here they be naow! Where in tunket did you come from? Dumbed if you did n't skeer me, anyway!"

The other members of the camp household were as much surprised as Joseph, but Sam was most disturbed, for he felt almost certain that much of Antoine's disclosures must have been overheard by the intruders, who he suspected were hunting larger game than ducks.

"Beg pardon, gentlemen," said one of the newcomers, a brisk, wiry little man with a sharp face and a business-like, official air. "Don't wanter intrude, but we 'd jes' like to light aour pipes 't your fire. Can't scare up a match betwixt us. Got a flint an' steel, but lost aour punk," and without waiting for permission he stepped to the fire and thrust a dry twig of cedar into it, wherewith when ablaze he lit his pipe and then offered it to his companion, a tall, sallow man all of whose movements were deliberate if not indolent, except those of his restless, searching eyes.

"Here, Clark, light up. This 'ere 's better 'n punk or a match."

But Clark had just begun to whittle a charge from a huge plug of peculiar light-colored tobacco, very different, as Sam noticed, from the black nail rod and twist to which he was accustomed, and he also noticed that the stranger's pronunciation of the few words he spoke bore a marked similitude to that of Jim's guest. When he had generously offered his "raal Ol' Firginny leaf" to each and lighted his own pipeful, so fragrant that those who refused regretted having done so, the visitors seemed in a hurry to go, but he who was the spokesman returned, after they had gone a little way, to ask in Yankee fashion for the loan of the scow.

"I s'pose you could n't let us take you scaow boat a spell to go aout an' see 'f we could n't git tew three ducks, could ye? We hate to go hum 'thaout a feather. They 'll make fun on us so. We can't git a thing huntin' 'long the shore."

Sam shook his head. "I'm turrible sorry, but we got tu use aour boat jest as soon as we git some grub."

"We 'd fetch it back in a couple o' hours," urged the man whom his comrade called Baker. "Guess you c'n let us have it as long as that, can't you?"

"No, got tu use it right off," said Sam. "Come, Antwine, hain't ye got the victuals 'most ready? We want tu be off tu rights."

Reluctantly relinquishing the design of borrowing the boat, Baker and his comrade hurried away up the bank of the creek. Sam watched them with unfriendly eyes till they disappeared among the trees beyond the landing, saying to himself as much as to his companions:—

"Consarn 'em! They won't git no boat o' aourn tu hunt niggers."

Uncle Lisha and Joseph stared at him in puzzled inquiry, and Antoine, with an abashed face, devoted himself to his cookery.

"What is 't, Samwil?" the old shoemaker asked at last. "I can't make head nor tail on 't."

"Why, you know what they ast you, an' you heard what Antwine said 'baout the darkies an' so did they, a-sneaking up behind of us at just that onlucky minute; heard all they wanted tu er they 'd ha' ast me some questions. They 're arter that 'ere runaway chap, an' I don't cal'late we 're a-goin' tu help 'em much, be we?"

Uncle Lisha snorted a contemptuous negative, and Joseph Hill said:—

"It don't seem 's 'ough that was what we come here for, not ezac'ly."

"Prob'ly Ah 'll s'pose, Sam, you blem me all up, but Ah tol' you, seh, Ah 'll ant to blem. Ah 'll ant s'pose dere was anybody but wese'f goin' for heard me tol' Onc' Lasha an' Zhozeff de new, an' Ah mus' tol' dat," Antoine said in deep dejection, as he set the dinner on the table and the hungry crew gathered about it.

"Oh, I do' know 's I blame you none. The' hain't no use in cryin' over spilt milk, an' we 'll jest tend tu aour business an' let other folks tend tu their 'n, if it hain't the pootiest 'at ever was. Say," he continued, as if dismissing the subject, "when we git done eatin' le' 's take the scaow boat an' all go over an' see that 'ere boat f'm Canady."

The Canada Boat

When the dinner of one course was finished, the simple service of iron and tinware was left unwashed without fear of disparaging feminine comment, and the voyagers embarked, Sam and Antoine at the oars, Uncle Lisha steering with a paddle, and Joseph as passenger and general observer. In these capacities he took his ease so far as he could with a hand on either gunwale and hitching from side to side at every slight lurch of the staunch craft. This he continued to do after the black depths of the creek were passed and they voyaged across the shallow head of the bay, where the oars grated on the sandy bottom and the golden mesh of reflected sunshine twisted and tangled its elusive threads among the caddis worms and mussels, a half arm's length beneath the rippled surface.

Over among the red maples of Lewis Creek could be seen the naked mast of the Canadian craft, its gay pennon lost in the brilliant foliage that it flaunted against. But the incessant gabble of the crew and their snatches of French songs would have guided our voyagers to the vessel without any visible indication of its whereabouts, and following it up the stream a little way beyond its last bend, they came to the boat at its moorings.

The jolly little captain was very polite, and welcomed them as possible apple sellers in English quite as good as Antoine's, if somewhat different from it, having evidently been drawn from a well not entirely undefiled with h's.

"Mek youse'f welcome, mah frien'," he cried, with his shoulders lifted to his ears and his palms hospitably spread. "Go hall hover mah boats. He was you boats, han' 'e was good boats, hif Hah say hit mahse'f. Oh, 'e good sloops. Han' if you gat happle for sol' Hah ready for bought she han' paid you ten cen' pour baskeet 'f she was mos' hall red happle, han' medjy him mah baskeet, hant' ol' more as t'ree peck," and he gave a contemptuous kick to a basket which could hold at least a bushel and a half.

The visitors gave the odd-looking and not very cleanly craft as complete inspection and as unstinted praise as would satisfy their curiosity and her captain's pride, smothering themselves in the garlic-reeking cabin as long as they could hold their breath and then stumbling forth into the fresh outer air.

"I hain't got no apples tu sell myself," said Sam to the little captain, "but I do' know but what I c'ld send you a man 'at has. Come aout this way a minute, won't ye? Say, captain," he continued when they had got beyond the hearing of the others, "haow long afore you 're a-goin' back to Canady?" Sam picked up a stick and began whittling it, wherefrom the shrewd Canadian, having had some experience of Yankees, augured that a trade was impending.

"Wal, Hah don't mos' know, me. Mos' likel' Hah go day hafter nex' day hif de peop' brought dey happle. But," he continued, curiously watching the shavings curl slowly away from the keen knife, "hif you can sen' it me some very good red happle, Hah could waits hanodder one day."

"No, guess I don't want tu keep you waitin'," said Sam. "Be you goin' stret hum? Goin' tu stop anywhere on the way?"

"Ah, no, no, no, bien no. Hah han' goin' let mah happle rot 'fore Hah cood sol' she. Hah go fas' Hah cood."

"S'pose you c'ld take 'long a passenger tol'able cheap?"

"Wal, seh, mah fren'," said the captain after some consideration of the proposal, "hif de mans was clever for behave hese'f, han' paid me one dollah 'fore 'e go, Hah will took it, me, han' dat was more sheaps 'e can go hin stimboat, yas, bah t'under! yas, more sheaps 'e can go 'foots."

"Yes, if you feed him, that 's reasonable 'nough," Sam assented.

"Oh, no, no, no," cried the captain, "for dat 'e mus' heat 'ese'f. Hif Hah heat 'im, Hah mus' hask more as dat."

"Wal, then, we 'll hev him eat himself," Sam agreed with a chuckle. "I sh'd wanter be tol'lable well paid myself if I 'd got tu eat him. All right, captain, I guess he 'll be here 'baout the time you start," and having concluded the negotiation he threw away the neatly whittled stick and pocketed his knife.

"Mos' likel' your frien' was be goin' on Canada for 'ees 'ealthy," said the captain, shrugging his shoulders and winking at Sam.

"He 's a-goin' there tu extend the ary of freedom," Sam answered with an imperturbable countenance.

Sam and the captain returned to the boat, where Antoine and his compatriots—who, though not old acquaintances, had mutual knowledge of some—were swimming with violent gesticulations in a babbling torrent of gossip, on whose brink Uncle Lisha and Joseph sat in gaping, wondering silence, now turning their puzzled faces upon the Canadians, now slowly upon each other. Their amazement increased when the captain also plunged in and contributed his full share to the confusion of tongues.

"Good airth an' seas!" Uncle Lisha gasped in a loud whisper to Sam, "it hain't no more like talk 'an a passel o' hens hevin' a cacklin' bee in the mornin', an' I can't pick nothin' aout on 't on'y now an' then a 'wee' and' a 'sackeree.' I b'lieve the dumbed critters is jest pertendin' they 're a-talkin' an' don't understan' one 'nother no more 'n they would if they was a-whirlin' hoss fiddles at one 'nother."

"Wal, they 'pear tu git ahead wi' the' vis'tin' some way," said Sam, regarding the animated group with an amused smile.

"I do' know fer sartain," Joseph remarked, after deliberate consideration, "but I kinder cal'late the heft o' the conversin' is done by signs, an' the gab is jest hove in for sort o' fillin'. Seem 's 'ough that was the way on 't, but mebby 't hain't."

"Wal, they beat ten women tu a quiltin'," said Uncle Lisha, "an' I give it up. Say, Samwil, you be'n a-buyin' the boat?"

"Wal, no; on'y a sheer on 't. Cal'lated it 'ould be handy for Joseph to go huntin' an' fishin' in."

Their attention was attracted to a heavily laden wagon that came jolting over the rough pasture, announcing its approach with a rumble and creak that began now to be heard above the voices of the Canadians, till at last their interested attention was called to the fact that a customer was arriving.

"Wal, if there hain't a load of apples comin' a'ready," said Sam. "I guess this feller sent on word ahead 'at he was a-comin'. We 'll wait an' git a pocketful an' then be off."

While the captain and his customer were pitting Canuck and Yankee shrewdness against each other in sharp bargaining, Sam and his comrades tasted, and selected their pocketful of the mellowest and least sour of the common fruit, that but for the advent of the Canada boat would have gone to the cider mill, and they then departed. Antoine went most reluctantly, for he was still oppressed by unspoken words.

When they were at home again—for so they at once began to call their temporary abiding place—they fell to picking their ducks—a task whereof many hands made light work—beguiled by Sam's and Antoine's relation of the circumstances of the day's incidents.

"Naow," said Sam, laying apart a couple of the finest ducks, "if the' hain't no objection, I b'lieve I 'll take them 'ere up tu Mr. Bartlett. There's more 'n we c'n use anyway. Mebby it 'll be kinder late afore I git back, but you need n't tew, if it's dark fust, on'y jest set aout the lantern tu one o' the landin's." There being no demur, he embarked at once on this mission.

A Side Track of the U.G.R.R.

The shadows of the trees that skirted the west shore stretched far across the marsh and channel as Sam drove the canoe up the creek with quick, strong strokes quite regardless of the throngs of incoming waterfowl that swept past him or those already arrived that arose from the marsh on either hand and the open water before him, for he had left the temptation of the gun behind him. When he entered the East Slang all lesser shadows were dissolved in the overwhelming shadow of the Adirondacks, and when he stepped on shore at the old camp landing the twilight was thickening into gloom in the woods, through which he took the now dimly defined path and hastened toward the log house of the negro.

When he came in sight of it, it was a dark blotch in the clearing against the faint light of the afterglow, with one spot of light in it, where a candle shone from its single front window. As he approached he heard the voices and frequent laughter of his acquaintances of the morning, with the softer voice of a woman sometimes breaking in. He knocked at the door and the voices were suddenly hushed, and in the stillness he heard the puff that blew out the candle, followed by excited whispers and cautious steps across the floor. He knocked again, and the woman's voice demanded:

"Who's there?"

"It's me! Sam Lovel! the man 'at was here this mornin'. I want tu speak tu the man they call James."

There was more whispering before Jim asked, jerking out the words with the characteristic nervous twitches of the head that Sam could almost see in spite of the intervening door:—

"What d' you want? Be you alone? Can't you talk through the door?"

"I don't want tu holler," said Sam in a low voice, answering the last question first. "It's suthin' 'baout the man 'at you call your brother er cousin. He wants tu be makin' himself sca'ce raoun' here. I'm all alone, an' you need n't be afeared tu open the door."

After more whispering inside, the door was unfastened and cautiously opened far enough for Jim to thrust his head outside and assure himself of Sam's identity and that he was alone. Then the door was held wide open and the visitor invited to enter by a jerk of the head and motion of the hand. The door was closed so quickly behind Sam that it nearly caught the skirts of his coat. By the glimmer of light from the stove he saw the lilting, dancing negro of the morning transformed into a stern, threatening giant confronting him with an axe uplifted above his shoulder. The figure of a woman shrank behind the stove, with a child, wide-eyed with fright and wonder, clinging to her gown.

"You need n't be afeared tu light your light an' see who I be," said Sam. "The' hain't nob'dy else."

While Jim relighted the candle with a splinter the others looked intently at Sam, as his features grew distinct in the increasing glow, when, being assured that his honest face masked no evil purpose, the tall negro lowered his axe, and the woman, a handsome mulatto, sat down and took the child upon her knee.

Sam told them of his suspicion that the visitors at camp were in search of Jim's guest. "And naow," he said in conclusion, "the chances is they 'll be here arter you to-morrow. I 've laid in with a feller tu take ye tu Canerdy on his boat, but he won't go afore to-morrow night or nex' day, an' you 'll hafter lay low either in the woods or up tu Mr. Bartlett's. I cal'late his haouse is the best place, an' I come tu take ye up there an' tell him abaout gittin' on ye off, an' if that suits ye we 'll be a-moggin' soon as you c'n git ready."

"I 'se ready," said Bob, snatching his hat and coat from a peg on the log wall and moving toward the door.

"It don't take Bob long tu pack his trunk, no sir," Jim said with a nervous laugh. "Lord, haow you did scare me when you knocked. Twice in one day is 'baout often 'nough to scare a man in one day, yes, sir! But naow you 're putty nigh scarin' of me ag'in. You s'pose them fellers r'ally was huntin' arter Bob?"

"I 'se ready," Bob repeated as he drew a small pistol from his coat pocket, and turning stooped to the candle light to examine the cap. Replacing it in his pocket, he turned to Sam and said:—

"I s'pec 's you 're gwine ter sot me 'cross de run, Marse Lovel?"

"The run? Oh, the Slang; yes, I was cal'latin' tu, an' tu go up tu Mr. Bartlett's with ye. I want tu see him. My canew 's up there tu the landin'."

"What! you did n't never come clean raound to the Slang to-night? You might ha' come right acrost the crik no time."

"I did n't know who might be a-watchin'," Sam answered. "The longest way raoun' 's the surest. Come, le' 's be a-moggin'."

"I 'se done b'en ready," said Bob. "Goo'-by, Nancy; goo'-by, little Jimmy. De good Lawd bress ye an' ta' keer on ye."

He shook hands with the woman and laid his huge hand on the child's curly head, and then stretched it out to Jim.

"Goo'-by, Jeems, er is you gwine 'long?"

"You stay along wi' me, Jim," said the woman anxiously.

"I guess mebby you 'd better," said Sam.

The two negroes looked at him suspiciously, and exchanged questioning glances.

"I guess I 'll go a piece," Jim said with an emphatic jerk of the head.

"All right, suit yourself. I only cal'lated it 'ould look better if anybody come. S'posin' yu put the light aout ag'in, so the' can't nob'dy see us goin' aout."

Jim blew out the candle and the three went out into the night, now lighted only by the stars and the flicker of the northern lights.

They took their way across the clearing at a brisk pace, Jim taking the lead as being most familiar with the path, Sam next, and the runaway in the rear. The latter cast frequent glances behind and started nervously when an alarmed bird fluttered suddenly from a bush, or some night prowler scurried among the fallen leaves and dry twigs, while Sam and Jim held steadily on, quite regardless of such harmless sounds. Feeling their way more slowly along the unseen wood path, they came to where they saw the stars again, then saw them repeated in the still water of the channel, and then were at the landing. There was a soft splash in the channel like the cautious dip of an oar.

"Fo' de Lawd," Bob gasped, starting back and thrusting his hand in his pocket, "dem fellers out dar layin' fo' me. My Gawd, Marse Lovel, you ain't de man to fool a pore niggah what 's bein' hunted to de eends of de airth!" and he tried to scan Sam's face in the dim starlight, but holding aloof in a half-crouching attitude that might be a preparation for either a fight or a run.

"I guess it hain't nothin' but a mushrat or a duck," Sam whispered, looking intently in the direction of the sound, "but mebby Jim hed better shove aout there in his canew an' see."

Jim pushed his dugout to the edge of the channel and presently jerked back a loud disjointed whisper.

"Everything 's all right. Jist as clear 's a Christian's eye. Yes, sir, jist eg-zackly."

With this assurance Bob took his place in the canoe where Sam had already kneeled, with his paddle in his hand, and he now pushed out and laid his craft alongside of Jim's.

"I do' know jest where I 'm a-goin' tu land," he said with a questioning inflection.

"You go up 'baout fifty rod an' you 'll come tu the John Clark place, where ol' John Clark allus used tu fish. You can run right up to the hard bank there. Mr. Bartlett's is the furdest north in that string o' lights. You put right straight for it an' you 'll strike a big holler where a brook runs, which you cross it an' follow up the north bank an' you 'll hit the secont road right by his haouse. I guess I won't go no furder an' I 'll bid you good-by, Bob, an' good luck to ye."

"Goo'-by, Jeems; ta' keer yo'se'f, boy."

They shook hands across the gunwales and the bark canoe slid silently up the channel, breaking the smooth surface with wake and paddle strokes that set the mirrored stars a-dancing and startled the sleeping ducks to sudden, noisy flight. Without greater incident the brief voyage was made, and the two men set forth across the fields, guided by the house light and the deep-cut watercourse to which they presently came. They approached the first road with scarcely a precaution of secrecy, for there was not a house upon it nearer than the tavern at the corner, where the bar-room lights shone out with hospitable gleam.

They were beginning to climb the fence when they heard the sound of a wagon and voices in low but earnest conversation close at hand and drawing nearer. Then they saw the intermittent glow of a pipe, and as they sank back and crouched in a weed-grown fence corner they caught a whiff of its odor.

"Fo' de Lawd," Bob whispered, sniffing it eagerly, "I hain't felt de smell o' no terbacca lak dat sence I done lef' Ol' Firginny."

Sam laid a cautionary hand on his arm. "What be they talkin' 'baout?"

The wagon stopped almost in front of them, and as its clatter and the footfalls of the horse ceased, the guarded voices of the occupants were distinctly heard.

"I tell you the rwud cross lots is consid'able furder on," said one. "The' hain't no gap ner barway here, fer I c'n see stakes an' caps tu ev'ry corner."

Sam held his breath while he knew that two pairs of eyes were closely scanning the fence and the very corner where he crouched beside his companion, whose hand he could hear stealthily creeping to the pocket that held the pistol.

"I reckon yo' ah right," the other occupant of the wagon said at last, and Sam recognized the smooth voice of the quiet visitor at camp; "but 'pears like we 'd come fah enough."

"No, sir," the other rejoined emphatically, "the 's a reg'lar rwud when we come tu it, an' it runs through a paster. This 'ere 's a medder; I can see a stack a-loomin' up."

"All right," the other conceded, "go ahade and hurry up yo' cakes, foh I 'll be bound Baker and his man 's thah with the boat foh now."

The driver spoke sharply to his horse, and the wagon went rattling down the road at a rapid pace.

"Wal," said Sam, rising and letting out his long-held breath, "I cal'late you stayed to Jim's 'baout as long as was healthy for ye."

"Sho 's yo' bawn, Marse Lovel! Dat 'ar man saoun' des lak Cap'n Clahk," Bob whispered excitedly. "De shaapes' man faw huntin' niggahs dey is in all dem pahts. Lawd, if I did n't t'ink he was lookin' right squaar' at me."

"Wal, he hain't a-huntin' on his own groun', an' that makes lots o' odds. My sakes, won't they hev fun a-hoofin on 't raound the head o' the Slang in the dark! It would be tew all-killin' bad if they should break the' necks a-tumblin' through the woods."

When the two came to the broad stage road, no one was astir in the quiet neighborhood, and leaving Bob hidden in an adjacent fence corner, Sam went to Friend Bartlett's kitchen door and knocked, and presently a handsome young woman came forth. Her plain dress wore some un-Quakerly adornments, but her face was so kindly that Sam felt sure she must be in full sympathy with her parents in all benevolent work.

"Good evenin', Miss Bartlett; I fetched up a couple o' ducks tu your father, an' I wanted tu speak tu him abaout a little business."

"Yes," she said, with a questioning affirmative, as she took the proffered ducks. "Thee may leave any message for father with me. Why, these ducks are very nice, and I 'm sure he 'll be very much obliged to thee. Won't thee come in?"

Sam declined and she stepped out, closing the door behind her.

"You tell your father," Sam hastened to say in a low voice, "'at the' 's som'b'dy arter that nigger an' they 've faound aout where he was hid, so I fetched him up here."

"The colored man at James's? Where is he?" Margaret Bartlett asked anxiously.

"I did n't cal'late tu hev nob'dy see him but your father, an' hid him in the fence aout here. But he can't stay there all night, an' what be I goin' tu du with him?"

"Thee must put him in the barn, in the bay on the west side of the barn floor. No one will go there, and I 'll tell Father when he comes."

"All right, an' you tell your father 'at I 've laid in wi' a Canuck 'at's a-buyin' apples tu take the nigger tu Canerdy in a day or two. Your father 'll want tu take daown a lwud to-morrer an' find aout when, an' we 'll git the nigger there tu rights."

"I wish thee would n't call colored people niggers," said Margaret.

"Why," said Sam, "That's what he calls himself, an' I rather guess from his looks he is one. Good night. I 'll mow him away all right."

Groping his way into the unknown interior of the barn, guided only by feeling and a knowledge of the common internal arrangement of barns in general, Sam led his charge to this safe retreat, and bidding him good-by departed on his devious, dark, and solitary way back to camp.

As he silently passed the landing where Jim's dugout lay he saw the light of a lantern glimmering unsteadily along the wood path and heard the hunters returning in bad humor from their unsuccessful quest, stumbling and grumbling over the rough trail.

"Wal," said Sam to himself, as he listened to their floundering progress up the wooded bank of the Slang, "you faound the holler tree, but the coon was n't in it. By the gre't horn spoon! I 'd ha' gi'n a fo'pence tu ha' be'n there an' seen 'em an' seen Jim shake that head o' his 'n."

When he reached the mouth of the Slang he heard the regular sound of oars and saw another light steadily advancing up the channel of the creek, shining far along the quiet water before it, while glittering reflections flickered out like floating sparks where the wake stirred the rushes.

Sam ran his canoe into the weeds till the other boat had passed. The lantern shining on the face of the man in the stern revealed the features of Baker, the other visitor at the camp.

"You planned it fust rate," Sam soliloquized again, "but it 's a dre'f'l poor night for huntin' niggers. Oh, you cussed slinks! I don't lay it up so much ag'in that other feller, for that 's the way he was brought up; but you—V'monters—huntin' niggers! Damn ye! I 'd lufter sink ye in the mud!"

So, by turns boiling with wrath and chuckling over the discomfiture of the slave-hunters, Sam pursued his way to where the candle was burning low in the socket of the tin lantern which was hung out to beacon him to the upper landing.

The northern horizon was glowing with the pulsating flame of the aurora, and the dark forest of the eastern shore echoed at intervals with the solemn challenges of the horned owls, remotely answered by their brethren who held sway over the somber realm of the Porterboro woods that stretched their dark expanse along the west bank of the South Slang and beyond the sluggish rivulets of its source.

"'Cordin' tu the signs we 're a-goin' tu git some sort o' fallin' weather," Uncle Lisha remarked as he gave an eye and ear to these prognostics of a storm.

"The north'n lights is shinin' tol'able bright," said Joseph, peeping through the trees at the celestial display.

Antoine rolled himself off his seat on to all fours, and in that position intently regarded such glimpses of the flickering arch as could be seen between the tree trunks that stood in black relief against it, then turning his searching gaze to the creek, descried a light moving about in the black shadows of the farther shore.

"Look, see dar!" he said in a suppressed tone of alarm, as he pointed to the moving light.

The Canadian watched the light till it vanished in fitful gleams among the woods, and then he turned and stooped to the campfire to rekindle his neglected pipe.

Before seating himself at the fire he looked again in the direction where the light had disappeared. If he had been given the vision of an owl he might have seen a boat with two figures in it stealthily landing at the farther shore; but the faint light of the aurora, that barely defined in dimmed silver the course of the channel, revealed nothing to him.

The owls had quit their dismal calling, and not a sound was to be heard from the woods or waters save the occasional splash of a fish or a waterfowl or a muskrat busy with its nightly labors.

"What ye s'pose has become o' that 'ere tormented boy?" Uncle Lisha demanded sharply, after some inward fuming at the apparent apathy of his companions, "or don' ye car' whether he 's draownded or lost in the ma'sh? Why don't ye say suthin'?"

"Wal, Ah guess Sam gat hol' 'nough for took care heese'f of it, prob'ly," Antoine answered with some sharpness. "He 'll ant leetly boy, ant it?"

Uncle Lisha deigned no reply to the Canadian. Then after a moment of intent listening, "I 'm a dumbed good min' to holler. I c'n make him hear if he 's alive within a mild o' here."

As he drew in his breath for a mighty shout they heard disturbed waterfowl, one after another, nearer and nearer, taking sudden flight, the flutter of uprising and cries of alarm continually drawing nearer, till at last the thump of a paddle was heard at the landing, and then the lantern began to sway and undulate, now hidden behind a tree or knoll, now shining brighter till its sprinkled light disclosed Sam's illuminated legs quite close at hand.

"Wal, folks, here I be," he announced as he let the full light of the candle upon his face through the open door and then extinguished it with a puff.

"An' high time 'at you was," and Uncle Lisha spent his hoarded breath in a growl. "What ye be'n shoolin' raound these 'ere ma'shes for, a-ketchin' the fever 'n' aig an' freezin' tu death? I 'm a tarnal good min' ter shake ye, so I be. Sed daown there by the fire an' warm ye whilst I put on some more wood. An' say, Ann Twine, hain't ye got a col' duck for him an' a hunk o' bread? I know he's hungry."

"I ain't a mite hungry, ner cold nuther," Sam declared, seating himself by the fire and preparing for a restful smoke. "On'y a leetle mite tired. I stayed tu Mr. Bartlett's longer'n what I meant tu an' it's kinder slow poky work a-keepin' the channel in the dark, 'spesherly in the Slang. I 'm sorry you got worried."

"Sho, I wan't worryin' none, but I was a leetle riled," said the old man as he ran his hand down Sam's long shank. "Why, your laigs is kinder damp. You want tu dry 'em good 'fore you go tu bed!"

"Say, Sam," Antoine whispered cautiously, "Where you was, hein?"

Sam cast a scrutinizing glance upon him as he answered, "Why, up to Mr. Bartlett's. Where d' ye s'pose. Le' 's go tu bed."

The Canada Boat Departs

In prompt fulfillment of the night's prophecies, the morning, dawning dully through a thick veil of clouds, brought a drizzle of rain. This fell with such a drowsy patter on the canvas roof that the inmates of the camp felt little inclination to bestir themselves till impelled to do so by hunger.

Then Sam and Antoine crept out and after inspecting the lowering sky set about building a fire and making other preparations for breakfast, though Uncle Lisha advised a cold bite in the shelter of the tent.

"No, sah," Antoine objected as he moved around the fire, quite regardless of the slow drizzle of rain except when the drip of an overhanging bough aroused a spiteful sputter of the pan wherein two split ducks were frying. "We 'll ant goin' for discourage de inside of us wid col' victual w'en de rine comin' on de aoutside. Ah tol' you, if mans wan' have hees heart warm he 'll gat for had hees stommack warm. Fetch de dauk in de coop, Sam. We 'll can't sit aour table in de rine," and he swung the kettle over Uncle Lisha's imperiled legs to a place inside the tent and Sam bestowed the sizzling frying pan beside it. "Naow Ah 'll was goin' for heat. Dat was de bes' t'ing we can do w'en it was rine, 'cep' go feeshin'."

"An' I cal'late tu stick right by ye, Antwine," said Joseph from behind a duck's wing that he was gnawing, holding it with both hands. "I hain't the kind er man tu desart a friend in no sech scrape, don't seem 's 'ough I was, not as I feel naow."

Uncle Lisha filled his pipe and went out to enjoy it by the fireside under shelter of his blue umbrella, and Sam, after providing a present supply of firewood with a few axe strokes, wandered out to the bluff overlooking the creek.

Far or near there was no visible sign of human life, nor amid the continuous purr of the rain, the contented gabble of the ducks, the whistle of passing wings, the raucous call of some estray or laggard, and the metallic clatter of the kingfisher, was there any sound of it except from the quarter where the Canadian boat was taking in its cargo.

Thence through the heavy vaporous atmosphere came the lumbering of laden wagons, the rumble of their discharging freight, and then the brisk rattle of departing empty wagons, all mingled with the shouts of teamsters and the vociferous jabber of captain and crew.

For one who had no apparent reason for being interested in fruit trade, Sam was uncommonly well pleased that the rainy day was not hindering it, and having assured himself of the fact he returned to camp.

"Wal, Samwil, what ye diskivered?"

"Nothin' but water an' ma'sh an' woods, lookin' lunsomer 'n they did a hundred year ago, fer there hain't even an Injun in sight. I heard the Frenchman lwudin' his boat, though."

The afternoon was spent in the tent. Uncle Lisha discoursed of the past and Antoine of various men in Canada who were always the heroes of his tales, while in the breaks of conversation Sam several times went out for the ostensible purpose of a general inspection of the weather, though the examination was mostly confined to the direction of Lewis Creek.

Late in the afternoon the wind freshened from the northeast, the tossed branches dropped sudden showers upon the canvas with a startling, ripping sound, and amid the sullen murmur of the windswept woods and the louder patter of the driven rain could be heard the regular wash of the rising waves and the shrill whistle of frequent flocks scudding in from the lake.

Then Sam saw the Canada boat gliding down the unseen channel, the great square sail stalking between the trees like a gigantic ghost, till at last it walked forth upon the vexed lake amid the taller phantoms of mist and vanished in the thronging host.

Sam reentered the tent with a satisfied visage and remarked:—

"Wal, that 'ere Frenchman 's got started fer Canerdy with his apples."

"An' like 'nough a blackbary," Uncle Lisha added, with a significant twinkle in his eye.

Sungahneetuk

In the morning, when eating breakfast, no plans were laid for spending the day, and after the meal no one made the usual preparation for departure, but all idled about the camp as if without a present object in life but the mere pleasure of existence.

The day was one to invite indolence, the sun bathing the earth in such a mellow warmth that it soon dispelled the morning chill and left no use but pipe-lighting for the fire, which burned with a lazy flicker of transient flame and lazier drifts of smoke jets from snapping embers and brands.

Unruffled by the breath of the sleepy air, nor broken at all save where some waterfowl languidly cleft their surface with a silent wake, lake and creek bore the motionless doubles of painted shore and reedy margin, and the deeper azure of far peaks and cloudless sky; while from the tranquil scene arose no busier sound of life than the lazy call of a duck or the faint noises of farms so remote that they seemed beyond it. Near at hand, but no more obtrusive, there was a drowsy hum of warmed flies and the slow chirps of crickets and the light scurrying of a chipmunk among the leaves.

"Wal, seh, boys," said Antoine, breaking the silence of the circle as he arose and stretched himself with a yawn, "dis was too pooty day for lose it. What all you goin' do wid it, hein?"

"It is a turrible neat day an' that 's a fact," Joseph declared with unwonted decision, after a slow and careful contemplation of earth and sky. "An' I be thankful 'at we ain 't obleeged tu waste it a-workin'. It allus did kinder seem tu me as 'ough 's if it was a-sorter heavin' away o' the Lord's blessin's tu spend a ri' daown pleasant day a-workin'. Some 'at I misused that way years and years ago lays heavy on my conscience yet."

"Naow, Jozeff, don't be no harder on yourself 'an what other folks is," said Uncle Lisha, in mild sarcasm. "You must have an almighty tender conscience an' an almighty good mem'ry. I can't remember but precious few such misduin's tu lay up ag'in ye."

"Wal, the' 's more 'n I wish 't the' was," said Joseph, staring retrospectively into the smouldering embers as if they represented the cold ashes of the past. "It does seem 's 'ough it was weeked, most 'specially 'long in the fall, an' winter comin' on, when the' won't be no rale pleasant days aou' door tu speak on, for a feller tu be a-breakin' of his back diggin' taters, a-humpin' up ag'in the blue sky, with his nose an' eyes tu dead tater tops an' naked sile, when ev'ything looks so putty all around, an' it a'most the last chance o' seein' on 't, or putty nigh, mebby. Then take it in the winter when the' does come one o' them kinder stray days 'at got left over aouten fall, er comes afore its reg'lar time in spring, a feller do' want tu be a-tunkin' at a tree julluk a woodpecker, an' lose all the good on 't, 'ceptin' what sunshine soaks intu his back. Then ag'in come spring you jest wan' tu thaw aout an' git the good on 't yourself, an' not be tapped julluk a maple an' have your sap b'iled daown for other fo'kses benefit. Take it in summer, it 's tew hot most o' the time tu work, anyway, an' when the' is a comf'table day it seems 's 'ough a feller ort tu jest lay in the shade an' see things blow an' grow an' git ripe erless go a-fishin'.

"I don't s'pose it 's sca'cely right," Joseph continued, "but sometimes it 'most seems 's 'ough I putty nigh wanted tu cuss the man 'at invented work; he sartainly did begin a tormented sight o' trouble."

"Not no gre't for you, Jozeff," Uncle Lisha commented, and went on to say, "I do' know as I hanker arter work, but if I hed me my tools here an' a shoe tu mend, jes' for knittin' work, I cal'late I sh'ld enj'y myself tol'able well."

"Work kinder goes ag'in the grain when it interferes wi' huntin'," Sam said, thrusting a cedar twig into the dying embers and watching its tardy kindling, "but then the work gives a better relish tu the huntin' when you git it."

Sam's comrades were in delicious, semi-torpid enjoyment of a morning nap when he quietly left his place among them and set forth in fulfillment of a promise made to himself of a day alone in Sungahneetuk, the fish-weir river of the old Waubanakees. He was not unsocial, but yet at times was fonder of solitude than of company. Like a true lover of nature, he desired not to go with a crowd to woo his mistress.

Sam put his gun in the canoe for company or from force of habit, but took no pains to find use for it. His paddle strokes fell so noiselessly that the waterfowl sitting in the edge of the marsh were first notified of his approach by the sight of the canoe's prow nosing its swift way past their hiding place, or of the paddler's slightly swaying figure and the flash of his dripping blade. Others dozing full-fed were not aroused till the wake of the canoe shook the walls of their rush wigwam, and then with shaken quacks and squeaks of terror sprang to needless flight. A flock of low-flying teal came upon him so suddenly that he instinctively ducked his head as they swerved upward and swept over him, and great fish dashed from beneath his stealthy keel with a startling surge.

Rounding a bend, he came to the foot of a long reach, in which nothing animate could be seen astir but a solitary grebe wrinkling the glassy surface in widening circles at various points of departure and return, in his explorations of the nether watery world. Sam let the canoe drift at the will of the idle current, while he curiously counted the moments of the agile diver's disappearing.

Then his wandering gaze became fixed on a great hawk that came cruising low over the apparently tenantless marsh. With short, restrained beats of his broad pinions the falcon ranged the silent cover till suddenly, with a sharp, downward slant, he swooped into its depths, wherefrom, in the same instant, with a clamorous outcry of affrighted squeaks, a hundred wood ducks burst upward with a startling, thunderous roar of wings, threshing water, sedges, and air. As suddenly as they had risen they settled with a resounding splash in the open water of the channel, where they sat motionless, silent, and alert. The baffled marauder mounted heavily from the weeds, and wheeling a moment above the vigilant congregation, each member of which was ready to dive at any sign of attack, he recognized the uselessness of a further attempt and sullenly retired.

Then he entered the stream's gateway, gorgeous with the autumnal colors of the water maples. Looking around and backward, he could imagine himself in the solitude of the primeval wilderness, for there was no visible sign of man's intrusion on the wooded banks at either side, nor on the silent lake, nor on the rugged crags of Split Rock Mountain, and these were the bounds of vision.

A few rods upstream the illusion was dispelled where the cleared bank opened to an old pasture. The turf was cut with wheel tracks of wagons that had brought apples to the Canadian boat, signs of her recent presence that set Sam wondering how it fared with her contraband freight.

Passing the next bend, he was between wooded shores, where ferns and other moisture-loving plants crowded one another in rampant growth. Ducks frequently arose before him, singly and in flocks, taking wing from the water or jutting logs, out of range before he discovered them or could bring his unready gun to bear on them. He saw that shots were only to be got by prowling along on foot, and ran in behind a little island that hugged the left bank. It was crowded with great trees; most conspicuous among them was a towering elm and an immense buttonwood, whose trunk shone unearthly white amid the forest shadows, like the ghost of a giant, and all were embowered in a tangle of wild grapevines.

As Sam stepped on shore he caught a glimpse through the treetops of a flock of ducks whistling with lowering flight toward some spot below him and back from the stream. Thither he cautiously made his way and presently saw an open space among the trees, toward which he made a stealthy approach under cover of a clump of alders. When he reached this he discovered a narrow lagoon lying close before him. It was some twenty rods in length, bordered by a growth of wild rice and covered with duck weed. A great branchless tree lay lengthwise of it at the nearer end, an inviting roosting-place for wood ducks, a score of which were occupying it with heads uplifted and alert, or comfortably resting on their mottled breasts or tucked beneath their wings, the males resplendent with bright color, the females shining with gilded bronze, yet all strangely inconspicuous in nature's nice adjustment to their environment, never failing to blend them with the hues of her changing seasons. As many more swam idly to and fro, meshing the green scum of duckweed with a network of watery paths.

If Sam was aware of a qualm of conscience it came too late to withhold him from the unfair chance, and he raked the log with such deadly aim that more than half its happy crew tumbled overboard, killed outright or, in the last extremity, splashed aimlessly, sorely wounded, struggling instinctively toward the cover of the weeds, while the affrighted survivors jostled each other in flurried flight, knowing not what to make of the catastrophe which had befallen their comrades, but wheeled and pivoted in confused wonderment till Sam came forth to secure his victims, when they took flight, yet returned to circle and hover overhead, reluctant to leave a haunt where man so seldom intruded. Another shot fired to secure a cripple served to convince them of its present unsafety, and when Sam bore away his abundant trophies he left the pool as silent and deserted as it is today, when it is known to every gunner of this region, and even the poor heron and bittern avoid its precincts.

A smart breeze ruffled the green water of the bay with waves that flashed like fire in the broad glade of the low sun and flecked the far blue of the lake with leaping whitecaps as the canoe slid over the long undulations of the shallows toward her port.

A flock of golden eyes took flight before her, their wing beats ringing like the quick clangor of tiny bells, and flocks of teal and dusky ducks whistled past, coming in early on the favoring breeze from their day's outing on the lake. One by one a company of herons forsook the shallows beneath the cliffs and sagged on slow vans toward the woods of Little Otter, and high above all an eagle made stately progress through his aerial realm. The wash of waves was left behind when the canoe entered the creek, and presently it slipped in at the landing, where Sam found his friends already returned and awaiting his coming.

Unexpected Visitors

"Wal, here you be, boy," said Uncle Lisha, "an' I 'm glad tu see ye, for it 's a-gittin' consid'able ca'julluky aout yender for your milkweed pod. Good airth an' seas! What a snag o' ducks you got! Sixteen, sebenteen, eighteen, nineteen! Yes, sir; nineteen! Jullook o' there, Ann Twine; he 's skunked the hull caboodle on us! Le' me see, you got three, an' me an' Jozeff—wal, we hain't caounted aourn yit."

"Pooh, dat ant notings!" said Antoine, contemptuously poking the pile of ducks with his toe. "Ant he 'll gat honly nanteen dawk in dat crik all to hese'f? Dat ant much for do, an' what leetly feller dey was! One tam w'en Ah 'll leeve in Canada Ah 'll keel forty wid club; yes, seh, an' dey was gre't beeg feller. Yes, seh, dey was geeses."

"Sho, Ann Twine, I guess they was in the aig."

"No, seh, dey was in Canada, sem Ah 'll tol' you, an' if you 'll ant b'lieved me Ah 'll goin' tol' you de trute. You see de way of it, he come on stubbly graoun' for pick de hoat was jus' sow, an' he steek hees foot on de mud so he can' pull it, an' den he froze heem fas' 'cause it mos' winter; so den Ah 'll ant not'ing for do honly knock hees head of it."

"What be you a-tellin'?" Uncle Lisha groaned. "Oats jes' sowed on stubble in the fall! Du, fer massy's sake, lie reason'ble if you must lie."

"Oh, Onc' Lasha!" Antoine said, in an injured tone. "If Ah prove mah storee you 'll ant b'lieved it. Haow you s'pose mans was goin' for rembler everyt'ing was happen in hees laftam w'en he happen so many, hein? It was two tam Ah 'll keel forty wid stick, one tam in de sprim an' one tam in de fall! Come, le' 's go on de camp. De patack was mos' all bile, prob'ly, an' de dawk ready for cook. Sam, you wan' save dis leetly feller?" touching the ducks again with a scornful toe.

"Sam Hill," said Joseph, just finding words to express his admiration. "If that 'ere hain't a harnsome mess o' feathers. Samwil, if you 'll let me pick them tu the halves, M'ri 'll be more 'n willin' 'at I come, or leastways she 'd ort tu be, seem 's 'ough."

"You c'n hev the hull on 'em tu feather your nest, for all me," Sam replied. And so they all set forth toward the camp.

As they drew near it they were astonished to hear the unmistakable sound of female voices, and singularly familiar ones. Sam coming first in sight of the place signaled silence and a halt to his companions, who gathered close at his back, and all stood and stared in wonder not unmingled with dismay upon the unexpected invasion of the camp.

Two women were nosing about, turning their sunbonnets like telescopes this way and that in diligent inspection of every object, now focusing a common center of interest, now separately, in search of new diversions and discoveries. These movements were accompanied by remarks which were not very flattering. The faces were indistinct in the depths of the sunbonnets, but there was no mistaking the forms, motions, and voices of Aunt Jerusha and Huldah.

"I don't b'lieve they 've swep' up sence they be'n here," said the first, making a slow inspection of the fireplace and its littered surroundings.

"Swep'?" the other returned sarcastically. "Why, they hain't got so much as a hemlock broom, I warrant ye, which they might easy enough, for jullook at the cedar a-growin' all araound."

"I know it," Aunt Jerusha acquiesced, "jest as good if not full better, not scatterin' itself so bad."

"An' will you look at that 'ere fryin'-pan?" cried Huldah, holding off the utensil with gingerly hands at a distance, yet bringing the muzzle of her bonnet to closer inspection. "I can caount the leavin's o' three cookin's in 't, plain."

"Sam Hill, hain't I glad M'ri hain't here tu see that 'ere," Joseph whispered, "an acre o' feathers would n't caount ag'in leavin' on 't so; wal, mebby that 's settin' on 't high, say half an acre."

"An' see them pertaters. I 'll be baound they 're all b'ilin' tu pieces," cried Aunt Jerusha, fluttering over to the pot and peering into it while she blew away the steam. "Yes, they be, true 's you live. Can't you take 'em off, Huldy?"

"'T ain't likely there 's no sech a thing as a holder. I da' say they use a bunch o' leaves or a dirty stockin'," said Huldah, rushing to the rescue of the potatoes; "but thank goodness I 've got my apron," and she whisked the kettle off, keeled it and set it by the fire in a trice.

"Or mebby the' hats," Aunt Jerusha suggested, still dwelling on holders. "Jest think on 't, Lisher might ha' fetched his luther apron." And Uncle Lisha gave Sam an appreciative dig in the side with his elbow.

Then the two women backed off a little to take a comprehensive view of the scene, making inquiries and responses of, "Did you ever?" and "No, I never," till they fell into a fit of laughter which they were obliged to sit down to finish, while the spectators made a silent exchange of imbecile grins. When the camp inspectors had exhausted their mirth, they discovered the tent and flew to it. Now their heads were thrust far inside in minute inspection, now withdrawn and the muzzles turned to each other with divers nods and shakes of assent and dissent, accompanied by spasmodic movements of their bodies, all of which gave evidence of invidious remarks and indulgence in unseemly mirth. All this was endured in silence by the spectators of the inquest till the older woman began poking at the contents of the tent with a long stick, when Uncle Lisha could restrain himself no longer, but rushed forward and shouted at the top of his voice:

"Hello, you women; what you duin' in there!"

Thereupon the intruders backed out of the tent, and facing about showed the rightful occupants a far bolder front than they could muster, caught as they were in all unseemly ways of housekeeping.

"Why, Lisher Paiggs, haow du ye du?" cried Aunt Jerusha, beaming upon her husband, and Huldah called out heartily:—

"Haow be ye, Sam, an' all of ye?"

"Good airth an' seas, is that you?" Uncle Lisha shouted. "Why, I thought you was couple o' schoolgals a-snoopin' raound. Wal, seein' you ast, I do' know 's I 'm none the better for seein' you, considerin' haow you talk abaout aour haouskeepin'."

"Wal, naow, Lisher, you can't deny but it 's a leetle mite thick under the nail," said his wife.

"By gosh, Aunt Jerrushy," cried Antoine, coming to the front, "you was come de wrong day. Dis ant aour day for wash de dish. We jes' daown to de lake for see if dere was waters 'nough for wash to-morry, an' we make off aour min' we got for wait till he rise."

"Haow come ye tu come, anyway?" Uncle Lisha demanded. "Sed daown an' make yourselves tu hum, an' tell us 'baout it," and he waved them hospitably to one of the fireside logs. "Aour gal 'll git tea ready tu rights. Come, Miss Ann Twine, you want tu be gittin' aout your sweetcake an' plum sass an' jell, for we got comp'ny."

"Ah 'll gat all of it in de pettetto keetly, an' de res' of it Ah 'll gat pooty soon," Antoine answered promptly, and began bustling about the fire, heating the frying pan and scouring it with a stone—as he would never have thought of doing but for the presence of the guests. They eyed his movements, but politely refrained from audible comment. Then seeing the ducks, they fell into a poultrywives' admiration of them.

"My, I never see sech harnsome ducks," cried Huldah, "an' you got all them sence you come here?"

"Why, I got these tu-day, jes' myself, an' I do' know what the rest on 'em has got," Sam answered.

"Haow come ye tu come?" Uncle Lisha shouted. "Good airth an' seas! that's what I want tu know," while Joseph could not find a chance to inquire after the welfare of his father or to ask what message M'ri had sent.

"What was 't you was sayin', Father?" Aunt Jerusha asked at last. "Haow 'd we come? Why, we tackled right up the waggin an' come along. But we never tol' nob'dy 'at we was a-comin' here. The' 'd ha' be'n objections, no eend on 'em, if we 'd ha' tol'. An' so you see, Huldy she hed some dried apple 'at she wanted tu trade off, an' we jest fixed it up betwixt us 'at we 'd fetch it daown tu Vergennes an' stay over night tu Cousin Chase's an' then come here! An' so we did, an' here we be. Hain't you glad tu see us? You don't act as if you was, not turrible."

"Why, yes, we be tew," Uncle Lisha protested; "but you see, you took us kinder onawares."

"We did n't hev time tu put on aour tother clo's," said Sam.

"Wal, tu tell the truth an' not no jokin' abaout it," said Aunt Jerusha, "we fetched daown all on ye's tother clo's as fur as Cousin Chase's an' there they be."

"You did n't never, Jerushy Paiggs," said her husband incredulously; but she nodded repeated affirmatives and smiled serenely.

"Wal, then, what did ye for? Be you goin' tu sell 'em or be you goin' tu take us to meetin' or a-visitin', or what is 't?"

"No, not nary one," said she after a moment's enjoyment of her auditors' mystification; "but tu the caravan 'at 's comin' nex' day arter tumorrer. We cal'lated you 'd plan tu go to 't, an' we 'd go tew, on Bub's 'caount. His gran'pa an' gran'ma's goin' tu fetch him, an' we wa'n't a-goin' tu hev you raound in your ol' ev'yday clo's."

"Good airth an' seas, if I had n't clean forgot it!" Uncle Lisha declared in genuine surprise at his forgetfulness of so important an event.

"Forgot it!" Aunt Jerusha exclaimed with mild scorn; "that 's a likely story, an' it all pictured aout in red an' yaller ev'ywheres. Anyways, it is naow up to Danvis even ontu folkses' barns, an' ev'ybody 's a-goin'."

"On Bub's 'caount, I s'pose," her husband remarked, bestowing a wink upon the company. "I do' know what we 'd all du if it wa'n't for that boy."

"I don't nuther," Aunt Jerusha assented heartily. "But it don't signify. We 're all a-goin' an' a-goin' lookin' somehaow. Oh, you need n't think me an' Huldy did n't fetch aour tother bunnits," as she detected a quizzical glance at the gingham sunbonnets.

"An' we fetched along a loaf o' bread an' some butter, an' some b'iled aigs an' some quick pickles," Aunt Jerusha continued, casting a doubtful eye upon Antoine's panful of fried duck, "'cause we did n't know but what you might be gittin' short; but I will say it smells better'n it looks.

Then Antoine announced supper and the embarrassed hosts led their guests to the repast, which they attacked with no great zest, having seen the cook wipe on his trousers the fork with which he turned the contents of the pan, and use his hat for a holder. Yet they praised what was set before them, while making a meal mostly from the provisions they had brought with them. Then they helped to clear the table and made the dishes cleaner than they had been since their first use here.

After this all the company gathered around the fire, the men smoking, Aunt Jerusha regaling herself with snuff, Huldah unwontedly idle for lack of knitting, while all the latest Danvis news was told and with judicious omissions all the adventures of the camp, and so well did the visitors enjoy their first taste of this life that they decided to lodge in the tent, where a luxurious bed was prepared for them with a double allowance of cedar twigs.

At sundown the north wind died, but the pulse of waves still beat upon the beach in regular recurrence above the slumberous murmur of distant shores. A company of bitterns were performing a farewell rite on the eve of migration, uttering uncouth squawks as they wheeled high above the marshes in awkward gyrations, and frequent flights of ducks were whistling past and splashing into channel and marsh.

The busy air was filled with sounds that were strange to Huldah's ear; the shuddering cry of a screech owl and the sad monotony of the crickets were the only familiar ones among them all. These with the slow wash of waves were the voices that her dreams shaped themselves to, when with a lingering sense of strange environment she fell asleep.

Women's Day

The full light of morning had chased the shadows from the camp and even possessed the recesses of the tent when the drowsy inmates awoke and crept forth yawning and shivering in the unsunned air until the rekindled fire warmed them.

Then the women folks got the tidiest breakfast the camp had ever known, and when all save Antoine, who sulked on his faded laurels, had eaten it with great relish, Huldah went out and feasted her eyes full of the wonder and beauty of the lake, where it doubled painted shores in the glassy mirror of near waters, its far expanse melting into ethereal hills and further sky, where distant islands hung in the blended azure.

Then while Joseph and Antoine, forlorn bachelors by brevet, kept camp, the reunited couples embarked in the scow for a cruise along the shore of the bay.

The experience gained while voyaging on the canal and the Western lakes put Aunt Jerusha quite at ease on these quiet waters, and with such an example before her Huldah was too proud to show any trepidation and too sensible to affect it.

"Wal, Huldy," said Uncle Lisha, watching her as he steered while Sam wielded the oars, "you be a nat'ral born sailor, an' you never in a boat before, I 'll warrant. Why don't you jump raound and squawk ev' time the boat jiggles?"

"Why, I hain't no time tu, the' 's so much tu look at," said she, her eyes roving far and near over the unfamiliar landscape. "Hain't them pine trees? We don't hev no sech tu home. An' if there ain't the Hump, for there can't be no other like it—an' hain't that Tater Hill? My, what a ways off they be, so blue they don't look much nigher 'n the sky. I should hate tu live so far from 'em all the time. Oh, look at that boat, an' hain't that a black man in it? It sartainly is," and she pointed across and up stream to where Jim was paddling out of his marshy harbor.

"Why, yes," said Uncle Lisha, "that 's one o' your husband's friends, Huldy. You 'd admire tu see what comp'ny he keeps when he 's daown here,—Injins an' niggers an' I do' know what all."

"Quakers an' shoemakers," Sam supplemented.

"An' you hain't no idee what cadidoes he cuts up," the old man continued, regarding his audience with a solemn countenance, "a-helpin' Quakers steal runaway niggers away f'm the owners. Yes, sir, he done it an' he da's n't deny it," and Uncle Lisha frowned benignly on the culprit.

"Why, Samwil," Huldah said, in a low voice, beaming affection and admiration upon her husband, while Aunt Jerusha laid a gentle hand upon his shoulder.

"Wal, no wonder both on ye 's mad an' he 'shamed, but we won't tell on 't if he don't du it ag'in," said Uncle Lisha.

"Sho, Uncle Lisher, what nonsense hev you be'n a-s'misin' up," Sam demanded, with a bold assumption of innocence.

"Good airth an' seas, boy! don't ye s'pose I know brand when the bag 's ontied? Wha 'd ye go over tu that Canuck's boat for? Sellin' apples proberbly. Wha' 'd ye kerry them ducks up tu Bartlett's for? Thought they was starvin' proberbly. What made ye so tickled when ye seen the Canuck boat p'intin' for Canerdy? Turrible glad tu git red on him, wa'n't ye? Oh, you be almighty cunnin', hain't ye?"

Sam's downcast eyes discovered something on the boat's bottom which promised a change of the subject of conversation.

"Why, if there hain't a trollin' line an' hook wi' a piece o' pork rin' an' red rag on 't all rigged for fishin'. It must be Antwine had it, but I don't know when. You put it aout, Huldy, an' mebby you c'n ketch a pickerel."

"Me? My goodness, I could n't never. I 've ketched traouts, but I can't never ketch a pickerel, I know. Would n't I feel big tu, though?"

The line was let out, the boat was slowed down to the proper rate of speed as it skirted the channel, and Huldah held the hand line with a grip that showed a determination to be hauled overboard rather than relinquish it. When the boat reached the mouth of the creek her resolution seemed about to be tested, for the line tightened suddenly with a jerk that drew her arms out to their utmost stretch.

"Whoa! whoa! Back up your waggin, Sam," she cried. "I 've got ketched on a lawg or the hull bottom of the river."

"You hain't nuther!" shouted Uncle Lisha, at once recognizing the cause of the intermittent strain. "It 's a fish, an ol' solaker. Pull stiddy, Huldy, stiddy. Oh, good airth an' seas! If you c'n on'y git him! Keep a tight line on him!"

"I sh'ld think he was a-doin' that," said Huldah, her voice shaken by the beating of her heart, though she presented an outward appearance of coolness. Foot by foot the big pickerel was drawn toward the boat till the cold gleam of his wicked eyes could be seen, and then by Uncle Lisha's direction he was given line, then hauled in again till the old man could get a grip on his gills and toss him into the boat. Huldah gave a great gasp of relief and was ready to cry for pride when Sam swung his hat and gave a lusty cheer that was echoed by Jim, who had been watching the struggle and now came paddling over, jerking his head and laughing and offering congratulations while yet twenty rods away.

"I tell ye what, Mr. Lovel, he is a good one!" Jim cried, as he ran his canoe alongside the scow and looked at the fish with a sort of proprietary pride and with almost as much satisfaction as if he had caught it. "Yes, sir, he is a good one, Mr. Lovel. Is it Mis' Lovel 'at ketched him? Well, ma'am, you handled him just as well as ever I ever see anybody. Yes, sir, you did. Could n't no man done better—could n't myself. Naow, if you want tu try it, you might troll aout raound the island. Mighty good place that is for ol' big fellers," and Jim emphasized every item of praise and advice by a jerk of the head, continuing both till the crew of the scow passed out of hearing, and Huldah remarked, still gloating over her captive:—

"Wal, Uncle Lisher, Samwil might find wus comp'ny, for he 'pears tu be a real sensible, candid sort of a man."

When they entered the lake Aunt Jerusha was induced by much persuasion to take the line and a chance of distinguishing herself. She held it anxiously and under continual protest of inability to do so at all.

As they coasted along the gray northern wall of Garden Island she was thrown into a fever of excitement by a tug at the line. It was a pickerel, which, by dint of stout tackle and good fortune, was brought to boat, and in spite of her protested indifference to such a capture, she rejoiced over it exceedingly.

They landed on the island, and with Sam acting as guide explored its interior. The garden-like bloom of its shrubbery no longer verified the island's name, but there were evidences of it in the abundant black clusters of viburnum berries and scarlet haws of wild roses, and there were yet enough blue and white blossoms of asters to make the place pleasant to flower-loving women.

Then all went over to the east end, where Aunt Jerusha found some stranded clam shells and all found arrow points of flint on the narrow strip of gravelly beach.

"It does beat all natur' haow the critters made 'em!" said Uncle Lisha, pondering over a handsome hornstone arrow-head. "We could n't, wi' all the tools we got."

Then they strolled back to their humble craft and coasted along shore toward camp. Antoine was at the landing to receive them and was profuse in his compliments to the anglers when their trophies were shown him.

"Bah gosh, Aunt Jerrushy! Bah t'under, Ma'am Hudly! You bose of it beat Onc' Lasha an' Zhozeff an' Sam for feesh, an' 'mos' me, w'en Ah ant try. Prob'ly if Ah 'll was go wid you, you ketch lot of it. But you do pooty good, Ah tol' you."

The next morning the preparative bustle of departure began, and though no one openly confessed it, each felt a shade of sadness as the place grew bare and desolate where such pleasant hours had been spent.

"It beats all natur' haow a feller gits wonted tu a place where he 's hed a good time, an' hates tu leave it," Sam said, as he turned away, "but it 's hopesin' we 'll come ag'in."

"What 's sass for gander 's sass for goose, an' when you come ag'in I 'm a-comin' tew," said Huldah decidedly.

"If de hwomans was comin', Ah 'll ant, me," Antoine declared; "it was spile up all de funs for try to live too pooty."

"Wal," Uncle Lisha sighed, "it hain't noways likely 'at I 'll ever come ag'in."

"But if ye du, Lisher, I 'm a-comin' tew," Aunt Jerusha said, as they departed.

The last ember snapped out in dull explosion and the last thin wisp of smoke dissolved in the colorless air, and amid the silence of desertion the falling leaves began the slow obliteration of man's transitory sojourn.

The Caravan

Toward the middle of the afternoon Uncle Lisha and his friends entered the outskirts of the little city, where the unusual appearance of a camping outfit attracted considerable attention and was generally believed to be one of the side shows belonging to the coming caravan.

It presently gathered a following of boys, and when Sam drew rein in front of Cousin Chase's tidy house these were joined by several grown-up and no less curious idlers, and all surrounded the wagon in an interested group.

"It's a nigger show, I bet ye," one boy confidently asserted.

"Yah. What you talkin' 'bout?" cried another contemptuously. "It 's the Injin show! Don't you see the canew? An' that black feller up there 's one of 'em; the ol' chief, he is."

"My, don't he look ugly, though?" loudly whispered another, staring in fascinated horror at Antoine, who, overhearing these remarks, at once fell into humoring them.

"Yas, sah, Ah 'll was big Injin, me! Ant you see haow Ah 'll was sca'p dis hol' mans?" He lifted Uncle Lisha's hat, displaying the shining bald pate, and then after a moment's impressive silence continued, "Wal, seh, boy, Ah was tore off you hairs jes' lak dat 'f you 'll ant ta' careful. You want for hear me spik Injin more better as Angleesh?

"Cangra musquash nawah alamose woisoose chunkamug peskegan. Ooop!"

His audience listened with deep admiration to the first specimen of aboriginal eloquence which they had ever heard.

"You want to go on and turn to the left to get to the show ground," said a florid gentleman of leisure, dressed in a drab fur hat, blue coat, and tightly strapped trousers, and he pointed up street with his cane, which he then tucked under his arm, while he took a pinch of snuff and meditatively surveyed the occupants of the wagon. "I hope you folks don't have any tight-rope dancing and the like," he continued with a deprecatory air. "That's contrary to the laws of the State, you know."

"Wal, naow, that 's tew bad," said Uncle Lisha in a grieved voice, and indicating Joseph with a jerk of the thumb, "for this 'ere young man is turrible hefty on the wires."

The florid gentleman thought he recognized the blush of modest merit in Joseph's abashed face, and with a sly wink at Uncle Lisha said in a husky undertone:—

"We might fix up a leetle private entertainment—in a barn—you know, to-night. Select and quiet, you know."

"No, sir! We 're law-abidin' folks," said Uncle Lisha with virtuous decision. "Say, can any on ye tell me whether no Ab'm Chase lives in this 'ere haouse. Good airth an' seas! If he don't come an' tell us where tu go pooty soon we sh'll hefter hev a show tu git red o' the folks."

"Say, mister," an eager boy whispered, clutching Sam's knee, "if I 'd fetch water for your hosses, won't ye let me go in for nothin', me an' my little brother; he hain't bigger 'n nothin'! We hain't got no money. Will ye, mister?"

"Why, Bub," said Sam, "we hain't no show. We jest come tu see the show, that's all."

The boy stared incredulously into the honest face till assured there was no guile in it, and then retired in disappointment, leading his little brother.

Now the front door of the house opened and Abram Chase came hurrying out in a state of excitement quite incongruous with his smooth-shaven face and plain, neat attire, when he found his Cousin Jerusha's husband and his friends standing unwelcomed at his threshold and surrounded by a crowd of curious idlers.

"God zounds! Lisher, what be you settin' there for? Why did n't ye come right in? Back up a leetle an' haw right in here an' drive tu the barn. Clear aout, boys. What be you a-hengin' raound here for?"

As he opened the great gate and the wagon was driven into the barn, the crowd realized its mistake and dispersed, the blue-coated gentleman sauntering up the street in dignified indifference, while the boys made a joke of their disappointment and tried to out-jeer one another.

"Ya-ay, Kelly, how much 's the tickets to your Injin show? Ya-ay!" and Kelly retorted:—

"Ya-ay, Smithy, 'baout as much as it 'll be to git int' your nigger show. Ya-ay!" and both factions shouted "Ya-ay!" with a clamor like that of a congregation of crows, and Uncle Lisha was impressed by the depravity of town boys in calling each other by their last names.

"Well, Lisher, haow be you, anyway?" Abram Chase inquired, when, after a bustle of general hospitality, he found time to give attention to individuals. "An' haow be you, Samwil? An' hain't this Joseph Hill?"

"Wal, I don't sca'cely seem tu know whether no it 's me 'r a Injin 'r a balance master 'r some other sort o' show feller," said Joseph, feeling his head and looking at his short, stumpy legs to assure himself of his identity. "I was beginnin' tu 'xpect Uncle Lisher'd hev me a-stannin' on my head 'r a-turnin' summersets 'fore I knowed it."

"Bah gosh, Ah 'll give more for see dat as all de show dey had to-morry," cried Antoine. With that he departed to his numerous compatriots in the "French village" at the other end of the town, and the others went into the house, where Cousin Chase's good wife was entertaining Jerusha and Huldah.

Henceforth till bedtime these town mice and country mice compared experiences, now to the envy of one, now the other.

When morning came no one thought of anything but the great event of the day already heralded in the gray dawn by the rumble of the heavy baggage vans. Habitual early risers were out betimes full clad, to admire the teams of large, handsome horses and gayly painted wagons, and slug-gards came forth half dressed with garments in hand and unshod feet, rubbing sleepy eyes and fumbling at buttons with alternate hands as they blinked at the lumbering procession with a fellow feeling for the drowsy drivers and the weary showmen asleep on the jolting piles of canvas.

The vans rumbled past, transferring the present interest to the show grounds, and the brief excitement of the street subsided temporarily while the citizens breakfasted.

Then the first influx of sightseers came hurrying in, fearful of being late, though they reported the caravan two miles behind, delayed at the last stream by the elephants refusing to cross the bridge. Gradually the incoming tide of sightseers increased, some on foot, whole families in heavy farm wagons, and young fellows with their sweethearts in the cumbersome single pleasure wagons of those days, some of which had boxes shaped like bread trays, others square ones substantially framed and paneled, with high-backed seats cushioned with russet-colored leather and perched at such a lofty height that ascent and descent were not to be lightly undertaken.

At last the grand triumphal chariot appeared, blazing and glittering with scarlet and gold, and drawn by four white horses driven by a liveried driver, behind whom the band was enthroned, blowing lustily on brazen bugles, French horns, trombones, and ophicleides, all in time to the thunderous beating of a bigger drum than had ever been heard at a general muster. Then came two elephants, one of whom bore a howdah in which the lion tamer sat dressed like a Roman gladiator and quietly smoking an incongruous pipe. These were followed by four camels ridden by Arabs, whose genuineness became doubtful when one was heard to address his beast with "Git on wid yez, ye spalpeen." Then came the train of closed mysterious cages, some silent, others giving forth growls and screams of strange beasts and birds.

Close upon these came a crowd, hurrying for fear of being late, though it was two hours before the advertised opening of the show. Uncle Lisha and his party, reinforced by Mr. and Mrs. Purington, Sis and her nephew Bub, were early upon the ground, eagerly enjoying all the novel sights and sounds of the busy scene.

The little group of Danvis people passed on to where a peddler mounted on a cart was auctioneering his wares.

"Oh, just look what I 've found tucked away in a corner, an' I thought the last blessed pair was sold yesterday," he cried, stretching to arms' length a pair of puckery rubber suspenders that smelled infernally of sulfur. "Just look. Stretch like a deacon's conscience. Long enough for any man. Short enough for any boy. Oak-tanned luther ends an' gold buckles, I guess, but mebby they 're brass. Don't let your women folks wear their fingers aout knittin' galluses for you, but walk right up an' buy a pair of these beautiful e-lastic suspenders, worth one dollar tu any man, but I sell 'em for half that money, an' tu-day, seein' you all want tu save a quarter to go int' the show, I 'll let you have 'em for quart' of a dollar a pair, an' I 'll say no more an' take no less."

Such a generous offer was not to be withstood, and the new-fangled suspenders were passed out to the crowding purchasers till it seemed as

if the red cart could have been laden with nothing else, yet the enterprising proprietor was continually discovering some new article, and each
more tempting than the last. Now it was a ring or brooch, now some
cheap and tuneless instrument, now pocket-combs, side-combs, and
back-combs, jack-knives, distorting hand glasses, song books, lives and
confessions of criminals, and so on, changing as often as interest flagged.

There were numerous booths where refreshments of mead, spruce
beer, and great cards of good old-fashioned yellow gingerbread were
temptingly displayed, and the familiar, obese and blue-frocked figure of
Old Beedle was present, dispensing foaming glasses of innocuous beer
from a cask in the tail of his wagon, and with them such kindly words
and genial smiles that it seemed to his juvenile customers as if they were
receiving a great deal for a cent.

There were peripatetic venders of apples in baskets, and homemade
molasses candy on boards, both wares cried by the youthful Canadian
dealers at the usual price of "Two of it, one cen' 'piece."

Noisiest of all were the tooters, vociferously proclaiming the wonders
of the side shows, the fat woman and the strong man, the albino negroes
and the man without arms, and the waxworks of Monsieur Jonsin from
Paris, all of which were now on exhibition and each to be seen for the
small sum of twelve and one half cents.

The twanging of the banjo, the thumping of the tambourine, the
voices of the performers and the laughter of the audience sounded
smothered and echoless as they beat against the canvas walls, yet were
most attractive to the outsiders who crowded about the narrow en-
trances.

As Joseph Hill stood in rapt admiration of the colossal portrait of the
fat woman, counting the coins in his pocket with his fingers, he was
startled by hearing his name called in a familiarly imperative tone, and
looking in the direction from whence it came, saw the gaunt form of his
father standing upright in a lumber wagon, brandishing his cane toward
him with one hand and with the other restraining young Josiah from
leaping to the ground. Maria, who with her daughter Ruby occupied a
portion of the seat from which the patriarch had risen, was frantically
shaking a handkerchief toward her husband, and Pelatiah, who as driver
sat in front with two of the smaller children, had his breath indrawn and
his mouth made up, to add his voice to the family call.

"Wal, if this don't pooty nigh beat Sam Hill," Joseph exclaimed, as he
hastened over to them. "Seem 's 'ought I thought o' most ev'b'dy a-comin',
but I swaow, I never thought o' you a-coming', Father."

"You did n't, hey? An' you could n't hear me when I did come, a-gawpin' at that 'ere pictur'," Gran'ther Hill scolded in a cracked catarrhal voice. "What is 't a pictur' on, anyway? A elephant dressed up in women's clo's? I 'll bate they hain't got no sech a critter."

"It's the fat lady, Father," Joseph explained, "an' the white niggers. Haow come ye tu come, Father?"

"Fat lady and white niggers," the old man repeated scornfully. "By the Lord Harry, what is this cussed world a-comin' tu when *shes* 'at goes raound showin' their carkisses like hawgs tu a cattle show calls theirselves ladies, an' niggers calls theirselves white! I come 'cause I was a mine tu! Did n't you? Did you s'pose the' wa'n't nob'dy but you a-comin'? Don't ye s'pose Josier wanted tu come, an' Ruby an' t' other young uns, an' du you s'pose I was goin' tu let 'em come daown here along wi' M'rier and' Peltier and git lost an' eat up? That would be smart!"

"Why, I 'm glad you come if you can stan' it," Joseph declared. "Be you middlin' well? An' you, M'ri an' Ruby, an' 'mongst ye, an' you tew, Peltier? Oh, M'ri, if I hain't got the almightedest snarl o' feathers! Wal, not sech a turrible sight on 'em, but sech neat ones you never did see a'most."

"Yonder comes Lisher an' Jerushy an' Lovel an' his wife an' young un, all comin' tu ask what I come for, I 'll lay a guinea," said Gran'ther testily, "an' if there hain't that 'ere cussed Pur'nt'n woman an' her man. I hain't nothin' ag'in the beasts, but I swear I wish 't they 'd eat her. Young Gove, drive your hosses up tu the fence an' hitch 'em! Sed daown, Josier, 'fore I knock ye daown. G' 'long!"

The horses were driven to the nearest hitching place and given a bundle of hay from the hinder end of the wagon, whose occupants were by this time overtaken by their townsfolk in spite of Gran'ther Hill's attempts to elude Mrs. Purington.

"Wal, I should think you 'd 'a' hed more regard for your health, Capting Hill," the tired dame panted, fanning her hot face with a folded handkerchief, "an' I don't see what you let him come for, Marier. It 's jest flyin' in the face o' Providence."

"Damn my health, marm, it 's ol' 'nough tu ta' keer of itself," the veteran declared, standing very erect and looking fierce. "Haow d' ye s'pose M'rier was goin' tu help herself? The' hain't nob'dy flew yit; but I wish t' the Lord Harry they would, higher 'n Gilderoy's kite, an' never light this side o' glory halleuyer."

"I 'm dreatful glad you come, Cap'n Hill," said Sam, shifting Bub to his left arm that he might shake hands with the old man. "They say the' 's a bustin' old painter an' some wolves."

"Yis," said Uncle Lisha, "an' some Injins; but they won't le' ye kill 'em, 'cause they hain't got but a few."

"Hev they got all them?" the veteran asked eagerly. "Come, let 's git aour keerds an' g'w'in t' the carryvan afore the young uns dies o' waitin'. Take a holt o' my hand, Bub. For'a'd, march."

As they approached the thronged precincts of the ticket wagon and Sam detached himself from his party to enter into the struggle for tickets, he was accosted by his impecunious youthful acquaintance of yesterday, who was now standing forlornly apart from the crowd with his little brother, looking with longing eyes at the blue and yellow cards as they were passed to the outstretched hands by the imperturbable ticket seller.

"You wa'n't one of 'em, was ye?" said the boy, with a melancholy smile of recognition.

"Hello!" Sam responded cheerily. "Hain't you shavers goin' in?"

The boy shook his head in sorrowful resignation.

"The big fellers got all the jobs, an' I hain't got no money."

"You wait here till I come back," said Sam, after a moment's hesitation, and then shouldered his way into the crowd, through which his tall, strong figure enabled him soon to reach the wagon. Presently emerging from the press somewhat flushed and rumpled, but smiling, he returned to the boys and handed the elder a couple of half tickets. "There, Bub, you an' the little chap go in an' see the hull caboodle on 't," and Sam rejoined his friends before the boy could give audible expression to his thanks and astonishment.

Joining the drifting tide of mixed humanity, our Danvis friends were carried with it inside the great tent into a world of strange new sights, sounds, and atmosphere. If this was not the perfumed breath of Araby, these were the beasts and birds and reptiles of the tropics and far countries of the earth, this medley of discordant sounds that frightened children and startled their elders,—the natural every-day voices that had shaken the torpid air of Indian and African jungles.

The keepers, who walked unconcernedly in front of the cages and were the familiars of the uncouth elephants and camels, bore such impress of strange experience and wide travel as made them quite different from ordinary mortals, and speech with them an overwhelming honor.

"Yes, that 'ere is a boar constructor or animal condor," Solon Briggs explained to his neighbors, whom, with his wife, he had joined near the front of the cage in which a great serpent was coiled. "I s'pect that was the specie that onderminded the humern race of mankind by temptin' of

Eve, 'cause you see he 's cal'lated by the dimensions of his len'th for reachin' arter apples. An' that 'ere is the rile tiger, so called on account of his allus bein' riled, an' that critter that 's got stripes jus' like him is called zebray on account o' his resemblin' a jackass. An' anybody 'ould know them was lierns, only the female specie hain't got no mane. An' hain't them elephants the curisest freak o' humern natur'? It does appear 'at if they was pervided with another pair of visible organs in the behind of 'em they might perceed back'ards jest as well as for'ards, hevin' a tail on each end of 'em. That 'ere is called the backteryan camel on account o' his hump."

"Poor creetur's," said Aunt Jerusha, "I should think they 'd git dre'f'l tired o' goin' humped up so all the time."

"Them is what they kerry water in when they cross the desart of Sary—she 't was Abram's wife," said Solon.

"Briggs must ha' made most o' these 'ere animals hisself, I consait, he 'pears tu know so much abaout 'em," Gran'ther Hill growled sarcastically. "Come, Josier, le' 's go an' look o' the painter an' them wolves; I want tu see suthin' 'at I know suthin' abaout myself. There!" he continued, as, leading his grandson and followed by Sam and Pelatiah, he halted in front of the cages of these animals, "that 's the sort o' pussycat an' dogs 'at used for tu be a-yaowlin' an' a-yollopin' raound yer gran'ser's campfire when he was on airth the fust time. Ah, ye ol' yaller cat! You sneakin' whelps! Yer gre't gran'marms knowed me."

He shook his cane at them, and the panther spat at him and the wolves slunk into a corner as if each recognized in him an ancient enemy of its kind.

Presently the attention of all was drawn to the performance of the elephants, when one huge beast made its majestic progress around the ring with a howdah of delightedly frightened children, and the other walked with slow and ponderously careful steps over the prostrate form of the keeper.

Then a pony ridden by a monkey ran in the ring, at which time Antoine made his appearance. Having been entertained by many friends, he had arrived at a condition to fully enjoy the show. Now he was in a bellicose humor, thirsting for a hand-to-hand encounter with the bear, now he was affectionate, desiring to embrace every one, including the equestrian monkey.

"Say, Sam, Ah wan' kees dat leetly nigger. Ah luv heem more as Ah luv mah fam'ly, bah gosh! Ah 'll was nabolition mans, me, an' Ah 'll wan' stole dat leetly nigger. Sam, ant you wan' help me stole dat leetly nigger?" and so maundered on till, to Sam's great relief, his attention was directed to the band and he began to dance in front of it, dividing the attention of the audience with the clown, who, with the ringmaster, made the nearest approach to a circus that was then permitted in our virtuous commonwealth.

The humor displayed by the clown in his ancient jokes and repartees was irresistible, and when after turning a succession of somersaults he ran his painted nose against a center post of the tent, Aunt Jerusha declared:—

"He's the quickest witted man I ever see, but the clumsiest creetur, for one 'at 's so spry by spells. Eunice Pur'nt'n, if you 've got your camphire bottle, you le' me hev it an' I 'll go an' rub some on his nose, for it 's painin' on him turribly, I know it is."

Mrs. Purington never ventured far from home without her bottle of camphor and smelling salts, and possessing herself of the first, Aunt Jerusha hastened forth to offer a balm for the supposedly injured member, while audience and actors looked on in silent wonder.

"Here, you poor distressed wretch, le' me put some o' this sperits o' camphire on t' your nose. It 'll take the soreness aout if it does make it smart some," she said, approaching the clown, who left off his lamentations to stare at her in dumb surprise. "Le' me rub some on 't right on," she urged, "or put it on yourself if you 'd druther."

"Thank you," he said politely, "if you 'd be so good, just a drop," and he soberly submitted to the operation while the paint came off his nose on to the tips of her fingers. "Thank you, dear old lady," he said in a low voice, "and bless your kind heart. It 's done me ever so much good."

He returned her to her place as politely as if she had been the finest and fairest lady in the land, and then tripping back to the center of the ring he propounded another conundrum.

"Why is the old lady's heart like my nose?"

"Wal, sir, why is it?" the ringmaster demanded.

"Because it 's tender, of course," was the answer, and there was tremendous applause.

"Oh, dear, it 's tew bad, it 's tew bad!" Aunt Jerusha sobbed, almost in dismay at having attracted such general attention, "but if it done him a mite o' good, I hain't sorry."

Now the performers retired from the ring, the lively measure of the galop changed to a solemn andante, and the audience breathlessly awaited the grand event of the day.

There was a clang of bars and an opening door, and the lion tamer entered the den, driving the snarling beasts to one end of it, from whence they came one by one at his command and sullenly performed their parts.

"Oh, dear suz!" Mrs. Purington wailed in a tearfully restrained voice, "they 're a-goin' tu eat him, I know they be, an' the show folks expex it. That 's what makes 'em play so solemn on the music, jus' for all the world like a fun'al hyme tune. Say, mister," she piteously appealed to a showman who stood near, "won't you go an' tell him tu go right aout o' there? It don't seem as if I could stan' it tu stan' here an' see him eat up right afore my face an' eyes."

"Don't be alarmed, ma'am," said the showman, "there 's no danger. The last man they heat was so tough and disagreed with 'em so bad, they ain't 'ankered harter human flesh sence. More 'n hall that, 'Err Driesbach is a Dutchman, han' the beastises can't habide the smell o' saurkraout."

She only half believed this and kept her smelling bottle in hand till, greatly to her relief and that of most of the audience, the brave lion tamer backed out from the royal presence, and the band burst forth in a jubilant strain so loud that it set the elephants to trumpeting and all the carnivora to roaring and howling.

Every one was glad that this part of the show was over, but alas, it was all over, and even now the shutters of the cages were going up and the canvas walls were going down, and the crowd dispersed except the few who lingered for a last look at the camels and elephants, and such as were fooled into parting with their money to see the hurried, final exhibitions of the side shows.

Before the afternoon was much further spent the Danvis people were on their homeward way, and a little after nightfall their own mountains closed around them and again shut them in from the busy world of which they had had such a brief but memorable glimpse.

*   *   *

The lives of the Danvis folks resumed their ordinary tranquil course. For me, time has touched them as lightly as it has the crowns of their own mountains, which centuries have not changed.

I find myself forgetful of the lapse of fifty years, thinking of my old friends as yet alive, preserving the quaintness of speech, the homely pastimes, the simplicity of dress and manners, and above all the neighborly kindness that belonged to their day and generation untouched by the strifes and ambitions and changes of the busy world that chafes and beats around them, and without a desire for a part therein.

The uneventful day is spent. The shadows of the mountains and the early twilight creep across the quiet valley. Out of the dusk and deepening gloom, homestead lights shine forth like stars in a nether sky, and after a time go out, one by one.

I cannot say Farewell, as if the lights of my old friends were extinguished forever, but only,—Good Night.